Between the Bridges

Up Beaver Creek Book III

Sue Fagalde Lick

Blue Hydrangea Productions

South Beach, Oregon

Between the Bridges

Up Beaver Creek Book III

Sue Fagalde Lick

To all the friends and neighbors who love and support each other, no matter what

Contents

PART I

1. Is Someone Singing?

Sunday, May 24, 2020

"ROCKY! COME! Where are you, boy?" Nothing. The golden retriever has a mind of his own, and he doesn't understand what dangers lurk out here off Beaver Creek Road, a narrow gravel road that winds up and up through the woods overlooking the Oregon coast. He doesn't know about bears, cougars, other dogs defending their territory, and camouflage-wearing rifle-toting hunters who'd just as soon shoot a dog as an elk. Especially one that belongs to that "rainbow house" up the road where the lesbians live.

Actually, just one lesbian, my friend Dakota, and me, PD Soares. It has been almost a year since Dakota's partner Maryann died, three years since I lost my husband, Tom. Last summer, when I found myself needing a place to live, Dakota invited me and Rocky to move in.

The dog is still wandering, totally oblivious. "Rocky! God damn it!" Sorry, God.

Dakota could make him mind. Something about her deep voice and her take-no-shit personality, I guess. Maybe that she's older, 51 to my 43. Dogs, cats, kids, and men take one look at her and say, "Yes, sir, whatever you say." Me, with my soft don't-want-to-make-anybody-mad voice, they don't even hear.

"Rocky!"

My dog, given to me as protection after I was attacked by a would-be rapist, is almost two years old. He wasn't much help at first, but he's my best friend now, even when he drives me crazy.

I've never been this far from the house before. But it's Sunday, and I'm not in a hurry. It's beautiful here in the spring. The Scotch broom are loaded with yellow flowers. Pink wild roses poke out through the sword ferns. New cones decorate the conifers. After a rainy winter, the weather is cool but comfortable. But where is my dog? Despite graduating from obedience class, he's still 85 pounds of puppy. Once he ventures beyond our property, it's all a wonderland to him.

I hope he didn't splash through the creek that trickles on my right. I'd rather not get my shoes wet.

"Rocky!" If only I had the ears and nose of a dog. I hear a squirrel chirping somewhere and smell pine trees, dirt, skunk, and bear shit, but no dog.

Wait. Over the rumble of the ocean and traffic on the Coast Highway a few miles to the west, I hear something. Singing? It's faint, but it is definitely not a bird. I leave the road and follow the sound, splashing across the creek over tree roots, rocks, and pine needles. I keep looking back, trying to mark my way, afraid I'll get lost.

I've got my phone, but it doesn't do any good up here. No service.

The voice is growing louder. A woman. Is that an autoharp?

"Hello!" I call.

The singing stops. "Hellooooo." She sounds old. "Who is there?"

"A neighbor. Have you seen a big yellow dog?"

"Say again?"

"A dog?" I keep walking toward the sound even as the road behind me disappears in the trees.

"This one?"

I speed up and trip over a branch, landing on my hands in the mud. "God damn it."

Again, I'm sorry, God. I crawl to my feet, brushing off the dirt and leaves.

A few more steps, and the trees open into a clearing with a small white house and Rocky running toward me, tail a-wag. Behind him follows a woman in a flowered dress and hand-knit brown sweater, her gray-brown hair falling out of a loose braid. I'd guess she's in her sixties.

"Hello," she says. She nods toward the dog nuzzling my hand. "He must be yours."

"He is." I fumble in my pocket and come up empty. "I'm sorry. I don't have a mask."

"Don't bother. We don't have the virus out here."

"Well, I'll keep my distance. I work at the hospital, so I might have picked up some germs."

She nods.

"I'm sorry my dog is bothering you."

"Oh, piffle. We're having a nice visit. In fact, he said he loves my oatmeal cookies."

He said? Okay. That dog will eat anything, from used tissues to toothbrushes. "I'm PD Soares (SWAR-ez). I live with my friend Dakota in a house down the hill from here."

"The postmistress? Yes, yes. So sad about her wife. Cancer, wasn't it? I had it in my breast and survived, but that poor girl . . ." She shakes her head. "Are you Dakota's new partner?"

I chuckle. People always think that. "No. I'm straight. I'm a widow—to a man. My dog and I needed a place to stay and Dakota needed company, so we decided to share the house. She's still grieving pretty hard."

"Well, I'm glad she's not alone. PD. What kind of name is that?"

"Initials. I was born Priscilla Donatella O'Leary. People called me Cissy. I hated it. When I left Montana a couple years ago, I decided to change my name, my look and my plan."

Why am I telling this stranger the story of my life? I never tell anyone my real name.

"I understand. That's quite a name. I am Eugenia. It's very nice to meet you." She reaches out a hand then pulls it back. Social distancing.

"I heard you singing."

"Oh yes, I love to sing. The music keeps me company."

"I'm a singer, too. And I play piano. I used to perform, but since the pandemic, there's no live music anywhere."

She smiles, showing a missing bottom tooth. "There is music here."

Rocky rolls at her feet with his legs in the air. This dog is not shy. I ought to go home, but it feels great talking to someone who isn't sick or dying or petrified of getting sick or dying. "Do you live here by yourself, Eugenia?"

"Yes, I do. Have for a long time, since my hair wasn't gray. Why don't we sit down? You've walked a long way, and you're a guest."

"Thank you, but I really should keep my distance and take this crazy dog home."

"What is his name?"

"Rocky."

"Ah." She ruffles his thick fur. "Well, come again, Rocky, and bring your friend PD."

I hesitate. I don't know how to find my way back.

As if she can read my mind, she says, "Thataway, past the rain barrel, is a logging road that hooks up with Beaver Creek Road. If you go that way, you can't get lost." She glances at my shoes. "You won't get your feet wet either."

"Thank you."

"Take a cookie for the road."

I am hungry. "Thank you." Delicious. I pull Rocky's leash out of my coat pocket." Come on, Boy."

He looks from Eugenia to me and stands up slowly.

I hook him up, and we head off just as it begins to rain.

Soon, Eugenia is singing again. I don't recognize the song. It sounds like the song of the trees to me.

I can't wait to ask Dakota about Eugenia. I wonder why she never mentioned her.

2. Spring Storm

"LONG WALK," DAKOTA comments as Rocky and I straggle up to the front porch of the rainbow house, where she stands smoking and staring into the dimming light.

Rocky shakes the rain off his fur as I shuck my jacket and soggy shoes. "Yes, it got longer than I planned. Rocky took off and introduced me to a woman named Eugenia. She says she knows you."

Dakota stubs out her smoke in the can of sand she keeps on the porch. "Oh, yeah, I know 'er. She's, um, one of a kind."

"I like her. Very old-fashioned."

"Did she offer you some cookies?"

"Yes."

Dakota laughs. "Loaded with pot, my friend. How do you feel?"

"I feel pretty good actually. She said Rocky had one, too."

"That shit's bad for dogs."

"He seems okay."

"Well, great, you're both stoned. And wet. Are you hungry? I've got dinner for us."

"Did you cook?"

"Nah, I went down to the diner. Dry yourself off, and I'll towel off the dog. P.U., nothing like the smell of wet fur."

Rocky has a lot of it, lush, reddish gold, and forever in need of brushing.

"What are we eating?"

"Spaghetti."

"Yum. I'm starving."

Down the hill in Seal Rock, our friend Diana Peacock owns Diana's Diner. It's across the Coast Highway from Seal Rock State Park, which has stunning rock formations and wild surf. And yes, seals. Sea lions, actually. Normally a tourist destination thronged with visitors exploring the beach and gift shops, Seal Rock is almost a ghost town now.

Thanks to the COVID-19 pandemic, Diana can't offer seating inside. She has worked out a takeout system like the old 1950s drive-ins, minus the girls on roller skates. You park out front, call in your order on your phone, and Janey, her daughter, brings it out. You can eat in your car, take it to one of the beach overlooks nearby, or take it home. Everybody wears masks. Janey and Julio, the dishwasher, disinfect the trays, menus, even your window frame just in case somebody got some virus on it.

Janey's brother Jonas, who normally runs a taxi service, has gotten into the act, too. For $3 extra, he will deliver a meal to your house. He also runs errands for people. Nobody's calling for cabs these days, so he does what he can. With two sets of twins at home, both under age 5, and a house in Newport, north of here, he's got to earn money somehow. His wife Molly makes some money baking for the diner. Her pies and pastries are real diet-killers. She calls her business Molly Cakes. When COVID lightens up, I can picture a cupcake sign on one side of their car and Jonas' peacock taxi logo on the other.

The takeout system is better than going out of business altogether when most restaurants are closing. So many people are out of work now. I'm lucky to have my steady job in admitting at the hospital. No chance it will go out of business.

When I first came to Oregon, I house-sat Janey's Uncle Donovan's cabin just up the hill from the rainbow house, but he came back to town sooner than expected and kicked me out. I hadn't pulled together enough money to buy or rent a place by myself, and Janey's apartment had been condemned, so we became roomies, sharing a sweet gingerbread house overlooking Yaquina Bay. Janey was young enough to be my daughter, but we got along—until the landlord decided to take her house back.

I moved in with Dakota, and Janey moved to Corvallis. She was studying music at Oregon State and working at her uncle's art gallery when COVID closed everything down.

A curly haired leprechaun on the short and round side, Janey claims to have lost 12 pounds ferrying food back and forth at the diner. Maybe I ought to try it. The gym used to be my happy place, but that's closed, too, and all these diner dinners are making me fat.

While Dakota takes the food out of its foil containers, I stand by the fireplace warming my backside, watching her. She's so tall she towers over the counter. She has always seemed a little gruff, but now she rarely smiles. She and Maryann lived together for years, but they were only married a few weeks. I was best woman at their wedding overlooking the beach at Seal Rock. We all knew what was coming, but the wedding was beautiful.

Our rustic two-bedroom house doesn't look much different from when Maryann lived here, except that my piano has replaced her sewing machine near the front window, and we squeezed my sofa in against the opposite wall. The house is not fancy, but it is well-made and comfortable.

When you enter under the big rainbow painted over our front door, the kitchen is on the right, living room on the left, bedrooms and bathroom along the back. A door just past the long wooden table leads outside to the wood pile and Dakota's tool shed. She used to be a carpenter before she became postmistress, and she's still mighty handy.

Outside the house is forest. No lawns, no formal gardens. My Jeep Renegade and Dakota's old van, with rainbows painted on the sides, are parked on the gravel driveway up an incline from Beaver Creek Road.

As Dakota fills Rocky's bowl with kibble, he dives at it like he hasn't been fed in months.

"Let's eat," she calls.

Sitting at the big table across from Dakota, it always feels a little empty. This used to be the house where everyone gathered for parties or just to hang out. Maryann was mother hen to all of us, and the love of Dakota's life.

She was an expert cook, tending toward earthy, vegetarian fare. She was also a gifted fiddle player in our Seal Rock Sound band. She took care of everyone. Even when she was dying, she jumped to help me when I got in trouble. She even brought me blueberry muffins.

Dakota can do the basics in the kitchen, but she has made it clear she'd rather stick to carpentry and home maintenance. She'll keep the fire burning if I make sure we have something to eat. A lot of days, that means we eat takeout from the diner.

"Dear God, bless us and bless this food," I say.

Dakota waits for me to finish my prayer then fills her plate.

I load up and sprinkle parmesan on my spaghetti. "Eugenia lives out there all by herself."

"Yeah. She has since long before we got here. People call her The Witch."

"Why?"

"She's different. Out there alone. Growing pot and herbs. Raising chickens. Hasn't been to town in years, they say."

"How does she get food?"

"She grows some. Has some things delivered. I don't know what's in those packages I drop off every week."

"What does she do for money?"

"Social Security, I suppose."

I watch her twirl her spaghetti against a spoon. The sauce is thick, with ground sausage and mushrooms. It's even better than my Italian grandmother used to make.

"Well, Eugenia seemed nice to me."

"You were stoned."

"I was not." I glance out the window. It's dark now, even with daylight savings time, and still raining.

Lightning flashes, followed a second later by thunder. Rocky dives under the table. With all these trees around us, I'm nervous, too.

Dakota pushes back her chair. "Well, I'd better do the dishes while we still have light."

"I'll do them. You got the food." Not that there are a lot of dishes to wash. But this house has no dishwasher, and we both hate having dirty plates and silverware piled on the counter.

In five minutes, I'm finished, drying my hands on an embroidered dishtowel I brought from Montana. Dakota restocks the wood, and we settle in. She plays solitaire while I open a book I picked up at the library's drive-through window. It's quiet except for the thunder, the occasional snap of a log in the fire, and the swish and snap of Dakota's cards.

Down in civilization, it's 2020. People are wearing masks and running scared of the coronavirus nicknamed COVID-19. And for good reason. We started slow here in Lincoln County, but then COVID hit the coast like a second tsunami. Work has truly been a nightmare. We're running out of beds, and it takes hours for the mask lines on my face to fade.

Here in the woods, nothing seems different. We have the Internet, made better by the new tower installed after the tsunami. Oh, did I mention we were hit by a massive earthquake and tsunami two years ago? Trashed half the town. Just as we were recovering, COVID hit. Now, when I'm not working, I read, knit, play my piano, cook, and walk the dog. Dakota putters around the house.

Maybe I'll bake something tomorrow. I've got stew makings for the crockpot. It can cook while I'm at work—if the power stays on. No guarantee of that.

Boom! Another thunderclap. Rocky tries to climb into my lap. He's too big, but I cuddle him as best I can. "That was a big one, hey boy?"

You'd think winter would be over around here by now. You'd be wrong. We get rain on the Oregon coast from Halloween to Fourth of July. Despite plants starting to bloom, May still feels like winter.

I'm just about to finish reading a chapter in this novel about an Episcopal priest turned detective when everything but the fireplace goes dark.

"Shit," Dakota says. As she lights the fat candle that always sits on the table, the wall phone rings. "You know who," she says.

I do. I wade through the darkness to answer. "Hi, Dad."

"Hey, kid. Dark over there, too?"

"Darker than a cave at the bottom of the ocean."

"You girls got everything you need?"

"Of course. How about you?" My father, who spent most of his life in California and wandered a while before buying Donovan's cabin, is not used to our weather yet.

"I've got my camping lanterns. Want to come keep me company?"

"It's too late, Dad. We're settled in for the night."

"I figured. It's lonesome out here."

"I know."

"Are you working tomorrow?"

"7 to 3."

"Keep safe."

"I try."

"I'll bet the dog's not liking the thunder."

"Nope."

"Well, tell Dakota I'm expecting a package tomorrow."

"Okay. Good night, Dad."

"Sleep tight."

It's strange having my father here. My parents got divorced only a few years ago, long after my brother Andy and I were grown. Dad had retired from teaching and wanted to travel. Mom, who had a busy social life, wanted to stay home. They split. I hardly spoke to my father while he satisfied his wanderlust. Then bam, I came home after visiting Mom in California last year to find him and Donovan both at the cabin, all buddy-buddy, and Dad buying the place. I still can't believe it. I move across three states to start a new life, and then my father moves in just up the hill. If there weren't so many trees in the way, I could see his place from our porch.

Maybe I should introduce him to Eugenia. She seems to be in his age group. Maybe not his type, but hey, slim pickings.

Do I want a stepmother? God, no.

As I hang up, Dakota asks, "Is he lonely?"

"Yes. He invited me to come over. I said it's too late."

We're quiet, listening to the rain and the crackle of the fire. Maybe it's the remnants of Eugenia's pot cookie or maybe it's sitting here in the dark, but I feel like talking. "Dakota, I know you miss Maryann a lot."

"More than I miss booze."

"What do you mean? I've never seen you drink."

"I have a little problem in that area."

"I didn't know."

"I don't talk about it, but sure, back in the days when I did construction full-time, it wasn't unusual for me to join the guys at the Flounder in Waldport or this little bar we used to have here, Pepe's Pub, couple blocks south of the diner. Most of the guys had wives at home making dinner for them, but I didn't, so I lived on tequila and taco chips. I don't know how I ever got home in one piece."

"Were you living here?"

"No. I had a trailer in a little park between here and Waldport. It was all beat up when I bought it, but I made some improvements, and it did the job until Maryann gave me a reason to build a house."

"What happened to the bar?"

"Tree fell on it in a big storm, kind of like this one. Pepe decided to go someplace warmer and drier. Phoenix, I think."

"How did you stop drinking?"

"It's Maryann's fault. She kissed me and said, 'I like you, but I am not hooking up with a drunk.' So, I went to AA and quit."

"It must have been hard."

"It was. I chopped a lot of wood that year." She pulls the band off her braid and shakes out her kinky hair. "I'm going to bed."

"Will it bother you if I play the piano a while?"

"No. That'd be nice." She looks out the window at the rain sheeting off the edge of the porch. I'm sure she's missing Maryann. On a night like this, they could go to bed together and snuggle. Maybe more than snuggle.

Just like I could if Tom was here. Sometimes it hurts as if the bone down the middle of my chest is broken.

Dakota's grief is fresher than mine, but it never goes away, and we can't stop each other's pain.

I slide onto the piano bench, open the lid, and center my fingers on the keys, feeling the black keys rising among the white. What song goes with thunder? Don't say "Thunder Road." I'm not playing that. Or Garth Brooks' "Thunder Rolls." "Stormy Weather?" I'll just let my fingers wander a while and pray the lightning doesn't hit anything close by.

Stormy spring, it's a stormy spring . . . thunder rumbles in May like an angry bear . . .

Needs work. Speaking of which, I dread tomorrow at the hospital.

People in masks, people coughing, people bleeding, people who can't breathe . . .

Minor key. Definitely a minor key.

3. The Virus

Monday, May 25, 2020

WHICH MASK SHALL I wear today? I choose the orangesicle-colored one from the half-dozen hanging on my gearshift lever. I wear my homemade ones over the hospital's ugly standard n95 masks.

I no longer bother with makeup because it just stains the mask, and most of my face is hidden anyway. By 10:00, I'll have a headache. Jackson, who works with me, says it's from a shortage of oxygen.

When I first moved up here, I worried about the drive from Beaver Creek into Newport. The first two miles of gravel road are a little gnarly, but then I reach pavement and a relatively straight shot through four miles of marshland to the highway. From there, it's six miles to the Yaquina Bridge over Yaquina Bay, and two more blocks to the Newport Samaritan Communities hospital.

On a vacant storefront just past the bridge, someone has spray-painted *Stay safe; wear a mask.*

I gulp in a big breath as I walk toward the ER entrance and strap my face in.

"Good morning," I tell the guards in the tent by the door. All the other entrances are closed. Everyone has to go through here.

A tall guy in scrubs and a blue windbreaker checks my name tag. "PD. Good morning. Have you been exposed to COVID or had any symptoms?"

"No."

He scans my forehead with a thermometer. "Have a nice day."

I know I've got it relatively easy. Jackson and I work behind a plastic barrier, and we don't get hands-on with patients. We send those who might have COVID to wait in what used to be the children's playroom. We hand out masks like candy because a surprising number of people still aren't wearing them, living in denial or protesting the governor's mandate.

I hate wearing a mask, too, but people are dying. Hundreds of thousands of people. Not here yet, but we know it's coming.

We make patients come in by themselves. Except for children, who can bring one parent. People get mad, and I don't blame them. I think about how Andy and I sat at our mother's bedside for days when she had her heart episode last year. Now, she'd just be lying there alone with no one to talk to, no one to question the doctors, and nurses running around covered from head to toe in hats, masks, gloves, and gowns.

We can only see people's eyes these days, but those eyes look worried.

When this started in March, quickly moving from a rumor to a pandemic, people were afraid to touch anything—mail, groceries, furniture. Now we know the virus doesn't live long on surfaces, but we still have hand sanitizer everywhere. Staff is required to use it every time we go in and out. We make patients stop for a dollop, too. My hands are raw.

In the waiting room, half the chairs are blocked off with yellow tape because they're too close to the other chairs. Part of our job now is to wipe the chairs with sanitizer every time somebody gets up.

At some clinics, they don't even let patients sit in the waiting room. They make them call from their cars and come in when it's their turn. It's crazy.

Now wherever I go, I see masks on the ground, run over by cars, soaked in puddles, or abandoned in the grass. They remind me of used condoms. No one wants to pick them up for fear of catching the virus, so they stay until they rot.

And yet, some people insisted on gathering this year as usual for Easter. We had a big rise in cases the following week. Imagine sharing a joyous Easter dinner, kids hunting for eggs and all that, and a week or two later, several of your loved ones are dead.

It's a hell of a virus. Jackson was one of the first to get it. He said he was sure he was going to die. Within 24 hours of the first little cough, he couldn't catch his breath. He felt like he had a sack of cement on his chest. Achy and weak, he didn't eat for days. Nothing tasted right. When he got a little better, his boyfriend started leaving food outside the door. He crawled out to retrieve it and take it back to bed. He hated that they could only see each other over the phone. "You don't want this, PD," he said. He claims he still has no energy.

Elective procedures have been canceled. Knee replacements. Cataracts. Hernias. No room, and the doctors don't want their patients to risk exposure. Wellness checks, canceled. Staff out sick in every department.

I know doctors and nurses who strip off all their clothes, shower and change before going home to their families. Some barely see their spouses or kids. I could have been one of them. I was studying to be a nurse last year when I realized I should be taking music classes instead. That's where my heart lives, even if I might never make a living at it.

It's easier not having kids these days. All the schools are closed. The children are supposed to attend classes over the Internet via a program called Zoom, where people talk and see each other through their computer microphones and video cameras. It doesn't work well, especially with children. How do you make them actually show up and do the assignments, and how are their parents supposed to work, assuming they still have jobs?

Patients are lined up at the window. The waiting room is full. Zelda from night shift needs to go home. The other night clerk, Angie, as big and blonde as Zelda is small and dark, is already gone. I sanitize my hands, log in on the computer and call the first person over, a middle-aged man with a beard down to his chest. And no mask. How did he sneak past the guard? I point to the box on the counter.

"Sir, I have to ask you to wear a mask."

"This is still a free country, ain't it?"

"I hope so, but we can't treat you unless you wear a mask. Please."

"Fucking commie lesbian governor."

As he fits the bands on the paper mask around his ears, I resist defending our bisexual governor who is a Democrat, not a communist. People are waiting to be helped. "Thank you. What brings you here?"

"I think I broke a rib."

"Which one?"

He points halfway up his left side.

"How did you do that?"

"Lost my balance and fell on the woodpile." At my puzzled look, he adds, "I might have been a little drunk."

"Ah. Any trouble breathing?"

"No, but it hurts like a m-f-er."

"I'm sorry. Have a seat and we'll call you in a minute."

At least it's not COVID, but that young woman coughing her guts out over by the door is a likely candidate. Her mask is halfway down her chin. I picture droplets of virus spraying all over.

I slide out of the cubicle. "Ma'am, I'm going to need you to wait in the other room. Anyone with a cough . . ."

She nods and walks past me to the kids' room, still coughing. I wonder if she got COVID on my sweater.

I used to love my job, but now, not so much. I'm not sorry I dropped out of nursing school to play music, but there's nowhere to do that these days. No gigs, no open mics, no jams. People try to play together online, but the sound is all messed up. It only works for solos.

Famous performers are doing concerts on Facebook because they're stuck in their houses like everyone else. I watched Keith Urban do one the other day from his home in Australia. His wife Nicole Kidman was dancing around. It was kind of fun.

Janey and some of her friends did an impromptu concert in the amphitheater behind the library. I couldn't leave work. Their only audience was a few dog-walkers passing by, but no one told them to stop, and she said they had fun even though the temperature was in the high 30s.

Maybe I should try making a video of myself performing. Put it on YouTube or something. Or I could jam with Eugenia. No masks, fresh air, pot cookies . . .

"Ma'am?"

I have a patient. "Sorry. How may I help you?"

"I have my father in the car just outside. He needs help right away."

"Does he have COVID?"

"Maybe. I don't know. He can't breathe."

"Okay. If he has the virus, you have been exposed and should be tested, but please go wait with him and I'll send somebody out there."

I get on the phone. "We have an emergency admission at the front parking lot ER door. Probably COVID. Can we send somebody out there stat?"

In a minute, three people in scrubs run by and out the door. I can't see what's happening, but I suspect the father is coming in the ambulance entrance. I hope those guys tell his daughter she has to wait in the car.

I hope my own parents stay healthy until this mess is over.

My breaks are the only thing that keep me from going nuts. Cafeteria closed, I bring snacks and lunch from home and make a point of going outside in the garden or walking down the road to where I can see the bay and breathe mask-free. If it's raining, I park by the docks and eat in my car, my safe isolation chamber.

Health officials say the pharmaceutical companies are working on a vaccine, but it's going to be a while.

After lunch, I ask Kelly, the head ER nurse, about the father-daughter duo.

"Dad didn't make it. They both had COVID. His had gone into pneumonia, and they waited too long. She can't even plan the funeral because she has to isolate for two weeks."

Tears prick my eyelids, but I will not let them fall. Not now. "What about that woman who was coughing in the isolation waiting room?"

"We admitted her."

"COVID?"

"What else?"

"PD," Jackson calls. "Your phone is buzzing."

"Gotta go." I silence my cell phone at work, but it has a distinctive buzz.

I have a text message from Diana. *Jonas and Molly are throwing a party for the girl twins' first birthday. You are invited.*

A party? Are they crazy? I know the twins will only turn one once, but we are not supposed to gather in groups. How do we eat birthday cake while wearing masks? What do I buy for one-year-olds?

"PD. I'm going to take my break," Jackson says.

"Sure." It's relatively quiet at the moment.

There's a follow-up text. Oh! The party is on Zoom. Two o'clock Saturday afternoon. There's a link. Diana will have slices of birthday cake at the diner for pickup, but we will not actually be together in one house.

The little girls won't even remember it. Their older brothers, also twins, will think this is how life has always been.

4. Who Wants Cake?

Saturday, May 30, 2020

"HI, AUNT PD, Uncle Dakota," five-year-old Ty and Tim scream into the computer. Molly whispers, "*Aunt* Dakota."

Dakota doesn't hear it. She's puttering around the kitchen, reluctant to participate in this whole un-party. "They can't see me, can they?" she asks.

"Not from over there, but they can hear you. Come sit down. Show your pretty face."

"Psh. Pretty. I'll just listen in. You're the social butterfly."

I'm not, but whatever.

When we first met Dakota, I was a little unsure of her gender. She dressed like a man, wore her graying hair in a ponytail, and spoke with a deep voice, but she's definitely a woman. You should have seen her at the wedding, wearing a dress with styled hair and makeup. Wow.

It is weird, this Zoom thing. Jonas and his family are at their house in Newport, his mom is at her place in Seal Rock, and Dakota and I are here on Beaver Creek. But it's the safest way to get together now.

The boys dominate the screen. "Guys," I say." "Where are Gabi and Hannah? I can't see them."

Molly nudges her sons. "Move out of the way, boys. You're blocking the camera."

I'm tempted to block my own camera. I don't enjoy staring at my face on the screen, especially today with a red mask rash on my chin.

The girls sit in side-by-side highchairs pulled up to the dining room table. Identical dimpled redheads (not fake like me), they've got bibs on and are playing with Cheerios on their trays. They're completely unaware of the laptop in front of them.

A new face appears on the screen.

"Hey, Mom," Jonas says from the background.

The boys jump in front of their sisters again. "Gramma, Gramma, it's our birthday!"

Diana's mouth moves, but we don't hear what she's saying.

"You're muted, Mom."

I can read her lips saying, "Damn it."

We wait while she finds the button to release her voice.

"I said to the boys, it's the girls' birthday. Theirs is not until June."

"No, it's everybody's birthday, Gramma," argues Ty, the louder one, who's wearing a red Spiderman T-shirt today. Tim's blue shirt features Superman. I sense a theme.

Molly leans in. "Let it go, Diana. You can't argue with a five-year-old. Especially when there are two of them."

"I know. I had enough trouble with their father and his sister, and they were a year apart. Where is Janey?"

"Coming in right now."

My friend appears on the screen, looking like she just fell out of bed. "Hey all. Sorry I'm late. What did I miss?"

"The naked dancing girls," Jonas says.

"Yeah, right. How are the kiddos?"

"Swell, if you like being outnumbered by people half your height."

"You love it, brother."

"Your turn will come, Sis. Where's Uncle Donovan? He's the only one missing."

"Don't know. Haven't seen him since I moved back home."

"Maybe you should call him."

"Maybe *you* should."

"Yeah. Well, I guess we're all here. Shall we open presents?"

"How?"

"Hold on." Jonas and Molly pile up packages on the table and encourage the year-old twins to rip off the paper. When they don't pay attention, Jonas does it for them. "Look! Dolls." He opens another and holds up two matching T-shirts imprinted with "I'm one year old."

"Is this present from you, Mom? It's a big one. Help me, Mol." Jonas and Molly unwrap two patchwork quilts, each with the girls' names embroidered on alternating pink and white squares.

"Thank you!" Molly says. "I didn't know you quilted."

"I've had time on my hands lately, so I'm learning."

Jonas reaches for one more gift. "What's this?"

"It's from me," Janey says.

"Well, let's see." He pulls off the paper. "Oh! Tiny maracas. Now that's useful, Sis."

"Next year, violins."

"You wouldn't dare."

"Try me."

It's our turn, but I didn't send them a physical present. Our gift feels lame. I type a computer link in the chat bar to the right of the faces. "We bought you a coupon for a month's worth of diapers at JC Market. I know, it's boring."

"No, that's great," Molly says. "We need it."

"It's from both of us," I say.

"Thanks, Dakota and PD."

The boys are looking glum. Jonas reaches under the table and pulls out two more presents. They rip into them and are soon pushing little cars on the table until Molly orders them to play on the floor.

Jonas scoops up the wrapping paper and ribbons. "Who wants cake?"

"We do!" scream the boys.

"I do!" we all scream in our squares. Molly lights two candles on a chocolate cake with flowery frosting, and we sing "Happy Birthday." She offers slices to the little twins, but the girls look puzzled. I have seen one-year-olds put their whole hands and faces into a cake, but these girls don't do that until Molly demonstrates. "Like this. It's good. Have some." Eventually they make a mess of the cake, chocolate all over their faces as Jonas takes pictures and the boys look up from their plates saying, "Ew, she needs a bath. Hannah, you're a slob."

Dakota and I eat the matching slices of cake she picked up at the diner earlier and wash it down with coffee.

In forty-five minutes, the party is over.

"Not like the old days," Dakota mutters as she heads out the door for a smoke. Soon I hear the clang of the ax. Firewood. Dakota's therapy. I wonder if she ever wanted kids. I suspect all she ever wanted was Maryann. Without her, she's lost. When Tom died, I had my church family and my music. Not that that makes up for losing a partner and the kids we might have had, but it helped.

I need a walk. Rocky, reading my mind, stands by the door. For grins, I stuff a harmonica into my pocket.

I COULD PRETEND I'm just taking Rocky for a walk, but I want to see Eugenia again. It's almost like she was something I dreamed or saw on a TV show for children. I was lost and worried about getting home before dark, and there she was.

This time, I take the road and retrace our steps, keeping Rocky on his leash. It's a beautiful afternoon, a rare break in the spring rain. Tiny white flowers on the blackberry vines and swaths of yellow Scotch broom offer hope of spring and summer. I'm ready for it. There comes a point every winter when I wonder if I should move back to California and escape the gray, soggy weather. But on days like this, I think, no, this is heaven. I'd be crazy to leave.

We pass Dad's cabin. His truck is not there. I wonder what he's up to, but it's none of my business. Since he moved in, we have been doing this dance, trying not to step on each other's toes. We're not used to each other anymore. I moved to Montana, he traveled all over the country, and a lot has happened since we lived in the same zip code.

Rocky stops to sniff elk droppings. They look fresh. I wonder where the elk are. Bears and cougars also linger in these parts. I'm okay with raccoons and rabbits and even garter snakes, but the animals that could kill me worry me a bit. I'm trusting Rocky to smell them before they smell us.

I think this gravel road is where we turn off. "Wait," I tell Rocky. He sits. "Good dog. Is this it?"

He looks around like he's really going to answer me. I listen for music or other sounds of life. Nothing.

"Well, let's try it. Come on, boy."

The road leads through moss-draped spruce and pines, salal and blackberries and more Scotch broom.

I'm beginning to think we're lost when we come upon a rain barrel with a bucket beside it. Chickens cluck nearby. If this isn't Eugenia's place, it's somebody's.

Fifty yards farther, we reach the clearing in front of her house. She's sitting on her porch with her right leg propped on a chair as she holds a bundle of something over her knee. Her faded dress is rolled up to her thigh. She's muttering to herself.

"Eugenia!" I let Rocky loose, and he runs to her.

She looked up and smiles, showing that missing tooth. "Oh, hello! It's PD and Rocky. I didn't know if you would ever come back."

"We're here." I squat next to her. "Are you injured?"

She scowls. "I banged up my stupid knee, tripped over the ax I left right in my own way. I could have cut my leg off, but the spirits were with me. It's swollen and sore, but my herbs will take care of it."

"What kind of herbs?"

"Ginger, cinnamon, turmeric, lemon oil. It always does the trick."

"How about ice?"

"Oh no. It shocks the system."

"Well, at least you're elevating it. That's good."

"You said you worked at the hospital, didn't you? You ought to know about natural remedies."

"Well, I work in admissions. I'm not a doctor or anything."

"Ah, doctors. What do they know?"

I start to answer "a lot," but decide to keep quiet.

"I'd offer you a cookie, but I ran out."

"I don't need anything. I just had birthday cake for a pair of one-year-old twins."

"Oh? Where was the party?"

"Well, the kids and their parents were at their house, and the rest of us attended by computer from our own houses."

"What do you mean?"

"Our computers have cameras in them, and there's this program called Zoom that let us see them and them see us while the kids ate cake and opened presents. It's not the same, but that way we don't expose each other to COVID."

"I don't understand why people worry about that stuff. When you can't even eat birthday cake at the same table . . . I don't know. When my kids were small, we all sat together. Everybody brought something to eat. We played music and told stories until it got dark and we hadn't even realized it was so late."

"That sounds nice. Where are your children now? You must have grandchildren and maybe even great-grandchildren."

Her face turns stony. "I don't talk about that."

"I'm sorry. I never had any children."

No response.

"I came here all by myself, but now my father, Jack O'Leary, lives in the cabin just up the hill from us."

"I see."

"Can I get you something? Water? Something to eat or drink? Tylenol?"

She shakes her head. "No, dear."

Rocky is barking at the chickens that wander freely around a cage with an open door. The hens and roosters don't seem to care, but I don't totally trust my dog. He certainly enjoys fried chicken on a plate. "I'm sorry. Rocky! Come here. I said 'come'!" When he reluctantly obeys, I hook his leash back on and return to the porch.

Eugenia is quiet. She pulls down her dress and stands, reaching for a long stick she's using as a cane. "It's not a good day for a visit, PD. If you don't mind."

"Oh. I'm sorry. We'll go. But I'm going to come back another time to make sure your knee is healing."

"It's fine. Thank you."

As she hobbles into the house, Rocky and I retrace our steps past the rain barrel to the path that will take us to the road and home. Maybe Dad is back by now. I'm feeling lonely all of a sudden. The harmonica feels heavy in my pocket. Rocky, plodding along at my side, seems to feel the same way.

The walk from Eugenia's house feels longer going home. As if mirroring my mood, a dark cloud hides the sun, and the air turns chilly. I looked forward to spending time talking, playing music, and getting to know Eugenia. I thought we could be friends. At her place, I could escape the sadness that clung to Dakota, the fear that permeated the hospital, and the emptiness in town. No masks, literally and figuratively.

I wonder what happened to her kids. Was there a husband? Must have been. She is probably divorced or widowed, but for how long? Did she once live in a city, work a job, put on nylons and high heels to go to church or concerts or dances? Who is she? And why do they call her The Witch?

A lot of people don't get along with their families, but it feels like something more than that. There's a deep hurt that caused her to shut down and send me away.

Maybe I could visit again and not ask nosy questions, limit my inquiries to 'what kind of chickens are those and what's your favorite song?'.

5. New Garden

MY FATHER STILL isn't home. No truck in the driveway.

Something else is different. Donovan's glass garden is gone.

What do you mean "glass garden," you ask. Well, Donovan is an artist who likes to make things out of found objects. Discarded glass is his favorite medium. Bottles, jars, teapots, plates, windows. When he can't find what he wants, he makes it. He created a whole glass garden with all kinds of flowers, a fountain made out of a pink toilet, and a sculpture fashioned out of wine bottles. It was crazy, but when the sun glowed off that glass, it was like rainbows you could touch. I hope it didn't get thrown away.

Not everybody likes Donovan's art. Let's not forget last year's April Fool's Day art show to which very few people came, and those who did come didn't buy anything. He was crushed, but these are rural people who like more traditional art and wouldn't pay more than 20 bucks for any of it. A lot of them depend on hunting and fishing for food. A fountain made from an old toilet? Not buying that.

I remember just before we started dating—oh, did I not mention that?—Donovan invited me up here to watch the sunrise, and he showed me his garden. It was like nothing I had ever seen before.

He could be so charming. But he suffered from bipolar disorder. Shortly after the tsunami, he tried to kill himself, cutting his wrists with this same colored glass. He had a reputation for disappearing for months at a time. People gossiped and laughed about him. It was his decision to break it off just before he moved to Corvallis, but I knew he was right. It's better that we just be friends.

Let's talk about something else.

Where the glass garden used to be, the ground has been cleared and plowed into rows, with little plants just starting to come up. Seed packets on posts identify what's under the dirt. Zucchini, artichokes, chard, kale

. . . Did my father plant all this? He never had any interest in gardening before. That was Mom's thing. She didn't do vegetables; she was all about flowers. In fact, after Dad left, this woman who hadn't had a job in 30 years went to work at a flower shop. She's assistant manager now. My brother is a landscape architect, so he got the garden bug, too. Dad never went beyond mowing the lawn—and he only did that if he couldn't make one of us kids do it.

I hold Rocky back from trampling the new plants and knock on the door. Nothing. I peer inside. Dark. No sign of life.

Rocky and I walk around the cabin. It sits on a slope and there's empty space under the back part where Dad stores his wood and tools. An outside staircase leads to a small balcony outside what used to be Donovan's studio. It overlooks Beaver Creek and a pasture full of black and white cattle. Donovan and I shared a kiss or two up there.

"Come on, Rocky." I take him around to the front of the house and sit on the porch step. "We'll wait a few minutes, see if Dad returns. For all we know, he left town and went traveling again."

If he doesn't come, we'll just go home, batting zero today.

Where could he go? Most businesses are closed. You certainly can't go to a movie or a bar or even up to the casino in Lincoln City to gamble. You can still buy groceries, but it's a quick paranoid dash, stopping to use hand sanitizer on the way in and out. Maybe he went to the beach.

I pull out my harmonica, breathe in and out a few notes, then try "The Water is Wide." I can't quite play it, so I sing it softly to my dog. "The water is wide. I cannot cross o'er . . ."

Rocky settles next to me. I pet his soft fur as I hold my harmonica in the other hand and play "Amazing Grace," "Jesus Loves Me," and "This Little Light of Mine." I'm playing "Rock-a-My Soul" when a car rolls into the driveway. "Grandpa's home," I say, getting up and pocketing my harp.

But it isn't "Grandpa." It's Miguel, a handsome guy about my age with whom Dad tried to fix me up last year. At the time, Miguel was interviewing for a job at the Hatfield Marine Science Center. We all went to dinner together, but I was not in the mood for a new beau, and I might have been a little rude. He works at Hatfield now, but this is the first time I have seen him since that awkward evening.

He drives a black Subaru with a kayak rack on top. Before he gets out, he puts on a mask. I check my pockets and realize I forgot mine.

"PD," he says. "It's nice to see you again. I was looking for your father."

"Me too."

"I thought I'd invite him to dinner."

"Where? Nothing's open."

"My house. I've got salmon to barbecue and some good things to eat with it."

"Sounds good."

He looks around, no doubt trying to think of what to say next. "Looks like he's got a new garden going here."

"Yes. I was surprised to see it. My dad was never a gardening kind of guy."

"Well, I hope it grows well. Looks like mostly vegetables. Maybe he'll offer some of his crop to the neighbors."

I pet Rocky and don't say anything.

"It's beautiful up here."

I nod. "Where are you living now?"

"South Beach. I found a house within walking distance of work. The slough is just a block away. Boats cruise by. It's very comfortable."

"Isn't Hatfield closed because of COVID?"

"The visitors center, yes. But we're still doing research and caring for the sea animals that live there. Most of the people working at the visitor's center were volunteers. I'm sure they miss it a lot."

A car approaches. We both look toward the road, but it keeps going.

Miguel studies me and Rocky. "Maybe I should adopt a dog."

"They're great company." I stare at my harmonica and wipe a smudge of spit on my jeans.

"Well, I guess I should go. Unless you'd like to join me for dinner?"

I swallow. Per COVID regulations, we're not supposed to mingle with other people, but after my rejection by Eugenia and my father doing his disappearing act, dinner with a new person sounds nice. I was such a bitch to Miguel last year, but I didn't want to be around any man at that point. Plus, I hadn't seen my father in ages. I wanted a chance to talk to him alone, but there was Miguel, all friendly and conversational, not understanding that we had private things to talk about. Still in his wandering phase, Dad was back on the road the next day.

"I need to take Rocky home and give him his dinner."

"Sure. Where's your house?"

"It's just down the hill."

"I can drive you."

"He'd get fur all over your car. We'll walk."

"I'll meet you there."

He's still a little pushy, but what the hell. Barbecued salmon sounds delicious. We'll wear our masks and keep our distance when we're not eating.

As Rocky and I walk down the driveway, Miguel leans out of his car. "Which house is it?"

"The pink one with the big rainbow."

"Excuse me?"

"Pink house. Rainbow."

"Now he thinks we're gay," I tell Rocky. "Maybe that's a good thing." I laugh and fluff my spiky red hair, which is just a shade redder than my dog's fur.

AT HOME, DAKOTA is folding sheets. She looks past us to the driveway. "Who's that?"

"Miguel. Friend of my dad's. He wanted to invite my father to dinner, but Dad isn't home, so he asked me instead."

"Is this a date?"

"No, definitely not. I'm sorry to abandon you."

"No worries. I'll eat a sandwich. Watch yourself with this guy."

"Oh, I will. He probably thinks I'm gay since I live here. I don't plan to argue the point."

"Come on, you're as hetero as they get. Now, Rocky might be queer, I don't know for sure. I caught him trying to hump my friend's male Dobie the other day."

I squat to look into the dog's brown eyes. "Rocky, you idiot. That's not how it works."

"Maybe it is for him."

"Right. I'll feed the dog before I go."

"Okay."

I'm in the bedroom trying to decide whether to change my top when Dakota hollers, "Hey PD, guess who's here."

I'm buttoning my white blouse as I come out. My father's truck is parked behind Miguel's car.

"Huh. Maybe I don't have to go now."

"Go. Have fun. Rocky and I will watch a movie or something. Just wear your mask. We don't want any virus here."

"Miguel mentioned a barbecue. I guess we'll be eating outside."

"Take your raincoat then. Rain's coming."

"Be good," I tell Rocky, who is busy crunching kibble.

"Hey, did you see Eugenia?" Dakota asks.

"Yes, but she kicked me out when I asked about her kids."

"Ah."

"Do you know what happened?"

"Only rumors. I'll tell you about it later. Your men are waiting."

Dad and Miguel have climbed up the porch steps, and Dad's about to knock on the door when I open it.

"Hey, guys."

"I hear you're joining us for dinner. Let's go, I'm hungry."

Who is this man who looks like my father, except he has a beard and plants gardens and hangs out with men twenty years younger than he is?

6. He's Perfect on Paper

IN DAD'S TRUCK, we follow Miguel's car down the mountain, through the marsh area, and turn right on the Coast Highway. The sun, muted by clouds now, hangs low on the horizon.

"Dad, where were you this afternoon?"

"Out with a friend."

"What friend? We're not supposed to congregate. COVID, remember?"

"She and I have agreed to trust each other. We will take every precaution, and if we get sick, we get sick. Same as you and me."

"She who?"

"My friend."

"Dad, are you dating?"

"I'm a single man, PD. I need companionship. You should be going out, too."

"I tried it. I'm taking a break."

Dad shakes his head. "Look, PD, you've had some bad experiences. Miguel, too. He's on his own now, with his ex-wife and daughter in New Mexico. And my own marriage of 40 years went belly-up. Think I'm happy about that? I am not, but that's the way it is." He slows for a car turning off the road at 143rd Street in South Beach. "I told Miguel about you being attacked and about Donovan. He knows about your divorce and Tom dying. Despite all that, he'd like to get to know you."

"Dad!"

"Hush. We were just two guys talking, and I love my little girl. I want you to be happy. I don't want you to be alone."

"I'm not. I've got Dakota and Rocky and lots of friends."

"Not that special someone."

"I had him. He died. Can we please change the subject? Or maybe you could tell me who the hell you're dating. Am I going to get a surprise stepmother?"

"Miguel says he got the salmon from fishermen at the dock in Newport. With the fish plant shut down, they're selling directly to consumers at fantastic prices. We should buy some, put it in the freezer for when we can have company."

What's this "we" business? I'll probably wind up cooking the fish. "Is it just salmon?"

"No, all kinds of seafood."

"Maybe I'll go there after work one of these days."

We pass an RV park with no RVs and Lost Creek State Park, which is closed. Where the road opens briefly to two lanes, a white Toyota zooms past us. At the airport, beneath the Welcome to Newport sign with its slogan, "The Friendliest," someone has hung another sign: *Be safe; wear a mask.*

Trees, trees, trees, glimpses of ocean.

Just past Hoover's bar and the Lighthouse fish deli, the Yaquina Bridge looms, its green arches featured on every sign, ad, and article about Newport. Damaged in the tsunami, it was closed for months. With one narrow lane in each direction, with pillars and designs carved into the stone, it is not adequate for today's traffic. We'd be better off with a new bridge like the one in Waldport that is now four lanes of streamlined driving, but the city hasn't gotten to it yet. Old-timers on the coast are sentimental about their ornate old bridges. Before they were built in the 1930s, you had to take a ferry to travel anywhere from where we live. If you missed the boat, you spent the night.

Miguel turns right just before the bridge, leads us past La Quinta Hotel and Pirates Plunder secondhand and collectible store, closed like everything else, and continues east two blocks, pulling into the driveway of a small celery-green house.

Dad parks next to him.

The house looks cozy, plain compared to the cottage Janey and I rented near the hospital, but it has character. Dad points out a wooden sea gull nailed to a post.

"Make yourselves at home," Miguel says, letting us in. He takes off his jacket and hangs it on a hook near the door. His beige v-neck sweater reveals smooth brown skin and well-shaped abs. The man has been working out.

"I'll start the barbecue," he says. "Help yourself to beer in the fridge and some hors d'oeuvres I made earlier."

Miguel is one organized man. Against the walls behind his brown leather recliner and matching sofa, his books are alphabetized in a series of shelves divided into fiction and non-fiction like a library. Ocean paintings dominate the walls. Pale light filters in through translucent white curtains.

"Nice place," I say to Dad.

"Yeah. He's a good guy, PD. I like him a lot."

"I'm sure he's great, but stop trying to fix me up."

"Fine. This is just dinner with friends. He doesn't know anyone here except the crew at Hatfield. He's probably lonely."

"Okay. Miguel, can I help with anything?" I call through the open door to the patio.

"No. We've got green salad and potato salad, sliced vegetables, hummus, and chips. The table is already set. I think we're good."

In the corner near the sliding door, I spy an electronic keyboard on a stand. "You play piano?"

"Not really. I'm taking lessons online. Your father says you're a pro. You can play something if you want to."

I think I will. It's something to do. While I play, Dad sips his beer, and Miguel prepares dinner. The music comforts me.

We eat at a small wooden table in the kitchen, a little too close for my comfort when we aren't wearing masks. The food is delicious. I've never had barbecued salmon before. Now I'm going to crave it all the time. I love the way it's crisp on the outside and sweet on the inside.

"Miguel, what did you put on the fish? It's so good."

"That's a secret." He nods toward a bottle on the counter.

"I see."

The sun breaks through the clouds, spreading a golden light through the house.

"Would you like to take a walk before dessert?" Miguel asks.

Dad and I are both ready.

Miguel leads the way past a half dozen old houses into an open area bounded by Yaquina Bay on the left and a marsh on the right. I have to say our host looks good from the back, too.

"Skunk cabbage," he says, pointing to where giant yellow flowers poke out of massive leaves.

They do smell kind of skunky.

Birds are making a racket in the brush. Like robins with a new repertoire. "Miguel, what are those birds?"

"You know, I'm not sure," he says. "We can look them up when we get back."

We keep walking as the bay on our left narrows into the Yaquina River. In the distance, we can see boats, houses, and a massive blue natural gas tank.

Loud honks erupt nearby. It sounds like a trombone duet. An opening in the bushes reveals a pair of geese. "Hey, I know what those are," I say.

"Yeah, they're a lot of fun. Sometimes they even come walking up the street into our yards."

I notice a sign on the right that says *Fish passage study*. "Are you involved in that, Miguel?"

"Indirectly. We consult with the Mid-Coast Watershed Council. The objective is to provide safe passage for young salmon passing through here and under the highway. We've built a culvert, and it works pretty well."

"I guess fishing would be discouraged here," my father says.

Miguel looks puzzled then laughs. "That would be correct."

As we walk on, trees on both sides block most of the fading sunlight. "How far does this go?" I ask.

"Not much farther. The road dead ends at Idaho Point. It used to be a commercial campground. Maybe a dozen families live there now. I've gotten to know some of them."

"You can walk to work?" Dad asks.

"Sure can. Unless it's pouring rain, I do walk. It's about a mile and a quarter if I take the roads, only a couple blocks if the tide is out and I can walk through the estuary."

"So, you get your exercise."

"I do. I joined the gym here in South Beach. When it closed, I turned my spare bedroom into a gym. I'll show you later."

"PD was a gym rat, too."

"Dad . . ."

It's true. When I first moved here, I was always at the gym. I lost a bunch of weight and really got in shape, but with everything that has happened, I've slacked off. I know what my father is thinking. I can work out with Miguel in his home gym, and romance will bloom. Sweating is so sexy.

"Between work and school, I don't have much free time, but Rocky keeps me moving up at Beaver Creek."

The sun ducks behind the clouds, and the wind picks up. I bury my cold hands in my sleeves. It's about to rain.

"Ready to go back?" Miguel asks.

We walk in silence, our shoes tapping the pavement. A truck passes, and Miguel waves. This is another small community between the bridges, just like Beaver Creek but at sea level.

Back at the house, Miguel's kitchen feels warm after the cold breeze outside.

"Sit and relax," he says as he takes a carrot cake out of the fridge.

"Did you bake that?" I ask.

"No, I bought it."

I don't confess that I had chocolate birthday cake a few hours ago. I really do need to start exercising again. Meanwhile, I savor the cream cheese frosting and the irony of something made from vegetables that is so fattening.

When our plates are clean, my father stands. "Thank you, Miguel. This has been wonderful. We'll have to do it again in our neighborhood."

"I would love that. Have a good night, you two. PD, I hope to see you again soon. My gym is open to you any time."

Any other guy would be hinting at more than running on a treadmill and lifting weights, but I think Miguel is truly just offering his gym.

"Thank you," I say. "I appreciate it." Not that I'm ever going to come work out here.

In the truck, heading south, Dad says, "That was fun."

"It was."

I can see he wants to say more but is afraid to set me off.

"Hey Dad, what's with your garden? Are you suddenly becoming Farmer Jack? And where are Donovan's sculptures?"

"Well, he came and got them. I don't know what he's going to do with them. I decided, what with the pandemic and things running short at the grocery stores, I'd give gardening a shot. The critters are giving me a challenge, pulling plants out as soon as they emerge from the soil, but I'm hoping in a few months we'll have enough for our own little farmers' market."

"That would be great. I want to restart the Between the Bridges giveaways next month when the weather ought to be better. Maybe we can offer some produce."

"If God and Mother Nature cooperate."

After the tsunami, Maryann started this monthly charity giveaway for the people who had lost their homes and businesses in the disaster. Our little community between the bridges into Newport and Waldport was stranded when the bridges went down, and we kept it up after the bridges reopened. We gave away donated food and clothing and served free breakfast. We connected people with services, whether they needed carpenters to rebuild their houses or counseling to move past the trauma. COVID put a halt to everything. But I think the need is greater than ever, and Maryann made us promise to keep it going.

"If your garden doesn't work out, we'll beg for donations from the grocery stores and restaurants, like we did last year."

"Either way, I'll help."

"You'd better."

He smiles and nods. More and more, I'm getting to know Jack O'Leary not just as my father but as kind of a cool older man. I don't think I really knew him before. He was always busy and, well, I was a stupid kid. I think the divorce gave him a kind of freedom he had never experienced before. It wasn't great for Mom, but he seems like a new man.

Back at the rainbow house, Dakota has fallen asleep in the easy chair, but Rocky greets me at the door. I let him out for a quick constitutional, and then we head for bed, overfull and pleasantly weary.

There's a note on my pillow from Dakota. "A woman named Beverly from your church is gathering singers for a Zoom Mass at nine a.m. tomorrow. She hopes you will come." Her phone number follows.

Beverly? Lizzy's the choir director. I don't know who Beverly is. I was going to join the choir before COVID hit, but I kept putting it off. The virus gave me a good excuse to sleep in and watch Masses online from the cathedral in Portland and my old church in Santa Cruz.

Is Our Lady of Grace reopening? Will anybody come? Maybe I'll go just to find out what's what. At least it's a chance to sing.

"What do you think, Rocky?"

He wags his tail. Well, all right then.

As I settle into bed, Rocky beside me, I think about Miguel. He's handsome. I like his smooth brown skin, his perfect smile, and his thick hair. He has just the slightest touch of a Spanish accent. He's nice, normal, smart, gainfully employed, and has a cozy house. He's even trying to learn to play the piano. The ex-wife and child in New Mexico are no problem. Everyone has a past. On paper, he's perfect. But there's just no spark.

Maybe I'll never find that spark again. I pull Rocky closer. He groans, sighs, and falls asleep.

7. Zoom Mass

Sunday, May 31, 2020

I WAKE TO A DEEP Sunday morning silence. Rocky is asleep beside me, his doggy lips turned up in a smile. I wonder what he's dreaming about.

I need to get up and dressed. Why am I doing the church choir thing again? Didn't I do enough in Santa Cruz and Missoula? Besides, this can't be like an ordinary Mass. The doors have been locked since the second week in March. Last month, the archbishop said we could admit up to 25 people, but our church stayed closed. Some churches have been distributing communion to people in their cars. Other parishes offer online Masses, but not Our Lady of Grace. Our priest is old-school. I think if he had his way, we'd be chanting the Mass in Latin, and women would still have to cover their heads. I'm amazed we're joining the Zoom Mass crowd.

I slide out of the covers, do my business in the bathroom, and make coffee and toast for breakfast as quietly as I can. Just as I'm about to sit down and eat, Rocky wakes up and wants to go outside. I stand on the porch as he trots around the yard, lifts his leg on a couple of trees and stampedes back, ready for his dog chow.

It's okay. The fresh air feels good, and my stomach is jumbly anyway. In Missoula, I held down the alto section even when Tom was really sick. After he died, I only missed one weekend. I needed people, and I needed to do normal things. But when I left Montana, I thought I left all that behind. I was going to be a different kind of musician. Now here I am choosing an outfit for church and wondering what we're going to sing. Will we have to wear our masks? How will we breathe?

Never mind. Somewhere in the Bible it says if you have a talent, you're supposed to use it. So, I fluff my hair, grab my purse, and kiss the dog goodbye.

Dakota peeks out of her room, her hair loose and wild. "Church?"

"Yep."

"Have fun."

It takes 20 minutes to travel down the hill and into Newport to Our Lady of Grace, a rectangular brick building whose steeple can be seen for miles over the one-story businesses that surround it.

There's one car in the front parking lot. Used to be a busy place, with church ladies in the hall preparing coffee and pastries for after Mass and sometimes the Knights of Columbus making breakfast, but there's no more of that, thanks to COVID. No religious education, no Bible study, no socializing after Mass.

Okay. Mask on. Blue one today.

The front door of the church is unlocked. Inside, it's chilly and dimly lit. Bulletins from early March fill the rack. The holy water fonts are dry. The book of special intensions lies open. The last handwritten entry says Erma Hughes has the coronavirus. I wonder if she survived.

Morning light beams through the stained-glass windows onto empty pews. To the left of the altar near the piano, an older woman with peacock-blue hair is conferring with a tall Hispanic priest. Where's Fr. Clarkson?

They're both wearing masks. I guess I'm stuck with mine.

"PD. Hi. I'm Beverly Bacon. Thank you for coming." Her voice is gravelly and her head shakes.

"Happy to. Where is Lizzy?"

"Oh, she's afraid of spreading the virus to her elderly parents, so she asked me to step in. I'm good at leading but terrible at the piano. I'm glad you're here."

"Am I too early? Where's the rest of the choir?"

"They're not coming. Ronny Mae has gone to stay with her daughter in Bend. And Willa refuses to leave her house. Did you read that article where a whole choir got sick after rehearsing together? Apparently singing really spreads the virus. I can't blame anyone for staying home. I just figure I'm old. If I go, I go with the Lord. Besides, we'll wear our masks and be six feet apart. "It's going to be just you and me and Father Rigoberto. We call him Father Rigo. Father, this is PD Soares."

We start to shake hands then stop ourselves and nod. I think he's smiling behind his black mask. "Nice to meet you, PD. I hear you're very talented."

"Father is subbing for Father Clarkson, who has taken a leave of absence," Beverly says.

"Is he all right?"

"I think so. I guess he figured it was a good time to relax for a while."

"I'll let you girls work on the music. The songs look fine," Father Rigo says, heading for the sacristy.

"Now, what I was thinking was—can you play and sing at the same time?"

"Yes."

"If you would play the piano, it would be a huge relief because my hands shake so bad I miss every other note. I could take the lead in the singing, do the high parts, the psalm and gospel acclamation. You can sing with me or do harmony if you want."

"What are we singing?"

"Here." She spreads the handwritten list on the piano. "I took a chance on some newer songs. Do you know them?"

"In my sleep." Oh, thank God, they're not the moldy old ones Father Clarkson likes. I wonder how the congregation will react. But what the heck, they're not here.

"I've got a book ready for you. Father will start the Mass around 9:30 or as soon as Billie is ready with the camera. Everything will be as usual except for nobody in the pews. We'll invite parishioners to sign up for 20 slots next week, but we'll use this time to get our act together. Father said he would give us Communion, only the host, of course. Hopefully a few people will watch on Zoom."

"How do they even know about it? I didn't hear anything."

"It's pretty last minute this week, a practice run really, but it was on our Facebook page, and we'll email the bulletin to everyone. Father Rigo wants to bring people back together whatever way we can. He's even going to do Bible study on Zoom this week. Maybe you could tell your friends."

"Sure. Do you know Janey Peacock? She ought to come sing with us."

"I called her. She said she had to work with her mother at the diner, but she'll try to be here next week." She checks her watch. "Shall we warm up a little?"

I settle on the bench at the electronic piano, the kind that has umpteen different "voices" and lots of automatic rhythm sections. I used one like this in Missoula when I subbed on piano. I don't need all that stuff. All I really need are the power button and the volume control.

From the piano, I have a clear view of the altar and the choir. Half the pews are behind me, but there's nobody in them anyway.

I fumble into the first song. I'm nervous, and I haven't had a chance to practice this music. The piano feels different from my old acoustic one. My voice is raspier than usual. Beverly has a distinct vibrato, but at least she's willing to do it, and she is on pitch.

The door opens. Someone's coming in.

That must be Billie. About Janey's age, wearing a red leather baseball cap over her blonde ponytail, Billie rushes in, out of breath. She sets up a tripod with her iPhone as the camera, adjusting, staring at the altar, adjusting a little more, talking to herself. "Let's see, Father will be there and then . . ."

She's ready by the time we have gone through all the music.

I dash for the restroom. I have never seen it so clean, wastebaskets empty, paper towel holders full. No one has been using it.

As I pass the sacristy, I see Father Rigo putting on green vestments. We have skipped all the way from before Ash Wednesday to Ordinary Time, missing Lent, Easter, and all the other spring feasts with purple, white or red vestments. Father's lips are moving. He's either praying or practicing his homily.

As Mass begins and the priest walks in, I'm surprised to hear him singing with us. What a nice voice! I hope he sticks around.

Where the folks are supposed to respond, it's just me, Beverly, and Billie. Instead of leading the Mass, Father watches Billie to make sure she is ready for each transition. After we start the offertory song, for example, she stops us. "I'm sorry, can you start again?" When Beverly misses a line in the psalm, Billie tells her they'll record it again after Mass.

There is no altar server or lector. Billie goes up to the ambo to do the readings. Then Father reads the gospel and preaches to an invisible congregation. Billie keeps gesturing at him to look at the camera. After the Eucharistic prayers, Communion takes 30 seconds. It's all like this weird secret ritual. Because of my mask, I have my usual headache, and I can't get enough air. Every time I take a big breath, I suck in a mouthful of cotton. When the camera is on Father, I lift the mask a little and gasp.

After Mass ends and the camera is off, I close the piano and rest my head on the lid.

"Thank you so much, PD," Beverly says. Her drooping mask has left grooves across her wrinkled face. "I was scared I would have to do this alone."

"You'd do fine."

"No, I don't like to sing solos. I'm a choir person, not a performer. That's more your thing, I guess."

"Used to be."

"Anyway, we survived. I would hug you if I could. Will you come back next week? Please? I'll make you an accompaniment book so you can practice at home."

"Sure. How do people find the link to watch this?"

"Billie's going to send it out. In fact, she said she's going to put it on YouTube so people can watch the Mass whenever they want. We can even watch ourselves."

"I don't know if I want to."

"Me either. Well, thanks, PD. I'll be in touch. If you can bring Janey, it would be a big help. She has such a beautiful voice."

"I know. I'll work on her."

When I walk out, it feels like I'm getting out of prison. I was concentrating so hard on the music and the camera that I didn't experience much religion. Sometimes I think I'm more likely to find God on a mountaintop or walking on the beach. But don't tell anybody I said that. I'm trying to be a good Catholic. Speaking of which, I invited my father, but he said, "No thanks." That's between him and God.

The streets are empty as I drive south. There's still a lot of morning left, and the weather is decent. The beach calls to me. The state parks are closed, with sawhorses and tape blocking the entrances, but I have found a couple places I can park and walk to the sand, including one near Ona Beach, right at the turnoff to Beaver Creek.

No crowds. No mask. Just the ocean waving in and out as if nothing was wrong. Just like it did the day before and the day after the tsunami. I guess you just never know.

8. The Pandemic Hits Home

Wednesday, June 10, 2020

IT'S GETTING WORSE. The ER and Urgent Care are backed up. There was a big outbreak at the fish-processing plant on the Bayfront. We're running out of ICU beds and ventilators. When we try to send patients to the bigger hospital in Corvallis, they say they don't have any room either.

Governor Brown has ordered all Oregonians to stay home unless it's absolutely necessary to go out, and then we have to wear masks. We're getting more outbreaks. Four cases among employees at McDonald's, four at Georgie's Beachside Grill, three from a family gathering. We've got six people on life support.

The biggest problem is the fish plant. Most of its employees are immigrants from Mexico and Central America, and they don't speak English. The health department is going crazy with testing, tracing, and trying to convince people to isolate.

Schools and businesses are closed, every event from concerts to soccer games is canceled, and grocery stores are bringing food ordered online out to people's cars. We're back to paper and plastic bags because we're not allowed to bring in our cloth bags lest they carry the virus. Stay home, we're told, but some people are still working because they can't afford not to, and others don't understand that the governor's order does not allow parties, sleepovers, or, ahem, barbecues. I sure hope we didn't screw up last weekend by having dinner at Miguel's house.

Most people who come to the hospital are aware of the rules and nice about the whole thing, but every now and then we get a stinker who thinks we're all nuts to be worrying about this virus. *Hell, it's no worse than the common cold.*

That's not what I'm hearing. The numbers . . . dear God. The first death was reported in China in January. By Feb. 10, over a thousand people had died, and cases were showing up in the U.S. By March 11, over 4,200 people had died, and the World Health Organization declared it a pandemic. Within a few days, everything shut down. I'd never seen anything like this before.

People talked about the influenza epidemic of the early 1900s. Who ever thought this could happen again? By April, more than a million cases had been confirmed worldwide, including half a million in the United States, and over a hundred thousand deaths here. It's not slowing down. The experts are supposedly working like crazy to come up with a vaccine, but right now, we've got nothing. You survive it or you don't. It's like the flu on steroids.

In the early stages, it's hard to know whether you have the Coronavirus or just a cold. People are being infected with COVID by friends and relatives who have no symptoms at all. I've even heard you might be able to get it from your dog or cat. Rocky refuses to wear a mask.

We have drive-up testing set up outside our urgent care building. People make an appointment online, then pull up in their cars, have a swab shoved up their noses, and wait for a text message with the results. If it's positive, they are supposed to isolate for two weeks and inform everyone they have been in contact with. But if you don't live alone, how do you keep your family from getting it?

Hospital staff are tested once a week, first thing every Monday morning.

So far, I'm okay.

But it's hectic.

Dakota and I were hoping to have our Between the Bridges giveaway a week from Saturday. We were able to help a lot of people after the tsunami. The day we opened, a woman whose house was destroyed told us she had lost her cat. A man who was waiting in line said he had just found one. And it was hers. Amazing. Even better, he invited her to stay with him and his wife until she got settled. I wonder if she's still there.

The problems are different now. So many folks have lost their jobs. Their kids are home, and daycare is nonexistent. Stuck in isolation, something as simple as buying toilet paper or getting a hamburger becomes nearly impossible. Those of us who can are working remotely by computer and ordering necessities online, but what about the ones who can't? People like Eugenia all alone in their houses? Or the ones who might be sick, but don't have the strength to call for help? Especially when there isn't any help close by.

We are all very much aware that if anything big goes down, those of us who live between the bridges will be stranded. All it takes is an accident on the highway, a fallen tree, or a landslide where a chunk of asphalt falls off the road, and we're stuck. We need to help each other. Some people have never recovered from the tsunami, and now we have this other disaster going on.

I've been making myself crazy trying to figure out how to do this under the stay-in-place orders. We canceled Between the Bridges in April and May, and I'd hate to do it again. I suppose we could all meet online like that crazy birthday party for Jonas' twins, but then how do we deliver things to people?

Dakota thinks we should organize drive-up stations in the parking lot at the diner. People could pick up some pancakes and eggs, grab masks, clothing, nonperishable food or whatever from giveaway tables, and maybe fill out forms for insurance and unemployment, like we did before. It would be great if we could find someone qualified to administer COVID tests. Maybe someone from the nursing program at the college could do it.

I have a 10-minute break in the garden, time for one call. Two if they're short. I dial the diner, where Diana should be relaxing between the breakfast and lunch rushes.

"Hello?"

Her voice is scratchier than usual.

"Diana?"

"Yeah. What's up, PD?" She coughs. It's deeper than her usual smoker's cough.

"Are you sick?"

"I don't know. It's probably a cold. Or hay fever."

"You should get tested."

"It's just a runny nose and cough."

"Still."

"PD, I've got biscuits in the oven. What do you need?"

"Are you ready for next Saturday's Between the Bridges?"

She coughs again and clears her throat. "Geez, I forgot about that."

"That's why I'm calling."

More coughing. A nose blow. She's definitely sick. "Yeah, sure. If you think people will actually come."

"I don't know. But I need Janey's help if they do."

"Well, I can't spare her. Julio hasn't shown up for a couple days. I don't know what's going on there. If he wanted to quit, he could just tell me."

"Doesn't he work part-time at one of the fish plants?"

"Uh-huh. Why?"

"Over a hundred people who work there have COVID. They had to shut the place down."

"Oh, shit."

"Exactly."

"I guess I'll take the test."

"You can schedule it online."

"Everything's online now. Like that damned birthday party."

"Well, it was better than nothing. The girls won't remember anyway."

"No, but they could be my last grandchildren. Who knows?"

"What about Janey? She'll be having kids, too."

Diana starts coughing so hard I don't think she hears me.

"With everything that's going on, Janey's talking about moving to New York and performing on Broadway."

"The theaters are closed."

"I know." Cough. Wheeze. "Oh, there's the timer. I have to go. I'll make sure there's extra breakfast on Saturday. Nine o'clock, right?"

"Yes. Thank you."

Who's going to want breakfast cooked by somebody coughing like that? I'm getting nervous.

Jackson is at the window, waving at me. Break's over.

Next break, I'll call the college. No, wait, nobody's there. It's all online. I took my music composition class on Zoom last quarter. They canceled summer classes. If my friend Helen was still in the program, she could come and do COVID tests, but dang it, she moved to Portland. They probably wouldn't let us do it outside the hospital anyway. Too many variables. But we can help people schedule appointments.

That sounds an awful lot like my day job. Maybe nobody will come.

AT LUNCHTIME, I park on the Bayfront overlooking the fishing docks. When I call the college, hoping for at least a phone number or email address, I hear a recording telling me, "Effective March 16, all in-person classes are canceled due to the pandemic. Contact your individual instructors for information about remote learning possibilities. Students and staff will be notified when it is safe to return."

This is like living in the Twilight Zone. I find the program's Facebook group online and post a request for someone connected with the nursing program to call me.

Maybe we should just cancel the whole thing. But then I think about that one hungry person who might show up and find nobody there.

I pull my ham sandwich out of my bag and unwrap it, grateful to have something good to eat.

Usually, every parking space on the Bayfront is full. Tourists stroll from gift shops to Ripley's Believe It or Not to the restaurants to the floating docks where sea lions provide free entertainment. Now I've got the place to myself. The sea lions are barking, and a gull flying past sounds like he's laughing, but there are no people around. Spooky.

I almost expect to be arrested for being out of my house.

The phone startles me. Janey. "Hey."

"Hey, PD, Mom's sick."

"I know. I talked to her this morning."

"No, I mean she's really sick, just coughing her guts out. I went to help with lunch, and she hadn't cooked hardly anything. I had to scramble to put some food together. She has a fever and says she can't breathe. I don't know what to do."

I wrap up the rest of my sandwich. "Bring her to the ER. She might have the virus. Which means you have been exposed. She's not still at the diner, is she?"

"No. Only a few customers showed up. When they heard her coughing, they backed right out of there. I told Jonas to cancel his deliveries, and I took Mom home."

"Good. Bring her in. I'll be back at my desk by the time you arrive."

"Okay. Thanks."

It's one thing when it's strangers, another when it hits people you love.

I drive up the hill to the hospital. We've got to cancel the Between the Bridges event again. I don't think anyone will be surprised. Everything else is canceled. It's too late to stop the notice in the local newspaper, and people may have already seen the flyers Dakota put up. I'll ask her to take them down and notify everyone involved that it's off.

I call Dad from the parking lot. He was going to help.

No answer. Out again? Where does that man go?

Jeez, look at the line for testing. The line to enter the building is just as bad. Jackson must be losing his mind. Mask up, PD. There's work to do.

9. Dad's Lady Friend

DO WE BRING IN the bleeders or the coughers first? Tough call. The ones that come by ambulance bypass us and go straight in, but that still leaves a waiting room full of people who all want help right now.

"How's it going?" I ask Jackson as I sign in on the computer.

"Crazy. We can't send anybody inside until they clear a couple ER beds. There's no room upstairs to admit anyone."

"What do we do?"

"Beg for patience and look for beds in the Valley."

"Do they have beds?"

"Not many."

It's probably good no one can read our lips to see what we're saying behind our masks.

I call up the next person in line, a pale young woman in gray sweats. "Name and date of birth, please?"

I have processed a broken ankle, a nosebleed, a pregnant woman who is spotting, and two persistent coughs by the time Janey and Diana arrive. Diana is bent over, coughing hard behind her mask. As she starts to sit in a chair near the wall, I wave at them and shake my head. No, no, don't sit there. Janey pushes to the front of the line, causing some grumbling.

"Take Diana to that room over there with the kids' toys and stuff," I say. "She can't be in the regular waiting room."

"But what if—?"

Diana puts a hand on her arm and nods. "It's okay," she says, her voice like sandpaper.

"Janey, you have to wait in line, or these people will kill me."

"But."

"I know. Make sure you have her insurance information. We'll need to get you tested, too."

She rolls her eyes. "This is bonkers."

"I know."

The man at the front of the line holds up a hand wrapped in a bloody paper towel. "Can we move this along?"

"You're next, sir. What happened to your hand?"

"I had a run-in with the neighbor's German shepherd."

"We'll bring you in as soon as possible."

I'm not a drug-taker, but I'm thinking we need to set out bowls of Valium in the waiting room. The tension is so high the building might explode. I feel like I'll never get out of here. When I came to Oregon, I just wanted to sing and play the piano. What happened?

I finally get Diana and Janey checked in, but it's an hour before the nurse calls their names. As they pass my desk, Diana whispers, "Check on your father."

"What? Why?"

They hurry through the double doors.

I feel like I'm running a marathon. The line gets shorter, but it never goes away. We've got people lying on gurneys in the hallways. We're trying to find places in Albany, Corvallis, Eugene, and even Portland. Every hospital has the same problem. If they do have beds, they don't have enough staff or enough equipment, especially ventilators.

I'm scared somebody's going to die waiting for treatment.

If Diana and Janey have COVID, a whole lot of people I know may have been exposed.

I want to spend my 10-minute break in the chapel praying, but by the time I use the restroom, try Dad again with no answer, and spend three minutes breathing in the memorial garden, time's up.

By 3:00, I feel like I've been up for days and had too much to drink.

"Keep your mask," Jackson tells me as I lean over the computer to check out.

"It's nasty from wearing it all day."

"Mine too, but we're running low."

"Figures. I'll air it out at home."

He has stopped listening. "Hello, how can I help you?" he asks as a girl about 14 pushes a wheelchair to the desk with a person completely hidden under a gray blanket.

"My grandma is sick."

"Okay." He turns to me. "PD, go home. Zelda or Angie will be here in a sec."

I take one more look and hurry out the door.

Fog has settled over the coast again. It's chilly, but at least I'm outside. As soon as I'm within touching distance of my car, I rip off my masks and inhale. I can't help analyzing my breath. Do my lungs hurt or feel tight? Are they okay? Really okay? Is my throat sore?

In the car, I dial my father's number again. Nothing.

The radio news offers frightening statistics. It's becoming all COVID all the time everywhere. I punch it off and dig for a CD. Melissa Etheridge. From the pre-pandemic days.

I need a shower and clean clothes. I need food. I need a hug.

A half mile up Beaver Creek Road, I drive out of the fog into sunshine. Thank God. Might as well go straight to Dad's house and see what's up. If he's not there, maybe I can find some evidence of where he's gone. Maybe I shouldn't be so nosy, but I have a bad feeling.

As I pass the rainbow house, I realize I should have picked up something for dinner. With Diana's diner closed, there's no easy source between the bridges.

Dad's truck is in the driveway. Why isn't he answering the phone? Is he riding around with Miguel? Or his lady friend? Is she in there?

Up the steps. Knock on the door. Nothing. I peer through the windows. The lights are on. The fire is out. Oh, Lord. I'm getting flashbacks from when I found Donovan on the floor of his studio, bleeding from the wrists and going into a diabetic coma. I revived him with CPR while Dakota summoned an ambulance. No, I don't want to think about that.

As I turn my key in the lock, my heart is pounding. I put my mask back on.

"Dad?"

He moans from the bedroom. My father is curled on top of his bed in his underwear. His breathing is shallow, and his skin is on fire. He looks up at me, glassy-eyed. "PD," he whispers. "I—can't—breathe." He coughs, then fights to inhale. I see panic in his eyes, like a scuba diver who just ran out of oxygen.

Dear God, help. "Did you take anything for it?"

"No."

"Okay. Can you walk to the car, or should I call for an ambulance?" He shakes his head.

Thank God cell service is better here than it used to be. It was revamped after the tsunami. I tell the emergency operator what's happening. An ambulance is on the way.

I find my father's worn black wallet in the pants he threw off on the floor. His Medicare and supplementary insurance cards are inside. I grab some fresh clothes and check the medicine cabinet and kitchen sink to see what he's taking. Whoa. Prostate? Tranquilizers? I put the pill bottles in a plastic bag with his wallet and his clothes. The siren is getting louder.

I type a fast text to Dakota. *The ambulance is for Dad. I think it's COVID. Bad. I don't know when I'll be home. Don't come to the hospital. They won't let you in.*

It kills me seeing my father being hauled out on a gurney. Just a few days ago, he was healthy and fit, walking with me and Miguel . . . Oh shit. Does Miguel have it? Is that where Dad got it? Does that mean I'll get it too?

The ambulance guys look familiar, but I don't know their names. I don't know if they know I work at the hospital. I'm still wearing my badge. Doesn't matter. I'm in daughter mode now. "Shall I follow you?" I ask the bald one.

"No ma'am. No visitors. But tell me your number so the doctor can call you."

"I work at the hospital."

"Yeah, but you can't go with him unless you want to wait outside in the car."

It will take them 45 minutes just to get him into the ER and assess his condition. He might end up far away from here, and I'm exhausted. I hand over the bag with Dad's stuff.

As they hook him up to oxygen and insert an IV, they ask him questions. He says, "Tired," "Elephant-on-my-chest," "I don't know." They're just about to close the doors when Dad half sits up. "PD!"

I lean in. "I'll see you as soon as I can. I love you."

He holds up his hand like no, that's not what he wants to talk about. "Call Diana."

What? Why? And then, head slap, I realize who his new lady friend is. I don't tell him she's sick, too. He doesn't need that extra burden when he's fighting to breathe.

"I will." Tears sting my eyes as they close the doors and drive down the hill. I retreat to the porch and sit. "Please God, let him be okay. I just got him back. Please."

Everything was fine this morning. Well, not fine at the hospital. But that was there. Home was okay. Now, no place is safe.

Something moves out in the garden. A rabbit settles in to chew on Dad's young plants. I jump up and wave my arms. "Get out of here! No bunnies allowed."

The rabbit scoots away, but I know it'll be back. I should ask Dakota how to make some kind of protective cover before the whole garden is eaten.

I look up at the sky and yell, "Can't we have anything nice for more than a minute and a half?"

No answer. Might as well go home.

In the driveway, Dakota wraps me in her long skinny arms.

"I might have germs."

"I don't care." She rocks me as Rocky paws my legs. A soft wind whispers through the evergreens.

"Breathe, PD."

10.It Gets Worse

JANEY'S PHONE RINGS four times before she answers with a quick "hello," not her usual singing greeting. I hear Diana coughing in the background.

"Janey, what's happening? Did you both get tested? Did they admit your mother?"

"Yes and no. We've both got it, but so far, I'm not too bad, just tired and a little congested. Mom can't stop coughing, but they said she doesn't need to be in the hospital. Plus, they have no beds. We're on our way home to isolate for two weeks or until we're well."

"Okay. Listen, my father has it. He just left in an ambulance. I didn't know he was sick. I thought he was running around having fun somewhere and that's why he didn't answer his phone."

Janey stifles a cough. "Sorry. He's got it that bad?"

"Yes. He can't breathe, can barely talk. His oxygen level is dangerously low. I found him on the bed, too weak to get up. I think he peed himself."

"Oh, PD, that's awful."

Dakota is stirring something on the stove. Dinner? I never finished my lunch. Doesn't matter. "Janey, did you know my dad and your mom were dating?"

"What? No. That's crazy. How old is your father?"

"68."

"And Mom's 52. That blows my mind. I mean, he's a nice guy, but the idea of—gross—I guess they made each other sick."

"Where did it start?"

"The dating or the COVID? I don't know. The COVID might have been Julio. He finally called in sick. He's had it for a week. I hope we didn't make anybody else sick. When was the last time you ate food from the diner?"

"A couple days. Spaghetti day, whenever that was. Dakota goes there more than I do. Listen, I'll drive down and put up a sign saying you're closed for the next two weeks."

"Jonas already did that. He said he'd collect the perishable food and pass it around."

"I—my cell phone is ringing. It's the hospital."

"Go."

A man who introduces himself as Doctor Armstrong asks if I am Jack O'Leary's daughter.

When I say I am, he asks if I have medical power of attorney for him. Oh my God. Is he on life support? Now I can't breathe. "What's going on?" I ask.

"His condition has not changed. He can still speak for himself, but if he takes a turn, he might not be able to express his preferences. You're the next of kin, correct?"

I feel dizzy. "Yes, but tell me what's happening."

"Your father has a severe case of the Coronavirus. We've got him on oxygen right now in the ER, and I'd like to admit him, but we have no ICU beds left in Newport."

"I know. I work there at the admissions desk."

"Then you understand. We are sending him to Corvallis."

"Okay. Doctor, is he going to be all right?"

"I'll be honest. This virus is so new we can't predict the outcome. We have no proven treatment. Antibiotics don't work. All we can do is treat the fever and help them breathe. Most people pull through, but given your father's age and the severity of his symptoms, we just don't know."

"Can I possibly see him?"

In the background, a voice calls a code over the loudspeaker. He sighs. "No. We can't let anyone in. Besides, if you were just with him, you need to isolate until we're sure you don't have it."

"But I need to work. Have you seen the lines in admitting?"

"I have. But anyone, including staff, who has been directly exposed has to stay away."

"Crap. Has he already left?"

"They're loading him in the ambulance now. You can call Samaritan in Corvallis in a couple hours for more information. I'm afraid that's all I can tell you."

"Thank you."

The phone goes silent.

Tomato soup bubbles on the stove.

Dakota turns around. "Corvallis?"

"Yes."

"Well, that sucks, but it is a bigger hospital with more doctors and more equipment."

"I know."

She ladles soup into a bowl then places it in front of me. "Eat."

"I'm not hungry. What about you?"

"I already had something. You need nourishment. It's going to be a rough week."

She sits opposite me, sipping coffee.

"The doctor says I have to isolate because I've been exposed. But I think I should go to Corvallis. I could sit in my car."

"For how long, PD? What if you get sick, too?"

"I don't want to be here if he—you know."

"There's nothing you can do."

"This is just wrong. All wrong."

"I know. Eat."

The soup tastes good. That's a good sign. One key symptom is a loss of taste and smell. Maybe I'll finish my sandwich, too.

"Thank you for this. But Dakota, what if I've exposed you to the virus?"

"I'm tough. I'll deal with it. God knows what's on all that mail I'm touching every day. If I croak, I can be with Maryann. It's all good."

"No, it's not. We need you to stay alive. No more hugs. What time is it?"

"5:15. No, your father is not there yet."

She goes out to smoke. Rocky follows.

I text Janey to tell her what's happening. She says Jonas is on his way with a load of food. I'd better hide in my room when he comes. God forbid I expose him and his wife and four kids.

I need to call Miguel and my brother, but I'll wait until I have news from Corvallis. If it's not good, I'm going there, no matter what Dakota says.

6:30. JONAS HASN'T come yet. I'm pacing up and down the driveway like a prisoner in the recreation yard. I hate this. I can't go anywhere or do anything. I can't see other people. I know, I know, millions of people are doing the same thing. Some places are totally locked down. I read something online about people in Italy singing at their windows every night. People in other places, including New York, have started doing it. In several countries, folks applaud the hospital workers when they come out at the end of their shift. In parts of China, people can be arrested if they're caught outside their homes without permission. I've got a whole forest to explore, as long as I avoid other people.

When I called a while ago, the ICU nurse in Corvallis confirmed that my father had been admitted and was holding his own. He has pneumonia, a common path for COVID. He's on oxygen but doesn't need a ventilator, and he seems alert and oriented. He just has to fight it off, she said. No visitors. No Facetime. He needs to rest. All we can do is wait.

I'm not good at waiting.

I call Andy in Santa Cruz.

"I'm on my way," he says.

"No. Stay home. I would love to see you, but don't come. I'm isolating, and they won't let you in to see Dad. It's killing me not to be there, but we both need to stay put and stay healthy."

"Shit. Sometimes I think Iraq was easier than this virus. Okay, for now, I'll hold off. But if anything changes . . ."

"I know. Can you tell Mom?"

"Sure."

Our mother is so scared of COVID she never leaves the house. The flower shop where she works is closed like everything else. She chides Andy for continuing to work at his landscaping business, but he says you can't catch COVID from a rose bush.

As far as we know.

"Okay, Little Brother. Here's a big socially distanced hug."

"Hah. Keep me updated."

"I will."

Work is another hard call. Zelda, working the night shift, has been promoted to supervisor. I can picture her pounding her desk in frustration. We were already short-staffed. I don't know who can take my place, but I have no choice. I'm out the rest of the week.

Calls done, I'm pacing the driveway again.

"PD, sit down. You're making me tired."

"I can't, Dakota. I need something to do."

"Play some music."

"I'm not in the mood."

"Read. Knit. Watch something on YouTube."

"I'm not sick. I don't want to act like I am."

"Go for a walk. Water your father's vegetables. All this pacing is confusing the dog."

She's right. Rocky is following me down the driveway, up the driveway, down the driveway.

"I'm going down to Dad's house and see if I can clean up a little."

"There's virus there."

"There's virus everywhere. I'll open all the doors and windows."

I start down toward the road then stop. "Hey, do you know a way to keep the rabbits out of his vegetable garden?"

"It ain't easy. They're persistent little buggers. Ya gotta watch out for the big animals, too. Elk will pick your garden clean. I'll work on something. Don't be too long. It's getting dark."

"I won't."

It feels good to walk, with Rocky bounding ahead of me.

The cabin lights shine through the trees. I guess I forgot to turn them off.

The garden is clear of rabbits and rodents, although I see some of the plants have been bitten off just above the ground. I find the hose and spray some water on them anyway. They look dry. Who knows? Maybe something will grow.

Inside the cabin, I work my way through the rooms, stripping off the bedspread and sheets to wash with my germy clothes. I throw away sandwich makings that have clearly been sitting out for a few days, wash dishes, and pick towels off the bathroom floor. Without my mother to yell at him, my father has become a slob, but it's his house.

He has turned what used to be the art studio into a study. His old roll-top desk is here. Bookshelves ring the room, and there's a telescope by the sliding door. I imagine he sees some pretty good views of the creek by day and the stars on clear nights. I hope he can come home soon. Maybe I can sleep on the couch and help him until he gets his strength back.

I hate that this is happening. Last year we had a scare with my mother. Her heart slowed down until she collapsed. The doctors found evidence she had had a heart attack at some point. We knew something was wrong because she never sat still unless she was sick. A new pacemaker brought her back to normal rhythms, and she's all right now, but it put the fear of God in all of us.

I know people my age start losing their parents, but I'm not ready. Not even close.

I never thought about setting up power of attorney for my father. We never talked about it. I mean, 68, that's nothing these days, and he was in great health. We're definitely going to talk about it when he gets better. And it needs to go both ways. If I get sick, who's going to take care of me?

Dakota's not family. Besides, she went through enough with Maryann. I wonder if she had the legal right to make decisions for her. They weren't married until close to the end.

Walking through the cabin, I miss Donovan's cats, Sasha and Hernando. They were good company when I stayed here, but he took them with him to Corvallis.

I go out to the balcony. It's too cold to sit, and I can't see much through the fog and deepening darkness, just memories. A sunrise with Donovan. Peaceful evenings here alone. Warm nights with Tom. Wait. Tom was never here. Nuts. We should be together in Montana, healthy and happy and telling bedtime stories to our kids. As if that could keep the pandemic from happening.

Life is just one stinking tsunami after another, isn't it?

Rocky starts barking like crazy. As I walk out to see what's up, something scrambles out of the vegetable garden. "Good job, Rocky. Well done. Let's go home."

It really is dark out here. No streetlights, no cars, nothing between the cabin and the rainbow house except trees and bushes and whatever animals are watching us. To my right is a steep drop-off. I hug the landward side while Rocky trots ahead, oblivious. He knows the way home.

The porch light is on for us. Dakota is in the kitchen unloading grocery bags.

"Jonas brought us some leftovers. Can't let it go to waste. What do you want to freeze and what do you want to eat?"

I'm too tired to think. "I don't care. Is there any pie?"

She looks through the bags. "Yes, apple and marionberry."

"Good. I'll have some apple pie for breakfast. Keep out some kind of meat and vegetables for tomorrow and freeze the rest, I guess."

"Okay."

"How is Jonas?"

"Worried. About his mother. About his kids getting sick. About not having any income. Oh, and he says your dad and his mom are sleeping together. Are they?"

"That's the rumor. I'm still trying to digest that bit of news."

"They could both do worse."

"I know. But it's weird. Anyway, I hope Jonas saved most of the food for himself. He's got six mouths to feed."

"He said he did. How are things at the cabin?"

"Bunnies in the broccoli. Too many memories. I'm going to bed."

Ten minutes later, I'm under the covers, Rocky beside me. I hear Dakota locking the front door. It's like the jailer locking my cell.

11.Waiting

Thursday, June 11, 2020

I CAN'T SLEEP. I keep swallowing to see if my throat hurts and putting the back of my hand to my forehead, checking for fever. Nothing. If I don't get COVID, I can escape in a few days. I know they'll be going crazy at work, but until the incubation period passes, I can't do a damned thing.

I have never been to the hospital in Corvallis. I know it's bigger than our small-town facility, although smaller than the major medical centers in Portland. I know we send people there for anything we can't handle in Newport, from brain scans to open heart surgery. I suppose once you're inside, hospital rooms are pretty much the same everywhere. A bed, a tray table, a monitor, an IV stand, a little closet for your things, and a TV on the wall.

I wonder if Dad has a roommate, if he has a window, if they gave him anything to eat tonight. If he's breathing any easier.

I need to spend more time with my father. When I was a little girl, we were buddies. He worked all week, but he took me fishing and hiking on weekends. He had a trumpet in the closet. Once in a great while, he would bring it out and we'd play a duet. He wasn't very good at it, rusty, he said. He played in the high school marching band, mostly to be around a girl named Eloise who played the flute, but he remembered enough to blast out a tune.

When I got to high school, I was glad he worked at a different school. It would have been weird to have my father, "Mr. O'Leary," as my teacher.

When he went traveling, unraveling his marriage, I was furious with him, but I understand a little better now why he did it. If he can just survive this thing, all is forgiven.

He's a handsome man, my father. Smart. And kind. It's no wonder Diana likes him. Or that he likes her. She's a little rough-edged, but she loves hard and gives everything she has to anyone who needs it. Plus, she knows how to have fun. More than once, I have caught her in the kitchen at the diner dancing and singing—off key—to "Footloose" from the Kevin Bacon movie or something from the Grateful Dead and you could just feel the joy. Sure, her first marriage went bust, and the guy she was about to marry last year cheated on her. Money is tight, and she works hard, but she has a deep faith in God and keeps her glass half full.

I hope she's okay. I wonder if Donovan knows his sister and niece are sick. Maybe I'll call him tomorrow. What's he doing now that he can't teach or run his gallery? Is he still making his crazy art? A thing like this pandemic could send him into a deep depression.

Which makes me think of my father's tranquilizers. I always thought he was the calmest guy in the world. Mom was the moody one.

Rocky is snoring. I'm glad Jonas got us this giant yellow dog. I snuggle up close, feel his warmth, and hear his heart beating strong and even. My monkey brain slows down. I sleep.

When I wake up, it's overcast. Gray. Not my favorite.

Deep breath. Swallow. Hand to forehead. I'm okay. If I can stay okay for four days, I can escape. How many hours is that? 96.

6:30. Too early to make calls. I slide out of bed and put on my robe. Rocky opens his eyes.

"Come on."

Cool air. Tonic. I stand on the porch and stretch, laughing as Rocky stretches, too, then trots out to do his business. He won't go far because he hasn't had breakfast yet. Later, I'll take him to Dad's house. Maybe I can find boards or something to protect the garden. Then what? Should I drive to Corvallis?

Rocky trots up the porch steps, wagging his feathery tail.

"What should we do today, Rocky?" His brown eyes sparkle. Usually I'm hurrying to eat, dress and go to work, but today I'm free to play with him. He probably thinks it's Sunday.

Oh Lord, what about singing and playing at church? I need to call Beverly. I hope she doesn't have to do the music alone.

"Come on, Rocky, let's eat and get dressed. Want to share some apple pie with me?"

He looks like he's smiling.

AT EIGHT O'CLOCK, the ICU nurse in Corvallis tells me Dad is still "holding his own," but his fever is high, and his breathing is labored.

"Is he eating?"

"He had some Jell-O last night but says he doesn't want breakfast. It's not unusual with this virus to lose your appetite. He can't taste or smell anything. We're keeping him hydrated via IV."

"Right. Can I talk to him?"

"Maybe tonight. It's still difficult for him to speak."

"Okay. How long will he be in the ICU?"

"Hard to say. A couple more days, or it could be weeks. We just don't know. He could start feeling better or take a turn in the other direction. I'm sorry I don't have better news."

"It's not your fault. Thank you for everything you're doing. I know it's hard these days."

"I appreciate that."

I call Diana's house next. Janey answers, half asleep.

"How's it going there?"

"Oh, PD, let a person sleep. That's all I want to do. Mom, too. She's still hacking up a lung, but she's futzing around in the kitchen. How's your dad?"

"Pretty sick but hanging on."

"Okay. I need to sleep."

"You're sick now, too?"

"Oh yeah. G'night."

DAKOTA HAS GONE to the post office to sort the mail and welcome the few customers still coming to the window. Later, she'll deliver mail to the homes around Seal Rock and Beaver Creek. When I heard her coughing this morning, I panicked for a minute, but it was just her usual morning smoker's cough. I wish she'd quit smoking, but I can't imagine her without a cigarette, and I don't dare say anything about it. It's one of the unspoken agreements that come with living here.

I pace around the house a while, then settle at the piano. A little blues riff in E, then I start singing whatever comes into my head. Pandemic blues, got the pandemic blues, virus on my shoes, waiting for the news, a thousand people dead, an aching in my head, coyotes in the shed, I'm in virus jail, afraid to touch the mail…"

Shoot, this is goofy stuff, but I activate the recorder on my phone. Maybe I'll come up with something I want to save. I could add a harmonica riff. *Chucka chucka waaah waaaah wee ooh, I got the pandemic blues.* I need some paper and a pen.

Pandemic blues, got the pandemic blues . . .

By 10:00, I have a song I kind of like. I don't know where I'm going to play it. Maybe I'll put it online. Musicians are putting all kinds of stuff on Facebook and Instagram these days.

I position my phone on the piano, start the video camera and perform my new song. It's just for fun. I throw in a hot blues lick at the end, add a couple glissandos for spice, and click off the video. Share? Sure. Off it goes to the Internet.

Well, that was fun. I open the binder of church music Beverly dropped off for me at work the other day. Might as well practice. If I'm not sick by Sunday, I'm going to go play and sing. With my mask. Six feet away from Beverly and Father Rigo.

I'm on the closing song when the phone rings.

"Ms. PD Soares, I presume?"

"Donovan. I was going to call you. How are you?" As I move to the sofa, I picture this bearded Santa Claus giant and realize I miss him.

"I'm fine and dandy. How are my sister and my favorite niece? Jonas tells me they have caught the evil virus. They're not answering their telephone, and I thought you might know what's up."

"They do have it. I guess Janey went back to bed, and Diana didn't feel like answering the phone. I saw them at the hospital yesterday. Diana had a terrible cough. Janey hadn't gotten sick yet, but today she's feeling it, says all she wants to do is sleep."

"Oh dear."

"I think they'll be all right though. The doctor sent them home. They're young enough and strong enough to fight it. I'm more worried about my father."

"Jack?"

"Yes, I found him at the cabin yesterday in bad shape. He's at the hospital in Corvallis now. ICU. Holding his own, but it could go either way, the nurse says."

"Dear Lord. Perhaps I should pay him a visit."

"You can't. No visitors allowed."

"Bollix. Well, I will send up good thoughts for one and all. Are you well?"

"So far so good, but I have to isolate, and I'm not good at sitting still. I wrote a song this morning. Pandemic Blues."

He chuckles. "That's my girl. I miss seeing you, PD."

"I miss you, too. Maybe in a few days I can escape to Corvallis, and we can talk—with masks, at a safe distance."

"I presume that precludes hugging."

"Yes. And I sure could use one now."

"Me too. Email me your song. I'd love to hear you sing again."

"I put it on Facebook. You can hear it there."

"Excellent."

We say goodbye and hang up.

Damn. When Donovan is well, he is a warm, funny, fascinating man. But when his bipolar problems get ahead of him, he's either suicidal or manic with a touch of mean.

If things were different, I could end up with Donovan and my father with his sister and that would make us . . . what? Reminds me of that old song "I am my Own Grandpa."

Would Janey be my sister or my niece? Or both? I need to take my temperature. I might be delirious. 98.3. Normal. So far.

12. Pandemic Blues

Friday, June 12, 2020

I NEED A HAIRCUT, but that's hard to come by these days. Most salons are closed. The few that aren't closed operate strictly by appointment, ask all kinds of questions, and require everyone to wear masks, which makes it hard to cut, style or dye hair.

My once spiky red hair is looking flat and brownish. A grown-out spike is hair with no style at all. Just a mop, literally. If mops came in brown. Well, a dirty mop.

I asked Dakota if she ever cut hair, and she gave me this shocked gaunt-faced look. Then I remembered the last hair she cut was Maryann's when she was losing her beautiful hair to chemotherapy. "I'm sorry," I said.

"Be glad you've got hair," she said and went out for a walk.

I am, believe me. But either I start wearing hats all the time or take my scissors to this mop.

Why can't our hair be self-limiting like a dog's? I picture Rocky's fur continuously growing until it drags on the ground like a train on a wedding gown.

The dog is lying in the bathroom doorway staring at me. I'm sure he has decided humans are crazier than usual these days.

Okay, I'm going to do it. Nail scissors or knitting scissors? Oh, wait. Deep in a drawer, I have the scissors I used to cut Tom's hair when he was too sick to go to the barber. That didn't turn out so badly.

If I ruin my hair, I have plenty of time to knit a hat.

All I have to do is follow the lines from the previous haircut. Okay, I'm looking in the mirror, holding up a hank of top hair, surrounding it with the scissors. One, two, three, cut. The scissors make a squawking sound.

Maybe my hair should be wet. No, I'd lose my place. Cut again. Again. Hair starts falling into the sink. I grab a towel and block the drain. Too late to back out now. Cut, cut, cut. About an inch from my skull. No, an inch and a half. Closer on the sides.

Now I'm having trouble breathing, but it's not COVID. I think I'm giving myself a crew cut. Like Dad had in the old pictures from before I was born. Oh my God, oh my God.

Stop. Brush it out. Style it. It's kind of short but not too bad.

I know a lot of people are letting their hair just grow, but that long-haired person who kind of looks like me was the old me, pre-PD. This me has interesting hair. It feels velvety under my hand.

Ah, it *is* too short. But who cares? I have some dye in the cabinet, but I think I'll let it be brown for a while. Ooh, wouldn't it be cool if I got it tipped or frosted or whatever they call it. I could dye it pink or peacock blue.

I check my temperature again. Still normal. Cabin fever's making me crazy, I guess.

Okay, here's the deal. If I still have no symptoms, I'll make an appointment to be tested by next Friday. If it's negative, I will resume normal life. If not, oh hell, I'd be sick by then. Wouldn't I? They say you can carry COVID and have no symptoms.

Show yourself, you bastard.

HAS A DAY EVER lasted this long?

I know. I am blessed. I am healthy, free, living in a great place, and gainfully employed. There are people with real problems. But I can't shake the worry in my gut while I wait to hear an update about my father.

I text Jonas. *Thank you for the food. It's a big help. I had a turkey sandwich for lunch. Delicious. I hope you and yours are healthy. How are Janey and your mom?*

He responds right away. Probably as bored as I am. *You're welcome. We had turkey sandwiches too. We are all fine. Janey and Mom are sick and miserable but feisty so I'm not really worried. I hope your dad gets better soon.*

Thanks, I reply.

I don't know what else to say. I love Jonas, but we honestly don't know each other as well as I would like. He's two years older than Janey, but he's a lot younger than me. He played drums in our band. His wife Molly is nice, too, but overwhelmed with her kids.

Hmm. If my life had turned out differently, Tom and I could have been like them, happily obsessed with our children. He wouldn't be an unemployed taxi driver, and I wouldn't be a pie-maker shut down by COVID, but otherwise, yeah, that was the dream. That and a nightclub or coffee house/piano bar with live music. We were going to call it "PD's."

What if I deep-clean the whole house? It's something to do, and a good cleaning never hurts. Luckily, the phone rings before I can begin.

"Mom."

"PD, how is your father?"

"Well, hello to you. Dad is in the hospital in Corvallis. He has COVID, and it has moved into pneumonia. He's on oxygen and not eating, but he's holding his own. The ICU nurse says things could go either way at this point."

"Oh no." She sounds about to cry. "Are you going to see him?"

"They won't let me in. No visitors are allowed at all."

"I hate this damned virus, Cissy. I pray you don't get it."

"Me too. I hear you're being very careful."

"You have to be. I remember all the stories about the influenza epidemic of the last century. People forget. These things kill people."

"I know."

"I guess you see that at work."

"I do."

"You shouldn't be working there. It's too dangerous."

"Mom, somebody has to. We take every precaution."

"I know, but I want to lock you and your brother in your rooms until this is over."

"We'd sneak out the window."

"Well, I pray for you every day. Your father, too. I still love him, you know."

"I know."

The little girl in me has always wanted my parents to reunite. Now that Diana is in the picture, I don't think that will be happening."

"Maybe you should say a rosary or two for your father."

"Sure. Good idea." I haven't prayed the rosary since my grandmother's funeral.

She clears her throat. "I wish I could be there with you. Call me if anything changes with your father."

"I will. I love you, Mom."

"You too."

Her voice breaks as she says goodbye.

I swallow a wad of guilt for upsetting her. I know I didn't do anything wrong. I couldn't lie about this. I'm glad she's being careful. The way things are going, I could lose both parents, and I don't know how I'd survive that.

I take another look at my hair and shrug. I have another week to grow it out.

My phone dings with a text from Janey. *Look at Facebook. Your crazy song is going viral.*

What? I have to see this. Oh my gosh. She's right. On Facebook, my stupid little song has been shared 23 times and there are 56 comments with another coming in. Over 700 hundred people have clicked like, love, or the laughing emoji.

The comments range from "Love it!" to a gentleman who says he loves my sexy voice and would like to take me to dinner. The only problem is he lives in Chicago, and I suspect he might be a robot. I quickly type, "Thank you, everyone" and turn off my phone. What if I become famous for *that?* It's like Tiny Tim with "Tiptoe Through the

Tulips" or Paul Reuben's Pee Wee Herman. Nobody will pay attention to the serious music I hope to do.

People will "like" anything.

I start to the kitchen to make lunch then retreat to the phone and take another look at Facebook. Just in case, I add *Copyright PD Soares 2020* to my post.

13. Gabriel, Like the Angel

Tuesday, June 16, 2020

I'M GOING NUTS. It's the third week of June. The sun is out. I have read all I want to read, knitted until my knuckles ache, and telephoned everyone I ever wanted to talk to. I'm even tired of playing the piano.

I've got to do something. "Rocky, let's go for another walk."

The dog opens and closes his eyes, deep in his post-lunch nap.

Fine. I'll go by myself. I stuff my mask in my pocket just in case.

It's almost warm out. Let's patrol the estate. I'm not actually sure how much land Dakota owns. I know that beyond the green wire fence she put up for Rocky, her land stops somewhere between our house and the one south of us. The people who own that house live most of the year in Eugene. She's a professor at the University of Oregon. I don't know what he does. But how far east and north does our land go?

We don't have any formal gardens, although I'm thinking of planting some rhododendrons. They're big shrubs that bloom every spring with spectacular flowers in lots of different colors. I've seen red, pink, purple, yellow, and white rhodies. They remind me of my rose garden back in Montana. I'm not a garden geek, but I do like pretty flowers.

People call Portland the Rose City, but good luck with that here. Roses can't handle the weather, but rhodies love the cold, wet, windy, and once-in-a-blue-moon warm days. You see them everywhere. There's an annual rhododendron festival in Florence about an hour south of here. Or there used to be, before COVID.

God knows how much money cities are losing with no tourists, nothing open, and no special events.

I wonder if the nurseries are open. Most of them are outdoors, so why wouldn't they be? When I'm cleared to go among people, I'll have to go look. I could order plants online. People are ordering everything over the Internet. Dakota says she's delivering more than twice as many packages as before the lockdown. But I want to touch and smell the plants before I buy them.

Back to the yard tour. We've got spruce, pine, and Douglas fir, wild blackberries, ferns, and weeds in all shapes and colors, little purple daisies, yellow buttercups, and these white puffballs that are thousands of tiny flowers when you look up close. With nature providing so much, maybe we don't need to plant a garden.

Behind the house, Dakota has a woodshed stacked to the top with fresh-cut wood that keeps us warm. Another shed houses all kinds of tools and ladders and stuff. Some of my spare possessions, like china, Christmas decorations, nursing school notes, and clothes I'll probably never wear again, are boxed up in there, too.

Plain back door, no rainbow.

Oh, what's this? Leftover fencing material. Maybe I can steal some for Dad's garden.

Off to the east, there's an offshoot of Beaver Creek, barely a trickle most of the year, but it fills up in the winter.

I'm going to head north a bit.

Wait. COVID check. Swallow. Test for a cough. Feel for a fever. Lunch tasted normal. Still not sick.

I feel like I'm playing hooky from work.

Up the road, up the road. Dad's house looks so deserted. I keep seeing him in the back of the ambulance. Shake it off, PD.

I start to jog. A truck passes. I wave.

"Where's your dog?" the driver calls.

"Sleeping."

"Good for him. Be safe."

I should have brought music to listen to. I'll have to make something up. Running, running, running, feet stomping pavement, feet stomping dirt, arms swinging, heart racing . . .

"Excuse me."

I gasp as a young man comes toward me out of the trees. Why am I out here alone? I steel myself to fight him off. I'd run, but he might outrun me, and that would make it worse.

"What do you want?"

The man is tall and skinny, wearing stained and torn white pants and a long-sleeved white tunic. His golden hair hangs halfway down his back, and his blue eyes are so light they're practically transparent. "I'm sorry if I scared you."

"I'm still scared. Who are you, and what the hell are you doing out here?" I look for a rifle. Maybe he's a hunter. But as he opens his arms up like wings, his long-fingered hands are empty.

"I'm Gabriel, like the angel. I'm a wanderer looking for a place to sleep. The Lord told me to leave home, and I did, but I have had trouble finding refuge. The shelters are closed. I am not allowed to camp in the parks or on the beach, even though I am hurting nothing. The Lord promises a better life with Him in Heaven when we die, but here on earth, people like me are reduced to begging."

"I don't carry any money or anything when I'm walking."

"I understand. We're just two souls sharing the woods with empty hands open to the will of the Lord. I've got all my possessions in a bag back there in the trees. I don't want anyone to steal them. If you could maybe let me sleep on a little bit of your land, I'd be grateful. I would do chores if you had them. Do you know the story of Mary and Martha?"

"I do, but . . ."

The way he's smiling at me unnerves me. I wish that neighbor in the truck or somebody else would drive by.

A woodpecker pounds on a tree trunk. A squirrel chitters.

"Jesus said Mary chose the better way, dropping everything to worship him while her sister Martha was in the kitchen providing food. One needs both, love and food. What is your name, ma'am?"

I don't want to tell him, but he's staring at me with those weird eyes. "PD."

"PD, will you give this humble disciple a place to rest, perhaps a piece of bread?"

I want to be a good Christian, but this is too weird.

I shake my head, and I lie. Lie like a rug as my mom used to say. "I'm sorry. My husband and I are just visiting friends. We don't own any land here. I have to go back before they get worried and come looking for me. I don't know what to tell you. Maybe you could ask at the visitor's center down Beaver Creek Road."

I don't think anybody's there these days, but maybe he doesn't know that.

"I have been there. It's locked up."

"Maybe you could sleep on the grounds then."

"Only until the sheriff kicks me out. Do you think the people you're visiting would let me camp there?"

"No. They're kind of redneck. My friend George would greet you on the front porch with a shotgun, so I wouldn't mess with him." Lies, lies, lies.

"I see."

He's standing too close. I put on my mask. "Gabriel, you don't want to stand near me. I might have COVID."

"Oh, I'm immune to that."

"I don't think anyone is immune at this point."

"I am." He smiles, exposing brownish teeth.

I'm not going to argue about it. "Well, good for you. I'm not." I start to walk away.

His face turns dark. "You're really not going to help me?"

God, what am I supposed to do? "There must be some agency that helps the homeless."

"Come on, lady. They don't do anything."

Whoa, sudden change of personality. "I'm sorry," I say as I start walking back the way I came. "Please don't follow me. I-I was attacked last year, and I get nervous."

His expression softens. "Oh. Oh no. I would never hurt you. Say hello to your *husband*. Maybe I'll see you around."

He walks back into the trees as I break into a full-out run down the hill. Dear God, does he know I'm lying? Is he going to follow me? Near Dad's cabin, I slip on a patch of gravel and fall to my knees. I pull myself up and run until I'm safely inside the rainbow house.

Rocky is waiting by the door. I sink to the floor beside him. "That was scary, boy. I'm never going out without you again. You'd chase him away, wouldn't you?"

Rocky pushes his head into my lap.

God forgive me for lying. I know we're supposed to help the hungry and the homeless, but that Gabriel guy scared the poop out of me.

I pull up the legs of my jeans. My knees are scraped but not bleeding. I scrub them clean with a wet paper towel. The water stings, but it's no big deal.

Is four o'clock late enough to call the hospital in Corvallis? I can't wait any longer.

After a long game of pass the phone through the hospital system, the ICU nurse tells me Dad is doing better. His oxygen level is higher, his temperature lower, but he's asleep. Call in the morning, she says.

More waiting. But at least it's good news.

I startle at a noise in the driveway.

Dakota's home early. I want to throw myself into her arms. But I said no more hugs until I'm sure I don't have the virus.

"LET ME SHOW you where I keep the shotgun," Dakota says after I tell her about my encounter in the woods.

"What shotgun? I can't believe you would have one."

She gives me that squinty-eyed look she gets when I'm being stupid. "Look PD, we live in the wilderness. There are wild animals that might take offense at our being here. And there are humans who don't know how to behave themselves. Your guy sounds like he's nuts and might turn mean in a flash. So, your big lie is only half a lie. I would greet him with a shotgun. Follow me."

She takes me into her bedroom. Her dresser holds a toolbox, a hairbrush, and a photo of her and Maryann on their wedding day. She opens the closet, reaches behind the pants and shirts and pulls out a shotgun.

What I know about guns would fit—oh hell, I know nothing, and I don't want to know, but Dakota sits me down on the bed and shows me how it works. "This is a 20-gauge, break-action. If you want, we can go out and practice."

"No, that's all right."

"I'm serious, PD. Women alone are always at risk. It sucks but it's true, and when they find out we're gay—I'm gay—we're even more in danger." She touches the scar on my cheek. "You know. You were attacked between your house and the hospital."

"I wouldn't have been carrying a shotgun in the middle of Newport."

"No. But a little lady pistol would have come in handy. You were lucky you were able to fight him off."

"I know. I just thought it was safer out here."

"It's not a park; it's the forest. Don't walk without the dog anymore."

"I won't."

She hangs the shotgun up behind the clothes again.

"Dakota, would you have let that guy sleep on your property?"

That look again. "No."

"Okay. Good to know. Why are you home early?"

"Nothing left to do. No customers. People can call me if they need something. Are you making dinner tonight?"

"I thought I would. We've got some ham and potato salad and a ton of green salad."

"Sounds good. How's your father?"

"Better, but I can't talk to him until tomorrow."

"Diana and Janey?"

"Same. Janey's worse. But Jonas says they'll be fine in a few days."

"Good. You got any symptoms?"

"Not a one. I scheduled a test for tomorrow. If it's negative, I'm declaring my imprisonment over."

"Fine."

"Where'd you learn to shoot a shotgun?"

"My dad. He used to take me hunting."

"Did you like it?"

She sighs. "I didn't like killing things, but I did like spending time with my old man."

"Is he still alive?"

"No. He took off when I was a teenager and never looked back, but I heard he passed away about 10 years ago. Lung cancer."

Dakota lights a cigarette, goes out and walks around the yard. I know she's looking for Gabriel.

A shotgun. I might be better off hitting him over the head with Maryann's cast iron frying pan. Much easier to aim.

14. Someone New

I'M STILL IN MY nightgown when my phone rings. My heart lurches. Only bad news comes this early. It's the Corvallis hospital number. God, please let it be okay. "Hello?"

"PD. It's Dad." He sounds congested and hoarse, but at least he's talking.

"Dad, it's good to hear your voice. How are you?" I can hear the oxygen machine humming in the background.

"I'm better. Never been so sick."

"You scared me. Are you still in the ICU?"

"No. Regular room."

"Good. Do you know what number?"

He starts coughing. It sounds gurgly and painful. I feel it in my own chest. "Hold on."

"I'm holding, Dad."

The coughing goes on and on. Finally, he comes back and gasps out "231B."

A nurse comes on the line. "I'm sorry. He needs to rest. Maybe you can call back later."

"Sure. I understand. Tell him I love him."

The phone goes quiet.

I'm scared. Inside, I'm still the little girl who needs her daddy.

I've got my COVID test at 1:45. I need to be in line by 1:30. But that's hours from now, and Rocky is waiting at the door.

"Wait till I put my clothes on, boy. I don't suppose you'd let me drink some coffee first."

He barks as if to say, well, hurry.

Instead of walking toward Dad's place or beyond to Eugenia's, we turn left off the driveway and head south. In a half mile, the road will take a big right toward the ocean—or we can take South Beaver Creek Road toward Waldport. Whatever. I'm just walking to be walking. A rabbit sees us and scoots into the bushes. Rocky doesn't even notice.

It's going to be a nice day, a warm, sunny kind of day that makes a girl want to write a song. Maybe later. Something about walking in the woods where there's no disease, no fighting, no worry, where the trees are wiser than we are.

Near where the road turns, the creek widens out and there's a bit of a waterfall. Beyond, several horses graze outside a red barn. The grass is knee high this time of year, so lush even I think it would taste good.

As we approach the little dam, I leash up the dog lest he plunge into the water or irritate the horses.

It soothes my eyes just to stand here and look. Then my stupid phone goes off.

Caller ID shows Hatfield Marine Science Center.

It's Miguel, responding to my text.

"Hey, PD, hi. How is your father?"

"A little better. They moved him to a regular room. He's still coughing an awful lot."

"Poor Jack. Are you okay?"

"As far as I know. I'm getting tested later today. Then I'll know for sure."

"Where are you? I hear water."

"Beaver Creek. By the little dam where the road turns toward our place. It's pretty up here. The horses across the way don't care if I might have COVID. I guess you're still virus-free if you're at work."

"I am. Everyone is being very careful here. Like the horses, the fish and the octopus don't care."

"Probably not."

Awkward silence. He clears his throat. "I'd like to get together again, but considering the situation . . ."

"Right. Miguel, my signal is getting weaker. It's hard to hear you. I'd better go."

"Of course. Have a good day."

"That's my plan."

I nudge Rocky's leash and turn back toward home. God forgive me, I lied again.

THE COVID TEST isn't a big deal. No needles, no claustrophobic enclosures. You wait in line in your car, inch forward one at a time, open your window, fill out a piece of paper, then lean out while a technician swabs a giant Q-tip around in your nostrils. It's not a good feeling and it makes your nose drip, but whatever. They package it up, tell you that you'll hear from them, and you're on your way. You don't even get fries with that.

I need comfort food. I'm pulling out the ingredients to make muffins and soup for dinner when my phone rings again. It's the hospital in Corvallis.

I clear my throat and answer.

"Ms. Soares. This is Dr. Chen. I'm calling about your father, Jack O'Leary. His condition has taken a turn."

My heart stops. "What happened?"

"His fever has gone up to 102, and his lungs are full of fluid. I see he rallied a little this morning, but we seem to be back where we started. I would send him to the ICU, but they don't have any beds, so we're taking care of him here."

"Oh, God. Can I possibly talk to him?"

"No. I'm sorry. He's—kind of out of it."

"I understand. So, now what?"

"We work on draining the fluid and lowering his temperature. He was reasonably healthy before this, wasn't he?"

"Very. Just last week, he outwalked me. He's the kind of guy who can't sit still. Sixty-eight isn't that old."

"No, but there's still more risk at that age than say 40."

"Will you call me if anything changes either way?"

"Certainly. Try to have a relaxing evening."

"Sure."

I look around me at the flour, sugar, eggs, and seasonings spread across the counter. I don't want to do this anymore. I don't know what to do. I text Andy. He answers, *I'm coming up.*

No, don't, I respond. But I know he will, and I'm glad.

When my phone buzzes again, I expect Andy's rebuttal, but it's a text from the local hospital. *PD Soares, your test for the coronavirus was negative. Please continue to exercise caution by avoiding large gatherings and wearing your mask in public places.*

Whew. I'm free. Thank you, God, but what about my father? Is he going to die?

No answer, just the dog looking at me with his big brown eyes. I get down on the floor and rest my head on his belly. "Rocky, Rocky, why is life so complicated?"

Again, no answer.

IN SPITE OF ALL the insanity and most businesses being closed or limiting customers, a new pizza place has opened a few buildings south of Diana's diner. Might as well try it tonight.

It feels good to put on my jacket, get in my car, and drive away from here. I know it's only been a few days, but still.

As soon as I walk into the dimly lighted pizzeria, I want to turn around and leave. There are just three tables, set too close together. The guy behind the counter has a faded shirt wrapped around his mouth. It keeps slipping down his chin.

The masked older man in line ahead of me seems to have trouble understanding the menu. I don't blame him. There aren't many choices, and the prices seem awfully high. But he makes a selection, the unmasked man writes it down, and it's my turn. He adjusts his shirt-mask, but it doesn't stay up.

"Why don't I just take this thing off?" he says, throwing it under the counter. His face is sweaty and stubbled. "I don't know what the rules are now. Why don't you take your mask off, too, and show me your pretty face?"

I hate that kind of talk. It's like *what are you all worried about, little lady?*

"Are you kidding me?" I say. "You're supposed to be wearing a mask, especially if you're serving food."

"Relax. My wife went out to buy some masks."

"Right."

"What'll you have?"

I'm hungry, and the smell of tomato sauce has my stomach growling, but I don't even know if this guy washes his hands. God knows what he does in the kitchen. "I think I'll go somewhere else."

"What, because I don't wear a mask?"

"Because you don't seem to care about COVID or cleanliness or anything else. Plus, your pizzas are too expensive."

"Suit yourself."

As I stomp down the steps past the old man waiting for his pizza, a bunch of teenagers push in. No masks. No worries.

I guess I'm making muffins and soup after all. Reminds me of old Cissy the happy housewife. Ha. Just when I thought she was gone.

MAYBE A LITTLE BIT of Cissy mixed with a little bit of Maryann is a good thing. An hour after the failed pizza trip, the kitchen smells good and I'm relieved to have accomplished something. Rocky barks as the van rolls into the driveway. I'm about to rush out and shout, "Honey, you're home!" when I realize Dakota is not alone.

As this girl springs out, bright blue eyes, perky white-blonde pixie hair and the cutest yellow Converse sneakers, I feel all kinds of things. Puzzled because we're not supposed to gather with other people, worried that I didn't cook enough for three, and this mad jealousy, especially when I see Dakota is smiling like I haven't seen since before Maryann got sick.

I put on a welcoming smile like my mother taught me to do when she and Dad had old-people visitors I didn't want anything to do with. Especially when they called me Priscilla.

"Hi," I say, holding the door open. "I'm PD."

"This is Britt," Dakota says. "Smells like you're making dinner."

Britt? How young is she? Be nice, PD. "It's all ready. Homemade muffins and minestrone soup. Are you a vegetarian?"

Britt laughs behind her tiger-striped mask. "I eat everything."

And never gain a pound. "Great. I snuck in some Portuguese sausage."

"Yum."

How can anybody sparkle so much in the middle of a pandemic?

"I'll take your coat, Britt," Dakota says.

She shucks a green corduroy jacket, revealing a suede vest over a man's shirt and slacks. Could she get any cuter?

"May I use your bathroom?" she asks.

Dakota points the way, then returns to the kitchen where I am waiting to pounce.

"Where did she come from? What about COVID?"

"She just moved in near the post office, and we got to talking. I wanted to talk some more so I invited her here. Speaking of COVID, do you have it?"

"No. My test was negative. Has Britt been tested?"

"I don't know, but she seems mighty healthy."

Britt comes out of the bathroom just in time to stop me from asking Dakota if she plans on swapping spit with this girl. Or reminding her she's still grieving for Maryann. Then again, it's just one dinner, and she has a right to bring a friend home.

"Do you play the piano, Dakota?" Britt asks.

"Not me. PD is the musician here."

"That's great. I play a little." She sits and knocks out a few lines of "Fur Elise."

Don't touch my piano, I think. Such a Christian. Maybe Fr. Rigo could schedule a special hour-long confession for me. I'm going to need a lot of Hail Marys. "Dakota, if you set the table, I can put the food out and we can eat."

"I really appreciate this," Britt says, sliding off the piano bench and bending to hug Rocky, who is loving it.

Just serve the food, PD. Dakota has a right to have company in her own house.

Ensconced at the table, I have this crazy urge to demand we say grace together, even though we never do that, but I shut myself up, say grace in my head, and butter my muffin.

For a while, all we hear is the sound of chewing and spoons knocking bowls. Then the other two are talking about Seal Rock and mutual friends from the gay community. Britt just got here from Los Angeles, where she studied filmmaking at UCLA. She came here on vacation and loved it. Now, she has a grant or fellowship or something to make a film about our area surviving the tsunami and now suffering through COVID. She's thinking of calling it "Between the Bridges."

Wait, that's what we call our monthly giveaway gathering, I want to protest, but Dakota shoots me a look that says *don't*. I stare at the butterfly tattoo on Britt's neck and ask, "How did you come up with that title?"

"I started interviewing people, and I kept hearing that phrase over and over. People talked about how when anything happens to the bridges you all are sort of stranded out here."

"That's true," I said. "The night of the tsunami, my friend Janey and I actually snuck across the Yaquina Bridge into Newport. It was cracked and shaking and the cops were yelling at us, but Janey had to see if her apartment in Nye Beach was still standing."

Britt leans forward, spoon poised above her bowl. "Was it?"

"It was. But the bottom floor was badly damaged, and the building was condemned. We were able to retrieve Janey's stuff before it went down."

"Wow. Did you run back across the bridge that night?"

"No. One of our friends had gotten hurt in a fire. Janey went to her brother's house in Newport—while he and his family were stuck in Seal Rock. I went to the hospital to see our friend and wound up volunteering. Not long after that, I got a job there."

"PD, that's a great story. May I film you? Maybe you could show me where you crossed the bridge and where you went that night."

Dakota is smiling at me. "Why not?"

"Yeah, I guess. You should interview Janey though. She's a lot more entertaining."

"Okay. Can we get together tomorrow?"

"No. I'm tied up tomorrow. Plus, Janey has COVID."

"Oh no. I hope she's not too sick."

"So-so. Her mother, Diana, has it too, and my own father is in the hospital with it. It's not a good time."

"That's so scary. Well, let me know when you can do it. I want to collect all the stories. Where were you, Dakota?"

Dakota pushes her chair back and takes her dishes to the sink. "Good grub, PD. Thank you. Well, Maryann and I were visiting our parents in the Midwest and missed the whole thing. Not that there wasn't plenty of aftermath to deal with."

"Right." She watches me stack my bowl on my bread plate. "PD, can I do the dishes for you?"

"No, thank you. You and Dakota relax. I've got it."

"Let's, um, let's take a walk," Dakota says. "I'll show you my favorite trees."

Oh gag. They run off into the forest together while I scrub baked-on blueberries off my muffin pans and divide the soup into containers, two for the freezer and one for tomorrow.

They're still not back as darkness falls. It's none of my business. I settle at the piano to practice my church music. I guess I'm going to be there on Sunday.

15. Andy's Here

WE HAVE A congregation of one on Sunday morning. Andy sits in the middle of the church behind Billie and her camera as Beverly and I and Father Rigo work our way through the Mass. I feel for my brother. There's a lot of pressure to say the responses and sing along, with no books in the racks and no cheat sheets. I know he hasn't been to church in ages, something that bothers our mom a lot. But he's a grownup, even if he looks like a teenager slouching in his white shirt, jeans and sneakers, his orangey hair needing a trim. He grew up in the church, but I know he's only here today for me.

Andy arrived at the rainbow house all red-eyed and exhausted when I was having breakfast. After a big hug, I directed him to the muffins and melons and coffee and told him the latest news from this morning. Dad's slightly better, but still dicey. And no, we cannot visit in person or by phone.

Andy, pouring coffee into the biggest mug we have, said his business was still going well. Shari has been working from home, which is good under the circumstances.

"You mean COVID?"

"Well, that too."

"What do you mean?"

"What time do you have to be at church?"

I let him change the subject for now, but I'm going to have questions later.

When we left, Dakota was still sleeping. Last night while I was in bed reading, Britt dashed in and grabbed her jacket. Soon I heard Dakota lock the front door and climb into her bed.

Rocky sighed, which cracked me up because that's what I was going to do.

ANDY DOZED OFF a couple times during Mass. I had planned to show him Dad's garden, but it can wait. I let him crash in my bedroom while I call the hospital. No change. Dakota rises late, has her morning coffee and cigarette, then slides under the van to change the oil. I do my laundry, eat a little minestrone soup for lunch, and play my harmonica on the porch.

It's two o'clock when Andy staggers out, barefoot with his hair sticking up. He stretches and yawns. "Hey. Good morning, Sis. How's Dad?"

"About the same. Did you get enough sleep?"

"Maybe. What's the plan?"

"Well, our father has started a vegetable garden."

"He has?"

"I know. Not Mr. Green Thumb. But he did, nice little rows with little labels and little plants shooting up. Unfortunately, the rabbits think it's a buffet meant for them. So, I want to take you over there and get your opinion on what we can do to save the plants."

"I don't have a lot of experience with rabbits or other wildlife in Santa Cruz, but sure, I'd like to see it. I could take a peek at Dad's place, too. A log cabin, huh?"

"A log cabin. Well, made from a kit. Put on some shoes, grab a jacket, and we'll go. Oh, do you want something to eat?"

"What have you got?"

"Sandwich makings, soup, blueberry muffins . . ."

"I'll just grab a muffin. You're going to give me dinner, right?"

"Probably. I wish I could take you out to eat, but, you know."

"Call DoorDash?"

"Hah. Get ready. Let's go."

He wolfs down a muffin as we walk to Dad's house, then stands in the yard, nodding while I hold Rocky back. More plants are missing.

Damn rabbits. He squats, reads some of the tags, touches a few leaves, and then stands.

"Well, Doctor Andy, will it live?"

"I'm afraid I've got bad news and good news."

"Tell me."

"The bad news is this garden is toast. He's not going to get much produce out of it. The good news is he has a professional here who can redo the whole thing, construct an enclosure and promise a good crop in a couple of months."

"You'd do that?"

"Absolutely. I haven't had a chance to do anything with our father for years. I don't think he understands what I do. So yes, I'll research where I can buy supplies around here under the restrictions and start in the morning."

"Wow. You're all right."

"You didn't know that?"

Sigh. "I did. I miss you. Want to see Dad's house?"

"Sure."

It's a short tour. He looks around, admires the view from the other side, and collapses on the sofa while I take the chair by the unlit fireplace.

"I like it."

"Mom would hate it."

"I know. Not a chintz curtain or silk flower arrangement in sight. It's a man's place."

"Yes. You know my friend Donovan lived here before."

"Right. You guys dated for a while."

"Yes, we did."

"And?"

"He moved to Corvallis. He decided we should just be friends."

"Did you agree with that?"

"It was for the best."

Dad's cuckoo clock chooses that moment to go off.

Andy chuckles. "Whatever you say, Cissy. What shall we do now?"

"I'm thinking. I have this friend up the road. She's um, different. But I'd like to go see her. Last time I was there, she had an injured knee, and I think I said something stupid."

"Sure. Why not? Are you driving?"

"We can walk. It's not that far. Last time, I didn't get there because this homeless guy jumped at me out of the woods."

"Jeez. Did he do anything to you?"

"No, but he scared me enough that I just ran home. I didn't have Rocky with me. Big mistake. But with both of you there, I'm not worried."

"Big tough man defends weak little lady. Okay, I can handle it."

"Do you have a mask?"

He pats his pocket."

"Okay. Come on, Rocky."

A half mile up the road, we startle a garter snake, but it curls out of the way. No sign of any humans hiding in the trees. As we reach the rain barrel and walk into Eugenia's yard, she's taking laundry off a clothesline at the side of the house. "Hello!" she calls.

"Hi, Eugenia. Looks like your knee is better."

"Ginger always works. Who is this handsome young man? Your beau?"

Andy laughs and steps forward. "No, ma'am. I'm her brother, Andrew."

She looks from one of us to the other. "I don't see the resemblance, but my old eyes aren't what they used to be."

"Whose are?" Have I mentioned I recently succumbed to reading glasses? Makes me feel old.

"What brings you out here, PD?"

"We just wanted to visit. I was a little worried about how we left it last time."

She waves her hand. "I don't even remember. Would you like to sit on the porch? I have some cookies and lemonade.

"Sure," Andy says.

We settle in two rustic wooden chairs, leaving the rocker for Eugenia. As she disappears into the house, I whisper, "They're pot cookies."

"What?"

"Pot cookies."

He smiles. "Oh. Nice."

"Andy."

But Eugenia is back, holding out a chipped green plate with what look like sugar cookies. We each take one as she fills mismatched glasses with a greenish liquid. She settles into her chair and holds up her glass. "Cheers."

What can we do? We choke it down. The lemonade tastes like grass. The cookies taste wonderful, but I worry about getting too buzzed to make dinner. Never mind. The sun is shining, my brother is here, and Rocky is happily rolling in the weeds.

After Andy discloses he's a landscape architect, we tour Eugenia's garden, trading information about what grows well in this climate. Then we settle back on the porch.

I tell Eugenia about our father being in the hospital and Janey and Diana sick with COVID.

"Terrible," she says. "But they will be all right. Until it's time for the Great Spirit to take them home."

"Great spirit?" Andy asks.

"Yes. We don't know all the details, and I think the churches have it wrong, but there is a greater power. Haven't you felt it? The Native Americans certainly knew it."

"Sure."

"Now, I haven't offended you, have I? Sometimes church-going people are uncomfortable with my views."

"No, it's fine," I say. "I'm Catholic, but I believe we just have different names for the same creator."

She nods and reaches for another cookie.

"Hey, Eugenia, would you like to play some music and maybe sing a little? I have my harmonica."

"Well, yes I would."

Soon we're having a jam session. She offers old folk songs and Native American tunes. I play my Pandemic Blues and some oldies Eugenia knows. Andy adds lemonade-glass percussion. I haven't had this much fun in ages. But for our father being sick, life would be perfect.

As we start running out of songs, I ask, "What time is it?"

"I don't know, dear. I gave up clocks many years ago."

"I wish I could do that. Andy, I think we'd better head home and figure out what's for dinner. I hope we didn't miss any calls from the hospital. Eugenia, thank you for a wonderful visit. Please let me know if Dakota or I can do anything to help you. We'd love to have you over some time."

"Oh, I'm fine right here on my own. Young man, good luck with your father's garden."

"Thank you."

Rocky leads the way back to the road. I feel like skipping. That may be from the cookies. Or the lemonade, whatever was in that. I almost break into "Follow the Yellow Brick Road," but then a rusty black pickup comes roaring past us, turning toward Eugenia's place, showering us in a spray of gravel.

"What the hell? Should we go back and make sure she's okay?"

"It's none of our business, Sis. Maybe Eugenia has a gentleman friend."

"I doubt that. But yeah, we shouldn't butt in. I'm pretty stoned. How about you?"

"I'm a mellow fellow. And starving."

I'm glad we still have some diner leftovers. I'm not sure I could follow a recipe right now.

16. More Surprises

Monday, June 21, 2020

SUDDENLY IT'S MONDAY again. Everybody's back to work, Dakota to the post office, Andy to Dad's garden, and me to COVID Central. Andy checks on Dad mid-morning and texts that he's about the same. I wish I could visit him. I would bring him a book or something to do, slip him something good to eat, or just sit with him. We could maybe talk about all the things we never talked about. But instead, he's alone with a fever and no one for company except medical personnel whose faces are covered except for their eyes and who don't have time for chit-chat.

I text Janey. *How are you guys?*

Better but pooped. Could you maybe bring us some cough medicine, Tylenol and mint chocolate chip ice cream on the way home from work?

Of course.

The rest of the day, I don't have time to think. I'm too busy dealing with patients needing attention and complaining about the long waits. Their loved ones keep calling from their cars. Aren't they done yet? What's happening?

I don't have answers. If I can't fob them off, I check with someone inside. Too often, what's happening is nothing. The patients are still lying on gurneys waiting for someone to examine them.

At one point, I mutter to Jackson from behind my mask, "This really sucks."

He nods. "One hundred percent."

What a relief to finally escape when my shift ends at three o'clock. Zelda and Angie will have their hands full tonight, I'm sure. The tourists have invaded, and COVID has spiked.

The grocery store is nearly deserted as I dash to the medicine aisle across from the magazines. Where cough medicine ought to be is a big empty shelf. Ditto for Tylenol. Are that many people sick, or are they hoarding it just in case?

At least there's ice cream.

I make a quick stop at the pharmacy across the highway. The best they can give me is aspirin. I take it. They have one bottle of Nyquil left. I grab it.

Do we have some of this stuff in the medicine cabinet at home? Dakota and I both had bad colds last fall, but I don't remember if we used everything up. I'll check when I get home.

It's a relief to cross the bridge and get out of Newport, to drive around the curve at Ona Beach, into Seal Rock, and up the hill to Diana's house off the charmingly named Art Street.

When I knock on the door, Janey slides the living room window open and talks through the screen. "Thanks, PD. Leave it on the porch. I'll come get it."

I move closer to the window so I can see her. She's wearing pink pajamas, and her hair is a rat's nest. Diana, in a turquoise quilted robe, waves from the couch. The TV is on. "Judge Judy."

"How are you?" I call.

Janey's voice is an octave lower than usual. "Peachy. I keep puking. All I can keep down is ice cream and toast. Is that part of COVID?"

"I don't know. Maybe. Maybe you're pregnant."

"Shut up, PD." She looks back at her mother. "Mom, I'm not. Are you still okay? No COVID?"

"Yes. I tested negative." A garbage truck rattles by.

"What?"

I yell louder. "I'm fine. Tested negative."

"Good."

"They didn't have much medicine left. I got what I could. I'll bring you some of ours if we have it."

"Okay. Whatever." She starts to cough.

"Get away from the window. It's cold," Diana calls.

Janey crosses her hands over her heart as if to say she loves me, and slides the window shut.

As I back my car out of their driveway, I see Janey scurry out, grab the grocery bag and go back in. Like a mouse sneaking a chunk of cheese.

Instead of going straight home, I drive past Seal Rock State Park, still blocked off with yellow tape, and stop at a turnout overlooking the beach. I stand in the sun, looking down at kids climbing on the rocks.

The tide is out, leaving an empty stretch of sand, the same place where we watched people walk just before the tsunami swept them away. That seems long ago now.

I would like to dig my feet into that sand. I don't understand why they blocked the beaches off. Maybe to keep the tourists out. But they get there anyway. They park all over the highway and climb down, carrying their chairs, ice chests and surf boards.

I lean back against my car. I haven't done anything physical, but I'm worn out.

The waves go in, the waves go out. People die, people move away, tsunamis come, and earthquakes knock everything down. We build it again, and then everybody gets sick. Lord, is my life ever going to be normal? Without a husband and home of my own, what would that consist of? Will I ever stop working at that damned hospital? Will Dakota and I grow old together, living as platonic friends, her chopping wood and me playing my piano until we're too old and arthritic to move? Then what? What if she dies?

What if they all die?

It's getting to me. And I'm not one of those doctors or nurses watching people die alone or holding the phone for terminal patients so their families can say goodbye. The medical people are afraid to touch their own faces or any other part of themselves until they strip and shower after work for fear they'll be infected. Some do get sick despite every precaution.

I want to talk to my father. God, please let him be okay. I know you've got lots of people asking the same thing, but please. He's too young. We haven't had enough time together as adults. I know you have your own agenda, but please.

It's starting to rain, and I'm about to cry. Time to go home.

ANDY TAKES ONE look at my face and wraps me in a long-armed hug. He smells good, like he just showered. "Hard day?"

"Yeah."

"I'm sorry."

Rocky pushes between us. "Okay, okay. I love you, too. Where's Dakota?"

"She left a note. She's spending the evening with Britt. Her girlfriend?"

"I guess. She's new. So cute and perky you want to choke her. Anyway, I need to start supper."

"No need. I took care of it."

"What do you mean?"

"Well, when I was in town buying supplies for the garden, I ran into this guy who told me he was selling seafood off his boat, so I went down there and stocked up. I put some halibut in the freezer, and we've got fresh crab for tonight. I picked up some potato salad and wine at the store. Sound good?"

"Can I marry you?"

"No, that would be illegal in every state. Shari would not be happy. Get comfortable, I'll pour you a little pinot gris."

When I come back out in sweats, he's sitting on the sofa holding a glass out to me. I take the glass and sink down beside him. "This is a treat. Dakota doesn't drink, and I don't want to buy a whole bottle just for me."

"Well, enjoy it. PD. I need to offer a toast and give you some news."

"Dad's okay?"

"Not yet. This is something different."

"You're moving to Oregon?"

"No, I'm a Santa Cruz guy all the way. This is bigger."

My stomach is churning. "Stop torturing me. What?"

"Well, Shari and I are going to have a baby. I'm going to be a father."

"Oh my God. When?"

"Just before Christmas."

"Wow." Tears come to my eyes again.

He pulls me close. "It's good news, isn't it?"

I nod. "Yes, but all my life I have wanted to announce that I was having a baby, and I never will. I'm going to grow old without children or grandchildren while you're Papa Andy with a whole brood of red-headed descendants."

"We don't know they'll have red hair. Remember, Shari is not a redhead."

"That's true. But damn it." I slug him gently in the arm, "Why do you get to have kids and I don't?"

"Superior sperm, I think."

"Shut up." I take in a deep breath and gulp my wine. "We need to tell Dad."

"As soon as we can."

"He'll be thrilled."

"And you'll be Aunt—PD?"

"I guess. Not Cissy."

"Priscilla? Prissy?"

"Yuck. Stop." I grab a pillow and start to hit him, but Rocky thinks there's trouble and starts barking.

I give my brother one more hug. "Andy, this is wonderful news. Such a relief from all the death and dying. I'm going to love him or her ridiculously."

"I know."

"Are you and Shari going to get married?

He drinks the rest of his wine in one swallow. "We already did."

"What? Where? When?"

"New Year's Eve in Las Vegas. Mom doesn't know."

"She's going to have a fit. No church wedding? You are in so much trouble."

"We might do the church thing later when people can be together."

"I think you're going to have to."

"Shari's folks are not Catholic."

"I figured. Andy, my brain is going to explode. When are you going to tell Mom? Does she know about the baby? She'll want rings on your fingers."

"And bells on our toes. New subject please."

"Fine. What's happening in the garden?"

"It's a secret. I'm not going to let you see it until I'm done."

"How long are you staying?"

"A week or until Dad is sprung. Meanwhile, I have a present for you."

"Besides the gourmet dinner?"

"Come on."

He leads me and Rocky out to the back of the house where five rhododendron plants sit in big tubs. "I know you miss your roses. I also know that rhodies are the next best thing. I will plant these wherever you want."

"Oh, Andy. Thank you." I hug my brother again.

"I almost bought some cannabis plants, too. It grows really well here."

"I know. That's okay. Eugenia's my supplier."

"That's what I figured. Let's eat."

Dinner is delicious, and it's a relaxing night. Andy sleeps on the couch, Dakota comes in late, and I fall asleep in my own bed, spooning my dog.

My little brother is married and having a baby.

My fingers smell like crab.

17. Traffic Jam

Thursday, June 25, 2020

TWO AND A HALF WEEKS after my father went to the hospital, my phone rings while I'm driving to work. When I see a number from Corvallis, I pull off the road near 118th street in South Beach, expecting to hear from a doctor or nurse. It's 6:45 in the morning. It has to be bad news.

"Hi sweetie," my father says, sounding congested but way better than last time.

"Dad! Are you okay?"

"Better than I was. As they say in the old movies, my fever broke last night. I'm on the upswing. If my numbers stay good, they're going to let me out of here on Saturday. Could you come pick me up? Maybe about 10 in the morning?"

"Yes! Oh, thank God."

"I can't give you directions to the hospital. I couldn't see anything from the ambulance, and I wasn't paying much attention."

"We'll find it. I'll use my GPS. Should I bring anything?"

"Just enough gas in the car to get me out of here. Who's 'we'?"

"Andy's here."

"Hot dog. I'll see you kids day after tomorrow. Go now. Don't be late to work."

"How'd you know?"

"I know your schedule. See you tomorrow."

Is that the sun peeking through the clouds?

AS IT TURNS OUT, I'm late to work anyway. Traffic stops a couple miles north. All I can see is the white van in front of me, the butcher shop sign to the right that says "Get Your Ribs Here," and sun glinting off the rear window of the Toyota behind me. There are no cars coming from the other direction. Something must be happening on the bridge. I wonder how long I'm going to be stuck here.

Too bad the ferry that got people across the water after the tsunami went back to Washington. We could use it right about now.

A little Internet searching on my phone tells the story. A man was threatening to jump off the bridge. That happens sometimes around here. They hardly ever actually jump, but it's a hard, fatal landing if they do. Anyway, this guy was climbing over the railing hollering something, and somebody driving by got so distracted he didn't see a car stopped in front of him. Crash! Those of us caught south of the bridge are lined up as far as I can see.

We sit in our cars with the engines running, hoping to move soon. After a while, we shut them off to save gas.

A few cars turn around, probably giving up. You could drive all the way to Waldport, take 60 miles of winding road to Corvallis, then come back west on Highway 20. It would take a couple hours. By then, the bridge should be clear.

I text Zelda to tell her I'm going to be late. She replies with a row of frowny face emojis.

People are standing outside their cars. I decide to get out, too.

The wind blows through my hair and ruffles my jacket. It's cold and foggy. But it's kind of nice to be among people. I put my mask on.

A teenager comes jogging up from a couple cars behind, stopping when he sees me holding my phone. "Do you know what's going on?"

"Yes. Guy threatened to jump and then a looky-loo crashed into another car."

"Oh crap. I'm starting a new job today. I can't be late."

I shrug. "I need to get to work, too. Not much we can do."

"I'm going to run it."

"What?"

He waves at someone behind us and takes off on foot, passing cars until I can't see him anymore. I hope nobody stops him from walking across the bridge. That kind of energy deserves appreciation. I wonder what his new job is. So many businesses are closed. I hope it's not at the fish plant where everybody's getting COVID.

It's too cold out here. I get back in the car and text Andy. *Stuck south of the bridge. Accident has both lanes closed. Don't try to drive into town.*

No need, he responds. An early riser, he's probably already working on Dad's garden or planting my rhodies around the front porch. They won't look like much until next spring, but they will be glorious then.

I'm going to rest my eyes.

Forty-five minutes later, a honking horn wakes me up. The bridge is open. I drive to work, where I apologize profusely for what wasn't my fault and promise to stay late to make up the time.

Other than that, same old same old. Oh. Except that now when we walk out of our cubbyhole, we have to wear plastic shields over our masked faces, whether we're going to the restroom, wiping down the chairs, or monitoring the door. It's like looking through a fish tank.

We are not having fun.

18. Dad's Garden

"COME ON, PD!" Andy says as I drag myself out of bed on Saturday morning. "We don't want to be late."

"Andy, it's seven o'clock. We can drive there in an hour and a half. Maybe less. Give me a chance to wake up."

"You got gas in the car?"

"Yes. Unless you want to take your truck."

"The car would be more comfortable for Dad."

"Fine. I filled up yesterday on the way home. You can be the navigator."

I try to ignore him as I go through my morning ritual—dog, shower, dress, breakfast. But the house isn't that big. When did he start whistling? At least he's in tune.

Even Dakota, who rises after I do, is not thrilled by his impatience. "Have some herbal tea or something," she growls as she goes out for her first smoke of the day.

At 8:15, I surrender. "Let's go."

"Finally."

He sits with his knees up high like a grasshopper in my little Jeep Renegade. Maybe I'll let him drive back so Dad can ride shotgun.

"You're going to stay with him tonight, PD?"

"If he needs me to."

"We can take turns."

"Fine."

"Is there any food there?"

"I don't know, Andy. Look at the scenery."

Evergreens line the road and the Yaquina River flows by on the right.

"Uh-huh." He studies the map on his phone. "It says to keep going straight ahead for 50 miles."

"I know."

"You'll be turning off at—damn it. Lost the internet connection."

"That happens out here. We'll pick it up later."

"How do you stand it here?"

"Missing civilization?"

"Maybe."

Lord, I think, please let Andy take a nap so I can drive in peace. I know, not high on His agenda, but he grants me this favor.

My brother doesn't wake up until I cruise into the small town of Philomath and stop at a traffic light by a restaurant called Good Eats. "We there?"

"Not yet. Fire up the GPS."

"Got it. The turn is coming up. Left on Fifty-Third Street."

"Okay."

The hospital is easy to find, especially when you get close and see it towering over the nearby houses and shopping centers. It's a huge gray building surrounded by other gray buildings and parking lots. It's only 9:30, but I pull up near the main entrance to be ready. On deck, like in baseball.

That's when I see someone I definitely did not expect to see here.

"Oh my God," I say, throwing on the parking brake and jumping out.

"What? Is it Dad?"

"No," I say as I hurry toward the giant bearded man sitting on a bench outside the entrance. I'm unzipping my hoodie. It's hot here.

"PD, mask!" Andy calls.

"Damn it." I rush back, grab a mask off the gearshift lever and turn back toward Donovan Green. Even with a flowered bandana hung clumsily over his mouth and beard, I can tell he's smiling. He holds out his arms. I want to fall into them, but no. COVID, freaking COVID.

"Donovan, what are you doing here?"

"Wishing for a hug."

"I can't. But why are you here? Are you sick?"

"Fit as a fiddle. I talked to Jack last night, and he said you were going to rendezvous at 10. I thought I'd take a chance to say hello. Is that your little brother in the car?"

"It is. Andy!"

He comes out, stretches his long, cramped limbs and joins us. In ordinary times, the men would probably shake hands or slap each other on the back, but not today.

"Greetings, young man," Donovan says. "I remember you from Christmas at PD's place long ago."

"Oh, yeah. Hi. Can we find some coffee?"

"None here for the masses, sir. Only for staff. I checked it out."

"We'll go through a drive-through on the way out of town," I say, dialing the number for Dad's room on my phone to tell him we're here.

After we pass 15 minutes of awkward small talk, a nurse rolls our father out the door. He looks old. Pale. Skinny. He's wearing a blue hospital mask over his beard. He accepts the nurse's help getting out of the chair and into my car and sinks into the seat with a sigh. "Well, that was my exercise for the day. I have never felt so tired in my whole life. But they needed my bed for someone sicker."

I lean in and fasten his seat belt. "Are you sure you're ready?"

He shrugs.

Andy grumbles as he pushes the driver's seat all the way back and settles in.

Donovan leans toward Dad as I squeeze into the back seat. "I'm glad you've been released from jail, pal. I wish I could hang out with you, but the regulations are stiff these days. Hey PD, perhaps you could drive slowly past the gallery on your way out of town. It's worth seeing."

"Oh?"

"Just take a look. Andy, it's at 435 2nd street, near Monroe."

"Okay with you, Dad?" I ask.

"Fine."

Donovan blows me a kiss and walks off into the parking lot.

"Coffee?" Andy prods.

"Yes, coffee. I think I know where there's a McDonald's drive-through. We'll pick up some coffee, pass by the gallery and see what the hell Donovan is talking about. Then we'll go home, where we can all get some much-needed rest."

"Yes ma'am. How do I get to Second Street?"

I set the GPS on Andy's phone to guide us into the heart of town. A quick stop at a McDonald's, and we all three have coffee, which Dad holds like it's a magic potion. "Oh, I missed this," he says.

"You know this means we're all going to have to pee before we get home."

"*You* will," Andy says. "I'm fine. Gallery time."

Corvallis, bordered by the Willamette River and Oregon State University, is a true Oregon college town with a coffee shop on every corner, vegan this and natural that. A brewpub. A cannabis dispensary. A music store. Normally the streets would be full of students and faculty, as well as the other people who live around here. The college and most businesses are closed these days, and some have "for sale" signs in the window. But McDonald's never closes, and apparently Donovan J. Green doesn't either.

Andy pulls into an empty parking space at the curb in front of the gallery.

"Jesus," he mutters.

"Yes, Jesus." Donovan has crafted an image of Christ in a sort of grotto made out of stained glass that is absolutely glorious, but what does it mean? He's not even religious. And who would buy it? I wonder if the apostles and the Virgin Mary are nearby. Lying near the Messiah's feet are a big pink octopus and a snake made of green bottles. Off to the side, he has fashioned a donkey out of pots and pans, brooms and brushes with big beaded blue eyes.

"You used to date this guy?"

"Yes."

"A little nuts?"

"Maybe, but not too much." I lie. Sometimes he is plum off his rocker.

"Ay yi-yi," Dad sighs. I catch a little shiver.

"Are you cold?"

"Freezing."

I grab the blanket I keep in the back and wrap it around him. "Okay. We have seen it. Crank the heat, Andy. Dad needs to go to bed."

As we leave glass Jesus behind, I feel like making the Sign of the Cross or something. I do it small and bent over so Andy can't see me in the mirror.

"HEY, DAD?" I ask when he's settled in his bed. "Why didn't you tell me you were dating Diana?"

He chuckles. "You figured it out. We weren't sure how the families would take it, so we agreed to keep it quiet for a while. Is it all right with you?"

"I guess. It's kind of weird. She's a lot younger."

"It doesn't matter at this point in our lives."

"Do you want to know how she is?"

"Oh, we've been in touch."

I shake my head. "Dad, you're full of surprises."

"I plan to stay that way for a long time." He starts to cough. It goes on and on until he almost chokes. "I'm okay," he gasps.

"Sure. Would you like cough medicine or a slug of whiskey?"

He mimes taking a shot of booze. I bring the cough medicine I bought on the way home from work yesterday.

Dad could have used a few more nights in the hospital, but I guess as soon as it looks like you're not going to die, they send you home.

I hate seeing him like this. He's coughing less than he was, but he's still a little feverish and so weak he can barely walk to the bathroom without help. All he wants to do is sleep. I hate to do it, but I call Beverly to tell her I can't help with the music at church on Sunday morning. I don't want to leave my father alone, even though I know he would tell me to go.

While he's snoozing, I run down to the rainbow house to see what I can snatch for dinner. We need groceries or for the diner to reopen. Outfits like DoorDash and Grubhub are making a fortune in the big cities, but we don't have that here. If we don't buy some supplies soon, I could be fighting the rabbits for nubs of carrots and kale.

Dakota looks beat.

"Long day?"

She sighs. "Crazy. Everybody is ordering stuff online. I must have carried 200 pounds of packages to people's doors."

"What are they getting?"

"I can't always tell, but it seems like a little bit of everything. Books, clothes, air fryers and other appliances, build-it-yourself bookshelves. That shit is heavy."

"Do you have anyone to help you?"

"What do you think?"

"Right. What's Britt up to?"

"I don't know. She was busy making her movie today, I think. It's hard for her to understand that people around here don't want a camera shoved in their faces."

"I know what you mean. What do you want to do about dinner? I think I could work up a stir fry. Better use the salad fixings. They're starting to wilt. Do you want to join us at Dad's house?"

"Fine."

"Is there any wine left?"

"I wouldn't know." She flops down on the couch and peels off her boots.

"We don't need it."

Dakota has closed her eyes, but she's not asleep. "I dropped some mail and books at Eugenia's place."

"How is she?"

"I didn't see her. This guy was there, skinny, long blond hair like a white Jesus. He said Eugenia was busy inside, so he'd take the package. He looked like that homeless guy you met."

"Gabriel?"

"Yeah. Maybe she took him in. I also saw this little boy, maybe six or so, peeking out the window. When he saw me looking at him, he ran away, but I'm sure he was there."

"A grandchild? Or Gabriel's kid?"

"I don't know. There's that whole mystery about her children. I just don't know."

"I wonder if it has any connection with that truck we saw roaring toward her place the other day."

"What truck? What did it look like?"

"Black. Rusty. Probably a Dodge."

"Oh, that guy. He flipped me off the other day when I was delivering the mail. Apparently, I wasn't driving fast enough for him—or he hates rainbows. But I didn't see him or the truck today."

"I hope Eugenia's okay."

"She's tough. And her rifle makes my shotgun look like a toy." She stands and stretches. "I'd better get cleaned up for supper. Your new plants look good."

"They do. Andy says they'll make a rainbow of color when they bloom."

"Cool."

As she closes the door of her room, I focus on chopping celery, onions and carrots. I wonder what's going on at Eugenia's house. Maybe she's a better Christian than I am and let Gabriel camp on her land. Or even in her house. The witch and the angel. Interesting.

I'm still wondering about that as we eat dinner at my father's house. Dakota and I balance our plates on our laps as we sit by the bed. My stir fry is surprisingly tasty, considering I just threw together whatever we had.

Dad takes a few bites and sets his plate aside. "It looks good, but I'm not hungry, PD."

"At least you ate a little."

I finish my last few bites and take our plates to the kitchen.

"I'm going to head home," Dakota says.

"Okay."

"You sleeping on the couch?"

"Yeah."

"Let me know if you need anything. He'll be better tomorrow."

"I know."

The dishes done, I sit by the fire and knit until I hear a noise from the bedroom. He's up. I hurry to help.

"Dad? Are you all right?"

"I need to use the restroom. Then maybe I'll sit out there for a while."

"Sure. Great. Do you need help?"

"No. I can do it."

When he comes out, still hanging on to everything and moving very slowly, he sits in the easy chair. I wrap blankets around him.

"The fire feels good."

"Yes. Fall is coming."

"Thank you for doing this."

I pick up my knitting. I'm making Dakota a baby blue scarf for her birthday. "Hey, Dad, the doctor said I need to have power of attorney for your health care. Just in case."

A month ago, he would have told me there was no need, but now he nods. "Probably a good idea."

"Shall I bring home the paperwork?"

"Yes."

"It has to go both ways. You need to take care of me, too."

"I will, if I'm still here."

"Of course you'll still be here. A month from now, you won't even remember this. You'll be bopping around, dating Diana, and playing in your garden."

"I hope so."

"You will."

He sighs and says nothing.

"Did your parents or grandparents ever talk about the influenza epidemic in the early nineteen hundreds?

"Not too much. I have seen photos of people wearing masks, and there was one uncle, I think, who died of it. I did talk about it in my classes, but it didn't make much of an impression on the kids."

"We all assumed it would never happen again."

"Right."

"What was it like growing up in San Francisco?"

"Well . . . it was different."

Between coughing fits, he tells me about his childhood and his early years with my mother. I tell him about Donovan and my decision to trade nursing school for music. It feels good talking like this. To think I could have lost him and never had this chance.

Before long, he falls silent and closes his eyes.

"Time for bed?"

"Afraid so. But I'm glad to be home."

I help him into bed, give him his pills and a glass of water, and kiss him on the forehead. "Good night. Holler if you need me. I'm right here."

"Thank you. You're my favorite daughter."

"I'm your only daughter."

"I know. See you later."

I stir up the fire and knit until I can't stay awake. I turn out the light, too weary to even brush my teeth. As I lie down and close my eyes, my father starts coughing.

"Are you okay?" I call.

"I'm okay."

"Good." I'm going to be listening for him all night, but I don't mind. My father is going to get old and die. I intend to treasure every minute we can spend together.

Sunday, June 28, 2020

DAD AND I SLEEP in and watch the Mass online together in our pajamas. I pray someone else has volunteered to sing at Our Lady of Grace by now, but no. Poor Beverly is all alone, struggling on the piano, her voice wobblier than ever. Thank God Father Rigo has a good voice and pitches in between prayers.

"She needs you, PD," Dad says.

"I know. I'll do it next week."

"You're going to work tomorrow though, right?"

"Reluctantly, yes. Andy said he'd stay a few more days."

"Good. Where is he?"

"Putting the final touches on your garden. We'll check it out in a little while."

My brother has been hiding the garden from us both, temporarily using Dakota's fencing materials. But today as Mass ends, he comes in, wipes his hands, and pours himself some coffee. His shirt is unbuttoned, revealing floral tattoos along his ribcage.

"Ready for the big reveal?"

"Ready," we say, following him out to the garden.

Andy mimics a trumpet blast and slides the temporary fencing away.

"Aha!" Dad shouts, suddenly animated. "That's beautiful, Son."

It is. Andy has surrounded the garden with a white picket fence with gates at both ends and chicken wire above and underneath, so the critters can't burrow in, jump in, or fly in. In the middle, he has planted a blooming dogwood tree, circling it with rows of artichokes, pumpkins, squash, tomatoes, carrots and greens. Furrows in-between provide channels for water to run from row to row.

A white bench offers a place to relax.

"They call it Polywood. It's made of recycled materials and is guaranteed to withstand all kinds of weather."

"Hot damn. You have worked a miracle here. I could not have done that myself."

"I know, Dad. It takes a professional. Now all you have to do is water, weed, and harvest your crops. And you shouldn't be bothered by rabbits or anything else."

What about slugs and other bugs? I decide not to mention it.

"I don't know how to thank you, Andy."

"You'll get my bill." He looks serious for a minute, then laughs.

"Whew," Dad says, pretending to wipe sweat off his brow. "I suspect you're expensive."

"I am."

He and Andy settle on the bench while I run back in to trade my PJs for actual clothes. I hear Andy saying, "There's room for expansion in the corners, in case you want to plant . . ."

My phone is ringing. "Diana, how are you?"

"Much better. Do you think I could come visit your father tonight after dinner?"

"Well, you can't infect each other, I guess, so sure. Will you bring Janey?"

"Not tonight."

"Is she all right?"

"Just tired. Resting up. We're going to reopen the diner for take-out on Wednesday."

"That's good news."

I don't know what to say now that I know my friend is dating my father, so I say, "Well, I guess I'll see you tonight."

"Thanks, PD."

As I button my shirt, thinking I'd better go home and give Dad and Diana some alone time, I gaze out at the view from the study. The creek sparkles in a sea of green grass. The sky is the bluest blue, without a cloud. We are blessed. "Thank you, God. Anything you want from me, you got it."

19. In the Spotlight

Friday, July 3, 2020

WHY DID I AGREE to do this "Between the Bridges" interview today? I'm so wiped out all I want to do is throw my germy clothes in the washer and crawl into bed with a box of Oreos.

I barely had a chance to wolf down a sandwich before Britt was at the door. Dakota growled and went for a "ride."

Britt is setting up her camera. She's disgustingly perky in her little tiger mask and orange track suit. And her little butterfly tattoo. When I mentioned it to Dakota last week, she smiled and said, "Oh, she has more." I can just imagine.

This week, Dakota and Britt are kaput. When I asked about it, Dakota said only, "She needs to play with someone her own age." Indeed, I saw her doing just that one day when I was walking on the Bayfront. She was holding hands with an equally perky brunette as they watched the sea lions. So, that's that. She said that I'm the last interview on her list. Once it's done, she plans to go back to LA and make her little film. Fine. The sooner she crosses the bridge out of here, the better.

"I'm ready, PD."

"What do I do?"

"Sit down in the easy chair and relax. Take off your mask. I'll stand back here, ask some questions and we'll chat. Easy-peasy."

Sleazy, wheezy, kneesy, please me. I'm nervous.

I cover my eyes with my hands as she shines a bright light in my face. "Is that necessary?"

She tinkers with the lights. "Better?"

"I guess."

"All righty." She pushes a button and gives me a thumbs-up sign. "I'm here with PD Soares, who lives up Beaver Creek Road with her roommate Dakota Wells. PD, why don't you tell us a little about yourself?"

Great. What part of my fascinating self does she want to do know? I tell her I work at the hospital, I'm a musician, and I grew up in Santa Cruz, lived in Montana for a while and came here just before the tsunami.

"You told me an amazing story about crossing the bridge the night of the tsunami. Could you tell that story for our viewers?"

"Well, my friend Janey and I were trying to sleep at her mother's house that night, but we were having aftershocks every few minutes, and we couldn't sleep. I decided to sneak out and look around. Janey followed me, and we ended up driving north toward Newport. We were partially looking for our friend Dave, a park ranger who had not been seen since the tsunami, but also Janey really wanted to know if her apartment in Nye Beach was still standing. When we got close to the bridge, police officers had it all blocked off. Nobody crosses the bridge, they said. But Janey is a force of nature. She had me park my car by the marina. We climbed up the concrete steps to the bridge and ran across. It was shaking so much I fell and sprained my wrist. But we kept going, even though the cops were yelling at us.

"We made it. I had worked at the hospital in Missoula, and I wound up volunteering at the hospital in Newport. We slept at Janey's brother's house; his family was stuck in Seal Rock, where we had all gathered for Thanksgiving. After three days of aftershocks, we took a ferry back across the bay. Someone had broken into my car, but it was drivable."

"Was Janey's apartment still there?"

"Yes, but the city condemned it. Too much damage."

"What about Dave? Did you find him?"

"Not right away. A few days later, I was driving out Beaver Creek Road, fully intending to go back to Montana, when I stopped to answer a phone call at the boat launch and found Dave in the bushes at the edge of the creek. The tsunami had dumped him and his kayak there after he rescued a whole family. He was paralyzed from the neck down. He and his wife and daughter have moved to Portland where he can access the care he needs.”

“Oh my goodness. That’s terrible. Was the bridge open by then?”

“No. They airlifted him out by helicopter. His daughter and I drove the forest roads to Highway 20 and came into town that way.”

“Gosh. And you’re still living here.”

“Yes. I did go back to Montana to sell my house and pack up my things, but I wanted to come back to the Oregon coast and my friends here.”

Britt adjusts her tiger mask and straightens her kitty-cat earrings. “Here means Beaver Creek?”

“Basically, and Seal Rock, just south of here.”

“Is that a city?”

“Not officially. It’s really a state park and some tourist businesses built around it. Most of them are closed now and might never reopen. We’ve got Diana’s Diner and a fire station and the water company. In non-COVID times, you can buy stained glass, antiques, or fudge, but not groceries or gas. No medical services. No city hall or anything like that. There used to be a grocery store, just a little one that reminded me of the store in the old “Waltons” TV show, but the owner closed down after the tsunami.”

“I imagine a lot of people did.”

“Yes. Between the tsunami, COVID, and the economy, we’ve lost a lot of businesses. It’s isolated out here, but if someone came in and built all the big-city things we don’t have, it would ruin this place. We choose to live here because we like it the way it is. We might be missing some things, but look at the view. We have bald eagles and elk, beavers and bears, wild berries we can eat off the vine, and quiet. Most of the time, all we hear is wind and bird song.”

She consults her notebook. “You’re involved in a charity called Between the Bridges?”

“Yes, Dakota’s wife Maryann started that after the tsunami, figuring those of us trapped between the bridges need to help each other. It was great. We gave out food and clothing, helped folks rebuild their houses, helped them fill out FEMA forms, and just gave them somebody to talk to."

"Is that still going?"

"I'm trying to restart it. We had to shut down with COVID, but we're hoping to open up again when people start receiving the new vaccine. Maybe you could mention that we could use donations to our Between the Bridges project. A lot of people have needs that are not being met. Many are seniors who are afraid to leave their homes for fear of being exposed."

"Of course. I'll work on the donation part. PD, you're a musician. Are you able to do any performances these days?"

"No. No gigs at all. I was just starting to get some traction when everything closed. I am singing and playing at Our Lady of Grace. The church is pretty much empty. They record it and put it online."

"That's in Newport?"

"Right."

"And you work at the hospital in Newport?"

"Yes."

"If the bridge goes down, you can't go to church or work or the grocery store."

"Correct."

"This really is an island, a beautiful tree-lined island where the residents need to fend for themselves."

"Well, it's not so bad."

"I know. It's a very special place. But I'd have a hard time without my Starbucks and Trader Joe's . . ." She smiles. "Are you doing other music besides church music?"

"I am. I want to be ready to go all-out when things reopen. I have been taking composition classes online and writing a lot of music."

"Instrumentals or songs with words?"

"Both."

"Have you written any songs about this area?"

"I have. I was kind of inspired by this older woman who lives alone in the woods and sings songs like I've never heard before. It's like the voice of the trees."

"Do you think I could film her?"

"No. She would never go for it." Especially now, I think, when she seems to have company.

"Could I hear one of your songs?"

"Sure."

"Let me turn things around so I can face the piano."

I'm nervous as she rearranges, but the piano is my happy place, and my fingers know what to do as Britt listens intently.

"That's beautiful," she says, tapping her gold-polished nail against her mask. She nods to herself and pauses the recording. "I know this is coming out of the blue, but would you be interested in providing some music for my film? Maybe your own songs and some others with your musical friends from this area?"

"I would love that. I hope I have the skills."

"Judging by what I just heard, you definitely do."

"Well, let me know what you need and when."

"We have a few months. I'm aiming for the New Filmmakers Festival in LA next spring. I will pay you, of course, and you will keep the rights to your original music. We might want to make a sound-track album."

"Okay. This stuff is all new to me."

"No worries. I'm working with someone who knows all the ins and outs. We can do most of it online."

"Thank you so much!"

She turns the camera back on.

"Thank you so for sharing your story, PD. One last question. What does PD stand for?"

I shake my head. "I'm not saying. Use your imagination."

She chuckles. "All right. Thank you." She pushes the button and turns off the lights.

Whew. I'm sweating.

As she folds up her gear, she asks again. "Really, what does PD stand for?"

"I'm really not going to tell you. Did Dakota mention that that's not her real name?"

"No! What is it?"

"Never mind."

Speak of the devil, her headlights shine in the window as she parks behind my car. Britt's VW Beetle blocks Dakota's usual space.

Britt shoves the last of her gear into a big leather bag and folds her tripod. "Well, thank you. You're very photogenic. I think you'll like the results."

"Great. Have a safe trip home." I resist the urge to shake her hand.

"Oh, I will. Ciao."

She trips down the steps to her car, waving as she passes Dakota coming in.

"Hey," Dakota says and keeps walking.

"Nice ride?" I ask as she shuts the door behind her and Britt's taillights disappear.

"Swell. She going home?"

"Yup."

"Good."

"Hey, Britt's going to have me do music for her film."

"Swell."

"This is a great opportunity to get past the church music."

"I'm sure it is. I'm going to bed."

"G'night."

Rocky, who has been watching the whole proceeding, stands and wags his tail.

"One more trip outside," I tell him. "Don't ask me any questions, okay?"

He wags his luxurious tail. At least he's happy.

20. Fireworks

"DAKOTA, WHAT are you doing?"

From the piano, where I'm trying to compose music that sounds like Beaver Creek, I hear bottles clinking and see my housemate unloading the bottom cupboard to pull a fifth of Scotch from the back. Leaving everything on the floor, she unscrews the top and fills a juice glass.

"I'm having a drink. So what?"

"I thought you didn't—"

"Sometimes I do. Don't be such a prissyface."

Ouch! Dakota has never been mean to me before. I open my mouth to protest that I'm not—that—but decide now is not the time to defend my PDness. Besides, if you need to tell people you're cool, maybe you aren't.

"Okay," I say, playing some random arpeggios as she stomps outside. We're leaving the door open today because it's unusually hot around here. No rain for three weeks. Humidity way low. This is not normal for the Oregon coast. It must be climate change or something.

Maybe the heat is making Dakota cranky, but I think it's more than that. I mean, it's not even noon yet.

The thing with Britt was short, but it got to her. It was her first relationship of any kind since Maryann died. She had told me she didn't expect to find anyone else. I can relate to that. Pickings have been slim for me too lately. I was married twice, first to that fool I met when I was too young to know better and then to Tom. Maybe two husbands are all I'm allowed, and I used up my two before I was halfway through my life.

But if people do get two, Dakota could still have another one coming.

In the movies, you see all these gay bars and hangouts where people meet, but I don't think we have anything like that around here. I know she has some lesbian friends, but she's pretty shy, and with COVID, any get-togethers that might have happened are canceled. She sees people at the post office or delivering mail, but it's not the same. She's definitely not going to sign up for an online dating app. Neither would I. I guess you just do what you do and hope someone comes along. I was singing at an open mic when Tom showed up.

Ha. When I first moved into Donovan's cabin, Dakota thought I was gay, and she was kind of flirting with me. Surprise, I'm not. Sometimes I wish I did swing that way.

Maybe she's just depressed. So many people are sick or losing their loved ones to that bastard COVID. So many are isolated and unable to work, watching their businesses collapse while their kids receive substandard education because they can't go to school. Who wouldn't be bummed?

But if Dakota is an alcoholic, why would that Scotch be in the cupboard?

Maryann was so crunchy granola healthy that her parties rarely included liquor. When they did, I don't remember whether Dakota drank or not. I certainly have never seen her drunk. She did react rather strongly when I came home from Eugenia's stoned on pot. I don't know. In the mood she's in, I'm not about to ask.

Tires rumble up the gravel road. Janey's here. She'll lighten the mood. "Hey, Dakota, happy un-Fourth of July!" she calls.

"What's happy about it?"

"You know, freedom, America, rah, rah, rah. It's a little quiet without the fireworks. Stupid COVID, stupid fire danger. Just when we have a year we might actually be able to see the fireworks without fog and clouds in the way, we can't do it. But COVID can't stop me from singing." And she sings, "I'm Proud to Be an American—"

Dakota interrupts. "Janey, not today."

"Spoilsport. Is PD inside?"

I guess she nods because here she comes.

"PD-roo, how do you do?"

"Peachy-keen."

She leans in to whisper. "What's eating Dakota? Is she drinking?"

"Don't know, and yes, she is. Don't ask her about it. She'll bite your head off."

"I noticed. Wow." She plops into the easy chair while I spin around on the piano bench to face her.

"Are you all cured of COVID?"

"I'm great. I can even sing again." She sings a quick scale that ends in the stratosphere. Rocky looks up at the high notes, puzzled.

"I'm glad. Is the diner busy?"

"Oh, crap. Those tourists don't know when to stay home. Some places are open, but we're still doing drive-up until we can hire someone to help."

"Julio's not coming back?"

"PD, the dude made us sick, and he didn't bother to call us. So, no. Jonas and a couple of friends set up picnic tables in the parking lot so people can eat outside at a safe distance. Now I have to serve drive-ups *and* tables. Know anybody who needs a job? They have to be healthy, dependable, and speak English."

"Not offhand."

"Oh well." She studies the paper on my piano. "New song?"

"Sort of, yes. Britt asked me to do some music for that film she's making."

"The Between the Bridges thing?"

"Yes. I played her one of my songs, and she wants more. I'm really excited. There will be a soundtrack and maybe an album. I told her about you. Maybe we can sing some duets."

"Oh my God! That would be amazing! I could use it for my résumé for New York."

"You're really going?"

"I have to, PD. Broadway is calling me, and I'm not going to get anywhere singing in Seal Rock."

She's right. Whatever motherly doubts I have, I push them aside. "I can see you on the stage, singing your little heart out. Can you act?"

"Can I act? You bet. Before the tsunami and COVID, I was in every musical at school and at the Performing Arts Center. Hey, did you hear they're going to build a new community theater up above the middle school?"

"No, I didn't."

"Jonas does deliveries to this guy from the city whose wife spilled the beans."

"Wow. Remember when we tried to push for a theater last year and everybody dumped on us? They needed food and shelter, and we wanted show biz."

"Oh yeah. That was awful. Bad timing. Anyway, as soon as things open up again, probably next year, I'm heading for the Big Apple. Mom thinks I'm nuts to go there all by myself, but I'm going. Unless you want to join me."

"I don't think so. I'm too old to be an ingénue. I've moved around enough already. I just want to play and sing and write songs."

I still want that PD's Piano Bar dream that Tom and I talked about. Being in a band was good, too. Maybe I could form another band when COVID is over. PD's All-Stars. But New York? No.

Janey digs in my fridge and pours herself a glass of cranberry juice. "How's my future stepdad?" she asks.

"Better. Are Dad and Diana that serious?"

"I don't know. Mom seems awfully happy these days. I'm glad, considering what an ass Rick turned out to be. Can I eat this muffin?"

"Sure."

I miss Janey's brightness from our days living together, even though she can be such a child. Heck, she is young enough to be *my* child. That blows my mind every time I think of it.

Her mouth half full, she says, "Will you play me some of your movie music?"

"It's really rough."

"I don't care." She comes to stand over my shoulder, smelling of cranberry juice and blueberry muffin. I look at the sheet of paper I've been scrawling on and play. In a minute, she is humming a high harmony.

I hate to interrupt her, but I can't forget what I read online about drops of virus flying out with every note we sing and how that choir in Washington got sick. Some of them died. "Sweetie, can you put your mask on?"

She nods and I mask up, too.

I love harmony. I hum the melody while she sings the high part. Janey is also a flute player. I imagine hearing flute above the piano music, maybe with some soft percussion from Jonas.

We're blissed out on sugar and music when Dakota quietly comes in and pours herself another glass of Scotch before returning to the porch.

I'm not going to say anything. Neither is Janey. But we all jump when we hear a bang from northeast of here.

Rocky zooms under my bed. Janey and I look at each other and run outside.

"Dakota," I ask. What was that?"

"Fireworks, I guess. Or gunshots. It's Fourth of July."

"Yeah, but they're not allowed this year. I smell smoke. Is that coming from Eugenia's place?"

Dakota shrugs. "I dunno." She turns and goes inside.

"Let's go," I tell Janey. "Your car is behind mine, so you drive."

When Rocky sees us leaving, he noses his leash hanging by the door, but I raise my hand. "Stay, boy. Take care of Dakota."

I swear he scowls as he sinks to the hardwood floor.

"WHERE ARE WE going, PD?"

"Just follow my directions. It's not too far."

"Is there anything out here?"

"Surprisingly, yes. Rocky led me there a while back."

"Shouldn't we just call the fire department or something? I need to haul ass to the diner for the lunch rush."

"Turn right up here and then turn in at the driveway where you see the water barrel."

"You know there's bears out here?"

"And cougars and skunks and all kinds of animals. I know." My stomach is churning. I have no idea what we're going to find at Eugenia's place. What if the whole thing's on fire?

"Is this it?"

"Yes. Drive in until you see the house."

"Okaaay. Who lives here?"

"Eugenia."

"Wait. That crazy woman everyone calls The Witch?"

"Janey! She is not a witch. Just . . . old-fashioned."

"Uh-huh."

The house looks intact, but—"Hmm."

"Hmm what? I don't want to be thrown in the oven like Hansel and Gretel."

"That truck. I've seen it here before. Some guy driving really fast and wild. Dakota says he flipped her off when she slowed him down with her mail deliveries."

"Oh, great. Crazy lady and wild man. I'm starting to hear the theme song from "Deliverance.""

To be honest, so am I. "Park next to the truck, Janey. We can handle this."

As I open the car door, I smell the smoke again. It's coming from behind the house where Eugenia grows her marijuana. We head that way.

"Hello!" Eugenia says, waving us over to a rock-circled fire pit where weeds and something that looks like blue denim cloth are burning.

Eugenia's hair hangs loose. She has a dark smudge on her cheek and dirt on her faded dress. Her lips are smiling, but her eyes seem wary.

"Who is your friend, PD? You're always bringing me interesting people."

"This is Janey Peacock. Her mother, Diana, owns the diner in Seal Rock. We used to live together."

"I see. Such a pretty girl."

"Thank you. Ma'am." Janey is looking around, bug-eyed.

"Do you sing, too?"

"Yes. And I play the flute."

"Well, that's wonderful. Maybe you can join me and PD for one of our little songfests."

"Sure."

I clear my throat. "Eugenia, we came because we heard a loud bang and then we smelled smoke. We got worried. With the heat and wind and all, nobody is supposed to have fires out here."

"Oh, I didn't hear that. This little fire won't hurt anything."

"It could if the wind carries the sparks to the trees and grass. What was the bang?"

"Hah. I found this old firecracker in my shed and thought well, it's Fourth of July. I'm going to shoot it off. It made a pretty good explosion. Dust flying up all over the place."

"Scared the poop out of us," Janey said.

"Oh, I'm sorry, honey. I don't hear well, so it didn't bother me."

Janey knocks my arm and points toward the house. A little boy runs away from the window. It must be the same one Dakota saw.

Remembering how the woman got angry when I asked about her kids shortly after we met, I try to work around it. "Eugenia, whose truck is that?"

For just a second, she looks frightened, then she shakes her head. "Well, it's mine."

"I thought you didn't drive."

"Oh, I can. I just don't usually want to go anywhere."

"I understand. Sometimes I don't either."

"Do you live here all by yourself?" Janey asks.

"Yes, dear. Have for many years." She tosses a heap of Scotch broom onto the fire, and it flares up. "I'd offer you girls some cookies, but I'm afraid I ran out, and I haven't got a new batch made yet."

"That's okay. I'm on a diet," Janey says.

"Pssh. You look perfect just the way you are. Boys like something they can hold onto, not just bones."

Janey blushes.

A crash and a shout come from the house. "What's that? Eugenia, are you sure you're here by yourself?"

"Oh PD, you're hearing things. The cat probably knocked something down."

"I didn't know you had a cat."

"She just wandered in the other day and said, 'I'm going to live here now.' I said, 'Fine, happy to have you. Just don't bother the chickens.' "

Janey's looking at me, and I'm looking at Janey, and I really don't know what to do or say except, "Eugenia, would you consider putting that fire out for me? It makes me really uneasy."

She nods. "Okay, PD, for you. I have burned what I wanted to burn today anyway." She grabs a tin bucket. "Would you mind filling this from the rain barrel? My well is running low."

"Sure." I hurry past the car to the barrel and dip the bucket into the black water. It weighs a ton and the handle is digging into my hand as I carry it back. Eugenia and Janey are already kicking dust onto the fire. As I empty the bucket, the blaze fizzles out with a last puff of smoke. "Thank you. We should be going. Dakota will be wanting lunch, and I said I would cook."

I didn't, but who cares.

"All right. See you next time. I'm always around. I'll have cookies. You bring your harmonica, and Janey, bring your flute. We'll have some fun."

As soon as we're on the road, Janey explodes like that firecracker. "Holy crap. What the hell? Who is in that house? Is that woman on drugs or just crazy? What was she burning besides weeds?"

"I do not know, and I'm not sure I want to."

"Jeez Louise. Let's just get out of here."

"We're going. Hey, what's your mom cooking today?"

"Ribs, beans and slaw, plus red, white and blue cake. It's Fourth of July."

"Fattening."

"Men like girls with meat on their bones, remember?"

"Right. I wish they'd reopen the gym."

"Miguel has one."

"Hush. Take me to the diner. Let's beat the rush."

"We'd better stop and pick up your car, PD, because I need to get to work. Mom's gonna be steaming. We're gonna have a crowd, and she can't cook and serve at the same time."

"Fine. Janey, thank you for going with me."

"That's our thing, isn't it? Running into dangerous situations together?"

We slap hands. "For sure. Thelma and Louise, Janey and PD."

It's not until I'm driving back to the rainbow house with my stomach growling at the smell of barbecue sauce that I remember how Dakota said Gabriel was at Eugenia's house the other day. Was he the one making noise inside? Did he drive the black truck? Who is that little boy? I'm confused. And hungry.

Rocky greets me. Dakota's bedroom door is closed. I peek in. She's asleep—or passed out.

Oh well. As Tom's mother used to say when someone didn't want to eat what she offered, *Mais fica*. More for me.

Ribs, beans, and slaw. God bless America.

21. Devilish Angel

"MAY I SING with you?"

I startle hard. I thought I was alone in the church. Beverly has COVID now, and I'm practicing to do the Mass by myself. I look up at Gabriel, the homeless guy from the woods. Same long blond hair, same all-white clothing. At least he's wearing a mask now. But he still has those spooky eyes.

"Jesus. You scared me."

He does a yoga *namaste* bow with his hands in prayer position. "I'm sorry. I seem to have that gift with you, PD. I didn't know you played music here. I felt a call to find a church service."

I'm still trying to slow my heart down to normal. Gabriel's soft tenor voice is more disturbing than a drunken shout. A little like Anthony Hopkins in "Silence of the Lambs." *I know all about you, Clarice.* I wonder if he knows I lied about having a husband and a redneck friend with a shotgun, that I was just too chicken to give him a place to sleep.

Now would be a good time for Fr. Rigo to pop in, but all I hear is the old building creaking in the wind. "Usually Beverly leads the singing, but she's sick. I didn't know you were Catholic."

He spreads his arms wide. Again, I think of wings. "I am Catholic. I am Baptist. I am Lutheran. I am all faiths."

"Um—" Yeah, that's not how it works, but how do you argue with a guy who maybe thinks he has angel wings on his back? "Do you have any experience singing in church choirs?"

"I have sung in many church choirs. I probably know all the songs you're doing today."

"Really? Well, you're welcome to give it a try. I'm just practicing. We'll be sharing the Mass on the Internet live and later on YouTube."

"Oh, I don't get into that stuff. You turn on a computer or cell phone, and they know all your secrets."

"They who?"

"You don't want to know."

Great. He's crazy. He also needs a shower, but we are supposed to love our neighbor. "Grab a hymnal and we'll start with the opening song. I'm going to need you to stand over there where the choir stands."

Twelve straight chairs are set up on three rows of risers. No one has sat in them since March. Gabriel hesitates. "I need to go retrieve my stuff," he says.

Stuff? He lugs in several bulging black plastic bags and stashes them behind the middle chair in the second row. I see a box of vanilla wafers sticking out of one of them, a blue tarp out of another. "Gabriel, how did you get here? It's at least 10 miles from Beaver Creek."

"Kind strangers gave me a ride. They always do."

I hope he's not expecting me to chauffeur him back to Beaver Creek or wherever he's sleeping.

Oh, thank God. Billie is here now, setting up her camera. She studies Gabriel, then looks at me. I shrug.

"Okay. Number 175, first two verses." I start to play, and he joins in.

He has a nice voice. Very nice. But he still gives me the shivers. Isn't there a quote somewhere in the Bible about the devil having a pleasing voice? If there isn't, there ought to be.

As I play, I wonder if that was him in Eugenia's house the other day. Why would she lie to me about that? She's usually such a straight shooter. Does he know who the little boy is or who owns that black truck? Is there a black truck in the church parking lot now?

If the devil drove a pickup, wouldn't it be black? Jesus would drive a white truck, right?

Gabriel waves his hand like a kid trying to attract his teacher's attention. "Are you playing that quarter note correctly in the second line?"

"What?" I lean closer to the music. I forgot my reading glasses. "Here, on Lord?"

"Yes. I think you were cutting it short."

Now he's a music expert? "I'll count more carefully," I tell him. What I want to say is, "Shut up and sing. It's hard to sing and play at the same time, and I'm bound to make mistakes."

He wants to sing the psalm. I say no. I'm the cantor.

"Traditionally, a man sings—"

I cut him off. "Here and now, I do it."

He stares at the crucifix as if he has to confer with Jesus about that one.

When we get to the offertory song, he wants me to play it more slowly. I'm biting my tongue so hard I expect to taste blood any minute.

We're almost done when I notice Father Rigo standing in the doorway in his green alb. As we finish practicing the closing song, he strides forward.

"Good morning. PD, I guess you heard about Beverly. I hope she recovers quickly."

"Me too, Father."

He goes to Gabriel. "Are you new here?"

"I am Gabriel. I'm here to sing."

"Well, that's great. You have a very biblical name. Where do you live?"

"Here and there."

"I see. PD lives up Beaver Creek, comes all the way here for Mass."

"I know where she lives."

Is that a little earthquake I feel?

Father looks at me. "Is he a good singer?" I suspect he is asking more than that.

"Yes, Father. He has a nice voice."

He nods. "Well, it's almost time. Billie's ready, and the ushers are in the vestibule starting to check people in."

"Okay. We're ready."

Well, almost. I need to use the restroom before Mass. I grab my purse and go. Not that Gabriel would steal from me in church. Or would he?

He follows me. "Restrooms? I need to freshen up."

He sure does. I sink onto the toilet in the ladies' room with a sigh. *Lord, help me to play well and not scream at Gabriel. Let Beverly get well soon. Amen.*

I glance out the window on the way back. No black truck.

As I walk back across the front of the sanctuary, I count ten people, all wearing masks and sitting apart from each other. The parishioners are all kind of familiar by now, even though I don't know their names. Except, oh my gosh. Thank you, God. Sitting just to the right of the camera where Billie is fussing with the settings is Miguel. He waves. I wave back.

He's like the opposite of Gabriel, dark skin, brown eyes, nicely dressed in a pin-striped cotton shirt and black slacks. He works out at the gym at his house, which means he has muscles. If Gabriel acts up, Miguel can save me.

Where the heck is Gabriel anyway? It's time. Father nods at me from the doorway. I play and sing "Gather Us In." Father Rigo and the few people in the pews sing along, including Miguel. This might be all right.

We have finished the opening prayers and the "Gloria" and I'm singing the responsorial psalm when Gabriel walks across the front of the church, passes me and climbs to the second row of choir chairs. I have to focus on the words and music, but I hear him on the response, singing, "Taste and see the goodness of the Lord."

Oh no. He's conducting with his long skinny arms. I can't look over there. Too distracting.

During Communion, Gabriel doesn't just bow and hold out his hands like the rest of us. Leaving me to carry the song alone, he throws himself on the floor and tilts his head up with his tongue out. Father bends way low and places the host on it, but I can read his mind. *What's with this guy? I'm going to need to talk to him about how to receive Communion.* He smiles at the older man in line behind Gabriel and carries on.

Communion goes quickly. Thanks to COVID, we no longer pass the chalice with wine. I don't know if we ever will again. At the end of the line, I bring the song to a close and slip over to receive the host in my outstretched hands.

"Body of Christ, PD."

"Amen."

Miguel is kneeling in his pew, face in his hands. I ought to be in love with this healthy, handsome, devout guy. Why am I not?

During the closing song, "How Can I Keep from Singing?" I keep wondering what Gabriel will do after Mass. Will he ask for a ride or for money?

But he doesn't do any of those things. He slips out the door as Miguel comes forward. "Beautiful music, PD."

"Thank you."

"I could listen to you sing all day. But I'm guessing you're tired. I found a pretty good restaurant near my place. It has outdoor seating if it's not too cold. Would you care to join me there for brunch?"

I don't want to date him, but Gabriel scared me, and brunch sounds nice. "I would. Thank you. Where exactly is it? I can meet you there."

"It's just south of the bridge on the left."

"By the candy factory?"

"That's the one."

I follow him down the highway, over the bridge and into the parking lot of Off the Hook.

A cold breeze makes me shiver as I get out of the car. "Maybe we should eat inside."

He huddles in his beige jacket. "Good idea."

It's not crowded. Some of the tables are blocked off with "Reserved" signs so no two parties sit close together. Football games play silently on the screens hung in the corners. Beer signs dot the walls.

"Is this acceptable?"

"Sure. It's great."

A masked, multi-pierced waitress seats us, laying down menus. "Can I bring you something to drink?"

"Bloody Mary?" Miguel asks, his eyes twinkling.

"Tempting, but no. Just coffee."

"The same."

When she returns with our coffee, we remove our masks. There's something very intimate about it as our lips are revealed. His lips are thick and pink. I may not be in love, but I'm starting to be in lust. Is that terrible for a 40-something church choir lady?

Miguel is smiling at me again. His teeth are nice.

"I have to ask. Did you come to church just to see me?"

He shakes his head. "No. I didn't know you would be there. I just wanted to go to Mass, but if I had known, I would have come sooner."

The waitress is back. "What are you going to order?"

"I think I'd like a bowl of clam chowder," Miguel says.

"Sounds good. Me too."

As she walks away, Miguel leans toward me. "Maybe we can hit the candy store afterward."

"Uh-oh."

He glances at the TV. "49ers vs. Cowboys. Should be a good game."

Is he a sports fanatic?

No. His attention is back on me. "PD, how is it at work these days?"

"Crazy." As I fill him in, he nods and murmurs support. It's been ages since I had anyone to talk to like this. Dad is still getting over his illness, Dakota has been in a bad place, and Janey is all hopped up on Broadway. Oh! I can tell Miguel about the Between the Bridges film.

"I'm writing music for a movie."

"That's wonderful. I'd love to hear some of it."

"Not yet. It's too raw. How is your fish project?"

He laughs. It's a good laugh, wide open and warm. "The fish are going great. In fact, if you have time after this, I'd love to show you what's happening there."

Is this like "let me show you my etchings," the famous come-on line from the olden days? If we weren't in separate cars, if I didn't have a million things to do, if I didn't promise to make dinner for my father . . .

"I'm sorry. Not this time. I'm booked for the rest of the day."

"I understand. Weekends aren't nearly long enough. Another time."

"Yes. Definitely."

He reaches across and squeezes my hand. "Do you have time for chocolate?"

"I think I can manage it."

Is it okay to enjoy a man's company if there are no bubbles, just quiet comfort?

A COUPLE HOURS LATER, salad made, French bread ready for the oven, and pasta ready to cook, I've got my laptop perched on top of the piano as I work on a song, making up lines of music based on suggestions from my spring music class. Like use C, Em, and A7 chords to compose a melody. Or play a melody over a sustained low G. I love this. It's fascinating. I'm coming up with combinations I would never have thought of on my own.

I'm so wrapped up I don't hear Dakota passing through. Her voice startles me.

"What's for dinner?"

I take a deep breath, trying to calm my pulse. "Dad's coming, remember? We're having pasta carbonara and all the fixings."

"I might not be here."

"Oh?"

"Don't count on me." She heads out the back door toward the shed.

It has been like that since Fourth of July when she started drinking. She never seems drunk, just withdrawn and silent. I don't know what I should do about it, if anything. The only alcoholic I know well enough to ask is Donovan, although booze is just one little part of his problems. I don't want to talk about Dakota behind her back.

One thing's for sure. She is not a happy drunk.

I hope she isn't drinking during the workday. If she got fired or crashed the van, it would be awful.

Shut up and play your piano, I tell myself.

Dakota returns. "Well, that's a depressing song," she says as she grabs a beer out of the fridge.

I stare at her. Who is this?

Rocky has been pawing me. "Come on, boy. Dakota, if you're not going to join us for dinner, I think I'll take the food to Dad's house. It'll be easier for him."

"Fine."

Which is how I show up two hours early with an ice chest full of ingredients and cooking utensils for dinner.

"What's going on?" Dad asks, getting up from the afternoon football game he's watching on the little TV he usually keeps in his camper.

"I'm cooking here."

"Troubles in paradise?"

"Oh Dad. Dakota is drinking, and she acts like she hates me."

"Sweetie, that's just the booze. It's not about you. I would never have guessed she was a drinker."

"Me either." I stare at the TV. "Good game?"

"It's a rerun. They're not actually playing because of you know what."

"You like football enough to watch re-runs?"

He shrugs. "It's something to do. You need any help in the kitchen?"

"No, thanks. Relax."

The kitchen used to be my happy place when Tom was alive and I was Cissy. Something I could always do successfully and please the people around me.

By the time I put the bread in the oven, Dad is asleep. Good. I know he hasn't gotten all his energy back. I plan to spoil him rotten as long as I can.

"PD, YOU ARE a better cook than your mother. Don't ever tell her I said so, but man. If I had room, I'd eat another helping of everything."

"Thanks, Dad. Eat as much as you want. You're still recovering."

"Yeah, I'm always pooped. But at least I can taste food again." He pushes his chair back. "It's still kind of warm out. How about dessert in the garden?"

We retire to the bench. Things are growing well. Andy did a great job. The rabbits must be frustrated.

Wind blows through the pines. A robin warbles a serenade. The cheesecake melts on my tongue.

"I had brunch with Miguel this morning."

"You did?"

"I did. At this restaurant in South Beach. Dad, he's really nice."

"I told you. Will you go out with him again?"

"Probably. I don't feel any big sparks, but he's nice to be around."

"Sometimes that's enough. I hate to see you alone, PD."

"I'm not alone. I have you."

"That's not weird at all." He laughs.

I take our plates into the house and retrieve the wine bottle I hid from Dakota.

We watch the sunset, a beautiful orange sherbet swirl, and reminisce about childhood camping trips. Suddenly Dad stops talking and points. "PD, look."

Elk, three females, have gathered about a hundred yards away, grazing on the summer grass. The biggest one glances up at us then resumes feeding.

"They're magnificent," my father says.

Up close, they are huge, much larger than deer, not as pretty with their llama-like brown heads, tan torsos and white tails, but they move elegantly, all in step together.

We sit still and watch until something spooks them and they swoosh off into the woods.

"You don't see that in Santa Cruz," Dad says.

"Nope."

"Ah, PD, life is good."

"Yes." I smile at the father I came close to losing. It is.

PART II

22. Waves of Fire

Wednesday, Sept. 9, 2020

I'M CHOKING ON ashes. The bruise-yellow air looks like the solar eclipse in 2017 when it got so dark in the middle of the day the birds hushed and the streetlights came on. But that only lasted a minute. We've been breathing smoke for two weeks, and it shows no signs of stopping. Wildfires are burning all over the west, including a blaze only 30 miles from here at the north end of Lincoln City. We're safe for now, but that could change. I look around at the evergreens and alders, shrubs and weeds snugged up against the house. If a wildfire comes here, there aren't enough fire trucks in the world to stop it.

We used to think we didn't have to worry about fire because it's so wet on the coast, but the weather has gone crazy. It's Montana-summer hot, the humidity down from its usual 80 percent to 15, and the wind never stops. A perfect recipe for fire. This is not supposed to happen at the beach. Nobody has air conditioning. It's too hot inside and too smoky outside.

Ashes fall onto my hair and arms. They cover the cars in the driveway. Like snowflakes, they disintegrate when you try to grab them, but they're not half as pretty. They stink.

The sun is bright red. We're getting some colorful sunsets. Psychedelic, Dad calls it.

Sunset isn't for a couple more hours, but it's already twilight as I shelter on the porch while Rocky does his business.

Dakota is gone. Defying the call to avoid travel as COVID continues to rage, Dakota has taken two weeks off to visit her family in South

Dakota. She says as long as she eats and sleeps in the van, she ought to be safe from the virus. She will wear her mask around her folks.

"I just have to get out of here," she said when she left on Saturday. "You'll probably be glad."

"No. I'll miss you."

"I don't think anybody will miss me." Then she walked out with her duffel bag.

I don't know much about Dakota's family. They don't seem to call, and I've never met any of them, but I do know Dakota needs a change. She's still drinking and still depressed, looking older and skinnier. Whenever I try to ask her about any of this, she shuts me down in a hurry.

Selfishly, I worry this might lead to me not living in the rainbow house. What if she decides not to come back or that she'd rather I not be here? We joke about being the new "Golden Girls," two widows sharing a home, but we're different.

Wasn't there an episode where one of the Golden Girls had a problem with alcohol? Was it Dorothy? Never mind. The smoke is seeping into my brain. "Rocky, are you done yet?"

He looks up from the bushes at the side of the house where he has been sniffing something, wags his tail, and hurries to the porch.

"Come on."

At least I have the dog for company. I refill his water bowl, fill a glass for myself and settle on the easy chair. I don't feel like doing anything. It's strange being here alone. Dad is spending his nights with Diana, and Janey has a new guy. They met at the diner, which is the only place she goes.

I haven't seen Eugenia in a while. It's too smoky to walk there now, and I can't imagine sitting outside playing music. I did visit once in August. No sign of the black truck or the little boy, but Gabriel was there chopping wood for her. With his shirt off and his hair tied back, he looked almost normal. He comes to church intermittently, always in the same clothes. Always a bit, well, different.

Two more choir members, Ronny Mae and Willa, have come back, and Beverly has recovered, so our choir has grown to five now. Lizzy, our regular director, called to tell me she is coming back soon, but she wants me to stay on the piano.

We're getting about 20 people in the pews. Miguel is always there. Every Sunday after church, we have brunch, like a couple of old people. Sometimes we go for a walk.

A few times, I even used his gym to work out my frustrations. It was kind of nice running on his treadmill while he lifted weights. After a while, we changed places. I let him know I did not need help with the weights. He was fine with that. He was always there to spot me, but not in that sexist way other men have done, guys who assume I'm weak because I've got breasts.

We've had some sweaty kisses, but we have not had sex yet. Neither one of us has made a move. Maybe he doesn't feel the spark either. I don't know.

Spark. I shouldn't even say the word. All it takes is a lightning strike, a cigarette, a firecracker, a gunshot, or a *spark* from the bottom of a truck or a bulldozer. They had a list in the local paper the other day of things that could set off a blaze. I had no idea it was so easy to start a fire. The first time I tried to light a fire in the fireplace at Donovan's cabin, it was a total failure. Now, I'm a pro.

Rocky and I tried taking a walk yesterday. The heat strangled me like Saran wrap. Flies darted around my face and gathered in Rocky's fur, which looked reddish-brown in the weird light. The smoke stung my eyes. We hadn't gotten far before I started feeling faint. We gave up and went home. I tried to watch a TV show on the computer, but the Internet was out.

Work at the hospital is still intense. Ten people have died of COVID in Lincoln County, a small number compared to other places but a lot for here. Oregon is logging 200 new cases a day. I wonder how many of them will die.

Two more restaurants here had COVID outbreaks. At the same time, the state gave permission to reopen the movie theaters and bowling alleys. What kind of logic is that?

The first fires started in California, not unusual. In recent years, much of the territory between Redding and the Oregon border has burned. On my last trip to visit Mom and Andy, I saw blackened trees along the freeway for miles.

The whole town of Paradise was destroyed in 2016. California is burning again right now, but so is Oregon. There's a huge fire in Talent between Ashland and Medford, another east of Eugene, one up highway 20 east of Toledo, and the one above Lincoln City near Otis. Thousands of people have been evacuated, and hundreds have already lost their homes.

On the news, they keep saying the fires are only a few percent contained or not contained at all despite fire crews from all over the country working under hellish conditions. Wildfires have been a regular occurrence in the forest since time began, but now there are people, homes, businesses, churches, and cows in the way.

This guy from Otis who was interviewed talked about how he thought he was safe. Then suddenly he looked out his front door and saw the flames coming right at him. All he could do was grab his dog and run cross country because the roads were blocked. He ran and walked for two days, no food, no rest, just fear propelling him forward. He wasn't a young guy either.

Everything he owned is gone. The clothes he was wearing and his dog are all he has left.

It feels like the end of the world.

While Dakota is gone, I'm eating at the diner most nights just for company. I go home and change first to shed the hospital cooties. Diana is letting people eat inside now at tables spread as far apart as she can get them. Janey and Jonas are both helping. Everybody wears masks except when they're eating. I don't know how safe it is, but we're all trying to follow the guidelines set by the Centers for Disease Control and Governor Brown. Trouble is, those guidelines change every five minutes.

Diana's special tonight was fried chicken and mashed potatoes with peas and carrots. Plain, fattening, delicious. Janey sat with me for a while, sipping diet soda. Usually a little round, she lost 15 pounds while she was sick. She's happy about that. "No fatties on Broadway," she says.

I hold my tongue. The way I'm eating, old PD is going to need bigger clothes or more gym time with Miguel.

I guess I should work on my Between the Bridges music. Britt wants it before the holidays. She sent me some clips of the interviews and an outline of the film as a guide. I have sent her a few songs and instrumental background themes that felt somewhat finished. She made some suggestions, but overall she likes them. Eventually, she says, I'm going to have to record them through a Midi system with proper software so her tech people can edit them. I don't understand how that works yet. I'm just going to worry about the music.

What kind of music goes with fire? Not the peaceful singing-around-the-campfire kind of fire, the warm fireplace glow that heats the house in winter, or a flickering candlelight on a romantic evening, but fire that comes in waves like a tsunami and eats everything in its path. Oh, I think I know where to go with this. Give me some paper. Waves of fire, higher and higher . . . the words come easily. I hope the melody does, too.

My phone breaks my thought with a text message from Janey. *Did you know there's a fire up the Alsea Highway near Waldport? This guy just told us about it. It's not in town, but people on the outskirts are being told to get ready.*

Oh my God, I text back. Waldport is only a few miles south of us, just over the Alsea Bridge. That's too close. I read that wildfires can spread at 14 miles an hour under the right conditions. Could it leap over Alsea Bay or crawl up the river? Yikes!

What do I do if the fire comes here, especially without Dakota around? Should I get hoses ready, or is that just stupid? We're supposed to have to-go bags prepared for any kind of emergency. I haven't done that yet. As soon as I finish drafting this song, I'm going to pack a bag for me and Rocky.

Then what? Should I wet down the roof? Can I clear enough greenery away from the house to keep it safe? What about Dad's place? He's in the trees, too. Why didn't we do this before? Please, don't let it come here.

People receive three kinds of directives: *Level 1: There's a dangerous fire in the area. Get ready for potential evacuation. Level 2: Be set to evacuate at a moment's notice. Level 3: Go now. Leave immediately. If you don't, emergency services may not be available to help you.* Please God, don't let me get a knock on the door or a text telling me to do any of those. Where would we go? Everywhere around here is in danger of fire or COVID or both. The Newport hotels are full of evacuees from Lincoln City.

Wherever I go, I need to take my father with me. I wonder if the smoke is going to make him sick again.

Would Diana's house and the diner burn, too? God, please no.

Maybe I wouldn't receive a notice. The fires are knocking out electrical and Internet service, and the fire crews might be too busy to find these houses out in the woods.

The night of the tsunami, people were packed into the community college student union on blankets and sleeping bags. No social distancing. No masks. Everybody sharing food. A guaranteed super-spreader, as they call events where too many people gather and COVID runs rampant.

People are stupid. Even the president hosted an event where a bunch of the attendees got sick. It's a miracle he hasn't gotten it yet.

But if we have nowhere else to go, what choice do we have?

I think I'm going to pray the Rosary, if I can remember how. I never really got in the habit. That was my grandmother's thing. But it feels right tonight. Let me finish this song and put the whole music project in a bag in case I have to run. I'm not leaving my songs. I'll worry about clothes and food and other stuff later.

A wave of fire, growing higher and higher, pyre, desire, liar, mire, choir, wire, inspire, dryer, ire . . . Each rhyme inspires another line. Before I know it, I've got two pages of lyrics and a chorus that is mostly a wail. Exhausted and sweaty, I shove the pages into a tote bag and set it on the piano bench, ready to go.

I'm on my knees muttering "Hail Mary, Full of Grace" when another text comes in. It seems sacrilegious to interrupt the Rosary to read a text message, but I can't help myself. What if this is my notice to get ready?

Whew. It's not. Janey says they got the Waldport fire under control. They had a little one in Yachats, too, but it's okay. No homes lost.

Thank you, God. I finish the Rosary and pray for all those people who are not as lucky.

I want to talk to Dakota, tell her what it's like here and figure out what we should do if the worst happens. But she's in another time zone. It's late, and I'm not sure she would welcome a call. I could call Mom or Andy, but then they'd worry.

Diana gave me some frosted sugar cookies. I'm going to have one and go to bed.

Please God, let there be less smoke tomorrow.

23. Burnt Trees

Friday, Sept. 11, 2020

"D'YA SEE this?"

A burly bald guy from the next table at the diner tosses me a copy of the local newspaper. A picture of the burned area in Lincoln City covers half the front page. Nothing but foundations, fireplaces, and burned-out cars. You can see the streets and driveways, but the rest is gone.

"Buddy of mine lived up there. Just finished rebuilding his house, new kitchen, new deck and patio, new paint, put himself in debt up to the eyeballs, and it's all gone. One day you're eating and sleeping and watching TV in your house as usual, the next you're running for your life with only the stuff you can throw in the truck in a hurry."

"Where are they now?" I ask.

"Stayin' with friends in the valley. I said they could bunk with me and the wife, but it's too dangerous out here, they said."

"Yeah, it is," chimes in another man sitting with his wife near the window. "We live up the Alsea, and we got the call day before yesterday. Get ready. Luckily, they stopped the fire before it got to us, but it sure scared us. I don't know how you prepare to leave a place where you've lived for over 40 years. We've got livestock, goats, cows, chickens, can't put those in the truck. My wife packed some stuff, but we're too damned old to start over."

Janey comes around with the coffee pot. "You're not that old, Jasper."

"Wait'll you're my age, kid. You'll see."

"I'll be far away from here by then."

"Ha. That's what they all say," the bald guy jokes, and they laugh.

She looks at me for support.

"You never know," I say.

"Where you from, Ma'am?" asks the bald guy.

"California by way of Missoula."

"Oh, it's hot there."

"For sure."

"Whereabouts in California?" asks a younger man standing by the pie case.

"Santa Cruz."

"Nice place. My sister lives there. Kathy Wilson. You know her?"

"No. It's a big city these days."

"Too big. That's why we're all up here."

And so it goes. Strangers talk to each other around Seal Rock. It never happened like that in the Bay Area. You could be close enough to smell their breath, and nobody would say a word.

We're having meat loaf tonight, with mashed potatoes and gravy, and squash. I might cook something healthier and more interesting if I ate at home, but like I said before, I come for the company.

I'm pondering the pies when my father walks in.

"Hey, Kiddo," he says, taking the chair across from me. "If I'd known you were coming, we could have coordinated our time and eaten together."

"Sorry. I was starving after work."

"Well, sit with me while I eat."

"Sure." That decides it. Peach pie.

Dad tucks into his meat loaf like he's starving. That's good. He lost 20 pounds when he was sick, and he wasn't overweight to begin with. Diana has given him extra-large portions of everything.

My warm peach pie, with vanilla ice cream, is heavenly. I'm going to need more exercise to counteract it, but right now it feels good just sitting here with my father.

When he pauses to look up, I slide the newspaper over. "Look at that. Just awful."

"I know. I hope we're done with fire around here. We need a big dose of rain."

"Amen," says the bald guy on his way out.

When the dinner rush fades, Diana takes a break and joins us at the table.

I wince as she pulls down her mask and kisses Dad on the lips. *Hey, that's my father*, I want to holler, but I'm trying to be a grownup about this.

"Tired, hon?" Dad asks, rubbing her back.

She rests her head on his shoulder. "I could fall asleep right in this chair. I wish someone would open another restaurant around here so I could stop serving dinner or close up a couple days a week."

"What happened to that pizza place?" I ask.

"Shut down by the health department."

"Good."

"Somebody oughta open a coffee shop or something there. It's a great location," Dad says.

Diana shakes her head. "Not with this COVID stuff. You gotta be crazy to start a business now."

Everything comes down to the virus.

I push back my chair. "Well, I'm going to leave you two."

Diana smiles. "Better skedaddle unless you want to help with the dishes."

"I don't think so." I leave $15 on the table and head out.

ON SUNDAY, I wake up to clear skies and cooler weather. I'm happy to need a jacket for church.

Gabriel is waiting at the front door of Our Lady of Grace when I arrive. Beverly has the key.

He looks and smells a little cleaner these days, although I see he has his bags with him again, and his hair and beard are longer than ever. Very biblical. His skin is tanned, making his light eyes look even spookier.

We exchange good mornings and discuss the change in the weather. He's shocked when I tell him about the fire in Lincoln City. I suppose he has no access to the news.

"I'll pray for those people," he says."

We watch the cars passing by, looking for Beverly's old Buick.

"Have you been staying at Eugenia's?"

He sighs. "Sometimes. When the coast is clear. When it's not, I go, well, somewhere else, I'd best not say."

"Why wouldn't the coast be clear?"

Beverly parks near us, and he doesn't answer. She has brought Ronny Mae, robust and sixtyish, and Willa, tiny and very old, her short hair tightly permed.

"Hello, PD," says Ronny Mae. "Who is this young man?"

He bows and offers his hand. "My name is Gabriel, ma'am."

"Don't you go ma'aming me. I'm just Ronny Mae. Without all that hair, you'd look like my grandson."

He shrugs.

Beverly has the church door open. "Let's practice, ladies."

"Just a second." Ronny Mae hands out little white paper bags. "I baked again. Cinnamon rolls. Since there's no coffee and donuts in the hall anymore, take them home and enjoy."

Gabriel bows. "Thank you, ma'am. I'm sure I will."

Me too.

I'd like to use Miguel's gym this afternoon. I'm feeling chubby. But when we go inside the church, I don't see him. He hasn't missed Mass since that first Sunday in July, but his usual seat near Billie and her camera is empty.

I take my place at the piano. Gabriel, Willa, Ronny Mae, and Beverly are standing ready to sing when Miguel rushes in. I don't have time to wave hello. The whole church is waiting for me to play the opening notes. Deep breath. One two three four . . .

Willa has one of those wobbly soprano voices that cuts through everything. But look how she's smiling.

I wonder why Miguel is late. He probably just overslept. I assume brunch will happen as usual.

But no. After Mass, he stops by the piano. "I'm sorry, PD. I've got another commitment this morning. I can't do brunch today."

What kind of commitment? It's Sunday. But I don't pry. "Okay. We don't have do it every week."

"Thank you for understanding. We'll hang out another time soon."

Off he goes. I pick up my purse, my music, and my cinnamon roll and head out, leaving the rest of the choir, including Gabriel, chatting in the parking lot.

I'm not quite ready to go home. I cross the bridge, park by the south jetty and devour my cinnamon roll while I watch a sea lion cruising around the rocks and a fishing boat chugging out into open water. See, Miguel, I don't need to go to brunch every Sunday.

With the smoke gone, I guess Rocky and I will visit Eugenia and see what Gabriel means by the "coast being clear." With him, it could be anything.

I really should offer him a ride home on Sundays. I mean, I kind of know him, and I think he's staying in my general area. But I don't. I let him take his chances hitchhiking. God forgive me. There's still something about him that worries me.

HOME IN MY jeans and sweatshirt, it feels good not being smothered by ashes and smoke. Rocky and I have too much pent-up energy to just walk. We run full-tilt up the road past Dad's cabin until we're both panting and smiling. Yes, dogs can smile. Rocky's beautiful teeth are on full display. His tongue hangs out so long I want to grab it.

"Whew, good run, eh?"

He smiles.

Looking at the many shades of green around us, I think about those blackened trees along I-5 and the ones in the newspaper pictures from Lincoln City. The trees look kind of orangey brown. It's weird, like the whole forest turned sepia, like ancient photographs. Things grow back after a while, but the trees are never the same. In California, I saw road crews chopping trees down because they were so weakened by the fire they might fall in the next big storm.

I've brought some of my songs to share with Eugenia. Maybe she can add a little something to them.

Halfway there, a familiar voice calls my name from the trees alongside the road. Apparently, Gabriel made it back to Beaver Creek.

"Shush," I say as Rocky growls. "Hey, Gabriel. What are you doing out here?"

"Looking for a place to camp again."

"Can't you just set up anywhere in the woods?"

"It's technically not legal for us to be here, but where it is legal, people like me are robbed and beaten up. A homeless man in Waldport got stabbed last week. There's still a puddle of blood near the baseball field. You can just feel Satan in the air."

"That's awful. I wish there was someplace safe." Yes, our house, I think, but I'm not offering it, terrible Christian that I am. "I was headed to Eugenia's. Would you like to come with us?"

"No, I can't go there."

"Why not? I'm sure she would—"

"He said he'd kill me if I said anything."

"Who?"

"I can't say. Look, I'm going to head south, find a place somewhere else, along the creek maybe."

Rocky is quiet, but he seems uneasy, leaning against my leg. Usually, he rushes up to sniff people. "Well, we're going to keep going. We haven't visited Eugenia in a long time, and the air is finally clear enough to breathe."

"I wouldn't, PD."

"We'll be fine," I insist, although I'm a little uneasy now.

He looks skyward and clasps his hands. "Father, please protect this woman and this dog from the evil at that house and bring them home safe. Amen." He picks up his bags and walks down the hill while we continue up and around to the forest road that takes us to Eugenia's.

I hold Rocky tight on his leash until we pass the rain barrel. The truck is gone. Eugenia is feeding her chickens. I let him loose, and he runs to greet his friend.

"Hello, Rocky," Eugenia says. "How are you, boy? PD, you're just in time. I've made lemonade and a fresh batch of cookies."

The coast seems clear to me. Although you never know about sneaker waves.

"Are you by yourself, Eugenia?"

She looks at me, puzzled. "Well, of course. Look at this. Hermione has laid another egg. What a good girl."

I show her my bag. "I've brought some new songs to share with you."

"How wonderful. Relax on the porch and I'll fetch our refreshments."

Okay, I think my blond Jesus look-alike must be paranoid. Too bad I quit nursing school before we got to mental illness. Maybe I'm the one losing my mind. Either way, I think I'll stick to half a cookie today.

24. Parking Lot Concert

Saturday, Sept. 19, 2020

I'M IN LOVE with this borrowed keyboard and the way it sounds outside with the whoosh of the ocean in the background. The sun is out, and the air is just warm enough.

This lunchtime parking-lot concert outside the diner was Janey's idea. As if she doesn't have enough going on, what with work, college classes on Zoom, and Broadway. People are depressed from COVID and fire and unemployment, she said. Plus, she was dying to perform somewhere. So was I. I had all these new songs, as well as the old ones I love, and yeah, let's put on a show.

Diana said, "Fine, but not inside the diner." There isn't enough space, and she didn't want us taking tables away from paying customers.

"No problem," Janey said. "We'll do it outside."

She hung up flyers, borrowed a keyboard and sound equipment from one of her Oregon State friends, and convinced Jonas to wait tables while we're making music.

As a bonus, Molly whipped up a batch of her spectacular marionberry and cream cheese muffins. Janey advertised our show as Muffins and Music.

My stomach flutters as people gather around us. We haven't performed for an audience in over a year, what with the band blowing up and then COVID. It's just the two of us, piano, flute, and vocals. The picnic tables are filling up, and Jonas is bringing out extra chairs. Tourists, locals, and diner regulars are all here. Dad is sharing a table with some Californians he just met. A young couple in hiking gear watch from the tailgate of their Jeep. They're all waiting for us to entertain them. God, make me brave.

"Ready, PD?"

"Ready."

"Count us off."

We start with "Ain't She Sweet," an oldie, just to warm up. People sing along, and the applause is huge. After a few more familiar songs, I launch into "Between the Bridges," the theme for Britt's film.

People hush up and listen as my voice and Janey's flute soar out into the crisp air like soap bubbles.

This feels amazing. Only another musician would understand. Yes, people are talking while we sing, motorcycles roar past, and a dog starts barking, but that's what it's like gigging outside. We don't care. I'm already thinking we need to do this again, here and other places in the area.

By the end of two hours, as we finish our songs and the audience wanders off to do whatever they do on Saturdays, we are both sunburned, with sore throats and growling stomachs, but neither one of us would rather do anything else.

"You gals are so good," my father says. "Janey, that flute, and your voice . . . wow. Let me give you a hug."

"I'll take it."

As they wrap their arms around each other, I wonder if Janey will someday be my stepsister and call my father "Dad."

It wouldn't be horrible. At least she'd finally have a father figure in her life.

"What about me, Dad?"

He laughs and hugs me, too. "You are also very talented. I don't know where you got it from."

"Mom's side of the family?"

"Must be. Well, Diana's got a dishpan with my name on it," he says. "But really, good job, girls. I hope you do this every weekend."

We look at each other and grin.

"It worked!" Janey shouts.

"Sure did. Thank you."

More hugs.

I slip the keyboard into its leather case. "Janey, where did your friend get this keyboard? It's fantastic. I think it even has that Midi hookup that Britt was talking about."

"Um." She pauses in the middle of folding her music stand. "I think she said she got it at a music store up the Alsea Highway."

"There's a music store up there?"

"Yeah. Funky one in an old house."

"I've got to check it out." My piano at home is fine, but if I'm going to play away from home, I need a portable keyboard. My old one was smashed to bits in a car crash on the I-5 freeway last year.

The store is probably closed now because of COVID, but when things reopen . . .

When everything is packed away in the car, I look around and smile. Finally, PD is doing what PD came west to do.

25. Blackberry Cobbler

OUCH. MY BLOOD mingles with purple-red blackberry juice as I reach through the vines for the biggest, firmest berries. They're just glorious this year. Maybe the burst of heat a couple weeks ago gave them an extra push.

Rocky has claimed the lower berries for himself. He has a gift for pulling the ripe ones off with his teeth without getting poked by thorns. I don't know how he does it. His face is clean. Me, I'm a mess, but my bowl is almost full. I'm going to make the best cobbler ever for Dakota, who is coming home tonight. Finally.

She stayed in South Dakota longer than expected. Something about her brother being sick and business to take care of. I know how that goes. Last year I was gone way longer than I planned, taking care of my mother in Santa Cruz. When they released her from the hospital, everybody expected me to take care of her, and well, what are you going to do?

I talked to Mom on the phone today while sitting in the empty hospital cafeteria during my lunch break. Three of her friends have COVID, she said, but she's still okay. Not going anywhere she doesn't have to. Ordering her groceries online, talking to her doctors via "tele-med," wearing her mask every time she sets foot outside the house. She even makes Andy and Shari wear masks when they visit.

She has almost gotten used to the fact that they got married outside the church. They are still promising they will go to a priest and make it official before the baby comes in early December. It's a girl, by the way. I can't think about it right now or I will cry. I would give anything to have a daughter. At least, I have Janey in my life.

Anyway, Mom read me her recipe for berry cobbler, and I wrote it down. Then I heard my name being paged and I had to go. Things were backing up at the admissions desk, and *so sorry but we need you to cut your lunch short.* Fine. I had eaten my grilled cheese sandwich and needed an excuse to hang up the phone.

"I wish I could see you," Mom said.

"I know. Me too. As soon as I can take a vacation. Maybe I'll come for Christmas."

"That would be wonderful. You'll have a niece by then, and she needs to know her Aunt Cis-PD. Of course you might want to spend the holidays with your father."

"I see him all the time. He'll be so busy with Diana he won't even notice I'm gone. Mom, I need to go back to work."

"Who is Diana?"

Uh-oh. I didn't realize she didn't know about that. "Mom, Dad is dating my friend Diana, the one who owns the diner."

"Oh, that bleached blonde who smokes all the time? I thought she was engaged to someone else."

PD Soares, report to the admissions desk.

"Mom, I have to go. Diana was engaged, but it blew up. Now she and Dad are a thing. Who knows what will come of it, but they're happy right now."

"I wish I had someone."

"Me too. I really have to go back to work. We can talk later. Sick people are waiting."

"Fine. Go. Wear your mask."

"Always. I love you."

"Bye."

Now she's upset, and I feel guilty, but what can I do? She and Dad are divorced. Divorced people date other people. I did. That's how I found Tom. Now I'm kind of seeing Miguel, but I don't know what's going on with that. Not a word since his rapid exit on Sunday. Maybe he'd like to come over for berry cobbler. No, it's Dakota's first night home. When last seen, she was drinking, so . . . not tonight.

Let go of me, thorns. These things are vicious. My bowl is getting too heavy to hold, and there are way too many berries for me to pick. I'll leave some for the bears or whatever else is dining out here. Do elk eat berries?

"Let's go home, Rocky." He's lying on the ground licking his paws. Seeing me ready to go, he jumps up and leads the way at a trot.

A siren wails from the highway. Then another. Then the growl of gears. Fire trucks. I hold my breath until the sound fades as they head south. Not here. Thank you.

THE RAINBOW VAN is parked in the driveway next to my Jeep. She's home. Rocky races up the steps and paws at the door. Dakota comes out, smiling as he jumps up to kiss her face. Neither of us has the heart to holler "off!" as we're supposed to do.

"Hey," I say, putting down my bowl of berries and going for a hug.

My hands are full of juice and blood, so I hold them out as Dakota squeezes me. I inhale the faint smell of cigarettes. She's supposed to quarantine after travel. But we both live here, and we need hugs. It feels like it has been forever.

"I'm glad you're home." I pull back and look at her. Her eyes are clear, not darting away like before. "How are you?"

"Sober again."

"Thank God."

While I wash my hands, she carries my bowl to the kitchen, setting it next to a paper-wrapped package that looks and smells like fresh crab. This is going to be a feast.

"PD, can we sit down for a minute?"

"Sure." She looks so serious it scares me.

As we sit side by side on the couch, she strokes Rocky's thick fur. "I need to make amends. I am sorry for how I treated you before I left. I don't know how to live sober without Maryann. Used to be when I wanted to drink, all I had to do was look at her and know I could go another day without it. Now—"

"I know."

"Britt got me all out of whack. She's so cute and sexy, and I thought I might as well give it a shot. Maryann would tell me to go out and have some fun. So, I tried it." She rubs Rocky's ears; he moans in pleasure.

"Was it fun at least?"

"Yeah, kind of. I felt old and haggish next to her, but she said I was beautiful. As if. Every inch of her is perfect, I swear. And I'm . . . not. I know I'm an acquired taste."

"I think you're terrific."

"But you and I will never be lovers."

"No. I'm sorry."

"Don't be. I'm glad you're my friend. Imagine if I was here by myself. I'd be dead by now."

"No."

"Yes. There's no halfway for me. Anyway, I am sorry. I'm glad you and Rocky are here. I missed you. I missed your music, too. It's really beautiful, PD. I hope someday you can leave that hospital job and do it full-time."

"You and me both."

She looks out at the yard. "I missed these trees." She clears her throat. "My brother has early-stage Parkinson's. Watching him so determined to not let it stop him, I realized I was an idiot for wasting my life on booze when I'm perfectly healthy. I tossed the bottles and found some AA meetings. Got a silver chip for 24 hours sobriety. I'm hoping for the red 30-day one." She shakes her head. "I have all the colors in a box in my dresser drawer. I was sober for 10 years, damn it.

"Used to be I'd hang out at Hoover's and a couple other places— there aren't many bars south of the Yaquina Bridge, but I could name them all. I'll be going to meetings at the fire hall on Wednesday nights and maybe across the bridges on other nights. I need to find a new sponsor and work the program all over again."

"You can do it. I know you can."

"One day at a time."

"I'll take the beer in the fridge over to Dad's place so it's not here to tempt you."

"You don't have to."

"But I will."

"Beer isn't my poison, but thank you. You're good people, Priscilla Soares."

"You too, Annabelle Wells."

She gets up, towering over me. "What are you going to do with all those berries?"

"Make the world's best blackberry cobbler. I even bought ice cream."

"Hot damn. Crab and cobbler. Guess I'll unpack and stay a while."

"You'd better."

As I wash the berries and lay them out in the pan, I hear Dakota whistling. Sometimes I really wish I was gay. I could fall in love with her. But this is good.

Oops. I drop a couple berries on the floor. Rocky dives across the room and swallows them before I can pick them up. "Good dog."

26. Amber Alert

Wednesday, Sept. 23, 2020

MY CELL PHONE buzzes the next morning at work. Dakota. Urgent. Immediately I think "fire," although I have not heard about any new blazes here. That one yesterday was a house fire started by grease on the stove. The fire crew got it out right away.

All the patients are taken care of, so I answer my phone.

"Dakota, what's going on?"

"PD, I just got this Amber Alert, you know, for missing kids."

"Yeah?" She must be at the post office. I hear the printer running in the background.

"This child, kidnapped by his divorced dad from La Grande, looks just like that little boy I saw at Eugenia's house. At least to me. You saw him, too, didn't you? Let me text you the picture."

I wait while she sends it. Uh-oh. "I only got a glimpse, but it sure looks like him. What should we do?"

"Call the cops?"

"Last time I was there, Eugenia said she was alone. I didn't see any sign of anyone. That black truck was gone. But when I saw Gabriel, he was all nervous about something. He said a guy there threatened him."

"Hmm. I think we should call this number."

I picture the cops showing up at Eugenia's place. Would they come after her with their guns drawn? Handcuff her and put her in jail? "I can't believe Eugenia did anything wrong, that she would ever do anything wrong, except making pot cookies, and those aren't illegal here anymore."

"I know, but if that boy is there—Danny is his name—he might be in danger."

"I have an idea. Do you have anything to deliver to her today?"

"Let me check. Hold on."

People are coming in the ER door. I can't stay on the phone. *Hurry, Dakota. They're waiting now. Hurry.* Jackson is busy with a complicated case.

"PD. I have two packages for that address. There's another name on one of them. It's soft, clothes maybe."

"Well, here's my thought. When you go there, tell Eugenia you need to use the restroom, and when you do, look around, see if there's any sign of a kid. If there's nothing, you don't need to call anybody."

"Fine. I'll go there first. But if anything is strange, I'm going to call."

"Thank you. Dakota, I've got to go. This patient is bleeding."

"Later."

I slide open my window. "Good morning," I say to a mother and a girl about 12 who is holding a bloody dishtowel over her hand. "What happened here?"

COMING OUT OF the restroom during my lunch break, I see a familiar dark profile in the healing garden, a square bounded by the wings of the hospital building. Volunteers have planted roses, azaleas and I don't know what all. There's a brick path to walk and a bench to sit on.

Bent over, chin in hand, Miguel is doing a pretty good imitation of Rodin's The Thinker statue. I wonder why he's at the hospital. Maybe I should leave him alone, but I can't.

I push the glass door open. It's pleasantly cool outside.

"Miguel?"

He looks up, startled. "PD. I didn't expect to see you here."

"Well, I work here. At least you didn't check in through emergency. That's a good sign. Are you visiting someone?"

"No. Would you like to sit down?"

"To be honest, I sit all day. How about we walk around the garden?"

"Sure." As we pass by the roses, I notice a hospital bracelet on his right wrist. "Miguel, what's going on?"

He clears his throat. "This is embarrassing."

"We're friends. But you don't have to tell me just because I'm nosy."

"No, no. You've probably been wondering, and I need to get used to it."

"Used to what?"

He studies my face, his eyes the brown of dark chocolate, and I feel a nervous twinge in my stomach. "PD, I had prostate cancer."

Gulp. I didn't expect that. "Had? Is it gone?"

"I hope so. This was my two-year checkup. So far, I'm okay. I had surgery not long before I moved here."

"Chemo?"

"No, thank God. Radiation. Five days a week for four weeks."

"And then you were okay?"

"Basically. Except—" He looks like he's about to cry.

"Oh." Impotence. I grab his hand. "I'm sorry. Is that why we haven't—"

"Yes." He clears his throat. "And I want to, PD. You are so sexy."

"Me?" I laugh.

"You are."

As I hug him, our masks swish against each other. I think about my father having sex with Diana. Isn't that nuts, here in this sweet moment? Focus, PD.

"You are the nicest person, Miguel."

"Thank you, but you deserve a man who can give you everything, including, you know, fulfilling your physical needs."

"We can work around it. There are medical interventions, things they can do. Ask your doctor. Seriously."

He sees me checking my watch. "Do you need to get back to work?"

"Yes."

"Brunch on Sunday?"

"Sure. Maybe we can spend the afternoon together."

We lean in for a kiss. For once, neither of us is holding back. I want the whole package, but there are ways . . . Am I starting to fall for Miguel now? A little spark?

We pull apart as three nurses in scrubs come out, talking loudly, and settle on one of the nearby benches.

"See you Sunday."

Off he goes. What a morning.

JACKSON COVERS the mouthpiece of his phone and whispers, "Your cell was buzzing."

I have three text messages, all from Dakota. Can I go back to kissing in the sun?

No restroom at E's house. She pointed me to the outhouse in the back. I looked in the windows of the house, saw nothing. But—

Damn. It cut me off. In the outhouse was a little kid's book, something about bears, and there was a pair of little blue tennis shoes by the back door.

I asked Eugenia about the book and the shoes, and she claimed some church ladies came to visit and brought their child, and he must have left them. I could tell she was lying. As soon as I got back in range, I called in the Amber Alert. I'm sorry, PD.

Shit, shit, shit. I remember those burly sheriff guys I used to see at the gym before COVID. You might as well paint a red stripe across their necks. Short hair, beer bellies, egos bigger than their heads. What would they do to a person like Eugenia? Everybody knows she never leaves her house. She doesn't drive. How could she kidnap anybody? Then again, folks call her The Witch."

Where is she now? Home? Or in jail? Being grilled in some interrogation room or put in a cell with criminals? I admit all I know about jails is what I've seen on TV, but it can't be fun. Where is the boy? Did they find him and send him back to La Grande or call his mother to come get him?

How the heck am I supposed to work when this is going on and Miguel and I were just kissing and talking in the garden about sex? He had cancer. What if it comes back? Do I want to love another man who dies of this damned disease?

Great. Here comes another person coughing up a lung. I open my window. "Hi. Sounds like you have a cough."

"COPD. It's bad today."

"I'm sorry, Mr—"

"Fenton. Saul."

"Date of birth?"

"6-25-40."

I find him in the system and clamp a patient information form onto a clipboard. "Thank you, Mr. Fenton. You'll need to be tested for COVID to make sure you don't have anything else going on. Can you fill this out and wait in that little room over there?"

How I haven't gotten the virus yet, I don't know. My guardian angel is working hard, I guess.

27. Trouble

AFTER MY SHIFT ends at 3, I drive straight to Eugenia's house.

The black truck is there. Maybe I should leave. I don't have Rocky or anyone else to help if things go badly. But Eugenia is my friend. I need to know what happened.

As I park my car next to the truck, a heavyset man with a black stubble beard storms out the door. I don't have time to turn around and drive away. Saying a quick prayer, I open my window. I'll tell him I'm lost and hope he doesn't recognize me. Or maybe I'll just say I'm looking for Eugenia.

Before I can speak, he roars at me.

"Are you the bitch that got my mother arrested?"

"What? No. We saw the Amber Alert for a kidnapped boy and were concerned because we had seen a child here, but we know Eugenia wouldn't hurt anybody."

"Who's we?"

"My housemate Dakota and I."

"Oh, you're the lezzies from the house with that stupid rainbow. Even better. Why the fuck did you call the cops? They're saying we kidnapped Danny. Kidnapped! Come on. I just collected my own kid and brought him to his grandmother. We're his family, and he belongs with us."

"You're right. I'm sorry. I'll just go home. Pretend I wasn't here."

He leans his head in the window. He smells of sweat and something else. Evil.

"I don't think so. My ma's in jail because of you 'girls.' You ain't got any kids, do you? It takes a man."

"Listen—what's your name?"

"Why, so you can get me busted, too? My name is Trouble, and that's what you get for meddling."

Without looking away, I reach for my phone then remember there's no coverage out here. Help me, God.

Oh shit. There's blood on his black tee shirt. That's what I smell.

He catches me staring at it. "I killed a chicken. She wouldn't stop pecking at me, so I decided she would be dinner. Which my ma was going to cook with her dumplings and greens, and now she's in fucking jail."

His hands grip the car door. They're huge. There's a streak of blood among the black hairs on the back of his right hand.

"I'm sorry. Really. Just back away from the car and let me go home." He doesn't move. "Was your son here when the sheriff came? He must be terribly upset."

"No, he was in town with me buying supplies. He's fine. Taking his nap. All he knows is Nana went for a ride. Thanks to you."

"I didn't do anything."

"The hell you didn't."

A door slams. He steps back and glances at the house. The little boy, Danny, is standing on the porch wearing nothing but a pair of underpants. He's crying and filthy.

Something in me snaps. "Danny! Are you okay?" I open my door and start to get out.

Trouble catches me half in and half out and throws me to the ground. Holding me down, he reaches into the car and grabs my phone. Why didn't I keep my mouth shut? Why didn't I go straight home? God, he stinks.

"I don't have to put up with this shit. If I let you go in your cute little car, you're just going to pick up the phone and tell them all about me. I'll bet you have my license plate memorized."

"No, I didn't even see it."

"And I'm supposed to believe you."

"Yes. I don't even know what kind of truck that is. Listen, if you hurt me, you'll be committing another crime and you'll never get out of jail."

"What do you mean, *another* crime?"

"You know. Kidnapping." I struggle to my feet.

"I didn't kidnap nobody." He glances back at the house again. "Go back inside, you little brat!" His eyes widen as a car approaches, slows, and moves on. "Fine. Stand up. Get back in the car, bitch. Drive away. Go home to the other bitch and do whatever you people do. I know where you live. That house with all the damned rainbows."

He coughs in my face, gathers up saliva and spits, just missing my shirt.

"Give me my phone."

"So you can call and report me? Not a chance."

"It doesn't work here anyway."

He shows his filthy crooked teeth and tosses the phone into the rain barrel. It goes kerplunk and sinks. "It doesn't work anywhere now."

Well, now I'm as mad as I am scared. "Danny!" I holler as loud as I can. "Run down the hill to the rainbow house."

Trouble knocks me to the ground again and orders the boy to go back inside as he holds me down.

I can't believe this is happening. Last year, a man pinned me like this and almost raped me. That's where I got the scar on my cheek, from hitting the sharp edge of a brick when I landed. I fought that guy, and I'm going to fight this guy. I have to. There's no other way out of this.

But he's strong and mean. I'm pushing and kicking and getting nowhere. He's got my hands trapped so I can't gouge his eyes like I did with the rapist, and I can't get my legs around to kick him where it hurts. I'm not as strong as I was when I was working out all the time, before the tsunami, before the car crash, before COVID.

"Let me go," I plead.

"No. I'm tired of people telling me what to do."

"Papa," the little boy calls. "I'm scared."

"Shut the fuck up, boy, or I'll beat you. Get in the house. And you," he says, wrapping his massive hands around my throat. "You need to learn to shut up." He's squeezing. Dear God, is he going to kill me?

God, please help me.

I'm about to black out when someone says, "Get off of her, Louis." It's Gabriel. He's with two other men and Dakota, who is pointing her shotgun at my assailant.

They pull Trouble off me. "Run, PD," Gabriel says.

Before I can move, several black vehicles pull in, raising a cloud of dust. Lincoln County sheriffs.

"Ma'am, please put down your weapon." one of them orders Dakota. "We've got it from here."

Before I know it, one officer has Trouble in handcuffs, and another is leading Danny to an unmarked Ford.

Dakota folds me in her arms. "You okay, PD?"

"I think so." I'm dirty and bruised, traumatized, but not broken. "How did you all get here?" My voice is hoarse.

Dakota shakes her head. "You have the common sense of a loon. I just knew you'd be coming here after work. When you turned up late, I started up the road and ran into Gabriel and his friends. He said the black truck was back, so I thought, PD's going to get her damned self in trouble. I called the sheriff, told him what I knew, and here we are."

"Thank you. You're right. I don't have any common sense. That guy scared the hell out of me, but I was worried about Eugenia and about what he might do to the boy."

"He'll be okay. His mom is on her way. They'll probably let Eugenia out once they lock this guy in a jail cell."

"I hope so. Couldn't they charge her for helping him?"

"I don't know. Maybe."

"Ma'am," one of the sheriff's deputies says. "I need to get some information from you."

"Sure."

We sit on Eugenia's porch as he writes down my name, age, etc., and has me tell the whole sordid story. He asks if I want to go to the hospital to get checked out.

"No, I'm fine. I just want to go home."

"Sure. Let me take a couple pictures of those bruises on your neck. We thank you and your partner for your eagerness to help. But next time, let us confront the bad guys, okay?"

"I will."

"We'll be in touch if we need anything. You may be called as a witness later on. But that's all for now." He closes his report book. "That's a cute little car. How's she run up here on the rural roads?"

"Great."

"My daughter wants one."

"It's a good car."

The men in green and khaki leave. Dakota puts her shotgun in the van. "Let's go home. You can clean up, and then we'll see what Diana's serving for dinner." She looks around at Gabriel and his scruffy-looking friends. "You all come with us. Our treat."

"Can we bring our stuff?" one of them asks.

"Sure. Pile it in the van. You okay to drive your car, PD?"

"I'm all right. See you at home."

The rainbow van pulls out, and I follow in my Jeep. Out of habit, I reach for my phone, then remember it's in the rain barrel. Here come the tears. I peel off my dirty mask and let it out.

28. Ordinary Time

Thursday, Sept. 24, 2020

IT'S A RELATIVELY slow day at the hospital. Only one possible COVID case and the usual assortment of cuts, burns, sprains, and chest pains.

We even have time to chat. Jackson turns to me during a gap. The beads on his braids clack. COVID hair, he calls it. "What's new, PD?"

"Nothing much. We just captured a kidnapper yesterday."

"I see. An average day for Wonder Woman, right?"

"Exactly."

"I'd like to see you in that tight little outfit she wears."

"You're gay."

"Yes, but I'd still like to see it. Did you really capture a kidnapper?"

"Sort of. It will be in tomorrow's paper probably, but they said they'd keep our names out of it, just call Dakota and me "neighbors.""

"Good idea."

"But now you'll know."

"Uh-huh. Have you been eating your friend's pot cookies again?"

I laugh. "No."

A woman comes in alone, fussing with her mask. She leans on the chairs as she approaches the desk. "I'm so dizzy I can barely walk."

"Oh dear. Let's get you checked in."

Dizzy we can handle.

I'M A BIG FAN of ordinary time at church—no special services or special songs to learn, just that quiet time between Easter and Advent. I also like ordinary times for the rest of my life. That's the old Cissy in me who was content spending her day at home knitting, cooking, and playing music just for herself. I'm hoping that's what we can have now. The big fires are easing. Health officials are saying they'll have a COVID vaccine any day now. Wouldn't it be amazing to take off these masks and go wherever we wanted to again? Ordinary things like drinking coffee at Starbucks or walking into a yarn shop.

I'm sure Eugenia is wishing for ordinary time, too. She was released from jail shortly after Louis went in. She faces charges, but minor ones compared to the charges lodged against her son. Dakota saw her when she stopped to deliver the mail. She said she looked ten years older, had a black eye, and didn't want to talk. The whole thing must be traumatic for her. Being arrested. Her son in jail and her grandson taken away. She may never see Danny again, at least not until he's an adult, if he remembers he has a grandmother.

I wonder if she has other grown children. Are there more grandchildren? Why did she react so strongly when I asked about her kids last spring? Did Louis give her the black eye?

Someone's coming in the ER door.

"Hello," Jackson says. They nod and hurry past us toward the restroom. That happens a lot.

Dakota says Gabriel and his friends, the two men who were with him that day, are camping just south of Eugenia's property near an offshoot of Beaver Creek. They follow Gabriel like he's their leader. He does have that Jesus vibe. But who was that version of Gabriel who confronted Trouble? He sounded completely different. Whoever he is, I'm glad he's on my side.

The homeless guys have a pretty good setup with their tents and other gear, Dakota says. It's not legal to camp out there by the creek, but they're not hurting anything, and people have to live somewhere. I'm beginning to see the homeless as like me but with less luck and less money. I mean, what did I have when I came here? My car and barely enough cash to stay in the cheapest motel I could find until I got a house-sitting gig. I didn't have a job, just some rent income from the house in Missoula. The difference for me was that I knew I could always go home to my family in California. Not everybody has that.

When Andy and I were kids, we camped a lot in a little pop-up trailer. Mom hated it; Dad loved it. But my parents could afford to pay for a site in a nice campground. When we got tired of camp food, we could drive to the nearest town and eat at a restaurant. We had plenty of clean clothes, food, and fishing gear. It was a lark, not a necessity. Very different. I still wonder why Gabriel and the others are wandering the woods. I suppose I should just ask them. Maybe I will one of these days.

FRIDAY EVENING, while I'm chopping carrots and onions for a stir fry, Dakota brings in the local paper. "Here it is," she says. "Page one."

We read the report together, holding our breaths until we're sure there's nothing in there that identifies us. Whew. Neighbors. Nearby residents. A brief tussle but no one was injured, and the boy has been reunited with his mother in La Grande. The grandmother has been released, pending her arraignment on charges of accessory to a parental kidnapping.

"Look at this," Dakota says.

"Wow." Louis Matthew Renner, Jr. served eight years at the Snake River Correctional Facility for manslaughter in the death of his younger brother, Steven, in 2002. He has also been incarcerated for assault and DUII. His ex-wife, Charlene, called the La Grande police several times to report domestic abuse, but charges were never filed. He now faces felony charges of kidnapping and assault. Bail has been denied.

"Where is La Grande?"

"Northeast, near the Washington border. Redneck country."

"Oh." I sink into a chair. "I need a drink."

"Me too. Have some water instead." She fills a glass and hands it to me. "You're lucky that bastard didn't kill you."

"I know. He might have if you didn't show up with the cavalry."

"Someone has to take care of you."

I raise my glass to that.

29. Worrisome Questions

THIS SATURDAY'S Muffins and Music concert in the diner parking lot is not quite as fun as last time. The traffic noise bothers me more, and my throat is still sore from being almost strangled, but that's show biz. You play through it all.

My mood brightens when a red pickup pulls in and Donovan J. Green steps out.

He looks good, wearing his suede vest and a mess of jewels and pins, his white hair shining in the sun, and a green shamrock mask over his lush beard.

I finish the song and shout "Hey, Donovan! Good to see you."

"I missed you. I missed the family," he calls.

"Same here."

"Hi, Uncle Donny," Janey yells, then signals to start the next song.

I sing, "Summertime, and the livin' is easy." The song is short. There's lots of time for instrumental improvisation, me on the keyboard and Janey on her flute. We each win applause for our solos from the audience of locals and tourists. It feels good.

After a quick handshake, Donovan takes the seat next to my dad. A few minutes later, we take a break and join them.

"You're a sight for sore eyes," he tells me.

"You too. I have so much to tell you when you have time."

"Likewise, PD."

A young man walks out of the diner and sits across from Donovan. His hair is brown instead of gray, but he has the same build, the same beard, and the same eyes. It can only be Donovan's son.

"Trevor?"

He nods as he sets out soft drinks for both of them. "That's me."

"It's great to meet you."

"I heard you and Janey singing as I was coming in. You're good."

"Yes indeed," Donovan says. "Excellent musicians. The little one's headed for Broadway, she says. I believe she'll be a star."

What about me, I think, but I know that ship has sailed. I just want to play and sing, put out some recordings, and quit my day job. I still see that album cover with "PD!" plastered across the front in huge letters.

"Hey, Uncle," Janey says, going in for a hug. "Hello, cousin whom I've never seen in person before, only on a screen. You're bigger than I thought."

"You're tinier than I thought."

"I'm still growing. Hey, PD, we should do our last set before we lose our audience."

"Right." I'm a little nervous now as I return to the keyboard. I want to impress these guys.

I sure love this piano. Janey says I won't be able to borrow it anymore. The owner is moving away. I guess I'll have to go see if that music store where this came from is open. I could order something online, but I hate to do that without laying hands on the keys.

"Count it, PD."

"One two three four. 'Jeremiah was a bullfrog'"

Donovan cracks up. He sings along with us. I like his voice, not perfect but deep and warm. Pretty soon, everybody's singing with us, and it's fun. Then we slow it down with Sarah McLachlan's "Angel."

Near the end of the set, the fog comes in. The temperature drops 10 degrees in a minute. That's life on the coast. I'm not sure how we're going to do this in the winter. I refuse to sing in the rain, hail, snow and wind or when it's 15 degrees out. We'll need a new venue. But for now, considering everything that's going on, we're lucky to be here. We accept rousing applause and squeeze onto the barbecue table benches with Dad, Donovan, and Trevor.

Eugenia and all that went down at her house this week passes through my mind. I shake it off. Can't think about that now. I'm here after a successful performance, sitting with some of my favorite people in the most beautiful place on earth. Who needs anything more?

We don't sit long. It's too danged cold, so we start packing our stuff.

"Why don't you all come to my house," Dad says.

"I think we know the way," Donovan jokes.

Janey makes a frowny face. "I've got to stay here and *work*."

Soon Donovan, Trevor, Dad, and I are seated in the living room that once was Donovan's, was briefly mine, and now is my father's.

"My dear, what is your big news?" Donovan asks, kneeling on the floor to start a fire.

I look around and realize I can't tell him any of the stuff that's on my mind. At least not now. I haven't told my father about the events of the other day, and I don't intend to. Nor am I going to share Miguel's private medical problems. I probably shouldn't talk about Dakota's sobriety either. "Nothing," I say. "It just feels like forever since we've seen each other."

"Ha." He turns to Dad. "Young man, you look less green around the gills than you did the last time I saw you."

"I feel a lot better. I still get awfully tired though."

"They say the fatigue goes on and on," I offer from my limited store of medical knowledge.

"But I dodged the bullet. I'm grateful."

I lean toward Donovan. "What's new with you?"

"Well, the boy and I have moved into the 21st century. If people can't come to the gallery, I'm going to bring the gallery to them. Show them, Son."

Trevor pulls out an iPad, clicks a few keys and turns the screen toward me. "The Art of Donovan J. Green" says the heading over a stained-glass fountain in bottle green, cobalt blue, and beer-bottle brown. He clicks through the pages from one piece of art to the next, each with a description and a link to purchase them. There's the religious one we saw in the window of his store in Corvallis. There's a bio of Donovan, a list of past shows and awards—I had no idea he had won so many.

"That's wonderful. Are you getting many viewers?"

"Over a thousand followers," Donovan boasts.

"Pretty impressive," Dad says. "Maybe you should do that with your music, PD."

"Maybe, but sound is different from visual art."

Trevor sits back, thinking. "It could work. We would need some good recordings, and visuals to go with them, but yeah, it's totally doable."

"My boy is a genius," Donovan says proudly.

It shocks me to realize Donovan's son is probably closer to my age than he is. But he's way ahead of me on technology, that's for sure.

Trevor's on a roll now. "The music business has been heading this way for ages. When was the last time you bought a CD? Remember cassettes? Vinyl? COVID just sped it up. Artists are bypassing the big producers and putting on their own shows. You could do a Facebook live concert anytime you want. Just set up the camera and do your thing."

This guy is really into this stuff.

"I have seen a lot of artists doing that lately," I say. "But I still like a live concert best."

"Oh, for sure, but this way you can reach a much wider audience, and you can control the situation. No traffic noises, no sudden blast of cold weather, nobody chitchatting in the background."

"Nobody to get me a beer when I get thirsty."

Donovan chuckles. "There is that."

"Think about it," Trevor says.

"I'm certain my son would give you a family and friends discount if you asked nicely," Donovan adds.

"Well, I'm in the middle of this project writing music for a film being made by this woman from LA."

"Cool. How are you recording it?"

"I haven't gotten to that yet."

"What kind of contract do you have? Do you own the rights to the music so we could share it online?"

"I-uh." Oh my God, I'm an idiot. "We don't actually have a contract. She's a friend of my housemate's and when she suggested I do this, I got so excited I just started writing music."

Dad looks concerned. "Honey, you need to get the details in writing. I'd hate to see you do all this work for nothing."

"I'm sure it's fine. But I'll ask her."

Trevor nods. "Good. Communication is vital. You don't want to lose the rights to your own music or do a lot of work and never be paid for it. But, regardless of what happens with the contract, I'm serious about helping you promote your music. When you're ready to put something online, call me." He pulls a card out of his wallet and hands it to me.

I take a look. Trevor Green, Media Man. "You live in Corvallis now?"

"Yes, since June. I work remotely, so I decided to spend some time in Oregon and get to know my father better."

"That's great."

My own father is getting restless. "Coffee anyone?"

"No." Donovan stands. "We should get going back to the valley. It's a sizeable drive."

"I'd better go, too. I've got chores to do."

"I think you have earned a nap after that great concert," Donovan says.

I feel a pang. Dang it, after all this time, I still have feelings for the ever unpredictable but totally loveable Donovan Green. I go for another hug, and he kisses my cheek just above the mask. I melt.

This never happens with Miguel. Warmth but no melting. And it shouldn't happen with Donovan. I know all his issues.

I wonder how much Trevor knows about our relationship and about his father's history. Something to think about later. Right now, we're leaving. "See you soon, Dad. Thanks for coming today."

"Wouldn't miss it. Goodbye."

A gust of wind tosses our hair and grabs at our clothes. "A wee bit windy," Donovan says.

"A wee bit," I respond as we climb into our cars, leaving Dad on the porch waving.

In a minute, I'm back at the rainbow house. The trees and my rhododendrons are dancing. It's the kind of night where Mother Nature cleans house by blowing out all the dust. Wind makes me feel unsettled, as if seeing Donovan and hearing Trevor's warning about a contract didn't stir me up enough.

30. Get Ready

Saturday, Sept. 26, 2020

DAKOTA LOOKS UP from her book when I come in. "What's bugging you now?"

"Donovan Green. He was here. With his son. I still like the big guy."

"PD, he's like whiskey. Tastes great but it's not good for you."

"I know. What's new here?"

"Nothing. Oh wait, yeah, I'm having some friends over tomorrow afternoon. Just warning you in case you want to run away."

"I don't mind your friends. Do you want me to cook something?"

"No, I ordered some stuff from the fish place on the Bayfront. I just don't want you to feel uncomfortable."

"I won't. I think I'm going to be with Miguel anyway."

"Problem solved."

I sink onto a kitchen chair. "Not really. Can I tell you something? You can't tell anyone else."

"Sure. What?"

"Well, Miguel . . ." And I spill the whole cancer/impotence story.

"Oh man," she says. "Guess you need to figure out what you need and whether you want to risk losing another man to cancer."

"He says it's all gone."

"There are no guarantees. Why do you think he was seeing the doctor?"

"I know." Big sigh. Then a thought tickles my funny bone. "You never have to deal with that kind of penis problem, do you?"

She chuckles that deep raspy laugh I love. "No, I don't. Hey, how about a strap-on?"

"For me or for him?" My face is on fire. "Whoo. I'm going outside. Come on, Rocky."

We're circling the property when I catch a whiff of smoke. The fire in Dad's fireplace burned out before we left. We never lit ours. There shouldn't be anything burning outside around here with the burn ban in place. Most people know better. I can't imagine Eugenia burning anything now.

"Hey Dakota?" I call through the open door.

"Yeah?"

"Come out here. I smell smoke."

She sniffs. "That ain't a barbecue."

"Should we call someone?"

She already has her cell phone out, dialing 911. "I sure hope this is a false alarm."

My call catches my father asleep. "I'm sorry to wake you, Dad, but a fire truck is coming our way. We smell smoke. Can you smell it at your place?"

I hear him stumble out and down the steps. "Yes. It's not much, but it's there. I'll come down to your house."

"Okay."

The Seal Rock Fire Department, staffed by volunteers, is close to the diner. In a few minutes, we hear the sirens. Rather than take the sharp turn into our driveway, they park on the road. We run down to meet them. My father arrives a minute later.

Two young men and a woman in yellow and black turnouts climb down from the trucks. The woman nods at Dakota, who nods back, then looks at me. "You smelled smoke?"

"Yes," I say. "In fact, I think it's getting stronger."

The woman scans the area. "I smell it. Look. You can see smoke now off to the east."

"What's out there?"

"Couple farms, lot of trees and shrubs," she says.

"Is that near Eugenia's house?"

"That old lady they call The Witch? The one with all the police action last week?"

"Yes."

"I don't know. Raul, do you think it could be the witch lady's place?"

He squints into the darkening sky. "Maybe, but probably not. I think it's closer to the creek."

Oh Jesus. Gabriel and his buddies?

The other man is listening to his radio. "Someone higher up the hill just reported it, too."

"How big?" Raul asks.

"They couldn't tell."

"Let's roll."

"What should we do?" I ask.

"Sit tight. If there's any danger here, we'll let you know. You might pack a to-go bag just in case."

I don't want to hear that.

They ride off. "Dakota, I already packed my bag when you were gone. The fires were moving fast then, but they didn't come this far."

"I'll pack," she says, "but with any luck the wind will blow it the other way, and the firefighters will put it out before it gets very far."

"Please, God."

Half the stuff that was in my bag during the Waldport fire has gotten pulled out and used since then. Once again, I gather my music and my essential things, along with food for Rocky. As if I didn't learn my lesson before, I really want to go down the road and make sure Eugenia's place is safe. I want to check on our homeless guys camping by the creek, too.

Remember what I said about Ordinary Time? Seems like I haven't had any since Tom got sick four years ago. Apparently, it's not happening any time soon.

It's almost dark. I'm afraid of what this night will bring.

The air gets smokier by the minute. There's a roaring sound and a reddish tinge to the sky in the southeast. As Dakota packs, Rocky sits, stands, circles, licks his paws, and sits again. I'm doing stomach crunches in the living room. Dad is fussing with his phone, trying to get more information. None of us can relax, not when we might get the order to evacuate any minute, not when everything we own could be gone by morning.

I want to start loading stuff in my car. Dakota says it's too soon. It might be a relatively small fire they put out in a few minutes.

Or not. I remember with the last fire, they said pine needles, leaves and bark can blow around like flying matches and set things on fire far from the main blaze. The rainbow house could burn down. What then? Go live with my mother in Santa Cruz? Move in with Janey and Diana or with my dad? If our house burned, his would go too, wouldn't it? Unlike Gabriel and his homeless friends, we have jobs and insurance. We can recover, but . . .

I step out into the yard and look up into the smoky sky. "God, please put this fire out. Maybe you could send a little rain?"

In September? Not likely.

Dakota has finished packing and is outside hooking up a hose. Our water, coming from a well, is limited. I don't know if there's enough to stop a big fire. Remember all those old cowboy movies where the bad guys torch the barn and the neighbors pass buckets hand to hand, as if a bucket of water is enough to stop a fire when the structure is engulfed in flames. The barn always burns. But sometimes they save the house.

Ashes are landing in my hair now, and it's harder to breathe. I put on my mask, but it doesn't really help. "It's getting closer!"

"I know," Dakota says. An ember lands on the roof. "Shit." She extinguishes it with the hose, but there are going to be more.

"Where do you think it started?"

"I hate to say it, PD, but I think your homeless buddies might be involved."

"I hope they're not in the middle of this."

"Yeah. Watch for sparks, PD."

"I'm watching."

The phone in her back jeans pocket chimes. She pulls it out. "Holy fuck."

"What?"

"Check your phone. We got a 'Get ready' order."

Dad is standing in the doorway. "I have to go pack."

"Go. Do it fast, Dad. Do you want me to help?"

"No. I can handle it. You watch out for your place. I'll watch out for mine."

"Can I pack the car now, Dakota?"

"Pack it. I'll load the van." A car is coming up the road. "Who's that?"

"Diana. Heading for Dad's place. You think she knows what's happening?"

"Probably. If not, she will soon. PD, should we take food?"

"Yes. I'll help you in a sec." I toss my bags into the passenger seat. "Do you have an ice chest?"

"Big one in the shed."

"We can fill it with all the ice from the fridge and put in as much food as we can."

"What happens when the ice melts?"

"We'll worry about that later."

It's getting harder to breathe. Now that it's close to dark, I can see orange flames shooting into the sky to the east and a little south. Where the horses live? Damn.

In the shed, the ice chest is stuffed behind boxes of knickknacks, books and clothes I brought when I moved in. I push them out of the way, grab the ice chest, and hurry back to the house. I fill it with meat, cheese, juice, vegetables, and condiments.

A bottle of wine was hiding way in the back of the fridge. Dakota sees it just as I reach for it. "We can leave that."

"Of course."

She covers the food with ice cubes and closes the top.

I help her bag cereal and other edibles from the cupboards, leaving sacks of flour, sugar, and beans. What would we do with them?

"Where will we go?" I ask.

"Diana's?"

"What if she's in danger, too?"

"We'll camp at the beach. Water doesn't burn."

"No, it doesn't. But it does drown people."

"Just load the car, PD."

When our vehicles are stuffed, we stand on the porch. The fire crackles.

"That's close." Dakota says.

"Too close." Rocky is hanging beside me. "Should I go help Dad?"

"He's got Diana. She'll help him. Did she ever tell you about how she got flooded out of the house where Janey and Jonas grew up?"

"No."

"That's a story to tell, but not now." She pauses on her way to the van. "What the hell is that?"

Sirens. Two sheriff's cars speed by.

Eugenia?

"PD, I can read your mind. Don't even think about it."

"I wish she had a phone."

"She could try smoke signals."

"Not funny."

"Sorry." Dakota lights a cigarette.

I stare.

"Shut up. I have to do something."

More fire trucks rumble up the road. Reinforcements.

Our phones buzz. We look at each other. *Be set to evacuate.*

"Son of a bitch," Dakota says.

"Exactly." We go inside for a last look around. Dakota hugs Maryann's cookie jar urn under her arm. "Oh girl, I'm glad you missed this. Without you, it's just a house anyway."

So true. I left a house back in Missoula. Without Tom—yeah, it was just a house.

I don't have that much to lose. I cut my possessions way down when I left Montana and again when I moved here, but I love my sofa, my dishes, my books, that lamp over there, my bed, my nightstand, my clothes, a lifetime collection of sheet music, and my piano. I have a crazy urge to sit down and play something. If I was alone, I would. One last song.

I take another load out to the car, along with more sheet music, my knitting bag, as much yarn as I can carry, and Donovan's crazy fish clock.

I flash on the night of the tsunami when I parked on this side of the bridge. Everything I originally brought to Oregon was in my car because Donovan, in a manic phase, had just kicked me out of the cabin. When Janey and I came back a few days later, someone had broken out the back window and stolen everything of value.

Another flash: my broken keyboard on the side of the I-5 freeway.

You can't really hold onto anything. Father Rigo would say all we can count on is Jesus and the promise of eternity with him in heaven.

I'm having a little trouble finding comfort in that right now as I wait for my phone to buzz again with the *go now* message.

At least we have a little warning. It has been over an hour since we first smelled smoke.

Dad's and Diana's cars roll up the driveway. Both are loaded. Dad gets out first.

"You got the *be set to go* order?" he asks.

"We did."

"Well, this is a hell of a note. I was fond of that cabin."

"I know. Are Diana's house and the diner okay?"

"She hasn't heard anything so far. I guess the fire is not going toward Seal Rock."

She joins him in the driveway. "So far." She grabs my hand and my father's. "Shall we say a prayer?"

"Couldn't hurt," says Dakota, taking my other hand and Diana's.

"Our Father, who art in heaven . . ."

As we end with "the kingdom, the power and the glory," we raise our hands toward the smoky sky and say, "Amen."

Even Dakota, who doesn't do religion.

Dad looks around. "The wind has died down."

It has. That seems like a good sign. But then a sheriff's deputy drives up and parks behind our cars, leaving his engine running.

"Folks, I'm sorry, but it's time to go. You need to evacuate right now."

"You sure?" Dad asks. "It looks like it's easing up."

"It's still unpredictable. Just to be safe, I'm asking you to head down the hill to somewhere else."

"Well, adios," Dakota says to the house, walking to her van just as the lights in the house go out. I guess the power lines burned.

"We going to my house?" Diana asks.

"Where else?" Dakota says.

I lead Rocky to my car and into the small space left on the passenger seat. "See you guys there."

As I turn onto Beaver Creek Road, I take one last look. What's going to happen is going to happen.

31. Waiting to Hear

Sunday, Sept. 27, 2020

IT'S SUNDAY. STILL DARK. I didn't sleep much. I kept looking out the window, expecting to see flames, and checking my phone, expecting I don't know what. There isn't another order after *go now*. I'd like to see a text saying *Come back. Everything's all right.*

Beverly and the choir are on their own today. I need to know. Is the rainbow house gone? Are my father and Dakota and I homeless?

Well, maybe he's not homeless. He slept with Diana in her room last night. His robe was hanging in the bathroom. I guess we just need to accept that they are together.

Janey is in her old bedroom, and Dakota took the guest room. I don't mind the couch. I'm too antsy to sleep anyway. Rocky's sacked out on the floor. He tried to jump up on the cushions with me a couple times, but he's just too danged big to fit.

Now it's five a.m. and I'm waiting for daylight, checking my phone for news. Is the fire out? Has it spread? Where will it go next?

Diana is up first, already dressed. She needs to open the diner and start breakfast, assuming the diner is still there, and she still has customers. Soon Janey is up, too, yawning and muttering about how people deserve more time between shifts. "Isn't that the law, Mom?"

"I don't know, baby. I want to sleep, too. But hungry people will be expecting their eggs and bacon."

"And pancakes. And French toast."

"With hash browns."

"Morning, you guys," I say from the darkened living room.

"Hey, PD. Why don't you come with us? Get some breakfast and find out what's what."

"Okay. Thanks, Diana. I guess it's too early to call anybody about church."

Janey rolls her eyes. "You think?"

"Is Dakota still sleeping?"

"Snoring like a hibernating bear."

"What about Dad?"

"The poor guy just got to sleep," Diana says. "Let him rest. He's not all better from COVID, you know, and he's really upset about the fire."

"I know. Give me a few minutes to dress and take Rocky out to do his thing, and I'll meet you there."

I've got smoke in every crease and crevice. I think it's between my eyelids and my eyeballs. I stink.

As I dig fresh clothes out of one of the bags in my car, I inhale. The air seems less smoky. Did they get the fire out?

I grab a fresh mask, too. The purple one I wore yesterday, my favorite, is black with smoke.

Diana's bathroom is small and old-fashioned, with a claw-foot tub and rose-covered wallpaper. Little-kid pictures of Janey and Jonas share the walls with the two sets of twins.

I move quickly, changing clothes, washing my face, fluffing my hair with water, and brushing my teeth. I want to know. I need to know. Is our house still there? Is everybody all right?

Rocky and I take a quick walk around the yard, and I bring him in. "Rocky, stay."

His expression says, "Are you nuts?" but he stays. As I walk out the door, he trots into the bedroom to sleep with Dakota, his other mom.

THE DINER IS BUZZING when I walk in. The first thing I see is two Newport firefighters hunched over plates at the table closest to the door.

I walk right up to them. "Hi. I'm PD. My housemate and I had to evacuate from up Beaver Creek Road. Is the fire out?"

"It's contained," the older man says. "A new crew came in from Florence to give us a break."

"But it's smaller?"

"Yes. We lost some homes, but now it's confined to wilderness."

"Is our home . . . one of the ones that was lost?" Please God, let them say no.

"I'm sorry, ma'am. I don't know."

Radio chatter. "We've got to go, Jerry," the tall skinny one next to him says. They push back their chairs and head for the door.

"Wait. Can I go up there?"

"Up where exactly?" Jerry asks.

"Beaver Creek Road a couple miles past where it turns to gravel."

"Sorry. It's still under evacuation from the visitor's center up about four miles. Just hold tight. I know it's hard."

"Let's go," says the other guy."

"Coming."

I sit at the table they just left and rest my head in my hands. Janey sets the coffee pot down and falls into the chair beside me, stacking the plates with remnants of eggs, bacon, and syrup. "I'll bet your place is just fine, PD."

"Or it's a pile of burnt wood and ashes."

"No, it's fine."

"This isn't a Broadway musical; it's real life. Bad endings happen."

"Janey!" Diana calls.

"Mom, get off my back. PD, what do you want to eat?"

"I don't know. Toast. And coffee."

"Coming up."

I don't think I could keep anything else down, but my stomach is growling. Idiot stomach.

Dakota comes in, leaving Rocky in the van with the windows half open. We nod at each other. What is there to say?

The diner is slammed. Between tourists, regulars, and folks like us who can't go home, every COVID-distanced table is full, including the picnic tables outside. The workers wear masks. The customers take theirs off as soon as they have anything to eat or drink. I don't know how safe it is. COVID + fire. I guess you decide which is worse and hope for the best.

As soon as I finish my breakfast, Diana puts me to work pouring coffee and water and clearing tables. I don't mind. I need something to do while we wait.

I recognize some of the customers as neighbors and try to eavesdrop as I roam among the tables.

"I heard McCabe lost everything," big-bellied Jasper tells his tablemates.

"No. That's awful. And his wife with the cancer. God damn. Your place is okay?"

"Far as I know. The wind died down just in time, but there may be others not so lucky. He catches my arm as I pass by. "Hey, did you girls make out okay with the fire?"

I shake my head. "I don't know yet. Nobody has said anything, and we aren't allowed to go up there to look."

"Well, I hope you still got a house. That rainbow house is famous, you know."

"Really?"

"Oh yeah. That Dakota's a hell of a carpenter. Hey, warm up my coffee while you're here."

Around eight o'clock, I call Beverly to tell her I won't be at church.

She answers on the fourth ring, out of breath. "PD, I'm running late."

I tell her about the fire and having to evacuate.

"Oh, I'm sorry. I heard about the fire, but I didn't know you were in that area. How is your house?"

"I don't know yet. They won't let us in."

"I'll say a prayer. We all will."

"I'm sorry to desert you, but you'll have the ladies and Gabriel."

She is quiet for a minute. "Actually, we won't have Gabriel."

"What do you mean?"

"He's in jail, PD. I don't know if I ever mentioned my son is a deputy sheriff. They found Gabriel and some other homeless guys camping near where the fire started. They're pretty sure they're responsible."

"I can't believe Gabriel would do that. I mean, he's a little strange, but he's not stupid. He knows about the fire danger."

"How about the other guys?"

"I don't know much about them. Did he say anything about Eugenia, the woman who lives out there . . .?"

"No. PD, I'd better go. If I'm playing the piano today, I need to practice. Not that it's going to help much."

"I'm sorry to leave you hanging."

"No, no. Don't worry about us. I'll tell Father Rigo to add you to the special intentions."

"And the McCabes. I don't know them, but they lost everything."

"I will. Take care, PD. Bye."

I look across the restaurant and see a man holding up his coffee cup. He's silhouetted in the window. It takes a minute before I realize it's my father. I grab the pot and hurry over.

I kiss him on the cheek. "Good morning."

"I didn't get a kiss," Jasper complains.

"Hush. He's my father." This is kind of fun. Maybe I should trade my hospital job for this one. "Good morning, Dad."

"Hey, Cissy." For some reason, the old name brings tears to my eyes. My father grabs my hand. "It will be all right, kiddo. Worst case, you and I can hit the road."

"We still have COVID restrictions."

"I know. We'll figure it out."

"PD!" Diana calls. "I'm running out of silverware."

You'd think I worked here or something.

We have a second rush of customers, the late sleepers, I guess. My legs and feet are tired. That's what happens when you're used to a sit-down job.

THINGS FINALLY slow down enough about 10:15 for us to sit together and relax a bit, although Diana has her eye on the clock. The lunch crowd will be here soon. The chowder is warming, and the grill is ready for burgers and bacon.

Jonas rolls in with a taxi full of fresh-baked pies and muffins from Molly.

"Hey, Joney," his sister calls. "How's it hanging?"

"Long and hard," he grins.

"Jonas Peacock, watch your mouth," Diana says, her eyes sparkling as she tries not to laugh.

"Tell Janey to watch hers. Hey PD, Mom finally put you to work?"

"Payment for sleeping at her house. We got evacuated last night. Big fire."

"Oh, shit. You too, Jack?"

Dad nods. "The whole gang."

"Are your houses still standing?"

"Don't know yet," I say. I look around at the empty tables. Thanks to COVID, Diana no longer puts out ketchup, sugar, salt and pepper, or jam. Customers have to ask for them. But she has little vases of fake petunias on each table.

This diner feels like home. We were here the day the tsunami hit. We had just eaten Thanksgiving dinner and were playing a little music when things started shaking. We dove under the tables as pictures fell off the walls and crockery tumbled off the shelves. I remember Jonas' boy twins screaming. Once the shaking stopped, Dakota worked with the family to rebuild and refurbish the diner. Later our band, Seal Rock Sound, practiced here. Now it's our refuge from the fire.

What would we do without Diana and her family? Where would I be? I wouldn't have met any of these people, except my dad, and God knows where he would have settled.

Diana drains her cup. "Back to work."

"I'm going to help," my father says.

"Thanks, Jack. All volunteers accepted. You'll be paid in food and lodging, and maybe a little something else, in your case."

"Gross," Janey says as she starts wrapping silverware in paper napkins.

A truck rumbles out front. Then another. The Seal Rock fire crews returning. Is it over?

The three who answered our 911 call last night come in, heading straight for Dakota and me and Dad. "Good morning," says the man named Raul. His face is black with smoke and stubble, and he has bags under his eyes.

"Is the fire out?" Dakota asks.

"Just about. We've got guys checking for hot spots. We'll be watching it the rest of the day and probably through the night."

"What about our homes?" Dad asks.

"You've got the cabin up above the ladies' house, right?"

"Yes."

"It's fine."

"And our place?" I ask, my voice suddenly reduced to a hoarse squeak.

The woman, whose badge says Tess Garcia, answers. "You have some damage. Embers were flying so high and fast we couldn't stop them all, but it's not too bad. We did the best we could."

"Thank you," Dakota answers, resting her hand on Tess's shoulder. "I know you did."

"Can we go home?"

Tess sighs. "We're not supposed to let you in yet, but yeah, okay. If you run into anybody, tell them Tess said you could take a look."

"Thank you."

"How did it start?" Dad asks.

The third firefighter answers. "The sheriff arrested some homeless guys they found running away from the fire carrying all their stuff. They probably started a fire to cook or keep warm, or maybe they were smoking, but you just can't do that in these conditions.

"They're going to face some stiff charges. They aren't supposed to be there in the first place, and all burning is prohibited, even campfires, especially since the blazes up north earlier in the month. Anyway, we can all get some rest now. Until the next fool lights a fire or tosses a cigarette—or lightning strikes. Even a spark from a lawnmower can do it when it's this hot and dry."

"You guys want something to eat?" Janey asks.

"Maybe later, after we clean up," Tess responds. "Thanks."

"We owe you guys," Dakota says.

Tess shakes her hand, and they leave.

Dakota slaps the table and stands. "Let's go, PD."

"Wait a sec," Diana says.

She rushes to the kitchen and fills a bag with food for us. "Lunch, dinner, snack, whatever. Get out of here. Let me know how it is."

32. Walking Through Ashes

Sept. 27, 2020

Once again, I'm driving with my car full of everything I value. Once again, I'm not sure I have a place to live, but I'm not alone this time as I follow Dakota and Rocky up Beaver Creek Road.

Things look normal at first, the marsh area bounded by alders, the creek, and the hills beyond, but when I drive around a bend after the junction with South Beaver Creek Road, the landscape becomes the reverse of a snow scene, everything black instead of white. Trees reduced to blackened sticks. Ash-covered earth, remnants of buildings, a burned-out camper, blackened fences, a charred car.

The visitor's center is gone. I always thought that big concrete-floored building would be a good place to play music. Not anymore. Just a foundation and steps are left. I wonder if the state will rebuild. Maybe they'll decide it isn't worth it. It never got much traffic anyway, and it has been closed since the pandemic started.

Up and up the hill, black and more black to the right, almost normal in the ravine to the left until I reach the turn.

Where just a few days ago, I stood watching the horses and the waterfall, it's all black. The horses are gone, and all that's left of the buildings are concrete foundations, posts and twisted, blackened tractors. The water is still flowing, but only at a trickle because it's been so dry this summer. Pieces of burnt wood and a pair of eyeglasses float in the current. For a second, I can't breathe.

I turn onto the graveled section. More blackened trees, burnt fences, and orange-brown grass where two days ago, it was a dozen shades of green. Wildflowers, Scotch broom, blackberries, all toast.

The house below ours is ashes. The owners, whom I have never met, live in Eugene most of the year and haven't been around lately.

Our house is next.

Dakota is driving slowly, probably taking in the scene like me and maybe just as afraid to see what's left of our place. *Please let the house still be there.*

Here we go. The bushes that hid the view of our driveway are burnt and leaning every which way. Dakota pushes ahead into the drive, and I follow.

As we get out of our cars, she lets out a big sigh. The shed beside the house is blackened and partially burnt down, but the house itself seems to be untouched, except for a smear of black on the roof and walls. Rocky runs out to sniff around, coating his paws and fur with ash and soot.

"Thank God," I say moving toward the steps. Through the front window, I can see the house is just the way we left it. Dakota stands frozen, tears pouring down her cheeks. Her deep hoarse sobs break my heart.

I put my arms around her. "It's okay. Let it out. We can rebuild the shed, make it better. Maybe make a garage, maybe—"

"I know. I know. Shut up," she says between sobs. "I—Did you see how much was burned, how close it came?"

"Yes. I can't believe it. So much is gone."

As Rocky returns, she holds him, crying into his fur.

Her pain is not just about the house, and I don't know how to stop it. I don't want to cry. I want to unpack and pretend life is exactly the same as it was yesterday. But I didn't build this house. I didn't watch my partner die here.

"I'd better let people know," I say, pulling out my phone. Not in the mood to chat, I send a group text. "Shed is burnt, but rainbow house is okay. God is good."

I ignore the pinging responses and head into the house. We forgot to lock it.

"P.U!" Dakota says, wiping her eyes with her shirt sleeve.

It stinks, even though all the doors and windows were shut.

There's a gray layer of ash on everything. My eyes burn. We've got some cleaning to do. But at least it's all still here. I don't care about the stuff in the shed. I stroke my piano like an old friend. My finger comes up ashy. My dishes, my bed, the old shoes I rejected, I cherish it all now.

Is it overdramatic to say I fall to my knees, saying, "Thank you, God," about a hundred times? Well, maybe I do while Dakota carries Maryann's ashes back in, setting them on her dresser. I can't quite hear what she says to her late wife.

She blows her nose with toilet paper in the bathroom then goes out to fetch the ice chest. Together we unload it into the refrigerator. I'm glad we took the food. According to what I read online, it might not be edible if we'd left it. As it is, Dakota tosses the flour and other baking supplies we left behind into the trash.

That forgotten bottle of wine is still in the back of the fridge.

"Get rid of it, okay? Give it to your father. I don't trust myself."

"Me either." When I go out for the next load, I stuff the bottle under the passenger seat of my car.

We clean everything we can reach with wet cloths and mops. When we finish, there's still a layer of soot where we can't reach without the ladder that burned up in the shed, but it's better.

We open all the windows, grateful for fresh air. We throw our smoky clothing, towels, and bedding into the washing machine or in a pile on the floor beside it. It's going to take a few loads, but we're grateful to still have our washer and dryer in the nook by the back door, and even more grateful that they still work. The refrigerator hums, and the lights we left on shine. Kudos to the power company.

When the cars are empty, we close the door and collapse on the sofa. Rocky settles into a square of sunlight on the rug. He leaves black paw prints next to our shoe prints. Dang. I wonder how long it takes ashes from a wildfire to go away. We should leave our shoes on the porch for a while.

I would love for it to rain, but wouldn't all that ash turn into black mud?

I'm torn between going to the beach, letting the waves wash away all the smoke and fire and fear, and sitting on my sofa in this house we almost lost. Sitting here wins. The house smells of smoke and lemon-scented cleaning solution, but I can handle it.

Dakota undoes her braid and lets her hair fall around her shoulders. With her face still marked with tears and the wrinkles around her eyes and mouth more pronounced, she looks more fragile than I have ever seen her.

I hate that she had to go through this on top of losing Maryann and her constant battle to stay sober.

As she closes her eyes and falls asleep, a melody plays in my head. The fire wants a song. I'll go down by the waterfall and write it.

Rocky looks at me as I'm slipping out the door. I signal him to come along.

Maybe I'll call it "Walking through Ashes."

33. Visitors

LATE IN THE afternoon, I drive up the road to check on Eugenia, my new song playing nonstop in my head. As I turn in by the rain barrel, I see no signs of the fire, but the place looks different. The chicken coop is open; the chickens are gone. There are no clothes on the line, and I don't see Eugenia, who is usually outside during the day.

When I knock on the door, no one answers. I peer through the grimy windows. Nothing. Eugenia never leaves. She doesn't drive. Her son is in jail. Where would she go? Did she have to evacuate? But she'd be back by now. This feels wrong.

Like so much about this woman people call The Witch, it's a mystery. I don't know how to solve it right now, and I'm not really comfortable hanging out here alone. I'd better go home and finish my laundry.

When I pass Dad's place, the lights are on, and his car is in the driveway. Good.

Back at the rainbow house, where the burnt shed and the lingering smell of smoke are still a shock, there's an unfamiliar car in the driveway.

Company?

Dakota is sitting at the table eating pie with Tess the firefighter.

As I look from one to the other, wondering what's going on, Tess smiles. "Hi, PD. I hope you don't mind my dropping by. Dakota's not going to tell you because of our anonymity, but we met at AA and found we have a lot in common. I figured Dakota would be pretty shaken up by the fire and need a little support."

I nod. "Sure. You're always welcome. You saved our house."

"That wasn't me. I was just part of the team."

"Yes, but you helped stop the fire."

"I tried. I was telling Dakota you guys need to make a list of everything that was lost and call your insurance company first thing in the morning."

Dakota has already started writing things down on a notepad beside her plate. "I lost my tools, my ladder, some folding chairs, hoses, firewood, bird feeders, and shit like that. If I walk around out there in the morning, I'll remember more. What did you have in the shed, PD?"

I sink into a chair. "Um, an end table, a couple bar stools, some boxes of Christmas decorations, books, old clothes, and knick-knacks. Oh, the doghouse that Rocky refused to use was out there. There's probably more. I haven't looked at it in months."

"Well, that's a start. We have the cost of the shed itself, replenishing the woodpile, and repainting the house. I need to get up on the roof and make sure there aren't any burned spots."

"You think there might be?"

"It's likely," Tess says. "Be careful up there, Kota. You don't want to fall through a weak spot."

"No, I don't. I guess if we need a whole new roof, we'll take care of it. You want some diner pie, PD? It's cherry."

"Not now. I think I'll pull my stuff out of the dryer and rest a while. I'm wiped out, and I have to work tomorrow."

"Me too. Don't worry about dinner. The pie filled us up for now. Take it easy, Kid."

Kid?

I hear the two of them laughing as I put clean sheets on my bed, climb in, and curl around my dog. "Hey Toto," I whisper into his big silky ear. "There's no place like home. And Auntie Dakota has a new friend."

He needs a bath, but it can wait. "Dog, you stink like smoke, but I love you."

He licks my face as if to say *likewise, PD.*

IT'S STRANGE going back to work after the weekend that started with music and Donovan and ended with the fire. I feel like I was gone a lot longer than two days. I'm still a little traumatized. But I drag myself out of bed, put on my clothes and my mask and show up behind my Plexiglas window at seven a.m. Jackson is conferring with a young black man while a middle-aged woman sleeps in the waiting area, wrapped in a hospital blanket.

"Good morning," I whisper.

Jackson nods. He's staring at his computer and talking to the guy. Finally, he wraps a hospital bracelet around his wrist and sends him off to wait. Thirty seconds later, a nurse peeks out and calls the man in.

"Whew. That was intense," Jackson says. "He just got out of jail, and he thinks he might have an STD. Of course, he's embarrassed as hell. Anyway, good morning, Ms. PD. How was your weekend?

I stare at him. Doesn't he know? But then, how would he? "Well, did you hear about the fire up Beaver Creek?"

"Fire? No. What happened? Are you guys okay?"

"We had to evacuate, and our shed got burnt. The house got a good smoking, but it's still there, thank God."

"Wow. You never know what's going to happen next, do you?"

"No, you don't." We hush as a doctor and nurse come out and wake the sleeping woman. She tries to smooth her curly hair as she stands, clutching the blanket.

They take her to the other room. We can't hear what they say, but we do hear her shriek, "No! Please no!"

Murmurs. Attempted comfort. They lead her past us into the ER to say her final goodbye. There's nothing anyone can say as the facts sink in. You came in as a wife, and you're leaving as a widow. Your legs wobble, and you keep seeing how he looked. You can't believe the world is going on as if nothing happened, but you get in your car and you drive home to the house where he will never live again.

"Sad," Jackson says.

"So sad." My voice cracks. Pull it together, PD.

"Hell of a way to start the day. I'm going for coffee. Can I bring you some?"

"Please."

Jackson's a good guy. He never forgets I lost my husband to cancer, that I have this grief wound in my chest that never goes away. He's pretty quiet about his own personal life. I know he lives with another man. Most of his family lives on the East Coast, and they don't appreciate his lifestyle, but he still hopes they will accept it someday. I know he likes pink neckties and pink tennis shoes. He is always kind, even with the people who are rude and impatient. They're sick, they're hurt, they're worried. They don't mean it, he says.

Unlike me, he doesn't want to do anything else for a living. "I'm helping people. I've got a front row seat to what's happening. And I have my late afternoons off to play," he says. "Got my man. My house. My cats. I'm content."

Content. Have I ever been content? Maybe on those evenings with Tom when we cuddled on the sofa watching TV after making love, and everything felt right. Yes, I was content then. Now? I feel like I'm always running from a tsunami or a fire.

Customers. My God, how many of them are there? This poor mother, a tiny Latina woman carrying a wailing infant, has five kids following her like baby ducks. "Good morning. How can we help you?" I ask.

The mother shakes her head. "*No ingles. Pablo, venga.*" She calls her oldest son, who might be nine or ten, to translate. The baby has a high fever and diarrhea. I take their information and promise someone will call them soon.

Lord, let it be no big deal, I pray as Jackson hands me my coffee.

AT HOME HOURS later, someone knocks on the door, followed by Rocky's "invader" bark. Dakota is still at work, and I'm cleaning the smoke and general dirt in the bathroom. Dad and Janey don't knock; they just walk in. We don't see door-to-door salespeople or Jehovah's witnesses out here. I hope it's not another evacuation notice.

I put on my mask and open the door to a tall man in his fifties. "Hello?"

"Hi. I-um. Are you the one they call PD?"

"Yes. And you are?"

"Roger. Roger Petersen. I'm looking for my son, Jonathon. He's twenty-eight years old. Tall, skinny, long blond hair and beard. Maybe talking religious stuff."

"You mean Gabriel?"

"You know, I think he does call himself that. Anyway, do you know where he is?"

"Mr. Petersen, come in and sit down. Can I offer you some coffee, tea, or water?"

"Water would be great."

I fill a glass for him and one for myself. I've still got smoke in my throat.

He sits in the easy chair while I perch on the piano bench, my safe place. Roger looks like Gabriel. His hair is short but the same color and they have the same ice blue eyes. Except the father looks more tuned in to reality.

"I have bad news, Roger. Last I heard, your son was in jail. We had a fire out here over the weekend. He was camping in the area with some friends, and the sheriff thinks they started it. Maybe not Gabriel specifically, but they arrested them all."

"Oh, Christ. I saw the burned trees and buildings. I guess I need to go see him and try to bail him out."

"They don't allow visitors. COVID."

"That's right. Do you know if he has an attorney or anything?"

"No idea. Knowing Gabriel—Jonathan—he'd probably want to represent himself."

"Yup." He drinks half his water at once. I follow suit.

"Roger, can you tell me anything about him? He's been around a while now, and he seems like a good guy. He even sings in my church choir sometimes, but, well, he's different."

"That he is. You should have known him before. After he got out of the Navy, we worked together on the docks near Bellingham, up in Washington. He was strong and smart and normal. Talked about going to college. Then the accident happened. A cable snapped and a crate fell on top of him, hit him in the head. He suffered a traumatic brain injury, and we almost lost him. After that, his personality changed. He lost interest in everything he was doing before.

"Now, he will tell you he saw Jesus and was chosen to be the twelfth apostle to replace Judas. He took the mandate to leave his father and mother and follow Jesus literally. He traded his regular clothes for white cotton garments and sandals and took off. On foot. He left a fiancée behind. Broke her heart. It's like he was brainwashed. I mean, we brought him up Catholic, but this is way beyond, you know, what's normal.

"To you, he probably looks like any other homeless guy, a little crazy, probably on drugs, abandoned by his people, but he comes from a good home. His mother and I love him and want him to be healthy and happy. He has two younger sisters who really miss him."

He pauses to finish his water.

"I'm sorry," I say. We're quiet for a minute. "How did you know to come here?"

He pulls a dirt-stained, folded postcard from his plaid shirt pocket and hands it to me. Seal Rock, it says above a photo of the familiar rocks down the hill from here. The cramped printing on the back is so smeared I can't read it, except for "God bless you, Gabriel."

"That was the first we'd heard in over a year. My wife isn't well, but I knew I had to come and find him. I asked at all the shops that were open. At the diner, a young gal with curly hair said I should talk to you."

"That's Janey."

"Well, I'm grateful. At least I know where he is. He won't do well in jail, not if he keeps talking nonsense. And I hope he doesn't get COVID."

"He says he's immune."

"Of course he does." He groans as he stands. "Years as a longshoreman take it out of the old joints. Anyway." He checks his watch," I need to run over to the jail and see what's what, whether I can pay bail, hire him a lawyer, or whatever. Can you give me directions?"

I explain where the courthouse/jail complex is in Newport.

"Thank you. It sounds like you care about my son. I'm glad."

"You don't have time for this story, but he helped save my life a while back, so yes, I do care. I'm glad you're here, Roger. Good luck."

As he drives away, I say a prayer of thanks. Even angels need their parents sometimes.

PART III

34. Vaccinated

Tuesday, December 15, 2020

MY ARM IS killing me. It's red and feels hot to the touch. I barely felt the shot going in, but I sure feel it now. The nurse giving the injection said I might feel a little feverish and achy tomorrow. I guess we all might, but we'll have to work anyway.

I have never been in the military, but I couldn't help picturing rows of soldiers lined up for their shots before heading overseas. Except most of our crew were wearing scrubs or white coats and masks as we reported to the conference room for our first COVID vaccines. Civilians aren't getting them yet, but our jobs make us high risk and first in line. Sir, yes sir.

Seniors will be vaccinated next. Gradually, it will trickle down to younger adults. Nothing for kids yet.

I have signed up to help when we start offering the vaccine to the masses. I can't give shots, but I can organize and fill out forms. Anything to make this plague go away. We're all tired of this, and too many are still getting sick and dying. I can't forget how close my father came to passing away.

By the middle of last month, we were up to 250,000 deaths in the U.S.

Lincoln County has gone up to "extreme risk" again, with 131 cases in two weeks. Needless to say, we've been busy at work. At least with the vaccine, we have a better chance of not getting sick. I hope. I'm double-masking just in case.

It seems like the restrictions change every day. Restaurants open, restaurants closed. Open the schools, shut them down. It's getting better; it's getting worse. For God's sake, don't bring your families together for Thanksgiving. So, we didn't. Dakota, Dad and I ate our turkey dinner at the rainbow house. Diana and Janey were prepping carryout dinners all day at the diner.

As usual this time of year, it's cold, wet and windy. I'm bundled up in three layers of clothing, hat, gloves, and boots waiting for Rocky to do his business. "Come on, boy, it's freezing." What is that weed he's eating? At first, we were warned to be suspicious of every smoke-tainted growing thing, but now we've had so much rain I don't think it's an issue.

The rainbow van rattles up the hill and stops next to my car.

"Rocky, Dakota's home."

She looks pooped. I can't blame her. She's been spending every spare minute working on the house. She replaced the roof and repainted the outside of the house before the weather turned. Now she's busy inside the new garage, dry-walling, painting, putting up shelves and cupboards. She's even doing the wiring herself. At this point, she's buddy-buddy with the building inspector.

I can't help thinking *what if we have another fire and all that time and effort is wasted.* Am I becoming a pessimist in my old age? Maybe I am.

Speaking of age, I had a birthday in August. I turned 44. I had let my hair go natural, but when I found gray hairs among my natural brown ones that night, I decided to start dying it again. Yes, red, short and spiky. I don't care whether it's in style or not. It's my look. Think about Pink or Liza Minelli or Rod Stewart. They've had the same hairstyle forever. All you have to see is a silhouette and you know who they are.

But I'm never going to become a household name if I don't start playing music somewhere besides church and our living room. With this weather, we can't do our Saturday concerts outside the diner, and Diana can't give up space inside, with the tables having to be so far apart. Plans for the new performing arts center have been approved, but it's a long way from being actually built. Side thought: They should hire Dakota to work on it.

You know, this sounds weird, but performing is like sex. When you can't do it, you really miss it. Now I'm missing both. Nope, no action with Miguel. He has been in Baja California since early October doing a fish research project. Dad said he was going to spend a little time with his 10-year-old daughter in New Mexico before returning to Oregon. To be honest, it has been kind of a relief having him gone. When he comes back next week, we really need to talk.

I wrote a lot of music for the Between the Bridges film the first few weeks after the fire. But what Trevor said about getting a contract bothered me. I tried to talk to Britt. No luck. She didn't answer calls, texts, or emails. She ghosted me, as the saying goes. I finally mailed her a letter. Nothing so far.

What if all these songs go nowhere? Or worse, what if she steals them? The whole business has sent my muse running to her room and locking the door. I'm back to knitting again. Everybody's getting a hat for Christmas.

Meanwhile, Dakota's limping again. Bad knees. I suppose that's coming for me, too, along with menopause, wrinkles, and blood pressure pills. Rocky and I follow her into the house.

"How was your day?"

Dakota shrugs.

"Did you see anybody at Eugenia's house?"

"Nope. I'm holding her mail at the post office. You need to stop asking. And don't ask about Gabriel either. No sign of either one of them."

"Okay, okay. I got my COVID shot today."

"It hurt?"

"Not then, but it sure does now." I shuck my coat and show her my red and swollen arm.

"Damn. Want me to make you dinner?"

"No, I'm not helpless. How do you feel about scrambled eggs and pancakes?"

"That sounds great. Let me know if you need help."

I'm mixing up the batter when she pokes her head out of her room. "Tess is coming over later."

"For dinner?"

"No. After."

Fine. The woman is here all the time. I mean, I like her. She's great. Capable, caring, smart, funny. She has helped a lot with the repairs. But I'm starting to feel like a third wheel.

Whoa. I'm beating this batter way too hard. My pancakes will be full of holes. Focus, PD.

35. We Need to Talk

Sunday, Dec. 20, 2020

"How was your trip?" I ask Miguel when he comes up after the closing song at Mass. What I can see of Miguel's face above the mask looks darker than before. I guess he got some sun while he was working in Baja. Me, I feel pale and puny. The COVID shot reaction was no joke.

"It was fantastic. Good work, lots of sunshine, plenty of *cerveza*—beer. I got certified as a Level 2 diver."

"No kidding."

"Yeah, I have always wanted to do that. They had a program I attended after work, and now I'm cleared to go down to 59 feet."

"I guess that's where the cool fish live."

"Some of them, yes. But I want to go deeper, to become a master diver."

I can tell he's jazzed about this, but we need to leave the sanctuary. Most of the parishioners and the choir have already left. Father's waiting to lock the doors. I close the piano and put on my coat.

"Did you see your daughter?" I ask as we walk past the empty pews.

"Yes. She's so grown up. I'm missing a lot."

"That must be hard. What's her name?"

"Lucy. Lucinda."

"Would you ever move to New Mexico to be close to her?"

"No ocean. I hope I can bring her out here for spring break. Anyway, shall we do brunch?"

I hesitate. Since the fire, since that afternoon with Donovan, since a lot of things, I have been thinking I need to end whatever this is with Miguel. He is a "catch," as my mother would say, but I just don't feel it. If I'm spending all my time with him, I'll never meet anyone else, well, except the old guys at the diner. I did meet Eugenia's son. Remember what a charmer he was. We could have conjugal visits in prison.

"If you're busy, PD, that's okay."

"No, I'm hungry. Let's get a bite. But I have to take off after that. You probably have a lot to do, too, having been gone so long."

"Sure." He shivers as we walk out into the rain. "I can't get used to this weather."

"They say it's going to be colder tonight, maybe down in the teens. It could snow."

"I need to buy a thicker coat."

We take our separate cars and walk into Off the Hook together, claiming a table near the fireplace.

Coffee poured and orders given, Miguel studies me. "PD, is everything all right? You seem preoccupied."

I can't stop the sigh that comes out of me. "Miguel, I have to tell you something."

"What? Did something happen? Are you sick?"

"No, none of that." I look across the blocked-off table beside us to the waitress spraying and wiping tables and chairs.

"PD?"

"Here's the thing, Miguel. I've been thinking about our—our relationship, and I don't think it's going to go anywhere. I think we should just be friends."

Miguel stares into his coffee. "Is it because of what I told you, my cancer?"

"No, no. It's not that at all. I just don't feel a romance working between us. You're terrific, you check all the boxes, but, I don't know. Maybe I'm done with all that. Maybe I'm getting too old to start again."

"Old? You're not old at all, even though you just had a birthday. I brought you something." He pulls a little box out of his pocket.

Please don't let it be jewelry.

It is. "Miguel, no."

"Just open it."

Inside the box, wrapped in orange tissue paper, are red and yellow earrings shaped like macaws. Thank God they're not romantic at all. "These are great. I love them. Thank you."

I remove my pearl earrings and stash them in my wallet, then put on the bird earrings. I can feel them swinging beside my cheekbones.

Miguel laughs and reaches to pull the right one away from my mask. "A gift from a friend to a friend. It's okay, PD. I knew you didn't share my feelings. And I know you're still getting over your husband."

"I'll never be over that," I say as the waitress brings my eggs Benedict and his *huevos rancheros*. I guess he misses Mexican food, but I'm sure the stuff they make up here in Oregon is not the same.

We chow down and share what's happened since we last met, which is a lot. We're still talking long after nothing's left on our plates but egg goo and salsa. When the waitress comes around for the third time asking if we need anything else, it's time to go.

As we head out into the pounding rain, Miguel says, "This may sound tacky, but I might bring a lady friend to church with me next week. She was in Baja with us, and we kind of hit it off."

I hit him gently with my purse. "You dog."

"But PD, you said—"

"I'm kidding. That's fine. See you next week."

I'm about to close my car door when I have a thought and run to knock on his car window. He rolls it down a couple inches.

"Can she sing?"

"I don't know. I'll find out."

Rain is pouring into the car. He rolls up the window, and I run to my Jeep.

I'm glad that's over.

At home, Dakota and Tess are playing dominos.

I see they plugged in the tiny store-bought Christmas tree Tess brought us. Dakota didn't want to cut down a tree that survived the fire, and all my ornaments burned up or melted into shapes that didn't look very festive. This little tree came with ornaments and lights already attached.

Dakota scoots a domino into place. "You got a call, PD. Lizzy from your church wants to know if you'd perform at her friend's art gallery opening."

"During COVID?"

"I guess. I left her number on your bed."

I call. Sonia Sunflower—I'm not kidding; that's her name—sounds friendly, and I'm happy to have a gig on January 9 at a new gallery in Seal Rock. I ask if she wants Janey, too. She says no. She just wants some nice background music on the piano she has there, maybe some soft singing.

I can do that.

Hallelujah, I'm back in show biz.

36. Subpoenaed and Skunked

Wednesday, Dec. 30, 2021

AN OFFICIAL-LOOKING envelope is sitting on the table on top of my magazines. Dakota must have brought the mail at lunchtime. I have been summoned by the district attorney's office to be a witness when Eugenia goes to court on Wednesday, January 25 and when Louis goes later in the month. I don't know much about the kidnapping, but the deputy saw the bruises on my neck from when Louis tried to strangle me and insisted I press charges.

They interviewed me for quite a while the night of our adventure by the rain barrel, and now I guess I'm going to court. Happy New Year to me. Let's put this creep in prison. I'm eager to testify against Louis, but I don't want to say anything negative about Eugenia. Will I have to mention the fire she had that one day, where she was burning what looked like a child's clothing?

I'm definitely going to mention her black eye, which I'm pretty sure she got from Louis.

I'm already nervous.

The process starts with an interview with the deputy district attorney. It's scheduled for one p.m. a week from today, so I'll have to leave work early.

I'm supposed to be helping with the shots at the fairgrounds that afternoon. I hope I'm done in time to get there. You should see it. We've got maybe a hundred people at a time waiting in chairs and sitting at tables. We run through a routine. Fill this out. Answer these questions. Take the shot. Go to the garden room and wait 15 minutes to see if you have a negative reaction, make your appointment for the next shot, and call this number if you have any problems. My tasks vary, but I'm usually going down the tables getting paperwork and patients ready, right down to which arm and roll up your sleeve, so the nurse can just uncap the syringe and shoot.

Having already gotten the vaccine, I'm feeling a lot safer, but I'm still wearing the mask, fully aware there are no guarantees. They say new strains will be coming along that the vaccine might not prevent, but with any luck people won't be as sick.

The president finally got COVID. He passed it off as no big deal, but his staff wouldn't have hauled him to the hospital if it was nothing. Still, he got in a car and went for a joy ride while he was still supposed to be in the hospital. Like, see, no big deal. I sure hope those guys driving him around didn't catch COVID.

He's over it now, contending that people worry too much about it. Tell that to all the people who lost loved ones to the virus.

While I'm checking the rest of my mail, Janey texts. They subpoenaed her, too. She was with me on Fourth of July at Eugenia's when we smelled smoke coming from her house. I'm glad we'll be going to court together.

I wonder what's happening with Gabriel. Is he still in jail or did his father bail him out? Is he anywhere near Louis? They are like good and evil. Maybe I'll find some answers at the courthouse.

Saturday, Jan. 2, 2021

RAIN PATTERS ON my cap and drips down my jacket as Rocky and I hike toward Eugenia's house. The evergreens look grayish under the dark clouds, while the leafless alders look naked and dead. They will fluff out again in spring, but now, it's depressing. No wildflowers, no berries, just ragged vines and an occasional newt, an orange-bellied, slimy cousin of the lizards I knew back in Montana.

I kick at a stone and watch it skitter up the road. Rocky sees it and pounces, then looks back, puzzled. Not a ball, not food.

I unhook his leash. He knows the way, and there aren't any chickens left to abuse. I'm pretty sure that cat Eugenia mentioned was made up to cover noise from the little boy. Danny. He's probably traumatized by this whole thing. Imagine being stolen away from your mother and the only home you know by this mean man who forces you to hide in this house in the woods with an old lady he says is your grandmother. And then they both go to jail, and your mother comes, all crying and happy to see you, but you don't know if you'll ever feel safe again.

Maybe Eugenia read him bedtime stories. Maybe they had some good grandmother-grandson bonding time. I hope they did. But now he's gone.

Where is Eugenia? As I pass the rain barrel, the place looks deserted. Beverly said she was released from jail right after they busted Louis, but she's not here. No chickens, no Eugenia. New tire tracks mark the ground almost to the front door. That could have been the cops. But I don't think they went there. They were busy out here with Louis. I don't know.

As Rocky explores the chicken coop, I walk around to the back of the house. The garden is doing well, especially the marijuana plants. Should I pick a few leaves to take home? No. Dakota and Tess avoid the stuff to protect their sobriety, and I was never a big user. It's a pretty plant, its long, serrated leaves unfazed by winter.

In the vegetable garden, a big pumpkin pokes out of the leaves. It's starting to turn a little yellow, but I could probably make pumpkin bread or pie or something. I pluck it and hug it against my jacket. Then I pick a zucchini and two artichokes. It's not stealing if it was going to go to waste anyway, right?

I can't carry anymore. Out of curiosity, I try the back door. It's unlocked. I leave my dripping jacket by the door and shiver in the cold. The house looks much as I imagined: homemade curtains, an old wooden table and chairs in the kitchen, a sofa and rocking chair in the living room. A fireplace. Two bedrooms. A bathroom. Aha. Eugenia fibbed when she told Dakota she only had an outhouse.

Just outside the first bedroom, there's something on the floor. I set down my stolen vegetables to take a closer look.

Oh no. It's a red syringe cap. A few inches closer to the door is a package that held an IV needle. In the bedroom, the covers have been thrown off the single bed. Waffled muddy shoe prints mark the hardwood floor.

It looks like Eugenia was taken out in an ambulance. Did Louis hurt her that badly? But he has been in jail since September. I don't think they crossed paths after she was arrested. This doesn't make any sense. When I get back to work, I can look her up on the computer to see if she came through our hospital, but that's two days from now.

A photo on her dresser shows Eugenia with a man who must be her husband. It was obviously taken many years ago. She was beautiful, slender in a flowing dress, her dark hair curling nearly to her waist. The man looks like Louis. I hope he didn't act like him.

From a distance, Rocky yelps and whines. I run out, following the sound.

I smell him before I see him. Skunk.

A little east of Eugenia's property, my dog cowers under a tree, soaking wet, stinking and pawing at his face.

"Oh, Rocky." I don't want him close enough to be on the leash. "Come on. Let's go home."

Thank God, he follows. I think he knows he needs my help.

When I can get a signal, I call Dakota. "Rocky met a skunk. Be prepared for the big stink."

Tess must be back. When Dakota relays the news, she laughs. "We'll have the tub ready out front." More laughter.

Good. Let them handle this. I'm going to put my head under the covers and stay there until spring. Or tomorrow when I play the piano at church and face Miguel with his new lady friend.

I'M ASLEEP when the phone rings. I can barely say hello before my mother shouts in my ear.

"PD!"

"Mom. What's wrong? Why are you calling so late?"

"Shari's in labor. The baby is finally coming. The doctor must have gotten the dates wrong. They've been any-day-now for weeks, but our new little girl is almost here. They won't let me come to the hospital because of COVID, but they're going to send pictures the minute she's born."

I pull Rocky closer. His fur is damp, and he still smells a little of skunk, but it's tolerable. "That's great. Have they picked out a name yet?"

"Oh PD, they want it to be a surprise."

"Why? It's just a name."

"It's not *just* a name. It's her whole identity. I can't keep quiet about it a second longer. They're naming her after you."

"PD?"

"No. That's not a name. It's just initials."

"Not Cissy."

"No. Donatella. But they're going to call her Donni. With an i."

"Dear God. I hope her middle name is something simple."

"Marie for Shari's mom."

Right away, I think of "Donnie and Marie," pop stars from days gone by. Poor baby. "Not Pauline, after you? It would sound better."

"I'll get the next baby. If it's a boy, they'll call him Paul."

Sure. Of course there will be another one, and Mom will get the grandkids she has always dreamed of while her daughter is a complete failure in that department. "Did you tell Dad?"

"Andy called him. I didn't want to interrupt him and his girlfriend."

"Right. Text me in the morning to let me know how mother and baby are faring."

"PD, I thought you'd be more excited. This is your niece, your namesake. I'll bet they even make you the godmother."

"I'm thrilled for Andy and Shari. But I had a long day, and I have to get up early. I'm pooped."

"You're not getting sick, are you?"

"No. I'm vaccinated. Did you get your shot?"

"I did. It didn't hurt a bit. I feel great. Goodnight, dear. Aunt PD."

"G'night, Grandma."

Rocky, hand me the Kleenex. I might need the whole box.

Oh gosh. I left the pumpkin and other vegetables in the hallway at Eugenia's house. Whoever shows up there next is going to wonder about that.

Donatella Marie O'Leary. Poor kid.

37. Pancakes for Courage

Wednesday, Jan. 6, 2021

As I stare at the photos Andy texted of my niece Donni, I realize it's time to PD up and get over myself. I'm an aunt. That's good news. I should enjoy the umpteen baby pictures my mother has sent since Sunday.

I need to stop worrying about things that aren't even problems yet. Miguel did not bring a girlfriend to church, and we did not go to brunch. Fine by me. As for Britt and the whole contract business, the songs are mine. If she backs out of her end of the deal, fine. I'll do something with them myself, starting with my gallery gig on Saturday.

Meanwhile, I'm meeting with the district attorney today.

By the time I shower and dress, Dakota is at the stove making pancakes. Unlike the fluffy little things at the diner, hers are gigantic and usually a little burnt, but I like them. Ooh, she put blueberries in them. Must have gotten them out of the freezer. Blueberry season is not happening in January.

"What's the occasion?"

"Something to cheer you up."

"I'm okay."

"I thought you might be nervous.

"A little, but I'm just going to tell the truth. That's all I can do. I hope I can find out what happened to Eugenia."

"No record at the hospital?"

"Not that I could find."

"Damn. How many pancakes you want?"

"Just one and a couple eggs."

"Coming right up."

"I wonder why they haven't called you in to testify. You're the one who told the sheriff Danny was at the house."

"I don't know, but it's fine with me. I'm just the weird lesbian making pancakes. Hey, Rocky, I see you staring at me. You'll get your share."

"You're giving him pancakes?"

"Just one. Minus the syrup. He's a growing dog."

Rocky looks up at me as if to say, *see, I'm no fool, I'm getting a pancake, too.*

THE DISTRICT ATTORNEY'S office is on the first floor of the red-brick county building between the jail and Domino's Pizza. I nod at the deputy guarding the door and walk through the metal detector. My dress shoes echo on the linoleum as I follow the signs, peek through a windowed door, see a secretary at a desk, and enter.

District attorney Jennifer Jankosky is a tall blonde in a stretchy blue dress that pooches out in front with an advanced pregnancy. She shakes my hand and leads me to a conference room where a young male assistant is poised to record my words.

As soon as we're seated and done with introductions, I interrupt the DA's first question to say my piece. "I'm not going to be much help to your case. In fact, I should be testifying for the defense. I don't believe Eugenia Renner is guilty of anything. She's a good person who got caught in a bad situation. I think she was terrified of her son. The last time I saw her, she had a black eye, and she certainly didn't get it from the little boy. Louis must have hit her. She was scared. She had to do whatever he said."

"Ms. Soares, do you have children?"

I can't stop the sigh that comes out. "No. How is that relevant?"

"Parents and children have a special bond. Grandmothers, too. Wouldn't Eugenia break the law to be with her grandson? I might."

"I don't know.

"Because you're not a mother."

"No. Because it's a tough question. I believe Eugenia was afraid of Louis and had nothing to do with taking Danny from his mother."

"Did she talk to you about it? Did you meet the boy?"

"No. When I heard something making noise in the house, she said it was a cat."

"Did you believe her?"

"No. My friends and I had seen the boy looking out the window on several occasions."

"She was hiding him?"

"Yes, I suppose. But we didn't know that at the time."

"Let's move on to Louis. Is it correct that he attacked you on the afternoon of Dec. 9?"

"Yes. He was strangling me when the sheriffs came."

"That must have been frightening."

"It was."

I retell the story of that afternoon and mention that I was attacked by a would-be rapist last year, which made it doubly traumatizing.

"Why did you go to Eugenia's house that afternoon?"

"I was worried about her. I wanted to make sure she was all right."

"Is that all?"

"Well, no. We had heard about the Amber Alert for Danny, and I wanted to warn her people would be coming."

As soon as the words come out of my mouth, I know I have made a mistake. It sounds like I was going to tell an alleged kidnapper to run before the cops arrived. Ms. Jankosky raises her eyebrows, but doesn't follow up.

"I see. I have no more questions at this time. Thank you for coming in." She nods. Her assistant turns off the recorder and leaves the room, but I stay in my chair.

"Can you tell me what happened to Eugenia? She's not home, and it looks like an ambulance might have been at her house.

Ms. Jankosky stands with a groan, cradling her belly. "Mrs. Renner had a stroke. The person who delivers her groceries didn't see her around.

He called her name a couple times and was about to leave when he heard someone inside banging on a wall. He went in and found her. He said he had to drive a mile or so to get cell service before he could call 911."

"Poor Eugenia. Where is she now? How bad was it?"

"I don't have a lot of details. She's at the rehab place by the hospital. No visitors, thanks to COVID, so we're stuck with video conferencing. She and her doctor both say she will be able to testify when we go to court."

"And Louis is still in jail?"

"Oh yes. He's not going anywhere."

"When will this go to court?"

"Two weeks from today. You will be called to testify."

"I don't have much to say."

"You were there. You saw some things. And don't forget you're the victim of an assault. That's more than enough." She glances at the door. "I wasn't supposed to tell you all that about Mrs. Renner, but I can see you care. On the stand, I might have to push you about your intentions that day, but right now, I don't have time. I'm due in court in a few minutes."

"When is the baby due?"

"One month. I can't wait. Again, thank you, Ms. Soares. We'll be in touch."

The sun is popping out through the clouds as I emerge from the big glass doors into the parking lot. The beach two blocks away is calling me, but people are gathering at the fairgrounds for their shots, and I need to be there.

Tonight, we're a threesome again, eating spaghetti and meatballs from the diner. I'm getting used to having Tess around. She's good for Dakota, and I don't mind her that much, even though I'm jealous that Rocky is hanging out on her side of the table.

"Tess," I ask. "Do you know anything about an ambulance call to Eugenia's house shortly after that kerfuffle over the kidnapped boy and Louis being arrested?"

"I didn't hear about that. Let me check around."

She steps outside to make some calls, then reports back. "That's the house off the forest road northeast of here? The older woman who lives by herself?"

"Yes."

"She had a stroke. I guess she had been lying on the bed for quite a while. Nobody really knows because she couldn't speak intelligibly at first. Just, you know. It was messy. The crew transported her to the ER, and then it was out of our hands. My contact said she was trying like crazy to tell him something, but he just couldn't understand the words."

"The DA said Eugenia is planning to testify in court."

"Good. That means her condition has improved."

"I hope so. Thanks for checking."

"Anytime, PD."

Tess's phone beeps with a text message, and she pushes back her chair. "Duty calls."

"Anything bad?" Dakota asks?

"Car fire up the highway."

Dakota kisses her on the lips. "Be careful, my sweet Tess."

"I always am." She rushes out, and Dakota carries our plates to the sink.

Suddenly I feel very lonely. "Rocky? You want to go out?"

He jumps up, tag wagging, eyes shining.

Maybe we'll get eaten by a bear.

38. Tinkerbelle

Saturday, Jan. 9, 2021

I FEEL JITTERY as I gather my music and put on makeup, a velvet skirt and a frilly top. Art gallery openings in the movies are always posh affairs. People dress up, drink champagne, and eat canapes. The building is elegant, the art is striking. Even the music is high class. Sure, this is in Waldport, where dressed up means wearing your less-faded jeans, but we can do classy when we want to.

It would have been cool if the gallery were on Art Street, but no, this street was named for a fish. Looking for the address on Lizzy's note, I don't see anything that looks like a gallery, but that's the number, 373 SE Sculpin St. Shouldn't there be some kind of sign? Or multiple signs? Something on the highway pointing this way? Grand opening? Nothing.

Two pickups are parked near the door. A raggedy-dressed man and a sunflower-masked woman in what I swear is a Tinkerbelle costume stand outside the door smoking. They watch me as I pull out my music. Maybe the crowd came on foot. Or in a bus.

I wave and walk past them into the gallery.

Wait. Gallery? It's more like a thrift shop or a rummage sale. As I beeline toward the upright piano near the back, I pass crocheted booties, duck decoys, paintings that remind me of paint-by-number art, fused glass plates, tote bags, and unmatched tables and chairs. The hand-painted jackets hanging near the window are pretty, but how long would they last in this weather?

I'm the only person here. Oh, excuse me, I missed the ancient border collie sleeping near the door to what I assume is a restroom. There's a kitchen area in the back, but I see no sign of refreshments. Is this the right day?

The piano, at least a century old, towers over me when I sit on the hard wooden bench and play a scale.

It's out of tune. Maybe I'll get used to it? I doubt it. I'm quirky that way. Bad notes physically hurt. My piano at home is just a little off, but I'm going to have it tuned as soon as COVID allows.

I'm leaning over the piano, testing the yellowed keys, when the Tinkerbelle woman swishes in.

"Hi, I'm Sonia Sunflower. Are you PD?"

Now might be a good time to lie and get the heck out of here. *Nope, not me. PD? Who's that?* But I can't. My mother raised me with a conscience.

"Yes. Nice to meet you. Am I too early?"

"No, right on time. Feel free to make yourself comfortable and start playing."

"But there's nobody to hear it."

"They'll come." She floats away.

I'm supposed to be here from 11 to 2. I might as well see if I can play this thing.

Hmm. Very honky-tonk. This will not do for Handel or Chopin, not that I was going to play the heavy classics. Maybe some jazz, easy listening, light rock, plus my originals. I should have prepared something from the Roaring Twenties. Barroom songs from old cowboy movies. I could practice my Between the Bridges songs. If nobody's listening, it's all practice. I open my notebook and begin.

"That's beautiful," Sonia Sunflower says, then turns her attention to her phone. "No. No. I said no. You cannot drive the fucking car."

Such language for a Tinkerbelle—or a sunflower.

"Damned kids," she mutters, paying absolutely no attention to me and my music as she punches in numbers and talks to someone else, getting progressively louder.

I don't know whether to play harder or give up.

Tinkerbelle goes outside. Cigarette smoke and voices drift through the open door. A couple of older ladies come in. Good. An audience. I play my best. I sing one of my songs about Ona Beach, waves going in, waves going out, etc. But they're talking about tote bags.

It's as if I'm a freaking radio. Wait till I see that Lizzy again. She's the one who got me into this.

A few more people show up, one with a kid who questions why anybody would want to buy this stuff. Amen, son.

Tinkerbelle tinkers with some of the displays.

I check my watch. Forty-five minutes in, all the customers gone, I stand and walk around, stretching, looking at the art. I've got a stiff neck from looking up at the music from the too-low bench.

A flock of parrots made out of plastic dishes reminds me of Donovan's art. At least his is real art, not these things half a step up from yard sale fodder.

As I'm checking the price on a tote bag with a piano embroidered on it, I notice Tinkerbelle—Sonia Sunflower, whatever—putting on her coat.

"PD," she says. "I'm going to lock up while I go home for lunch. You'll have to leave while I'm gone."

"I don't understand. What if people come? What time will you be back? Do you want me to start again in an hour or what?"

She waves her hand in the air. "If you want to. It's all good. Thanks for coming."

She waits for me to put on my coat and leave.

Without another word, she summons her dog, locks the door, gets into her car, lights a cigarette, and drives away.

I'm all dressed up with nowhere to go. The few people who passed through don't even know who I am. Nobody asked. Tinkerbelle didn't say, although she could have. "Our music today is provided by PD Soares." She could have put up a little sign or something. Nope.

I got less attention than that poor old dog sleeping in the corner.

I'm not coming back. What's the point?

I drive across the highway to Seal Rock State Park and stand at the overlook where Maryann and Dakota got married. That was a beautiful day. Sunshine and happiness. Today, the gray air blends with the gray ocean. Everything is gray, and it's cold. The frothy tide is high, covering almost all the sand, so there's nowhere to walk.

I'm not alone in this parking lot. A young man and woman are making out in a blue Toyota a few spaces over.

Tom and I made out in cars, too. We'd lean across the brake lever and touch lips and tongues, and I'd start feeling excited all over, and . . . you know.

With Tom in the driver's seat, I felt safe and part of a couple, a family. Now, wherever I go, I'm just one aging woman with stupid red hair trying to be a musician. At this rate, I'm never going to be more than a hospital clerk and a church piano player. I'll be alone watching everybody else play with their kids and grandkids. When I get old, and my parents are gone, I hope Andy's kids will remember old aunt PD and send her a Christmas card.

I don't think that couple is coming apart for air anytime soon.

That piano was awful. Pretty on the outside with lots of fancy scrollwork, but what made Sunflower think anyone would want to play it? Am I too fussy?

Great, now I'm crying. Why don't I have tissues in my purse?

Here comes an older couple in a motorhome. Why would anyone go camping in December? But they do look happy.

I'm going home.

Tess's SUV is parked in my space. Damn it. Doesn't she have a home of her own? When she's not fighting fires, she runs a pet-grooming business. Shouldn't she be working on Saturdays?

She and Dakota are laughing at the table over empty plates with smears of catsup and French fry remnants.

"Hi, PD," Tess says.

Dakota looks peeved. "I didn't expect you home."

"It ended early. I don't want to go into details. Is there any food left?"

"PD, we're sorry," Tess says. "We didn't think you'd be here, so we just got lunches for the two of us at the seafood place by the bridge. I love their fish and chips."

Tess does look sorry, I'll give her that. But she also has that post-love glow on her stupid beautiful face. They must have showered after. Her terrific upswept hair, like mine except it's perfect and the gray hairs look like highlights, looks damp around the edges.

"They didn't have any food where I was." I go to my room, close the door and change into my jeans and sweatshirt. I need a walk.

As I'm tying my shoes, my phone dings with a text. Britt. Finally.

PD, call me. We have to talk.

This does not sound good.

And it isn't.

She answers her phone right away. "Brittpix Productions. Hello, PD."

"I have been trying to reach you for months."

"I know. Sooo busy. Just slammed. I'm doing a series of how-to films for Acme Hardware."

"Really. Like what?"

"How to operate a chainsaw safely, how to care for your lawnmower, what to do about gopher holes, stuff like that. They provide all the talent and the scripts. I don't know much about this stuff, but I'm sure learning. Did you know lawnmowers have spark plugs? Anyway, how are you doing? I heard there was a fire."

"Yeah, there was. We had some damage, but we're okay. Listen, I need to talk to you about getting a contract for this Between the Bridges music project. Just to be clear about who's doing what and to protect ourselves if any questions arise."

She's silent for a minute before coming back sounding much less friendly. "Okay, you mentioned that in one of your emails. Here's the thing. I can't sign a contract with you."

"Why not?"

"I think you misunderstood what was happening. I'm considering music from other artists, not just you. When it's time, I'll pick what works best for me."

"What? Are you kidding?"

"PD, that's how this business works."

"No, I don't think it is."

"Look, I'm a professional. You're new to this. I have to keep my options open just in case, you know, the music doesn't work."

I want to curse loud enough to blow off the new roof, but I'm trying to salvage something of this project and my dignity. If only I could keep my voice from wobbling. "But you liked what I sent you before. What am I supposed to do with all these songs and all this instrumental music I've composed?"

"You can send it to me. I'll listen. I just can't promise anything."

I want to scream, "You bitch!" I want to scream, "F-you. I wouldn't give you my music if, well I don't know, if something," but by the cool tone of her voice I know it would only hurt my case. Without anything in writing, I have nothing to stand on.

I'm almost 20 years older than she is. How could I be so stupid?

"PD? Are you still there?"

"I'm here."

"I'm sure your music is beautiful. Plug your keyboard into your computer, record it, and send it to me so we can see if you're going in the right direction."

"I don't have an electronic keyboard."

"Maybe you can rent one from a music store."

"We don't have a music store here."

"I'm sure you can acquire one somehow. That's all I can tell you right now. This project is taking longer than I expected, especially with the new hardware gig, and frankly, I'm running out of grant money. But that's show biz. I've got to go. Call me any time."

She hangs up, and I throw myself face down on the bed, whispering curses. I want to beat something to a pulp.

I don't know how to absorb this. It's not fair. But I should not have needed Trevor to tell me I needed a contract. I should have demanded my rights from the get-go. I trusted that bitch.

Now I have no lunch, no gig, no contract, no Christmas ornaments, and oh, shit, is that rain on the roof?

Just shoot me, okay?

Sirens scream from the highway. More fire? Come on, God. I open my door. Tess is gone. I guess she got called in.

"You okay, PD?" Dakota asks.

"No. Is there a fire?"

"Medical assistance in South Beach." She puts down her dish towel. "What's wrong?"

"Britt is considering other options for the music for her film."

"But you're local. Who else can write songs that really feel like this place?"

"Not some guy in LA, that's for sure. Trevor, Donovan's son, warned me I should have a written contract. When I pushed Britt on it, she ghosted me for months, and now she says she can't commit to working with me. She's considering other artists." I pull bread, cheese and mayonnaise out of the fridge. "I'm starving."

"What happened at the gallery?"

"It wasn't even a gallery. It was a glorified yard sale. The piano was horrible, and there was no audience. At noon, the owner said she was going to lunch, and I'd have to get lost until she came back. So, I came home. I'm done. End of story."

"Oh, PD. Don't you sometimes wish you were still 25 and stupid?"

"Hell, I'm almost 45, and I'm still stupid." I slap my sandwich together and take a bite, then open it up and add mustard. I wolf it down standing up and wish I had a beer to go with it. No beer here. Dad has some, but I can't face him today. Him and Diana. Why is everybody two by two except me?

The way things are going, I might as well change my name back to Cissy, put my gray hair in a bun, and go raise goats, maybe knit their wool into shawls. My parents will die. I'll get old. I'll collect postcards from Janey in New York and baby pictures from my brother. People will call me The Witch.

Rocky will die and break my heart.

He's watching me from the door, worry in his caramel-colored eyes. I put on my slicker, hat, and gloves and grab his leash. "Come on. Let's get out of here."

By the time we reach the road, I hear hammering from the new garage. Dakota is in her happy place. With everything burnt, I wonder what she'll put on all those shelves.

Shoot. It's raining too hard. When I pull Rocky back toward the driveway, he doesn't resist. "Want to watch a movie, boy? Maybe I can find some popcorn."

He runs into the house ahead of me, leaving muddy paw prints on the floor.

I am not enjoying this day.

As THE MOVIE CREDITS roll two hours later, my phone buzzes with a text message from an unfamiliar area code. Arizona. The only person I know from there is Trevor. Is something wrong with Donovan?

Hey PD. Did you ask about the contract for your music?

This is more than a text conversation. But I answer by text anyway. *You were right. She said no contract, can't commit, considering other artists.*

Wow. I'm sorry. Are you ready to put it all online?

He's a tad pushy, isn't he? *Not yet. I'm going to polish it up and force Britt to listen to it. Maybe on Zoom or Skype, I don't know.*

We could record a presentation with multiple tracks, photos, text, whatever, really dress it up.

We could, but I want to go old-school for now. Just the music. How is your dad?

Fine. Busy. Seeing someone.

Why does my heart drop? *That's nice. Tell him I said hi. I have to go now.*

I slam my fist into the wall. "God damn it!" Startled, Rocky jumps off the bed as Dakota peeks in.

"What's going on, PD? Killing spiders?" Tess is standing behind her, looking concerned. I guess her medical call didn't take long.

"No," I say, rubbing my sore hand. "Donovan is dating someone."

"Well, that's okay, isn't it? You're not dating him." She turns to Tess. "Donovan is her booze."

"Aha. I have had relationships like that. Not healthy to be with them, but you can't let 'em go."

"He's all right," I say. "Trevor is bugging me to publish my music online with all kinds of video and other elaborate stuff."

"Why not?"

"It's not ready, Dakota, and I haven't given up on Britt yet."

"You trust too much, PD."

Tess butts in. "I say good for you. Do it when you're ready. I brought some chocolate cake. Who wants some?"

"Not me. It stopped raining. I think I need another walk."

Dakota looks doubtful. "Now? It's dark."

Is it? The sun sets so early around here in the winter. "So it is, but I have to get out of here. Come on, Rocky."

He looks a little doubtful, too, but wags his tail as I hook on his leash.

Once we leave the lights at the house, it's so dark I feel blind. I click on my cell phone light. We stick to the road, heading south toward the waterfall and where the barn burned. I find a rock to sit on and listen to the rain-swollen creek running hard and loud. Rocky tugs, but I'm not letting him loose out here.

The cold air is refreshing, my breath coming out as vapor. If we sit here long, we'll freeze, but I had to get outside for a while.

I know I'm not dating Donovan anymore, but I hate that he is dating someone else. I wonder if his new girlfriend knows about his illness and his history. I'm not even sure Trevor knows. People might assume he's colorful, an artist. Which he is. But he's bipolar, has tried to kill himself more than once, and goes bat-shit nuts when he's off his meds. Not to mention his diabetes is tricky to manage. I want to tell her, whoever she is, what she's getting into.

Shit, I want to take care of him. I want to be the one hugging his big old self.

Whiskey, PD. He's your whiskey. What if I like whiskey?

Then there's the whole music thing. I didn't start writing music until a couple years ago. Now there's all this pressure to compete, to make a big deal out of it. I'm still learning. What if I say it's just mine, and I don't have to do anything with it? I don't have to share it with Britt or anyone else. At church last Sunday, the gospel said we're not supposed to hide our light under a bushel basket. I don't intend to, but I'm not sure what to do with it.

My God, I have a niece. Donni. I want to see her, hold her, and study her. I should be in Santa Cruz to welcome her. She'll be walking and talking before this stupid plague ends.

Then there's Eugenia—

Rocky stands, his ears wide open. "Woof," he says softly.

I listen for critters rattling in the bushes. It's time to go home. Maybe I will have some chocolate cake. "Rocky, come." He resists for a second, sniffing the air and looking around, then gives in to the pressure on his leash. As we head back up the road to the rainbow house, I sing, hoping to let any animals lurking around know I'm here and not to be messed with. "Swing low, sweet chariot, coming for to carry me home . . ."

39. Day in Court

IN THE HALLWAY outside Courtroom 2, Janey and I sit on hard wooden benches waiting to be called in for Eugenia's hearing. Witnesses aren't allowed to hear what the other witnesses say before they testify.

Janey sips from a mocha latte she picked up at the Starbucks drive-through. My mouth is dry, but I don't think I could digest anything.

It's a colorful group out here in the hallway. At least they're all wearing masks and keeping their distance from us and from each other.

"That one looks like a drug dealer." Janey nods toward a scrawny guy with a greasy brown ponytail.

"Not so loud. You might be right. Or he could be a murderer."

"No, he'd be in jail clothes then, and they wouldn't let him out in the hall."

"Right. Is that his mother?" I point to the pudgy gray-haired woman standing beside the "drug dealer."

"His supplier."

I can't help laughing. "I don't think so. She looks like a mom. What about that well-dressed man pacing over there?"

"Drunk driving. Not his first offense."

"How do you know?"

She watches the drug dealer crouch to retie his shoe. "My dad had some problems in that area."

"Oh, I didn't know that."

"Yep. Uncle D. too, of course."

"Did Donovan ever get arrested?"

"Once. He called Mom in the middle of the night to bail him out."

"Did she?"

"Nope. They released him in the morning. Took his license away for six months. Jack—your dad—doesn't drink too much, does he?"

"My father? No. He drinks a few beers now and then or a celebratory cocktail, but no. I have never seen him drunk."

"That's good."

She gets busy with her phone, while I lean back and close my eyes.

We have been sitting here over an hour when a bailiff opens the courtroom door. "Jane Peacock," he calls.

"That's me."

"Break a leg."

"Please silence your phone, Miss," he says before escorting her in.

Pins and needles dance in my stomach. I wish I could hear what was going on.

Fifteen minutes later, the bailiff summons me. "Priscilla Soares."

Breathe, PD, breathe.

Next to the witness chair on a big video screen, I see Eugenia sitting beside a young-looking man. Her long hair is gone, cut to a short bob. She wears a heavy white sweater over a tailored green dress, and she's wearing a little lipstick and mascara. She's not as old as I thought she was. A newspaper article listed her age as 63. She definitely doesn't look like a witch now, more like everybody's grandmother, but her lips sag a little on the left side, and her face is so pale it almost glows.

The bailiff interrupts my staring, nudging me to swear to tell the truth and sit in the witness chair. The judge, a red-faced older man enclosed behind Plexiglas much like our windows at the hospital, is way up high to my right.

As the DA approaches, her belly even bigger than before, our eyes meet for a second, but then I see someone else in the nearly empty courtroom that makes me gasp out loud. Gabriel is sitting in the back row. Masked, hair tied back, dressed in a button-up white shirt and blue slacks, he looks very different. I try and fail to catch his eye as Ms. Jankosky clears her throat.

"Ms. Soares, people usually call you PD, is that correct?"

"Yes."

"A family nickname or your choice or how did that come to be?"

"I chose it when I left Montana to start a new life after my husband died."

"I see. Did Eugenia Renner call you PD?"

"Yes."

"And you were friends?"

"Yes."

"Well, I have a few questions for you about your interactions with Mrs. Renner and her family."

"Okay."

They're the same questions as before, and my answers have not changed. Eugenia seemed frightened. Yes, I saw the little boy in the window. Seeing Gabriel leads me to add that our mutual friend, a homeless guy named Gabriel, told me Louis had threatened to kill him if he said anything about what was happening at the house.

"Who are you referring to when you speak of this Gabriel?"

I point to the bleached-Jesus man in the back row.

She turns toward the judge. "Your honor, I believe she is referring to Jonathan Petersen, one of our earlier witnesses."

The judge nods. "Noted."

"On the day Mr. Renner and his mother were arrested, the day he allegedly assaulted you, what caused you to go there?"

"I was concerned about Eugenia. My housemate and I had seen the Amber Alert and were afraid she was involved somehow."

"Why is that?"

"We had seen a little boy looking out the window, and he looked like the boy in the picture. I wanted to see what was what before we called 911. Maybe we were completely wrong."

"Why didn't you let law enforcement take care of it?"

Good question, PD. "I don't know. She's my friend."

"Would you have helped her avoid arrest?"

"No. I—I'm not sure what I would have done. I didn't want her to be in trouble."

"You do know that if you helped her conceal the boy, you would be guilty of a crime."

Is my face as red as it feels? "Yes."

"Did that occur to you then?"

"Not at all. Sometimes my desire to help jumps ahead of my common sense." Why is Janey, seated halfway back on the other side, making faces at me? I have to tell the truth.

"Let's go back to your confrontation with Mr. Renner. You said he tried to strangle you."

"Yes. He got violent with me. Luckily the sheriff's deputies arrived in time to stop him."

"This wasn't your first time being attacked."

Oh God. "No. I was almost raped last year when I was walking home from work. I was injured and he was strong, but I was able to fight the man off. This time, Louis had me pinned down. I couldn't move."

"That must have been terrifying. Is your assailant from last year in custody now?"

"No. He was never charged with a crime. And yes, it was terrifying."

"Thank you. No further questions."

On the big screen, Eugenia's eyes sparkle with tears. I'm sorry she has to deal with all this.

Gabriel/Jonathan is staring at me. I wonder what he thinks. And how does he happen to be here looking so, so normal? Did his father have anything to do with it?

The public defender adjusts his mask as he approaches the bench, toeing a taped line six feet from the witness stand. "Ms. Soares, how long have you known Eugenia Renner?"

"Since last May. My dog got loose and ended up at her place."

"How would you describe her living situation?"

"Rustic. Bare bones. She grows most of her food, gets her water from a well. She has no telephone, TV, or Internet. She doesn't even have a car."

"I see. And she lives alone?"

"Yes. Until her son and grandson came."

"You used to visit her?"

"Yes. I enjoyed her company. We're both musicians, and sometimes we would sing together. She always offered refreshments. It was relaxing being with her, especially after my hectic days working at the hospital."

"At the admissions desk, is that correct?"

"Yes."

"I suppose you see all kinds of people every day."

"I do. Especially now."

"Did Mrs. Renner ever speak of her children?"

I look at Eugenia. She looks away from the camera. "No. I asked about them shortly after we met. She got upset and asked me to leave."

"What did you think about that?"

"I didn't know what to think. It was strange. Now that I know more about the situation with her two sons, I understand why she wouldn't want to talk about them. But I was puzzled and a little hurt then."

A tear trickles down her face and leaves a dark wet spot on her dress.

"How did you meet Jonathon Petersen, the man you know as Gabriel?"

"I was walking my dog, and he came out of the trees. He had been camping there and was looking for a place to stay."

"Were you afraid of him?"

"At first. But I soon learned that he is a gentle soul."

"Did you offer him a campsite?"

"No. I was not comfortable with that. But Eugenia did. He was helping take care of things on her property until Louis came."

"And sent him packing."

"Yes."

"Did Jonathan Petersen tell you about the boy?"

"No. He said he couldn't say anything about what was happening at Eugenia's place because Louis would kill him."

"And Mrs. Renner didn't say anything either."

"No."

"Let me ask you this. Would you trust Mrs. Renner with your own little boy?"

"I don't have any children."

"That's unfortunate. But if you did?"

I fix my eyes on Eugenia. "Yes, I would. I would totally trust her."

"Thank you, Ms. Soares. You are excused."

"You are welcome to remain in the courtroom now that your testimony is over," the judge says.

"Thank you." I take a seat next to Janey.

The testimony doesn't go on much longer. A social worker affirms that the boy, Daniel Renner, appeared to be clean, healthy, and well-cared for. A therapist says Eugenia showed signs of fear and trauma when they met. A doctor testifies that x-rays showed she had several healed bone breaks. She also had a black eye that was still healing when she suffered her stroke, which paralyzed her left side. She is making progress in her recovery and may be able to return home in a few weeks.

Eugenia is called to testify last. Judging by the flowered wallpaper in the background, she is speaking from the rehab facility. I think I see the handles of her walker beside her. She stares at the computer, possibly the first one she has ever seen up close.

The judge has a computer screen open on his desk so he can see what we all see. His face appears in a small box on the screen next to Eugenia and her companion.

The bailiff swears her in, and the DA asks her to identify herself. Her speech is slurred and she can't say her R's. Sometimes she stutters. But she's determined to speak. I close my eyes and pray she can do this.

The DA begins.

"Mrs. Renner, I know this is difficult for you, so we will keep it short. Before this recent, shall we say visit, when was the last time you saw your grandson, Daniel Renner?"

"I-I-I never saw him before that."

"Never?"

"No. He lived in-in-in La Grande with his mother."

"Where was your son?"

"He was in prison."

"He was serving an eight-year sentence for manslaughter for the murder of his brother Steven, whom he killed by hitting him over the head with a shovel. Is that correct?"

She nods.

"I'm sorry. I need a verbal response."

"Yes."

"Did you know he was going to take his son away from his mother?"

"No," she says. "I didn't know."

"What would you have told him if you did know?"

"Don't do it. Leave the boy alone."

"Didn't you want to see your own grandson?"

She chokes back tears. "I did."

"But you wouldn't kidnap him?"

"No."

"Were you surprised when Louis showed up at your house?"

She nods.

"Ma'am."

"Sorry. I was s-s-s-stunned."

"Were you afraid of your son, Mrs. Renner?"

She brushes away a tear. "Yes. He was violent—like his father."

"Your husband was abusive?"

"Yes. That's why I left him."

"Back to the current situation. Louis wasn't at your house every minute, was he?"

"No."

"Why didn't you call someone when he was away from the house?"

"I have no telephone. I was afraid he would kill me."

"Have you talked to him since his arrest?"

"No."

"Do you want to?"

"No. Never. He—he is not my son anymore."

"Thank you."

The defense attorney takes over, asking basically the same questions and getting the same answers.

My stomach growls.

Janey whispers, "Me too. I'm starving."

It's 1:15, well past lunchtime. I sense they want to complete all the testimony before taking a break.

"Mrs. Renner, you say you were afraid your son would hurt you. Was Danny also afraid of him?"

"He was."

"Did you ever see Louis hit him?"

"Once. I tried to stop him. He knocked me down."

"Is that how you got the black eye?"

"Yes."

"You had a stroke shortly after you and your son were arrested. How are you feeling these days, physically I mean?"

"Getting better."

"I'm glad. Do you think the stress of this situation with Louis and Danny caused the stroke?"

She shrugs her left shoulder. "I-I-I don't know. Maybe."

"That's all I have. Thank you."

Court is adjourned until tomorrow morning. The screen goes blank, the judge heads out his door, and we go out ours.

It's raining.

Gabriel bolts from the building and is out of sight before we can ask him how he got out of jail and where he's staying now. And if he saw his father. We'll find out eventually, I guess.

Janey and I look at each other. "Mickey D's?" she asks.

"Perfect. Let's take my car."

We pull off our masks and wolf down French fries on our way to the parking lot at Nye Beach, then sit in the Jeep eating our burgers as waves froth beyond the rain-streaked windows. The wind blows the car so hard if feels like we're sitting on a boat at sea.

Janey points a French fry at my face mask collection hanging from the gear shift. "You got enough masks?"

"Almost. I like to match my outfits."

"Makes sense. A face without a mask is so 2019."

"I know, right."

When we have eaten enough to feel sane again, Janey sucks chocolate milkshake through her straw and sighs. "That was fun, wasn't it?"

"A blast."

"Did you ever go to court before?"

"Ages ago for my first divorce. There wasn't much to it. We had no kids or property to fight over. We just wanted it done. I also served on a jury once in Missoula."

"What kind of case?"

"Drunk driving with an injury. I forget the exact term."

"You mean he crashed and someone got hurt?"

"Yes. She. The defendant was a college student. Just a kid."

"Did you find her guilty?"

"We did. But she didn't serve any more jail time. She got probation, a fine, and a suspended license, and she had to attend a program for alcoholics."

"Sounds about right. What do you think will happen to Eugenia?"

"We're probably not supposed to discuss the case," I tell her.

"Who cares? We're done testifying. I don't see how they could find her guilty of anything."

"I agree, but she did know about the kidnapping and didn't tell anyone or do anything. She could have told Dakota or the guy who delivers her groceries. She could even have whispered it to me or you, and we could have called the law."

"Louis would have killed us both then."

"Hush." I stash my empty wrappers in the McDonald's bag. "Let's look at the ocean for a minute and relax."

Janey's not good at sitting quietly. She makes it maybe 30 seconds. "What's the deal with Gabriel?"

"I don't know."

"Where did he get those clothes?"

"Janey, I don't know any more than you do."

"We don't have to go to the courthouse tomorrow, do we?"

"No. We can, I guess, but I'm going to work."

"Me too. I don't earn any tips sitting in the courtroom."

"I think they'll pay us for mileage."

"Eight miles. Woohoo."

"It would buy one of your lattes. Shall we head home?"

"Sure. Drop me off at my car."

From the courthouse parking lot, we caravan across the bridge.

The rainbow house should be empty for at least another hour before Dakota comes home. I can work on my songs without an audience. I want to send them to Britt before she makes any decisions. I think they're good, but I need to make sure they're the best I can do. Maybe I'll record them on my phone and see if they sound as good as I think they should.

But I can't stop seeing Eugenia on that big screen, looking so beat-up and sad.

The thought of her lying in bed unable to move or speak or get help horrifies me. God knows how long she went without food or water. I wonder if this business with Louis and Danny and being arrested brought it on. That's a lot of stress for someone used to a quiet life in the woods.

How is she paying for rehab? I look at insurance information all day long, and I can tell you Medicare doesn't cover that kind of care for very long.

What if I'm alone when I get older and have a stroke or something and no one knows? Will someone show up to find me? Who? Will I have to wear one of those alert buttons around my neck? Will I have enough money to hire help? Will I have to move in with my brother and his happy family?

I can't answer any of these questions. Forget the music. I need a nap.

40. Giving Testimony

Tuesday, Jan. 26, 2021

I'M STARING AT A hospital waiting room full of patients who have all been checked in when my phone buzzes with a text from Janey. Eugenia has been found not guilty of all charges. The judge said she was a victim, not a criminal. It was on the local radio news, that baby boomer station Janey's Mom listens to.

Thank God. I want to run to the rehab place and hug Eugenia.

But I can't. A man is standing so close to the Plexiglas his breath fogs it up.

"How much longer? I have been sitting here for over an hour. I'm in pain. Don't you understand that?"

"I do. I'm sorry, sir. I'll ask where you are in the line."

"Please do."

Jackson, on the phone, rolls his eyes as I slide off my chair and into the ER. All the beds are full; doctors and nurses are moving full-throttle. I signal the head nurse, who rushes over. "What's up, PD. We're slammed."

"I know. I'm sorry. I've got a very anxious man in pain who wants to know how much longer."

"Name?"

"McKenzie."

She checks her computer. "I'll bring him in next."

"Thanks."

When I come out, he's leaning on the counter, breathing hard.

"You will be next, sir."

"Great. I'm not sure I can wait. Oh God! Oh-oh-oh." He's bent over, gasping.

"Where does it hurt, sir?"

"My chest. My f-ing chest."

Jackson sees what's happening and runs for one of the wheelchairs we keep by the door while I run back into the ER.

"Mr. McKenzie is having a heart attack."

Thirty seconds later, orderlies have him on a gurney rolling through the double doors. Either Mr. McKenzie is a terrific actor, or his condition was allowed to worsen because we're so damned backed up and short-staffed.

Sometimes I really hate this job.

At least Eugenia's not going to jail. That's one good thing.

I still have to testify at Louis's trial, but this judge has ruled that because there are so many witnesses and this case is likely to last at least a week, the witnesses can testify remotely via computer. Works for me. I can duck into the conference room, testify on my laptop, and go back to work. I don't think I want to watch the whole gnarly week of jury selection, cross-examination, and Louis' ugly face. I wonder if his ex-wife is going to testify. I'd love to hear her side of things, but this isn't a TV show, and I've got work to do.

Wednesday, Feb. 3, 2021

A FEW MINUTES after the court clerk texts me, the district attorney sends me the Zoom link. I'm set up in the hospital conference room with the doors closed, hoping nobody needs it for an actual conference. I explained the situation to the woman who schedules use of the room, but I couldn't tell her exactly what time it would be. I brought a Bible from home, just in case, but the bailiff doesn't seem to care what I swear on, if anything. I'm going to tell the truth anyway.

I can see my face on the big screen behind the witness chair, along with the faces of the judge and the attorneys. I need another haircut. Or a hat. I've got wrinkles around my eyes. And there's my scar snaking out the top of my mask. Is it really that visible? I'd never want to be an actress magnified huge on a movie screen. People could see everything. I think

I'm attractive enough, but not for this kind of magnification. Anyway, today I'm rooting for the district attorney, who in her purple dress looks even more pregnant than she did the last time I saw her. I hope her water doesn't break in the courtroom.

Her questions are pretty much what you would expect. What did I know? What did I see? What did Louis say? What did he do? Did I feel my life was in danger?

Sure did.

Things get trickier with the defense attorney, a different one than Eugenia had. He's a short bulldog of a man with a Midwest accent, and he goes after me right away.

"Ms. Soares, you know Mr. Renner is charged with kidnapping his own son?"

"Yes."

"His own son."

"Yes."

"Does that make any sense to you?"

"Objection," shouts the DA.

"Sustained," says the judge. "Please move on, counselor."

"Ms. Soares, when was the first time you saw little Daniel Renner?"

"Fourth of July. I saw him looking out the window at the house. When he noticed me, he ran away."

"I see. Was he playing hide and seek?"

"I don't know."

"Where was his father?"

"I don't know."

"But he wasn't there at that time?"

"No."

"The boy was free to leave. How could he have been kidnapped?"

"He was a very young boy in a house in the woods with no idea where he was."

"If you knew he was there, why didn't you do something?"

"I didn't know the circumstances until we saw the Amber alert."

"The public notice of a missing child?"

"Yes. My housemate saw the notice at work—"

"Where does he work?"

"She."

"Oh. She."

"She's the postmistress for Seal Rock."

"That's Annabelle Wells, also known as Dakota?"

"Yes."

Well now, everybody knows your real name, Dakota, and they probably think we're a couple.

"That's when you decided to go to the Renner house?"

"Yes, I wanted to check on Eugenia."

"And tell her and her son to hide the boy?"

"No, it wasn't like that."

"What was it like?"

"I wanted to see if she was all right and see if this boy was actually the one they were looking for. I mean, maybe it was a perfectly normal situation of a different little boy visiting his grandmother."

"Did you really think that?"

"I didn't know."

"Did Louis Renner or anyone there tell you they had taken Daniel away from his mother illegally?"

"No. Louis was too busy trying to strangle me."

"I see."

I squint at the screen, trying to see Louis, but all I can see is the attorney's bulldog puss in my face.

"One last question, Ms. Soares. If your spouse was keeping you from seeing your son, wouldn't you do anything to be with him?"

I swallow the blockage in my throat. I know it's a trick question, but I'm not the one on trial, and I have to be honest. "I probably would."

"Thank you."

"You are excused," the judge says, and my screen goes blank.

I sit back. I'm sweating under my arms, under my breasts, pretty much everywhere. Why did I think I could go straight back to work after this? But Zelda, subbing for me while I testified, needs to go home to her babies.

"How did it go?" she asks, putting on her coat.

"Oh my God. I don't ever want to do that again."

"I hear you. Take some deep breaths, drink some water. I don't want you having a heart attack here."

I settle into the still-warm chair. "No. Just a little panic attack."

Jackson glances over. "We've got pills for that."

"Hush."

I wonder who's on the computer screen now, trapped like a bug under glass. Is Louis looking daggers at them, making plans to get even?

At least I feel safe at the hospital.

Except from the virus.

Okay. Back to work. "Next please."

41. The Family You Make

THE WAVES ARE white and wild this time of year. Loud. Angry. Whoosh. Boom! When I stop at Lost Creek State Park after work for an ocean fix, the water is almost up to the cliff. Much of the area that remains is covered with driftwood, seaweed and litter.

Wind rocks my car. The only other vehicle in the parking lot is a beat-up van with cardboard covering the windows.

Through the rain streaking down my windshield, I stare at the gray sky and gray ocean, seeking the slightest glimmer of sun. There is none.

Just before I left work, I got the news that Louis Renner, Jr. was found guilty of parental kidnapping, child endangerment, and assault. Sentencing will come later, but he's going away for a minimum of eight years, the DA said.

Thank God. But I feel for that little boy. He must be terribly confused. He's taken from his home by this man he barely knows who tells him he's his father, who says now you live with me, and this is your grandmother. He tells you to hide and not talk to anybody, and you can't go to school or go out and play. You can't even call your mom on the phone. If you let anybody see you, you'll get a beating. While you're in town, your grandmother is arrested. Then the cops come and drag your father away. How does a kid recover from that?

How does Eugenia get over seeing a grandson for the first time, then having him snatched away?

I'm still troubled by the defense attorney's question about what I would do if I were not allowed to see my own kid. The real answer is that I would have at least partial custody if not full custody because I'm not a criminal or a drunk or any other things that would bar me from spending time with my child. But if I really couldn't see my kid, I don't know what

I would do. Some people might say I couldn't possibly know because I'm not a mother. I don't think a mother would know either.

I'm just glad that case is over.

The COVID situation is improving, too. Here in Lincoln County, we're back to "low risk" for now. More and more people are being vaccinated. I'm still helping after work. Next week, we're starting on Dakota's age group, 50-55. Diana too. We'll all feel a lot safer when the people close to us are vaccinated. We can even take off our masks for a while.

Not that the pandemic is over. Health officials are talking about a new variant that might be resistant to the vaccine. I suspect it's never going to go away completely.

On the happier side of things, I got to have a video visit on my computer with Andy's baby last night. She's gorgeous. Her skin is light, but she has curly black hair and dimples. Cutest baby ever. At five weeks, she doesn't do much, but I think she smiled at me when I sang "Jeremiah was a bullfrog." A minute later, she started crying, and Andy ended the call. My brother had bags under his eyes and hadn't combed his hair. Apparently, nobody's getting much sleep at their house, but Mom, aka Grandma Pauline, has broken her COVID isolation to help, so that's something.

I hope Andy and Shari are letting Dad talk to the baby, too. He deserves to see his first grandchild.

Back at the beach, it's starting to get dark. I should probably go home.

TESS IS HERE. Parked in my space again. But what is she doing by the piano?

Once inside, I see she's reading the lyrics of the song I wrote the other day, "Eugenia's Song."

As Rocky rushes me and jumps up for a full-body hug and kiss, Tess looks up.

"PD, these lyrics are beautiful. How does the song go?"

She wants me to sing it right now? I'm pooped, and I need to use the restroom. At this point, letting anyone hear these songs is like showing them the inside of my skin. But I'm going to have to let them out eventually. I hang my coat by the door and sit on the piano bench. I haven't written any formal notation for this song yet, just a lead sheet with chords and some notes to cue me. I close my eyes, clear my throat, and begin. "Floating among the pines, a voice . . ."

When I finish, even the dog is quiet. Tess sniffs back a tear. "That is so beautiful. I mean, wow. You have so much talent."

"God deserves the credit. Not me."

"Wherever it comes from, it takes my breath away."

"Thank you."

Now that I have a minute to breathe, I notice the white bags on the counter and Dakota pulling out plates. "Dinner?"

"The Noodle House reopened. Tess brought takeout."

"I hope you like Asian food."

"I love it." I'm starting to like this Tess woman. She loves dogs, brings dinner, and likes my songs. I found out last week at the vaccination clinic that she's 58. No wonder she seems so motherly. I wonder if she has any children. A question for another day.

Dakota lays forks and knives next to the plates on the table. She's not a chopstick girl. As I sit in my usual place on the side facing the door, I notice a folder next to her seat across from me. "What's that?"

She looks like I caught her doing something wrong, but Tess seems happy. "Dakota is going to train to be a volunteer firefighter like me."

"Really?"

"Really," Dakota says. "That fire scared the shit out of me. Next time, I want to know what to do and be one of the people helping to put it out."

"Makes sense."

"You want to sign up, PD?"

"No. Sorry. I'm already overloaded. Besides, we need to restart the Between the Bridges help gatherings."

Dakota nods, her mouth full of noodles.

"I think I heard about that," Tess says. "You gather resources for people who need housing, food, or whatever."

"Yes. Maryann started it after the tsunami, but there's still a big need."

"I know. I'm sure those people who lost their homes in the fire could use your help."

"Definitely." I busy myself with sweet and sour pork for a minute, washing it down with hot tea from the green pot Maryann loved. "I think it's great you're going to be a firefighter, Dakota. You're perfect for it."

"We don't just fight fires," Tess says. "We go out on medical calls, respond to car accidents—"

"Rescue cats stuck in trees."

"Right."

"Where does the training take place?"

"A lot of it will be on Zoom due to COVID, but then she'll do the practical part here or at the station in Newport."

"How long does it take?"

Dakota answers, "Eighty hours for the original certification. More if I want to rise to higher levels or become an EMT. One step at a time."

"How often would you be called?"

"Depends on what's happening," Tess says. "We can put ourselves off duty and unavailable if we have a doctor's appointment or something, but they want us to respond whenever we can."

"Well, I admire you guys."

Tess pats my hand. "I wish I had your talent."

Okay, we all admire each other, and we're one big gang of superwomen. Pass the fortune cookies.

Mine says, "Fame awaits." No kidding. I hope they're right. Meanwhile, I volunteer to do the dishes.

After watching the news on TV, Tess and Dakota retire to the bedroom. Soon I hear muffled giggles and gasps. I don't want to hear that. I take my harmonica out to the porch, Rocky settling at my feet.

He looks up at me, wisdom in his caramel eyes. He knows things have changed. There's a new dog in the pack.

I'm playing a medley of church songs when Rocky barks.

"What is it? Elk?"

Human footsteps sound on the gravel road below.

As quietly as I can, I creep past the cars to where I can see. Dark as it is, I recognize Gabriel's blond hair reflecting in the moonlight. I scramble down, Rocky at my heels.

"Hey, Gabriel!"

He stops. "Oh. PD. Hello." He bends and rubs his right ankle. Instead of his usual sandals, he's wearing the dress shoes he wore to court.

"Where are you going?"

"Eugenia's house. If I can make it that far. I walked all the way from Newport, and I twisted my ankle on the gravel section on the way up here."

"That's what? Eight miles?"

"Something like that."

"Where's all your stuff? Did you leave it at Eugenia's?"

"No. They took it."

"Who? The people at the jail?"

"No. Those guys I was camping with. While I was at the courthouse, they stole everything that didn't burn up in the fire. I have nothing, PD. But Jesus told his apostles *don't take anything with you, not even an extra cloak.*"

He limps a step toward Rocky to pet him. Wearing only his court clothes and a thin jacket, the man is shivering. The temperature is supposed to go down to the twenties tonight.

"Why don't you come up to the house and rest? I can make you some hot chocolate or something."

His eyes shine with tears. "That would be nice. I used to think most people were good, but now evil seems to have taken over. I keep asking the Lord for help and nothing happens. But maybe he sent me to you tonight."

"Maybe. Come on. Can I help you walk? Get you something to use as a crutch?"

"I'll be all right. I'd better stay on the porch though. I don't think Dakota wants me in her house."

"That's crazy. After what you did for me? But she does have company right now, so maybe, yeah. I'll run ahead and start the hot chocolate."

Well, this is a change of plans, I think as I hurry up the steps and into the house, listening for activity from the bedroom. All I hear is soft snoring.

I microwave hot water and stir in chocolate powder. In a few minutes, I'm back on the porch with Gabriel, who huddles in his coat.

"Here you go."

He accepts the mug with both hands. "You are kind. What one does for the least of these, you do for me."

"It's just instant hot chocolate. Sorry we don't have any marshmallows."

"They're full of preservatives anyway." He flexes his foot and winces.

"Is your ankle swollen?"

He nods.

"Why don't you put your leg up on the other chair? I'll sit on the steps."

He groans and maneuvers his foot up. The sole of his shoe is slick. It would be easy to slip on these gravel roads.

"Can I get you an ice pack?"

"No. I'm already freezing."

"Well, maybe a blanket." I grab the granny-square afghan off the couch and drape it over his bony legs.

"Thank you." He looks up at the sky. "Angels are watching us."

"Uh-huh." I don't see angels. I see clouds closing in on the moon.

My first sip of hot chocolate burns the tip of my tongue. I set my cup on the step to cool. "Gabriel, I was surprised to see you in the courtroom. I thought you were in jail."

"I was. Horrible place. Evil emanating from the walls and floors."

"How did you get out?"

"Oh. The Good Lord talked to the judge and made him realize the other men were the ones who started the fire." He gulps his hot chocolate.

I try my cup again. It's cool enough. "What happened?"

"I was off answering the call of nature when I heard them hollering, and then they told me to run. That's when I smelled the smoke. Denny, that was the bigger guy, smoked cigarettes, and he had this red lighter he always carried in his shoe. As we were running, he took that lighter out and threw it far away. The firefighters found it later."

"But there are lots of red lighters, aren't there?"

"This one had his initials carved into it."

"Oh."

"Did you tell the judge about all that?"

"Yes. The sheriff remembered I had my fly open when they arrested me. I didn't have time to zip up as we ran from the fire."

"Wow. Did they charge the other guys?"

"Just the one. Denny. They had no evidence to hold Mutt, so he took off. The lawyer asked me to stay around to testify for Eugenia. And then I had to testify against Louis, too."

"Of course. You were around and saw some of what he was up to."

"Evil. Pure evil. Not Eugenia. She is a good woman."

"I heard she was found not guilty."

"God is good. Through our attorney, she asked me to come to her house and help her when she comes home."

"Is that going to be soon?"

"Tomorrow."

"I thought it would be much longer."

He drains his cup. "Tomorrow. We will be each other's family. She said she lost two sons, but now I can be her son."

That's how it works around here. It's not the family you were born into, but the family you make. Look at me and Dakota and my connection with Janey's family.

But still, here's this homeless man on my porch on an icy winter night with nothing but the clothes he's wearing. What would Jesus do? I can't really invite him into the house without Dakota's okay, and I don't want to wake her up.

"I met your father. He was looking for you. Did you see him?"

He sighs. "He will never understand. He wanted me to come home. He wanted me to see a doctor. He thinks I'm mentally ill."

"He seemed like he was really worried about you."

"I know." Gabriel tilts his head back and drains his cup.

My hands and feet are going numb sitting out here. It's so cold it could snow. "When you're ready, Gabriel, I can drive you to Eugenia's house so you don't have to walk any farther. There could be ice on the way. You could slip and fall."

"I should walk. It's part of my penance."

"For what? Hang on, and I'll fetch my keys."

By the time I come out, he's already down on Beaver Creek Road. I catch up with him, reach over and push open the passenger door. "Get in. The Lord does not want you to freeze to death. Rocky, get in the back seat."

As usual, Gabriel smells like sweat. He sits silently as I drive the short distance to Eugenia's house.

It looks deserted and dark. He'll need to light a fire to keep warm.

"Will you be okay?"

"The Lord helps those who help themselves."

"He does. Let us know if you need anything. How is Eugenia getting home?"

"The social worker from the rehab facility is driving her. She's going to make sure Eugenia has everything she needs."

"Good. The hospital will probably send a visiting nurse and a physical therapist for a few weeks, and I know you'll help Eugenia. I'll come visit soon. Good night, Gabriel."

He opens the door and slides out, limping toward the house. Rocky leaps into the passenger seat. *Shotgun is mine*, he seems to be saying. I hug my dog.

42. Eugenia's Song

Saturday, Feb. 13, 2021

WHEN DAKOTA SAYS she and Tess are driving to the valley for the day, I'm surprised because she rarely goes anywhere, especially during COVID, but pleased because I will have the house to myself. It's the perfect time to record my Between the Bridges music. No one to comment, and Rocky's taking his morning nap. So far, he does not snore.

I unplug the wall phone, prop my cell phone on top of the piano, and lay out the written copies of the songs in order. I have 20 songs and an instrumental theme that threads them together. It should take about an hour of recording time, although I plan to stop now and then to rest. If I make a mistake, which is inevitable, I'll do the song again.

Okay. Push the button on the voice recorder app, take a breath and play. I start my little concert with my theme. It opens with a B minor chord, goes to a D, then F# minor and continues meandering like Beaver Creek until I progress up the scale to the key of G and start singing the song "Up Beaver Creek."

The thing about singing songs you have written for yourself is that they fit you. They fall into the sweet spots in your voice, and every word has meaning to you. If a progression of notes doesn't feel right, you can change it. The song is yours, personal and pliable.

I love singing other people's songs, too, but this is the best.

One song leads to another until I reach the end with a soft B minor chord, letting it echo just as the sun emerges from the clouds.

Thank you, God.

I stop the recording, save the file, and email it to myself for backup. Then, before I can chicken out, I email the recording to Trevor Green, the guy with all the big ideas about making this into an online extravaganza. Then, thinking *why not,* I send a copy to Britt. *Thought you should hear this before you make your decision.*

The sun is calling me out to play. "Come on, Rocky!" I grab my keys and my phone. We run down the porch steps, down the hill and onto the road, turning right. I want to bypass Eugenia's house and see how far this road actually goes.

But when we reach the turn, I can't help but look. I'm out of breath and need to stop anyway. I'm not nearly as fit as I was when I arrived in Oregon two years ago, when I lived at the gym. It's still closed for fear of COVID, and my muscles are going slack.

Eugenia is sitting on her porch, wrapped in blankets, with Gabriel beside her in the same clothes he wore last night.

Rocky barks. Eugenia cries "Hello!" and we hurry to the porch. When she holds her good arm out, I roll into it, hugging her hard. I can feel her rib bones. I'm still shocked by her bobbed hair and her distorted smile, but her green sweater smells like cinnamon. And pot.

"Sit down," she says as Gabriel gets up and goes into the house.

"Eugenia, how are you? I'm glad you're home."

"M-me too. I missed you."

"I'm sorry about everything. I can't imagine—"

She just shakes her head.

We watch Rocky poking around the empty chicken coop.

"What happened to your chickens?"

"Louis killed some of them, and a cougar got the rest."

"I'm sorry."

She stares at her lap.

Change the subject, PD. "Dakota is going to be a volunteer firefighter."

"W-wonderful."

"Yes, I think she'll be great at it. You know her girlfriend is a firefighter."

She looks up, a little spark back in her eyes. "Girlfriend?"

"Yes. Tess is a dog groomer when she's not fighting fires. Very nice."

"Ah."

A black cloud rolls over the sun, and the temperature drops. It's going to rain again. But I'll take rain over fire any day.

"Eugenia, I recorded my new songs this morning. Would you like to hear them?"

She nods. I find the file on my phone and push *play*.

As my piano and voice pierce the silence of the woods, Eugenia smiles. "Beautiful," she murmurs.

I lean back and close my eyes. In a way, I don't want to hear my music played back. I want to stick with the euphoric feeling I had while I was recording it. I don't want to hear the word fumbles and wrong notes. Few as they are, every one sticks out. I close my eyes.

I wake to "bravo, bravo" and the sound of one hand clapping against her knee.

"Do you like it?"

"I love it. PD, you have—c-captured this—place." She rests her good hand against her heart.

PD is not going to cry. "I'll add Janey's flute and vocals to the professional version, and I need you to play the autoharp and sing with me."

She points to her limp hand.

"I know. But it will get stronger. I promise."

Gabriel comes to the doorway. "Ladies, I've got lunch ready. Come join us, PD."

I didn't come for lunch, but I'm hungry. I never pictured Gabriel as someone who cooks.

Inside the old-fashioned kitchen, the round table is covered with a blue tablecloth, and Gabriel has set out bowls of vegetable soup, warm croissants, coffee, and oatmeal-raisin cookies. We even have cloth napkins and shiny silverware.

He helps Eugenia from the porch to a chair at the table.

"Are those Eugenia's special cookies?"

"No. Regular ones. I don't do drugs," Gabriel says.

"Well, this looks wonderful."

"People brought food for Eugenia. Ask and you shall receive."

"What people?"

"Social worker. Grocery deliveryman. Neighbors from up there."

He points to the north. We haven't walked that far, but I know there are other people up Beaver Creek Road. Houses, farms, and mobile homes are tucked away all over these hills and forest roads. A lot more of the neighbors know about Eugenia now, thanks to news coverage of the trial. One article included a photo of her. Another showed her house.

I hope nobody calls her The Witch anymore.

Gabriel says a short blessing, and we tuck into the food. Although Eugenia has said she's a nonbeliever, she echoes my "amen."

The house is cozy, with lots of homey touches, like the crocheted afghan over the sofa and the glass-fronted bookcase under a cuckoo clock. It reminds me of my Italian grandparents' house on their ranch outside Watsonville before it was sold and razed for a new subdivision.

"How did you happen to move here, Eugenia?"

"It's-it's a long story."

"I've got all day."

She sets down her spoon. "I ran away from my husband, Louis Sr., because he kept beating me, especially after Steven died. I was homeless like Gabriel for a while, sleeping in my car or camping in my tent until I met Zeke."

"Zeke?"

She pauses for a bite of soup, her weak right hand shaking as she lifts the spoon to her mouth. She has spilled around her bowl and on her dress. Gabriel mops up the spill with his napkin.

"I'm s-sorry," Eugenia says. "I have trouble talking and eating at the same time."

Gabriel jumps in. "She told me the story before. That's his picture over there on the bookshelf. Zeke was a contractor. He found Eugenia sitting by the creek, gave her a place to stay, and fell in love with her. And she with him. But she was still married and afraid if she tried to divorce her husband, he would kill her. Zeke wanted to be with her anyway. He built her this house from scratch. He installed all the appliances, did all the wiring and hooked pipes up to the well. They had 10 beautiful years together, living in sin, but God understood."

"I'm sure he did. What happened to Zeke?"

"Cancer," Eugenia said. "Slow cancer. He knew he was going to die, so he showed me how to take care of everything and left me enough money to never worry."

"He sounds like a wonderful man."

"Yes." She coaxes Rocky over and gives him a bite of bread. "We had a dog. Jasper. He died. Cougar got him."

"I'm sorry. Did Zeke know about your sons?"

She nodded, tears in her eyes. "He didn't mind. He said he would protect me from Louis Junior and Senior."

"Did your husband ever find you?"

Gabriel took over. "Louis Jr. told me his father died shortly after Eugenia left. He tried to beat up the wrong guy, and the Lord took his life. No doubt he's in hell now. That's where he belongs. All these years she hid from him, not knowing he wasn't even alive."

"Oh, Eugenia."

She shrugs and reaches for a cookie.

"Gabriel, I'm glad you're here to help her."

"She has no one else. Like me."

Eugenia raises her eyebrows, but neither of us says a word.

A couple hours later, I'm back home practicing tomorrow's church music when Tess and Dakota return in the van. Instead of coming in right away, they stand outside talking. Dakota says, "I'll get the dolly."

Forget the music. I have to check this out.

"Hey, PD," Tess says. "Guess what we bought?"

"What?"

She points to several massive cardboard boxes. "Dakota bought a whole mess of gym equipment. She's going to set it up in the new garage."

"What? Seriously?"

Instead of replacing the old shed, Dakota built a garage at the side of the house. She felled trees to make more space and worked like crazy to finish the structure before the rain started. It includes a covered area on the side that she has filled with firewood. Inside, she installed shelves and racks for her tools and for extra storage, but there's a big empty space where I thought we would park our cars. Maybe not.

Tess explained. "She needs to pass a fitness test for the fire academy, so she wants to start working out. I told her she's plenty fit, but she insisted. She said you'd like it, too."

"I would. I've really been missing the gym since COVID. I pinch a roll of fat at my waist. "I'm getting chubby again. This is great."

"I'll probably use it too. Some. I hate working out, but exercise helps ward off the evils of old age, so I'll do my time."

Dakota rolls out the new red dolly she bought to replace the one that was ruined in the fire. "Tess told you?"

"Yes. This is fantastic."

"It's for all of us."

"You should let me pay for part of it."

"We'll talk. Let's open that biggest box first, okay?"

I feel so giddy I wonder if those cookies at Eugenia's house were really just regular oatmeal-raisin cookies.

43. Fame and Fortune Await

I HAVE PEDDLED halfway to Canada on the exercise bike when my phone dings with a text. Trevor again? Leave me alone. I worked all day, and I want to ride this stationary bike in peace.

He is driving me crazy with ideas for my music. Look at this video. What do you think of this font? How about if the words roll over images of the area you're singing about? Let's do a Facebook Live concert. Let's start a YouTube channel. Can you write some text to introduce the songs? Etc. I'm starting to wonder if he has a touch of his father's mania. This certainly reminds me of the way Donovan went nuts making art with the rubble washed on the beach after the tsunami. Would the two men recognize bipolar tendencies in each other?

I peddle on. I have already lost three pounds working out in the rainbow garage gym. I'm sweating and a little sore, but I love it. I may be destined by my Irish-Italian genes to be short and chubby, but I'm going to fight it. A buff body will look good on my album cover and the promo pictures that Trevor keeps babbling about.

I keep reminding Trevor I'm still waiting to hear from Britt. Whatever she says, we'll make something of the music. But not right this minute. I just passed Seattle, which is 315 miles. If I keep going, I'll be in Vancouver, British Columbia by dinnertime. I always wanted to go there. Maybe when COVID lets up, I'll take a vacation. It would be lonely going without Tom, but there's no reason I can't travel on my own. I refuse to be one of those widows who can't do anything by herself. PD is tough. Adventurous. Priscilla not so much, but she's just going to have to get over it.

Vancouver! I did it. My legs shake as I slide off the bike and reach for my towel to wipe my face. I'll spray everything with antibacterial cleaner before I leave, even though it's just the three of us. You can't be too cautious. People are still getting COVID. Just this morning, six people from a Valentine's party tested positive. Two are in the hospital.

I stand outside the big door and breathe in the cool, wet air. Most of the ash is blended into the soil now. The owners of the house behind ours had it demolished and put the property up for sale. Dakota is thinking about buying it. Why, I asked. It's a good investment, she said.

She didn't elaborate, but I think there's more to it, maybe something to do with Tess, who lives in a mobile home north of Waldport. She could have it towed up here. Fine with me. Despite all our time together, this is still Dakota's place, and she can do whatever she wants with it.

She built a hell of a gym. In addition to the bike, we have a treadmill and a weight machine with multiple stations to exercise every part of the body. She even put an old stereo out here to blast music to make it feel like a real gym. It's terrific, and I don't have to deal with musclebound men giving me stink-eye while I work out.

As I go back in to start my upper body work, the phone dings again.

"For Pete's sake!" I go to silence it, but then I see the message is not from Trevor. It's from Britt.

I sink onto the exercise bike to read it.

Oh my God.

PD, I love, love, love your Between the Bridges music. You blew all the other composers out of the water. Please check your email. I have sent you a contract. Sign and return ASAP.

I think I just stopped breathing.

Before I can respond, another message arrives. *I have arranged for you and any other musicians you want to record in March at a studio in Salem. I will fly up to help. I think we should debut the film in your neighborhood if we can find a suitable venue. Meanwhile, you need to buy or borrow a portable keyboard with the right kind of hookups. The money I have sent to you via PayPal should help with that.*

Ding. One more message. *I am jazzed to be working with you. Say hi to Dakota.*

Forget exercising. I've got to check my email. And my PayPal account.

Out of the gym, into the house, start the laptop. You know how in the movies, people's computers are ready the second they open them? That's garbage. I'm sitting here waiting, waiting, and waiting. Come on, come on. Insert password. Wait some more. Then I have to open my email, and whew, there it is. There *they* are actually. Contract. Instructions. Payment. Open, print.

I read the pages as they come out of the printer. I need an expert to interpret them, but it all looks good to me. A thousand dollar retainer and four thousand more upon completion? Good Lord. Plus royalties? I still own the rights to perform and record? Perfect. I think. I'll be showing this to everyone I know before I sign it. Not that any of us know anything about the business side of music. Are any of my friends hiding a law degree somewhere?

I check my PayPal account. One thousand dollars to PD Soares. Hot damn. Next day off, I'm going to find that music store.

Thank you, God. Thank you, thank you, thank you. I came west to play music, and it's finally happening. I can't wait to get started.

But right now, I'm typing a group text to Trevor, Janey, Jonas, Diana, Dakota, Donovan, Miguel, and Dad. *Britt sent me a contract and a thousand dollar deposit for my Between the Bridges music! She loves it, and we're going to record in a studio next month!*

I sound like Janey with my exclamation marks, but I think this deserves it.

Speaking of Janey, picture the credits rolling, my name first on the music and then "Featuring Janey Peacock and Eugenia Renner." Yes.

Then the devil peeks in. Maybe I should ask for more money. What if this film is a disaster? What if it never gets made? There are provisions in the contract for that. I keep my thousand dollars and my songs, but that's the end of it.

Well, I could live with that. And I've got Trevor on my side. Maybe he knows an attorney.

This could be the start of a whole career, not only as a musician but as a composer. Maybe my friends and I will open a music venue in Seal Rock.

I know the area between the bridges needs a lot of other things. A grocery store. A gas station. At least one doctor to help if the bridges fail. I picture the doctor from the "Little House on the Prairie" TV show. He was so comforting. He couldn't save anybody from anything serious because he didn't have any drugs or medical equipment, but he was wise and kind. We need one of those. And a vet. And . . .

Yeah, but we also need a place to hang out and hear music and just be with friends. . . We could be open in the evenings when the diner is closed. Tom and I dreamed about opening PD's Place. Maybe I can make that dream come true.

I'm so excited I need to go back to the gym to work off my excess energy. But not right this minute. My heart is beating too fast. If we had any booze in the house, I'd call for a toast.

As I fall onto the couch, Rocky stares at me, wagging his tail. He's not usually allowed on the furniture, but it's a special occasion. "Come on, Boy."

He leaps into my arms and kisses my face. I swear that dog can read my mind.

The responses to my text roll in as I lean back, holding my big beautiful dog, and let myself dream.

Am I hearing violin music? Oh Lord. I might be going crazy. Maybe it's Maryann reminding me from over the rainbow bridge that a violin might sound good with this music. Or that she always knew this bedraggled woman who showed up on her doorstep one stormy day with a sprained wrist and broken ribs had possibilities.

44. No Happy Ending Yet

Thursday, Feb. 18, 2021

GOD HAS A WICKED sense of humor. I wake up Thursday morning with a vicious sore throat and a painful cough. Instead of going to work, I call in sick and schedule the first drive-through test I can find, which is at Walgreen's pharmacy at nine a.m.

At seven, Dakota knocks on my door. "Aren't you going to work?"

"I'm sick. I'm getting a COVID test at nine."

"D'you think you have it?"

A cough forces its way out before I can speak. "Yes. Damn it. Stay away from me."

"Sure. I'll go study at Tess's place tonight, but I'll keep checking on you. Do you want any breakfast?"

"No. Just lock up that shotgun, so I don't use it on myself."

"All right. I'll take Rocky out."

I pull the covers over my head and try to sleep, but my mind is racing. If I have COVID, God knows how bad it might get. Even if it's a mild case, I won't be able to sing at church or anywhere else. I will have to cancel the Between the Bridges gathering and tell the COVID shot volunteer coordinator I can't come. I'll be off work for at least two weeks, and I'll be trapped in this house again. Shoot, I was going to buy myself a new keyboard this weekend.

Maybe it's just a cold or the flu, something miserable but normal. Please, God.

I set the alarm on my phone for 8:30 and will myself back to sleep until the noise jolts me awake again.

I feel awful. Now, I'm shivering. I probably have a fever, but I put on my sweats and my coat and drive myself to Newport. The test, administered through the drive-up window by a man wearing a mask and rubber gloves, is quick and uncomfortable. I'm driving back up Beaver Creek Road when the verdict comes in.

Positive.

I knew it. I freaking knew it. PD cannot have a happy ending that lasts more than a second. Considering how often I have been exposed at the hospital, it's surprising it took almost a year for me to get the virus. I guess one shot wasn't enough. I was going to get a second dose of the vaccine next week.

I go back to bed, semi-dozing. It's cold, but I don't have the energy to light a fire. I throw my winter coat on top of my blankets and bedspread. When I get up around noon to use the restroom, my legs feel like they don't want to hold me. Aren't these the same legs that ran all the way to Vancouver the other day? Lord, I hate being sick.

Leaning on the sink, I get the thermometer out of the medicine cabinet and take my temperature. 101. Well, that's not good.

Back in bed. I need to let people know. I have exposed half of Lincoln County. No, not that many, but my co-workers, our patients, my friends, Dad, Diana, Janey, Dakota and Tess. Eugenia and Gabriel? Maybe. Shoot, I probably exposed the checker at the grocery store, the church choir, and Fr. Rigo. No, no, no, I wore a mask. Did I leave COVID all over the piano at Our Lady of Grace?

What if I die?

I know. I'm getting all Cissy, feeling totally sorry for myself. I'm relatively young. I'm healthy. I'll get over this. I wore a mask everywhere I went, and I haven't been to Dad's house or Eugenia's place since last weekend.

I am PD. I am not going to die. I will ride out the worst of it with rest and Tylenol, and I will find ways to amuse myself until I'm not contagious anymore. God was good to keep me well until I could get a vaccine that might make the illness less deadly. He kept me well and safe through Dad's bout with COVID, Andy's visit, the fire, and the whole business with Eugenia's son and grandson. We're not recording the Between the Bridges music until next month.

Just chill, PD. Breathe, as Dakota is always saying. It doesn't feel great, but I can still do it.

When I wake up again sometime in the afternoon, it is unusually quiet, the kind of quiet that makes me think of—I pull the curtain aside. Snow. In February. Come on! The robins already came back. Why does winter last so long in Oregon?

Then I notice something else. Rocky isn't here.

"Rocky?" I call in my wimped-out voice. Nothing. A cough rises up and bends me over. Fighting for breath, I call him again. "Rock! Where are you?"

What the heck? Is he curled up on the couch? I push myself out of bed again, put on my coat, and walk barefoot across the hardwood floors, leaning on walls and furniture, looking for my dog. "Rocky?"

He's not in the living room, but someone has lit the fire. I guess Dakota stopped by while I was sleeping. Did she take Rocky with her? She never does that, but maybe because I'm sick . . . ?

I stagger back to the bedroom and send her a text message. *Rocky is not here. Did you take him with you?*

She responds quickly. *No. He should be in the house.*

He's not.

Maybe he snuck outside while I was bringing in your lunch, chowder from the diner. It's in the fridge.

Not hungry. I'm going out to find Rocky.

Do you feel up to it?

No.

Wait. I'll come up and look for him.

But I can't wait. I picture my dog shivering in the snow. I pull my snow boots over my bare feet and go out. Shaking so hard I can barely stand, I scan the yard. We already have two inches of snow on the ground. It blankets the trees, the roof, and my car. "Rocky!"

Past the porch, there's nothing to hang on to, but I struggle along through the falling snow, looking all around the house, under the porch, and along the fence. My lungs feel like the cotton batting I used when I made quilts and pillows. I can't breathe. I cough air out, but I can't get enough back in.

"Rocky!"

Are those footprints? They're faint, already getting buried in new snow, but they lead to the road. I start to follow them down the slope.

No! My feet slip. I'm falling, sliding first on my bottom and then on my right side until I land against a tree. My shoulder hurts. My butt is wet. My dog is gone, and I can't breathe. I'm going to die alone and too young. I huddle in my coat and cry.

They say when you start to freeze to death you get sleepy and warm. I'm not going to freeze to death. The snow is only two inches deep, and it isn't 30 degrees below zero or anything like that. I'm just feeling sorry for myself. In a minute, I'll get up.

Now, the snow turns to rain, pelting my coat and washing the snow off the trees in clumps. It sounds so loud after the softness of the snow.

I can't just sit here. I've got to get up and find Rocky. I'm working on standing when Dakota rattles to a stop in the van. She opens the door, and Rocky jumps out.

I open my arms and he runs into them.

"He's soaked," I say.

"I caught him halfway to Eugenia's house," Dakota says. "What are you doing out here? You're already sick. You want it to turn into pneumonia?"

"I was looking for my dog. And then I fell."

She shakes her head. "Come on, let me help you up. I'm sending you both to bed."

As she wraps her arm around me and tugs me to my feet, I start coughing again. As hard as I try, I can't hold it back. "I'm going to make you sick."

"Shut up, Priscilla."

THE NEXT THREE days are a blur. Runny nose, cough, fever and chills. A bruised shoulder that makes it hard to get comfortable. Dakota brings me healthy food, cold drinks, Tylenol and cough syrup. Nothing tastes good. Rocky goes out now and then, but he always comes back. The phone rings and buzzes, but I ignore it. Everything can wait.

The nights are the worst. As soon as I begin to relax, I start coughing, and I can't stop. My stomach muscles hurt from coughing so much. My nose keeps running. Used Kleenex and soggy handkerchiefs pile up around my pillows, but I don't have the energy to deal with them.

On the fifth morning, Monday, I sit up on the side of the bed and realize I feel a little better. I'm not shivering. I shove the thermometer into my mouth and wait. Dakota is in the kitchen, probably eating breakfast. So far, she has not gotten sick. If I were her, I would have moved into Tess's place, but she has been here every day, taking care of me and Rocky and keeping everyone else away.

I'm getting weepy. It's sweet to have someone who cares so much.

My temperature is down to 99.5.

My mouth tastes horrible. I push myself up and walk on wobbly legs to the bathroom. I brush my teeth, wash my face, and run a brush over my hair. It's growing out again. I think I might let it be brown and a little longer. I don't need to prove anything anymore.

I need a shower, but I settle for running a wet washcloth over the critical areas and changing into clean pajamas. I'm not going anywhere anyway.

By the time I crawl back into bed, I'm wiped out, but I send a group text. *Better. Temperature is down. I will conquer this. PD.*

I turn on some folk music, close my eyes, and go back to sleep.

ON WEDNESDAY, March 3, after my fourth test, I finally receive a negative result. I no longer have COVID. I can return to the uninfected world. Praise God.

I'm still tired. Food doesn't taste right. My throat is raw from coughing. I'm not going back to work until next week. But I'm going to live. I'm going to buy my keyboard, record my music, and who knows what might happen after that?

I can do anything. I don't think I really grasped that before. But I'm forty-four, single, and healthy. I'm not rich, but I have enough money to splurge a little. I am so blessed.

Another group text: *Negative test. I'm free at last. Does everyone still feel okay?*

Responses pour in. *Hooray. We're fine. About time.* Dakota writes: *I missed you, kiddo. So did Tess. No COVID here.*

The best response comes from Diana. *Party for PD at the diner Sunday night. NOT on Zoom.*

Rocky is resting on the couch. Apparently, the rules have been relaxed since I retired to my room. I tumble down beside him. "We are free, boy. Free, free, free. What do you want to do? Where do you want to go?"

He wags his tail. I consider the possibilities—walk, beach, visit Dad or Eugenia—and realize I don't have the energy. I just want to stay right here, loving my dog and watching the trees and rhododendrons rock with the wind.

"Is this okay?"

Rocky sniffs my face and licks my chin.

I love my dog.

PART IV

45. Island Music

Saturday, March 13, 2021

IN SPITE OF THE FIRE last September, the forest is full of new life as I drive down the hill toward the highway. Just last week, as Rocky and I were walking, I saw the three-petaled white trillium flowers that are always the first to appear. The blackberry vines have sprouted little blossoms, and the giant yellow flowers of skunk cabbage are peeking out of the wet areas along the creek. Ferns and grass have turned the ashy areas green again. The woods are full of the buzz of saws and knocking of hammers as property owners rebuild and remodel.

I'm moving into new life, too. My experiences have taught me that life is short, and it's a sin to waste it. I'm slimmer from COVID and fitter from working out in the rainbow garage gym after I got my energy back. I'm taking in-person music classes again for the spring quarter and seriously considering a full-time career in music, both performing and composing. Maybe teaching, too. Lizzy, our regular choir director, is back at church, and she has asked me to stay on as pianist and assistant director. It feels right.

Janey's dreams may lead her to Broadway. I hope they do. Me, I'm thinking I might have to travel for my music, but the West Coast will always be my home.

I still need a new keyboard to replace the one that wound up in pieces beside Interstate 5 when I crashed my car last year. It needs to not only sound and feel good but do all the computer-friendly tasks Miss McKenzie, my piano teacher back in the '80s, never dreamed of. It's time to go shopping.

I miss the old Ocean Harmony music store in Newport. I miss Deuce, the owner, too. Before the tsunami, I loved jamming with Deuce and his buddies. He let me play the grand piano there. He's also the one who gave me my green harmonica. I've got it in my purse right now. I can only play in the key of C, but that works fine when I'm by myself.

The shop reopened briefly after the tsunami, but when COVID came, it joined the many businesses that went belly up. It's a marijuana dispensary now.

I was talking to Ronny Mae's grandson Benny at church last Sunday. He plays guitar, and I was trying to twist his arm to join the choir. No luck there. He asked if I had ever been to the music store in Alsea, about 30 miles east of Waldport.

"No," I said. "Somebody mentioned it to me, but I haven't been up there. It's in an old house?"

"Yeah, it doesn't look like much. You kind of have to hunt for it, but the guy there is great. He sold me my guitar, got it all set up for me and even gave me a few lessons for free."

"Does he have any keyboards?"

"He's got everything. When you get to Alsea, turn right at the post office. Take that street to the next corner and it's on the left."

"Is he open on Saturdays? I could go up next weekend."

"Sure."

We said goodbye, and I was almost to my car when Benny came rushing over. "PD, when you see Sam, the owner, don't ask about his family."

"Why?"

"They were out on the beach near Waldport when the tsunami hit. They didn't make it."

"That's horrible." I'll never forget the people we saw on the beach at Seal Rock that day as Janey's family and I stood up above, watching. We screamed at them to run, but they didn't hear us. The wave came in, and when it pulled back, they were gone. "I'll stick to music."

"Well, just thought I should tell you."

Between the tsunami and COVID, a lot of people have died too young. Sometimes I get this feeling that because my husband died of something ordinary, I don't deserve as much sympathy, and after two and a half years, I should be over it by now. But if you ever lose your husband or wife, God forbid, you'll understand. The loss sticks with you forever. There ought to be a place where we widows and widowers can hang out with each other and avoid coupled people who just don't get it.

I haven't driven Highway 34, also called the Alsea Highway, before, so this will be an adventure.

I spend the morning doing laundry and homework and head out after lunch. It only takes about 10 minutes to get over the Alsea Bridge and stop at Waldport's only red light before turning east. I pass a gas station, bank, library, community center, and fire station before the road leads out of town, following along the Alsea River. As I drive up into the coast mountain range, riverfront homes and boat docks give way to scattered cabins and farms.

Oh, for a straight stretch to relax, but this "highway" is one curve after another. I'm grateful for my experience driving Beaver Creek Road. Two years ago, I would have had a lot more trouble driving here.

The city of Alsea is not around the corner. Thirty long miles. Dog miles. No cell service. No traffic. A few wayside pullouts with outhouses. I stop at one and stand by the river for a while, watching the water sheet over flat white rocks. It's pretty, but I'm going to have to drive this road back, so I'd better get going.

Alsea. Population 220. Alsea School, Deb's Café, a grocery store, and a turnoff to see a covered bridge. Here's the post office. Right turn.

This street is so narrow, the trees hang over it from both directions, blocking out much of the sun. I realize I don't know the name of the street I'm looking for, but there are no signs at the intersection anyway.

A quilted treble clef sign hanging in the side window of the white, two-story house on the left, plus a couple of old pianos, a rusted drum kit, and pieces of guitars on the back porch tell me this is probably the place.

As I park as far off the road as I can, two massive mutts charge the chain-link fence surrounding the house, barking and flashing their teeth.

I keep walking, hoping I can get to the door without being eaten.

Okay, there's a walkway past the fence and a little sign pointing to the side of the garage: Island Music. What island, I wonder as I walk along stepping stones decorated with quarter notes, eighth notes, and sixteenth notes. The side door has a faded sign listing the store's hours and an out-of-date concert poster for a band I've never heard of. This does not look promising, but I'm here.

A bell rings as I push the door open.

"Hello," a voice calls.

"Hello," I answer. I can't see him. It's like twilight inside, lit by strings of colored Christmas lights, the windows blocked by floor to ceiling guitars, cases, stands, straps, amplifiers, cables, and bits and pieces of electronics I can't identify. I turn to the right and hit a dead end, then veer left and see a short shaggy-haired man who appears to be Hawaiian. He wears jeans, a heavy blue sweater and sandals with brown socks.

"What can I help you with?"

"I just wanted to see what you had here. Are you Sam? A friend from church recommended you."

"Sam I am. Who's your friend?"

"Benny Hoffman."

"Oh, yeah, Benny, that's my buddy, my unofficial son. Great guy. You play guitar?"

"No, I'm a pianist." Oh, that sounds snooty. "Keyboards."

"Ah. Follow me." He leads me through a tunnel of guitars into a back room with an old upright piano and a few basic keyboards leaned against the wall. I know already that I'm not going to buy anything here, but I can't resist the piano.

"Is this real ivory?"

"Yes. No plastic there. That piano is vintage. The old man who owned it lived to be a hundred years old. Played honky-tonk right up until six months before he died. I can still see his big old hands going back and forth, bass, chord, bass, chord, and then he'd surprise you with a run and a slide that'd knock your socks off."

"My kind of guy."

"Go ahead. Play around on it."

Since it's always in my head, I start the "Between the Bridges" theme. It's definitely not honky-tonk. As I roll through the chords, I can tell the piano needs tuning. It's damp in this room. Instruments need a dry space with an even temperature, and this is like anybody's garage on the coast, but still, I can feel the music in this old piano.

"That's nice. Keep playing." He leaves the room for a minute and comes back with a beat-up guitar and a stool. He sits, tunes, and starts to play along. I sing the melody, and he adds a tenor harmony. I close my eyes, enjoying this.

When I open my eyes, he's smiling. I can't see his lips because of his white mask, but I do see the crinkles around his eyes. He smells good. I don't know what it is, very different from my husband's hairspray and Brut scent. Way different from Donovan Green's earthy funk. Kind of like the ocean and old wood and soap all blended together.

"I never heard that song before."

"I wrote it."

"You've got talent, girl. I like your voice, too. I wanna buy your album. Hey, do you know this one?" He launches into "Five Foot Two."

"Sure do." As I put on my best honky-tonk imitation, he tries to dance the Charleston while he plays, nearly falling in the process. We both laugh.

I play the intro to "Jeremiah was a Bullfrog," aka Three Dog Night's version of "Joy to the World." He chuckles and jumps in. I take a solo, and then he does one, and then we segue into "Summertime," "Let It Be," "Ripple" and a whole lot of other songs.

Time is passing, but I don't care. I feel like I want to play every song I ever knew. Finally, he hangs up his guitar and flexes his fingers. "Would you like a beer?"

This is going past customer territory, but I can't resist. "Sure. But only one. I have to drive that highway back to the coast."

"Oh. That's a ways. We definitely want you to stay safe."

He climbs a couple steps and goes into the house, returning a minute later with two open cans of Coors. We clink cans and drink.

That first sip is always my favorite, icy cold, with steam coming out the top. I have a passing memory of the exercising, health food-eating fiend I was when I came to the Oregon coast two and a half years ago. Cissy, the goody two shoes who preceded the redhead who became PD, would not be sitting here drinking a beer with a stranger.

Sam chuckles. "What's your name? I forgot to ask."

"Oh, I go by PD."

"What does that stand for?"

"It's a secret." I sip my beer.

"Ah, very show biz. Do you live around here?"

"Outside Seal Rock. Up Beaver Creek Road. I came here from Missoula, but I'm originally from Santa Cruz."

"When did you leave Montana?"

"Just before the earthquake and tsunami."

He grimaces. "Good timing."

He takes down a red guitar, retunes and plays something sounding vaguely Hawaiian.

"How long have you been here, Sam?"

"Oh, so long I forget how long." His guitar-playing soothes me. I like the feeling of being surrounded by all this musical gear lit by red, green, yellow, blue, and orange lights. "I'm from Kona on the big Island of Hawaii. Ever been there?"

"No, but I'd like to someday."

"You should. It's beautiful."

"What brought you here?"

"Family stuff. My wife missed her family, and my kids wanted to go to college on the mainland. I, um. . ." He plays. "Hawaiian music uses a lot of sliding, like this. It's mellow, easy-going, got that island feeling."

"It's very pleasing to the ear."

"I agree." He pauses to tune again. "You got a husband and five kids in Seal Rock?"

I shake my head and play a series of arpeggios on the piano. "No. My husband died of cancer. We couldn't have children. It's just me and my dog Rocky."

"I see. I like dogs."

I'm aching to ask about his family, but I heed Benny's warning. "How did you manage to keep this shop in one piece with the earthquake and all? And then COVID. I mean, look at all this stuff."

"Well," he puts down his guitar, stands and stretches as I glance at my watch. Four o'clock already. I need to go home before it gets dark. He probably needs to close up, not that there are any other customers. "It was a mess. Oh my God. Things just, you know, instruments and gear everywhere, stuff falling on stuff. You probably saw some of the broken things out back. Good thing I had insurance. It took me months to get it this good, and I know it still needs work, but I had other things to deal with."

He picks up the guitar again and plays. I search the piano keys until I match his chords. He nods and keeps going. I don't know what this song is, but I like it. When it's over, he continues his story.

"Last March, I had to close for COVID. I could only sell online, and I'm not very good at that. This started as my personal collection. It grew and grew, and guys wanted to trade gear. I said to my wife, is it okay if I turn the garage into a shop, and she said, 'Sure, honey, it would be great if you could sell some of this stuff.'" He sighs. "She was not a musician, but she loved me, so she never complained."

He clears his throat. "I know I need better control of the temperature and humidity. This isn't a great location, but I haven't done much about it yet. Times are crazy."

"They really are."

He looks around the store. "If I'd been in here during the earthquake, I'd have been killed, but at least I'd be surrounded by music, right?"

"Not the worst way to go."

"Instead, I was shopping in the valley when the earthquake hit. It was a tough drive, and when I got home . . ."

He looks away, clears his throat again. "PD, I don't usually talk about it, but I lost my wife and my two teenage daughters that day. My neighbor told me the kids were on the beach. They wanted to see the tsunami. When the warning came, my wife went after them, but it was too late. The wave got them all. I don't know how to live without them. I just sit here with my music. That's why the place is such a mess."

"Oh, Sam. I don't—"

He waves his hand. "There's nothing anybody can say or do. You know. You lost your husband. It changes everything."

"Sure does." I drain my beer. "I moped for a long time. I did a lot of knitting. Ate too much and got fat. Then one day I ran out of yarn and decided to change my life. I rented out my house in Montana, cut off my hair, dyed it red and spiked it up straight. Tired of being chubby, I exercised myself into a skinny pile of muscles. I changed my name to PD and drove until I found a place where I felt like I could play and sing my music."

He shakes his head. "Takes guts."

"Or insanity."

"Maybe, maybe not." He eyes me for a minute. "I like the brown hair you got now. It's softer. You gonna tell me what PD stands for?"

"Maybe someday." I stand. My legs are stiff from sitting at the piano so long. "I need to get going. It's going to be dark soon and you probably need to lock up."

He shrugs. "Won't make much difference. I don't have many customers. Good thing I have other sources of income. I just flip the closed sign whenever I feel like it. So, you're not gonna buy this piano?"

"No, Sam. I like it, but I have my own old piano at home." I look around the store. "By any chance, do you have any sheet music?"

"No. Used to, but it got ruined when a pipe broke and we had a little flood. Nobody was buying it anyway. They're all going digital. Do you need any mics or amps?"

"Not today, but maybe soon."

"Maybe you could learn guitar. Or flute. Have you ever tried that? How about a harmonica? He points to a glass case loaded with harmonicas in every key.

"Aha." I reach into my purse and pull out the green harmonica I have been carrying around for two years.

"Oh, next time, we're gonna jam on the harp."

"Absolutely."

"You need to get harps in other keys. Let me give you my card." He grabs one from the counter and hands it to me. *Sam Kealoha, guitar, ukulele, vocals, luthier*. I give him one of mine. *PD Soares. Piano. Vocals. Original songs and covers for all occasions.*

"Cool. You Portuguese?"

"No. My husband was."

"Ah. I got a little bit of that in me, too. Lots of Portuguese in Hawaii. You gotta go there."

"I don't want to go alone."

"I'll take you."

"Sure." We're still strangers. But you never know.

"Okay, PD, come back soon. Oh." He stoops behind the counter and retrieves a CD. "For you. A little thing I did. Check my website, skislandmusic.com, for the whole catalog."

It sounds like this guy was a big deal in Hawaii.

"Call me if you want to order something. I can get just about anything. I'll keep it in the house, so it's temperature-controlled."

I know it's time to leave, but I still need a keyboard. I could order it at home, but what the heck. "You know, Sam, I did come in looking for an instrument. I need an electronic keyboard with a MIDI hookup and recording capability. I need something I can take to my gigs, assuming I'm going to have some as COVID lightens up."

He nods, thinking. "I know just what you need. Let me show you." He leads me behind the counter to his computer and pulls up pictures of keyboards. He scrolls, then points his brown finger. "That one. That's what you need. It's not cheap, but you don't want cheap. You want something that's going to last like my old guitar over there."

He's right. It's not cheap. But this is an investment in my future, and I have that $1,000 payment from Britt. "Does it come with a stand? Or a bench?"

"Let me see. No. I can add a stand and a bench. What do you think?"

"This is a big decision. But yes. Order it." I hand over my credit card.

As he rings up the sale, he says, "You're gonna love it. Guy I used to play with had one just like it. Smooth as silk, plenty of settings, loud as you wanna make it, all the hookups. You can make ordinary music with anything, but with a good instrument, it becomes magic."

I'm smiling behind my mask, but he must see the doubt in my eyes, too.

"I didn't hard-sell you too much, did I?"

"No, no. It's exactly what I need."

"This way I get to see you again when you come to pick it up. Or maybe I'll deliver it to Beaver Creek."

I'm blushing. "Sounds good."

As I open the door, the junkyard dogs erupt into a new siege of barking. "Are those your dogs?"

"No, they belong to the neighbor. He's a fisherman. When he goes out, he leaves them here because I have a fence to keep them in. Edgar and Poe. Can you believe it? They're not as bad as they sound." He walks to the fence. "Hey, boys, come here. Calm down. You want some dinner? Yeah, I'll feed you." They stop barking and wag their tails. "Drive safe, PD. I'll call you."

And then he's walking into the house, and I'm driving into the sunset on the Alsea Highway with a warm feeling inside me that isn't just the beer.

I don't have a CD player in my car. When I get to Waldport, I pull over and search for Sam's recordings on my phone. There he is. Oh, he's handsome without his mask. I push play. His music is sweet and warm, like a frosty piña colada on a sunny beach.

46. This is It

Sunday, June 13, 2021

TODAY IS THE DAY. The "Between the Bridges" film premieres in Newport at four o'clock this afternoon. As I wake up and stretch, it feels like a wedding day. Or maybe graduation. One of those big milestones. Thank God we can gather inside without masks again. Last month, the Centers for Disease Control proclaimed that in situations where most people have been vaccinated, it's not necessary to wear masks anymore. Finally.

I still have to wear a mask at work. That may never end. In health-care settings, it just makes sense. We still have influenza, colds, and all the other contagious diseases. And we had another big surge of COVID right after Easter. We went back into lockdown for a while after an outbreak at some of the restaurants and also at the jail, but things are much better now. Businesses are starting to reopen. The manager at the Drift Inn asked me to play for the supper crowd on the second and fourth Thursdays. Janey and I will be performing at the Beachcomber Days festival in Waldport later this month.

Trevor got me a featured performance next September at the Yachats Commons. It used to be an old school, but the renovated multi-purpose room makes for a great auditorium. Here in Newport, construction on our new performing arts center is just beginning after all kinds of wrangling at City Hall about this and that. I'll play there someday, too. Maybe with Janey. Maybe after she comes home as a Broadway star. I know she can do it. I hope she thanks me when she accepts her Tony award.

Janey sang and played her flute in the score for this film. I got Eugenia and her autoharp in there, too. At the last minute, Jonas added some soft drumming that really gave it a nice feeling. Britt found a bass player and a cellist for our recording session in Corvallis.

Those days when we all gathered in the studio were special. Absolutely exhausting but also thrilling. Singing into that big mic, I knew I was doing what I had always wanted to do. Zelda and Jackson weren't too happy about me taking time off from the hospital, but I had to do it. This is my dream.

Britt said they would have CDs of the music for sale at the opening. My songs are already online. Trevor helped me make a website and a YouTube channel. Now we just need to spread the word. I'm letting Trevor handle most of that.

Janey and I went crazy trying to find a venue with a big screen and enough seating for the millions of people who would come to the local premiere. Okay, I know, not millions, probably fewer than a hundred, but we did need a place worthy of the event. The LA premiere is going to be in this fancy theater where all the movie stars go. Here on the Oregon coast, between the buildings that were knocked down by the tsunami and earthquake and the ones that were put out of business by the pandemic, options were limited.

Beaver Creek and Seal Rock had nothing. The visitors' center would have worked if it hadn't burned down. We have a six-screen movie complex at the north end of Newport, but it hasn't reopened since COVID, and they don't do live events anyway.

"Let's do it outside," Dakota said. "Maybe under one of the bridges." I liked that idea, but no. Even in June, you can't trust the weather, and I wanted this to be fancy.

The aquarium has a nice theater, but it's too small, and they're still closed, reopening Fourth of July weekend.

I was ready to do it in somebody's barn just to nail down a place when Father Rigo said, "Why not do it here at the church?"

"In the sanctuary? Is that legal?"

He shrugged. "I don't think Jesus would mind. We've got the big screen we use for family movie night. There's plenty of seating, and you can have your reception in the new hall."

Rebuilt after the earthquake, the new hall is big and beautiful. Add some candles and white tablecloths, and it could rival any fancy dining room. Once COVID is truly gone, Father hopes to rent it for weddings and other events.

That clinched it. I looked around the church. The altar made a natural stage. There were plenty of seats, and I liked the idea of doing this in my spiritual home. "Yes. Thank you, Father. Thank you so much. Is there a rental fee?"

"Not for you."

When I told Britt, her reaction annoyed me. "Oh, how quaint," she said. "Is it a little white church like in the movies?"

"No, it's a big red brick Catholic church, like in real life."

"Oh. Send me some photos, and we'll make it work. How much is the rental fee?"

"He's letting me have it for free."

"Nice. I hope he doesn't care that I'm not religious."

"We won't mention that."

I have decided Britt is not someone I want to hang out with after we're finished with this film business, but I am grateful for everything she has done for me and my music. Thanks to her, my career might go beyond The Drift Inn and Diana's Diner. She does make beautiful films, and she has useful contacts.

This may be my big day, but I've got church this morning, same as every Sunday. Afterward, Janey and I and the other choir members will decorate the hall and set the tables. Diana is bringing clam chowder and fresh salmon off the docks while the rest of us are potlucking the side dishes. Molly is making a cake with a big picture of the Yaquina and Alsea bridges from the movie poster. Britt will probably think all this is quaint, too, but it's the Oregon coast, not Hollywood. If she wants to serve fancy canapes and champagne down there, that's fine with me.

Once everything is set up, Janey and I will go home and change our clothes. While we were in the valley recording, we bought fancy prom dresses and matching shoes at Stacee's, and we are going to look good.

We don't even have to play or sing at the premiere. We can just sit in the front row and take it all in. If somebody wants us to do some songs, we won't say no, but we don't have to lift a finger.

Everybody is coming. Britt and some of the people who helped with the film are flying in. Dakota, Tess, and Dad will be there, of course. Dad will pick up Eugenia and Gabriel on the way. I have invited co-workers from the hospital, neighbors, and pretty much everyone we know. All the folks Britt interviewed for the movie are on the guest list.

I may have invited the clerk at the grocery store and the guy who picks up our garbage. I may have put up flyers at the post office, on the bridge posts, at the state parks, City Hall, the college, and all over the hospital. And that was just me. Janey knows lots more people than I do. Dakota might have put a flyer in every mailbox.

Trevor and Donovan are coming, too. I wonder if Donovan will bring his lady friend.

That's fine with me. I've got Sam. That's right, we're a couple now. God is amazing. Just when I thought I would never fall in love again, he gave me this wonderful music man.

After my visit to his store, Sam and I started texting each other. *I can't stop thinking about you,* he said that first night. *Me too,* I replied. It went on from there. Me: *Hey, do you know this song by Eric Clapton?* Sam: *Do you know how to make meat loaf?* Me: *Have you ever been to Santa Cruz?* Sam: *What's your favorite color?* He sent me pictures of elk walking down his street. I sent him photos of my new niece.

By the time Sam delivered my keyboard to me here at Beaver Creek, we felt like old friends. He helped me set it up and try it out—oh my God, it sounded so good. We played some guitar-keyboard duets, and then we went for a walk on the beach. By the time we sat on the porch dumping sand out of our shoes, we knew this was it for both of us. Not a replacement for what we had, but something new and special.

Even Dakota knew. "Not whiskey," she said. "This one's a keeper."

Sam will be here soon. The only ones not coming are Andy and my mother. They're waiting for the LA premiere. It's about the same distance either way for them, but in Los Angeles they won't have to deal with the Dad-and-Diana situation. They'll be at a much fancier venue. Red carpet and everything. But this day with my friends in the place I have come to love beats all the red carpets in the world.

Janey and Sam and I are flying down for the LA event. Eugenia declined. This is enough, she said. I suspect she's right.

Yes. It's a special day. But first, let's start the coffee, take the dog out, and have some breakfast. PD needs nourishment.

SAM ARRIVES AT THE rainbow house just as I'm putting on my lipstick. Rocky barks when he drives up in his white Buick sedan, but when Rocky realizes it's Sam, he's all wags and kisses. They have become buddies since we started going out.

"Rocky, off!" I say. "Don't get fur all over Sam."

"It's okay," he says, brushing his black suit pants. He looks me up and down in my slinky green gown. "Wow. You're a knockout, PD."

"Thank you. You look good, too."

"I have this for you." He holds out a white corsage. "May I?"

As he pins it on, his fingers brush the top of my breast. I have that warm tingly feeling as he leans in for a kiss. "It smells good," I murmur.

"Are you nervous?"

"A little. More excited than anything."

"Good. Just soak it all in."

"Ah, you're an old pro. I have seen your web page. I have all your records."

"Old, maybe. Pro? Eh."

"You're only 50; that's not old."

"Thank you. Where did you get the pretty flowers?" He points to the bouquet of red roses and white chrysanthemums on the counter.

"My mom. Her note made me cry."

He plucks it out of the flowers. "'PD, my dear daughter, I am so proud of you. Follow your dreams. I'm with you all the way.' Sounds like she loves you."

I look forward to meeting Sam's parents in Hawaii. If we don't go there sooner, Sam says he will show me a "real Hawaiian Christmas."

Dakota and Tess emerge from the bedroom. Wow. Dakota looks so uptown in her white tuxedo and black shirt. Tess is wearing a low-cut purple dress with a matching shawl.

"You two are gorgeous," I gush.

"Are we ready?" Dakota asks.

"I think so. I'd like to be there when Britt arrives."

"She's driving from the airport?"

"Yes. She and her associates."

"She has associates, huh?"

"Be nice."

"Oh, I will." She winks at Tess.

Dakota has still not quite forgiven Britt for ending their relationship the way she did. It never would have worked. Tess is a much better match.

THE CHURCH IS PACKED and buzzing with conversation. Gabriel and my dad, both in dark suits, welcome people at the door and hand out programs. Britt and her crew sit across the aisle, looking very LA in their short skirts and suits.

It feels weird occupying the front pew with Janey, Eugenia and Sam instead of sitting at the piano, ready to play for Mass. Out of habit, I kneel, make the sign of the Cross, and say a prayer, mostly giving thanks, but I can't help adding, *Hey, Jesus, I hope it's okay that we're doing this in your house.*

Our house, I imagine him saying.

At exactly four o'clock, Fr. Rigo dims the lights and introduces Britt.

Her speech and those that follow are all a blur. As I stand for a bow, I see so many familiar faces—friends, family, parishioners, co-workers, and neighbors I met at the Between the Bridges giveaways.

The film begins with the piano. That's me, playing my "Between the Bridges" theme. Janey's flute comes in, then the soft strumming of the autoharp and a gentle swish-swish of the cymbal. Add cello and bass and my voice. It sounds earthy and clear.

While Gabriel remains at the door to watch for latecomers, Dad slides into the seat beside me. "I know that piano player," he whispers.

"Me too."

The screen shows the ocean at Ona Beach and then Seal Rock State Park. The camera pans from the rocks to a harbor seal to a gull riding the wind, then crosses the highway to Diana's Diner.

The music fades as Britt begins to speak. "Seal Rock on the Central Oregon coast is an island of sorts. Located between Waldport and Newport, Seal Rock and the neighboring community up Beaver Creek are the kind of places where everyone knows and helps each other. They have to. They can only reach the cities to the north and south by two grand old bridges, the Yaquina and the Alsea. When the bridges go down, whether through earthquake, high winds, or a car accident, the residents lose access to groceries, gas, medical care, jobs, and other things we city dwellers take for granted. Starbuck's. Churches. Law enforcement. Schools. Libraries and bookstores. There's not a single place here to buy toilet paper or dog food.

"Even a tree falling on the highway can throw their lives into a tizzy. They were stranded for weeks after the 2018 earthquake and tsunami, and again at the height of the COVID pandemic. A recent fire threatened to wipe out the whole community. But today, life is good . . ."

The piano continues under the narration then swells with "Eugenia's Song."

"Let's meet some of the people who live in the area between the bridges."

The camera takes us to Eugenia's house where she hangs clothing on the line as she talks. Then the music swells as Eugenia, Janey and I sing together, her voice and autoharp prominent. Next to me in the dark, Eugenia is smiling and singing along. She has transformed for the event, her hair, growing long again, pinned up on the sides and hanging in loose ringlets in back above a swirly maroon dress that shows a little bosom.

Instead of a walker, she's using a cane now, and her speech is close to normal. Her stroke didn't stop her from playing the autoharp for the film.

Dad leans close. "It sounds good, honey."

Britt has done a great job. I remember spots in the music that didn't feel as perfect as others, but I don't hear any glitches now. It's beautifully woven together, words and music and pictures. I glance back at Trevor, sitting with Donovan and a silver-haired woman in the third row. Trevor gives me a thumbs up sign. Donovan's eyes are fixed on the screen.

This isn't a quiet audience, especially when people and places they know appear. "Hey, that's me!" someone shouts. "There's old Tom. He'll talk your ear off." "Watch you don't get goat poo on your fancy shoes." Laughter.

Here's the rainbow house, shot before the fire, when Britt and Dakota were dating. In her narration, Britt calls it quaint and quirky. Maybe it is, but I love it. Britt hasn't seen the new garage gym. That's not quaint or cute or any demeaning adjective. It's a palace.

Gulp. Here I am, sitting sideways on the piano bench, talking about how I came here from Montana to do music after my husband died. I talk about our band, the Seal Rock Sound, and how after Maryann died and Janey and I lost our rental house, Dakota invited me and Rocky to move in. Oh, here's Rocky. He leaps right at the camera, his nose filling the screen as the audience laughs. He's at home today, missing his screen debut.

We move on to Donovan's/Dad's cabin and the view from the balcony, continue across the area that burned in September, and down the hill back to Diana's Diner, interviewing locals eating at the picnic tables outside. We meet Diana and Janey, both wearing masks, and Jonas dropping off Molly's pies and pastries. During her interview, Janey manages to sing a few notes because she can't help showing off. I love that girl.

The film goes on and on, up and down the road to each bridge and along the beaches, ending with a view of the waves at Seal Rock State Park for the two last songs and the credits. There's my name: *Music composed by PD Soares.* All the musicians and singers are listed, along with the many people who were interviewed or who helped in some way. Transposed over the ocean in the final shot are these words: *Filmed in Seal Rock and Beaver Creek, Oregon, 2021, a little bit of heaven between two bridges.*

The audience stands and roars and hoots and whistles and applauds. I'm getting hugs from all directions and hoping to God that my breasts stay inside my dress.

Sam looks on proudly and is not the least daunted when Donovan, a foot taller than he is, sweeps around and pulls me into a dramatic embrace. "My darling, you have exceeded my extremely high expectations." His voice is loud, piercing the clamor.

"Thank you, Donovan."

Trevor is right behind him. "This is going to make you a star, PD Soares. I'm already hearing from lots of people who want to show the film and share the music. You too, Janey Peacock. You're too terrific to ignore. I'd fluff up your web page and put as much content on it as you possibly can. Hit Instagram and TikTok and whatever they invent next."

"I'm on it," she says, dancing in place because she can't stand still.

Eugenia watches, alone in the crowd. After all these years in the woods, she doesn't know many people here. My father gallantly takes her arm. "What say we retire to the reception hall?"

"That sounds good."

Maybe now that Eugenia doesn't have to fear her husband and her son, she can start to venture out and become known to the community as the nice person she is rather than The Witch."

The crowd filters into the hall. It smells of salmon and chowder. Candles sparkle in the subdued light.

Someone taps a knife on a glass, and we hush as Fr. Rigo walks up front to say grace, reminding us that it all comes from God.

It does. I'm sure of it.

I feel as if all my worlds and all my identities have merged here. Music, religion, love, food, family, friends, neighbors, and co-workers. All the doors that seemed locked before are opening.

Dakota stands to make an announcement. "Ladies and gentlemen, thank you all for supporting these talented women in the making of this film and this music. I am very proud. But I want to remind you that some people are still having a hard time. Next Saturday, the Between the Bridges giveaways will start again at Diana's Diner. Nine to one. Bring something, take something, have breakfast, say hello. As the film says, we need to help each other. Thank you."

Applause. As she sits, my dear friend's face is red. She does not like to speak in public, but I'm glad she told people about the giveaway. I'm so happy we can finally do it again.

Between the entrée and dessert, I slip outside into the parking lot. They talk about the Big Sky in Montana, but tonight, stars fill the sky over Newport. Venus and a bright new moon hang over the horizon. The ocean hums as waves roll and break against the sand. I breathe in the clean, cool air and let out a big sigh.

Dear God, thank you. I will always treasure this day, this time. I miss Tom, but you had a reason for sending me here and putting so many things in place for me. Even Fr. Rigo is an important cog in this wheel. Our old priest would never have allowed us to hold the premiere here. Please never let me forget this moment and how amazing you are. Amen.

Behind me, footsteps. Sam slips his jacket over my shoulders. "It's chilly."

"I imagine it's warmer in Hawaii."

"It is. You'll see. But I'm happy here tonight." He reaches for my hand.

Janey breaks the spell. "Hey, you two, get back inside. Britt wants to talk to you, PD. You too, Sam. And we all want to cut into that cake."

"We'll be right there," Sam says, leaning in to kiss me. I close my eyes and soak it in.

47. Another Sunrise

Saturday, August 7, 2021

I'M BACK WHERE I started, watching the sunrise from the balcony at Donovan's/Dad's cabin. My father and Diana have gone camping in the California redwoods. They plan to continue down to Santa Cruz to meet the baby and visit Andy and Shari. Dad wants them to get to know Diana better. Is she going to be my stepmother? I don't know. Whether they get married or not, she's already my friend.

While Diana's gone, Janey and Jonas are running the diner. Molly is helping as much as she can while wrangling the two sets of twins. The girls are in the terrible twos now, but the boys, age 5, are turning into human beings. Next month, COVID willing, they'll start school, and Molly will have more freedom.

Some days, I envy her for having all these children. But there are other days when even Rocky, currently wandering the yard, is too much to take care of.

I'm staying here at the cabin to give Dakota and Tess some privacy. Where is that relationship headed? Somewhere nice, I think. I hope. I want Dakota to be happy, and Tess already feels like family.

Today's sunrise is a gentle one, no wild bursts of color, just hints of pink among the gray clouds and openings where a touch of blue shines through. Fall is coming. I'm ready to wear sweaters again.

Something about dawn feels sacred. God is opening a new day full of possibilities.

After the hullaballoo of Hollywood, it feels good to be back here by myself. The premiere was great, but I have gotten used to a simpler life.

We'll see if the connections I made at the premiere and other events lead to anything. The film and soundtrack recording are doing well. Not quite "viral," but we're attracting an impressive number of viewers and purchases.

COVID is a virus we don't want. But we do want our social media posts to go viral, meaning the whole world sees them.

While I was in California, I got to see Mom, Andy and Shari, and I met my baby niece, Donni, who is already eight months old. She felt so good in my arms. When she looked up at me with those eyes just like mine and smiled, oh my God. I didn't want to give her back. I still ache for the babies I'll never have, but I love being Aunt PD.

Andy claims she can already carry a tune. I hope so.

I'm meeting Sam for dinner tonight in Newport. We're taking our relationship slowly. We have both been through a lot. Plus, he's busy preparing to move his home and business to Seal Rock. He's not saying it's because of me, although the 70-mile round trip between here and Alsea is wearing us both out. His garage store is too small. It can't be brought up to proper conditions for storage of musical instruments, at least not according to the building inspector, so he needs a new shop. He says his house in Alsea is too big and too full of memories, so he's looking for a place in this area.

The new store was a gift shop that closed because of COVID. The former pizza parlor next door was also available, so he bought that, too. Sam has this plan to turn the pizza parlor into a performance space, maybe with a coffee shop or wine bar. It will complement the diner rather than compete. He's going to have the old upright piano from the store tuned and refurbished. I can't wait to play it.

We have not committed to each other at this point, but we have committed to the music. For today, that's enough.

As the sun bursts through the clouds, warming me here on the balcony, I hear Eugenia's autoharp.

She's playing in the key of C. Pulling my green harmonica out of my bathrobe pocket, I listen, set my lips to the metal plates, and play along. When she stops, I blow a riff, then wait for her to respond, and she does. It's perfect.

Acknowledgments

Like PD and her friends, I live in the forest between the Yaquina and Alsea Bay bridges on the Oregon coast. I am grateful to the neighbors who share this beautiful place with me, knowing that if the bridges go down, we're going to need each other.

Writers need other writers, too. I thank my writing friends from Willamette Writers and Oregon Poetry Association for their encouragement and support.

I am especially grateful to my beta readers Patricia Stern, Bonnie Dodge, Samantha Ducloux Waltz, Nancy Clifton Ballard, Stacy Smith, and Kathryn Ehlers, for seeing the typos and inconsistencies I could not see.

Many thanks to Erin Seaward-Hiatt for yet another beautiful cover. She is my go-to designer for book interiors as well. Visit her website at http://erindesignsbooks.com.

My writer friends said, "Don't write about Covid. Nobody wants to read that." But how could I take PD and her friends through 2020 without mentioning the biggest thing that happened that year? Thank you, dear readers, for taking another look at that most unusual time.

Finally, thank you to my co-writer, Annie Mae Lick, best dog in the world, who crossed the Rainbow Bridge not long ago.

About the Author

Sue Fagalde Lick spent many years earning an honest living writing for newspapers in California's Bay Area before moving to the Oregon coast with her late husband, Fred. When not writing books, essays, poems and blogs, she assumes an alternate identity as a singer, guitarist and piano player. Sue lives just above the tsunami zone in South Beach, Oregon, where she talks to robins, rabbits, elk, and the imaginary characters who live in her head.

Also by Sue Fagalde Lick

NOVELS

Azorean Dreams
Up Beaver Creek
Seal Rock Sound

Coming soon! *Back to Ona Beach*

NONFICTION

Childless by Marriage
Love or Children: When You Can't Have Both
Stories Grandma Never Told: Portuguese Women in California
Unleashed in Oregon
No Way Out of This: Loving a Partner with Alzheimer's

POETRY

Gravel Road Ahead
Widow at the Piano: Poems by a Distracted Catholic
Blue Chip Stamp Guitar
Dining Al Fresco with My Dog

For more information, visit www.suelick.com .